I0547039

Acknowledgments:

To mom, for everything.
To Sarah, for the great perspective.
To Dane, the Cartographer and Illustrator.

With love,
To Nik, my muse.

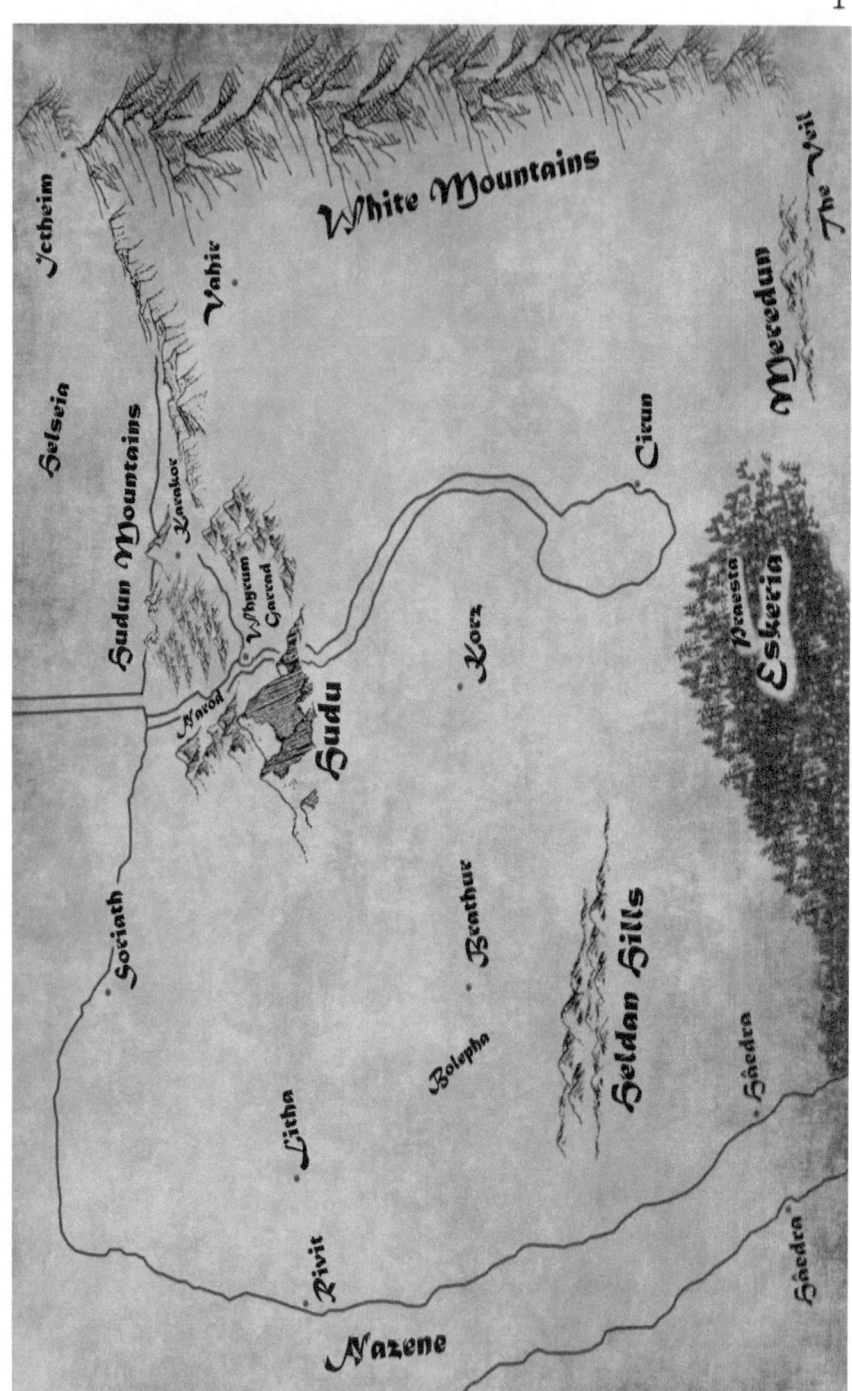

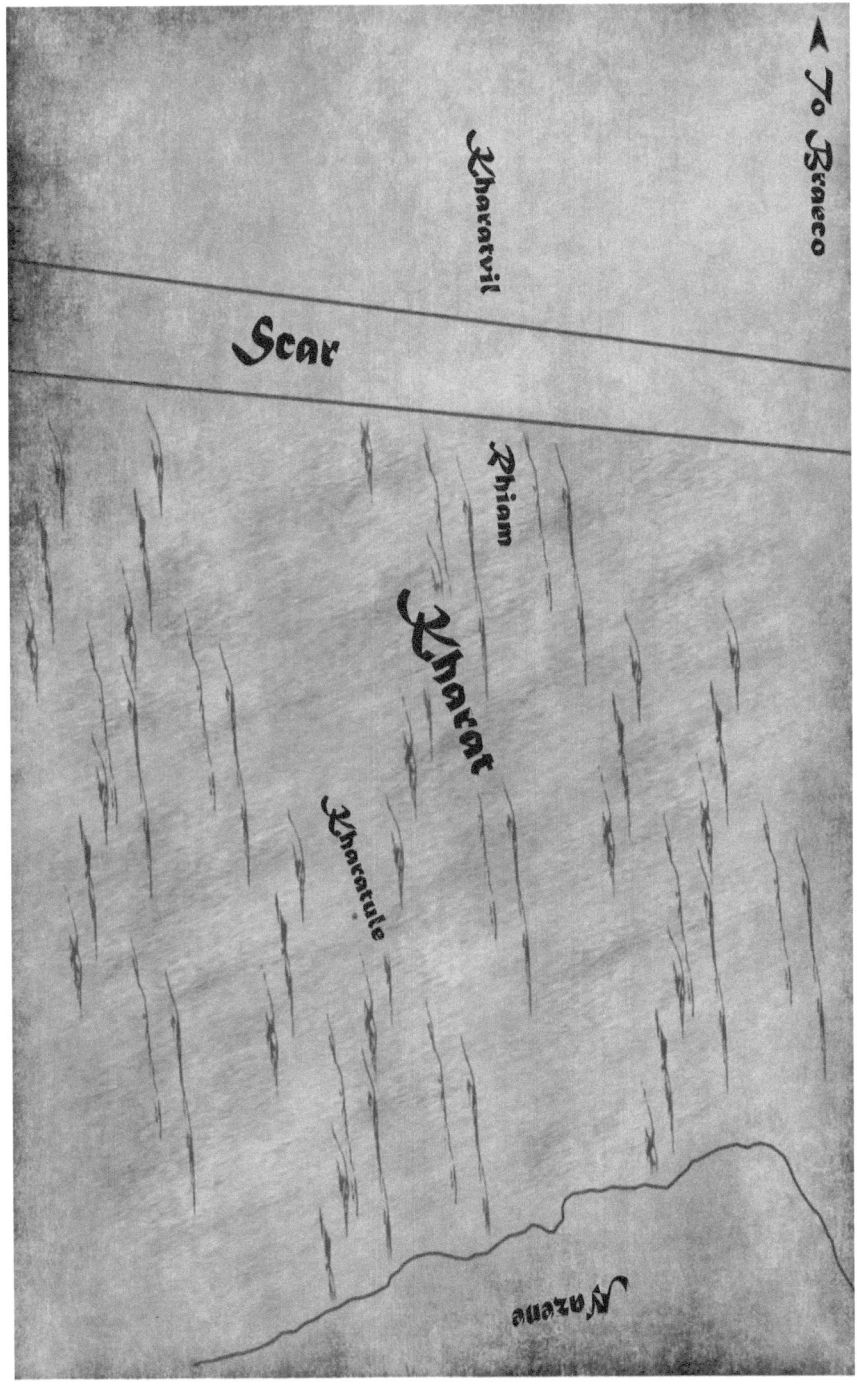

Alkurah:

Pawns of the Shadow

By Clint Foster

Some tales are woven by mouths from the Seia Wesrin to the White Mountains, and perhaps even beyond. Others are whispered in the dark, damp holes most befitting their horrors, and seldom befoul the light of day with their wickedness. Whether legend or myth, the passing of stories to younger generations seems an ancestral habit. Men speak in hushed, guttural tones, huddling about their scattered fires for warmth and safety. Elves weave songs into the trees, the ground, even the very air they breathe that Alkurah may remember the fairest of races to bless her surface.

But it is dwarves that *best* keep track of events in Alkurah. In immense, leatherbound tomes are written every happening that can possibly be recorded in collaboration with eyewitnesses from each event, as objectively as can be expected.

In time forgotten, before maps were traced and tales twisted by the mire of time. Before the first fires warmed the Hudun Mountains and the waters of the Nazene had yet to rush. Before even the gods themselves walked the world, and only creatures of darkness and fear stalked the shadow, there was Bol the father, ruler of the Alkui in their greatness.

However, the first of even the Alkui was Sypchallu. He is darkness, and shadow, and in the time before creation, before Bol, he was supreme. Sypchallu had no dreams of creation or life, and was satisfied with the cold and the darkness that came before. For time immeasurable, Sypchallu was the sole entity in the unending reaches of nothing. Until, born in the thunder of the beginning of the universe, the creator god broke the shadow with fists of lighning and war, and a crown of fire blazed upon his brow. Bol breathed life into the light, and allowed it to rise up against the darkness and cast down Sypchallu. The Lord of Darkness could not be destroyed, for there can be no light without shadows. However, Bol made use of near limitless power, and brought forth creatures equal in the agelessness of the Alkui. These he called the Eova, elves.

The Eova were born first within the mind of Bol. An idea. A mere shade of a thought of what may come. They were shy, and they did not wander far from his thoughts, for they feared being lost to him within the vast wonders of his mind. But the Eova grew in strength and magic, and they learned quickly, until they were ready to be let free into the darkness. Only there was not yet a world for them to occupy, so it was that Bol strode from his throne in the sun and made a world of his own flesh. For nine days he labored, carving mountains by hand and setting the course of rivers that would flow until the end of time. He showed the Eova his gift to them, and they had no way to thank him save words and prayers. Bol would not come to the world to guide his children in physical form, choosing instead to remain in the sun to keep watch over his children.

He became lonely, however, on his throne in the sun. He fretted for his children when the night came and he was no longer there to guide them, so he created the stars in the infinite void of space for the Eova to observe with wonder. When he realized the night was still dark, that his children cowered in caves when the sun set, and that Sypchallu began whispering once more in the shadows. Bol severed a corner of the sun, and he set it in equal orbit around his world, and so the moon kissed the night for the first time. The Eova worshipped the moon, that they called Lau, for it brought respite from the terrible night. They believed Lau and Bol were lovers, and that she had come from a far off place to keep him company in the skies.

Eventually, Bol came forth once more unto the sky and hewed the clouds and shaped the moonlight and the stars into a home, the Godhall. It had many rooms and stores of food to last until the ending of time, for it would be filled with the greatest of Bol's children, to feast and rest for all time. When it was finished, Bol returned to his throne in the sun to rest, and in his dreams he saw a family of the Alkui, of whom he would be most beloved. He created his brothers and sisters as he slept, and to each was assigned a different part of his world to watch over and keep beautiful.

To the oldest, Ong, he gave the beasts of Alkurah, such was the name he chose for his world. Ong ruled over the horses, and dogs, and livestock, and would come to be loved by men of the plains. He was, too, Lord of the seas and rivers. The burbling of streams, the roar of the Nazene, the trickle of drips that would otherwise have been silent, and the fury in the crashing of waves upon the shores were his voice and his might. Ong was merciful, though he could become wrathful if challenged, and loved his beasts and cared for them. He understood that their uses by the children of Bol would be many, and so did not begrudge the slaughter and the taming of beasts for the growth of the Eova.

Magic and starlight were Noc's domain. She soared across the sky on her steed, Satara, and gave the stars their twinkling that they appeared to teem with life. Noc existed in opposition to Sypchallu, though she was unaware of the Lord of Darkness for many long years. She would learn of him, however, for Sypchallu would suffer no rivals and was often thwarted plotting against Noc's works.

There was one Alkui not blood related to the rest, for she was not made of Bol's own mind and flesh. Elu came to be out of the dreams of the Eova, who so deeply loved beauty and art that they created her of their own accord. Her beauty was such that there can be no comparison to mortals. Dawn was her hair, with many hues of red and gold, and her eyes the open skies, and her skin fair and unblemished, like the first hours of snowfall before the travel of rough boots wears away her perfect stillness. Rather than being jealous and vindictive of their creation, Bol loved Elu, and gave her a room in the Godhall. He forgave the Eova their creation as they had not done it willfully, but he warned them against attempting their own creation in the future, for Elu was pure, but another such attempt may be soured by imperfection.

To Elu was betrothed Ula, the lord of music and art, because Elu had been born of the appreciation of those things. Their love would become legend, so that everything beautiful in Alkurah was said to be of their making, and everything dreary and dim was of their discontent. Thus the Alkui, the Gods, of Bol's own flesh and magics, became intertwined with the children of Bol, their fates woven into the same tale.

For many years, the Eova were given Alkurah to their sole possession, and they walked freely from the trees to the mountains to the seas that time has now forgotten, and they were all equals, and the world was beautiful and bright. They sang to the forests, and the forests sang back, and Eskeria resonated with the voices of the trees. They did not write, but the Eova would weave their magic into stones as they sang. These became totems of immense power, many of which would survive the ravages of time and war for eons to come. This was a time of boundless contentment, and the Eova gave unto the Alkui all the glory they deserved.

But peace is frail, and Sypchallu had not been destroyed. Bol saw beauty in the struggle of the dark and the light and he knew he could not eradicate his elder. In his weakened state, Sypchallu created weapons and trinkets capable of extraordinary destruction in the darkness within caves deeper than the oceans. There he forged armor to withstand the breaking of the world, weapons to strike down the Alkui themselves, and poisons so potent that the wielder could even control the corpses of the slain. He unleashed his evils upon the world whenever he saw the opportunity, and the Eova thwarted them time and again before their full terror could be wrought. Some they treasured and kept locked away, and the first thoughts of greed and selfishness entered their minds.

For centuries this continued, and the Eova slid into their jealousy and fear so gradually they did not even notice it happening, and it came to pass that they were sundered by their hatred. The Braeco, those of the Eova who settled in the oceans and did not explore Alkurah, content with the gifts Bol had given them upon the land that birthed them; saw their opposites as greedy and foolish. The Praesta, often lighter in complexion and of fairer skin, journeyed far to learn and grow wise. They were the explorers who first discovered the Hudun Mountains, Eskeria, the Nazene, and all other rivers and mountains. These they named after the feelings they had upon discovering them, and they sang everywhere they went, letting magic blanket the world in their wake. There was happiness, following the Sundering, as the Braeco built wonders beneath the Seia Wesrin and the Praesta explored streams and great woods that had never been disturbed, trees never climbed or spoken to, and lakes of such depth and clarity they seemed the greatest mystery of all. The world grew, and the Sundering seemed a memory to any but the Eova themselves, who bore their bitterness for one another as a badge.

After the Sundering, Bol strode from his throne once again and gave new life to the world. There were already beasts and creatures of flight, but there were none to challenge the Eova or to contest them in the aspects of mind and magic. The Eova would always be the eldest race, and they were beloved by Bol, but he felt they required a force within their world to show them they were not perfect, and that they could yet learn.

So, the mortal races were born, and dwarves sprung from the stone. Men, eventually, for they were weaker and slower and aged more quickly than the rest, crossed the White Mountains to the west.

Sypchallu took advantage of the Second Birth, and his grasping fingers found many willing to turn to his words, for it was a time of fear for the youngest races, and Sypchallu knew fear greater than all. Orcs and goblins he corrupted with his wicked magics in the darkness and shadow of the caves and damp places of the world, and were it not for his words they might have grown to be just and kind. They too were beloved by Bol, even in their evils, because he saw virtue in the difference of creatures. Centaurs, the halfhorse men that dwelt in the mountains and great Eskeria, and rarely conversed outside their tightly knit tribes. Trolls; strong, broad, lean, and well suited to battle and hard living. Their grayish-blue skin thick and tough, often crisscrossed with ritual scars and tattooes. Ogres, pale and massive with hides like stones, and often twice as tough. Lovers of travel and gentle learning, occasionally broken up by a good mauling. Dragons, mystic and wondrous. Unable to even be comprehended in their true majesty by some. And, eventually, giants, the youngest and dumbest of them all, grew strong on the bounty of Alkurah, and the world was bountiful and joyous.

When the Second Birth of Bol burst from his light, his new children scattered about Alkurah and inhabited all places they could find shelter and food. The trolls settled far to the north, and for thousands of years they built their kingdom in the frozen wastes, happy to hunt the toughest beasts in all Alkurah for their furs and food and glory. Creatures of the darkness haunt Ictheim, which is what the trolls call their home, for Sypchallu loved the frozen north above all places. Some believe trolls are not of Bol, but were born of Sypchallu in mockery of his rival's children. But trolls count themselves blessed that they are provided with food and honor, so long as they have the strength of body to seize it. In their distant past, they worshipped Sypchallu, who they called Shkaylhu, as it was he who provided them with meat and glory, but they too came to worship Bol their father.

It was the Eova who explored the swamps. The first sons of Bol wandered far and some used their gifts of magic with abandon. To the swamps, or the *meredun*, which means dark waters, there went a tribe of the Eova who would come to be known as the Vulkha. The Vulkha were pale and had eyes like oceans and hair of gold and they wandered farthest and their experiments with magic were wild and whimsical, but they did not come without cost. The *meredun* was born of magic used to attempt creation of life without Bol's breath, which Bol forbade in his first direct edict to his children. The Vulkha were destroyed, in a way, as Bol reached out and declared that each would live a life unending, but never would their glory be their own, and Alkurah would forget them in the shadows of their betters. Then they were scattered across Alkurah, and their minds were destroyed, their faces changed before they were set free, so they would not remember their pasts and the world would forget their futures. Such is the wrath of Bol.

With the creation of the *meredun* and the scattering of the Vulkha, the Sundering turned violent, as the Braeco believed it their duty to cleanse Alkurah of the Praesta. Although it was against his will, Bol did nothing to help either side, and there was war among the Eova, terrible and enduring.

Ogres would nestle in the *meredun*, eventually, following a period they call the Era of Wandering. They were largely left alone by the other races, for the most part because their speech was utterly alien to the others. They did not learn from the Eova, and grew apart from all other creatures. They roamed the Veil, an area south of the swamps filled with boundless magic and power. It was a place the Eova cursed, and they did not go there even in direst need. Ogres' tough hides and massive stature, as well as their robust natural defense against magical attacks, made for intimidating foes, and they have shared almost nothing of their exploration of the Veil with anyone but themselves. The Eova were jealous of their power, and sought to supplant them on several occasions, but were always denied. Ogres are wise beyond their speech, and often know more than they say, and their deeds would come to be known through Alkurah as those of wisdom and forethought. Often they were the sole factor to decide a battle or alliance, usually arriving unsought for in the most helpful possible location.

Across the grasslands and the milder climates settled humans. They were weaker in physical form than their brethren, but they made up for their shortcomings in sheer numbers. Unlike the Eova, who were whimsical and free in their youth, men were hard and serious and took little love in songs and beauty, save to preserve their own legacy. They built harsh cities, strictly for defense. Their structures were designed to keep unseen enemies at bay, and they spent little time making works of beauty. Humans learned much from the Eova, for Bol's eldest children saw themselves as teachers. By the time the two found each other, men had already developed their own speech. It was rough and lacked the precision of that of the Eova, with many words meaning dozens of things depending on the circumstance. Subsequently, many men took to learning the language of the Braeco, as the Praesta had fled to the southlands many decades before the coming of mankind.

The men of the north, who called themselves Koros, began a strong friendship with the dwarves, who were underway with the immense undertaking of carving the great city of Karakor from the heart of the Hudun's. The Koros were hardy, with thick beards and long dark hair they often left unkempt, and they wore strange furs that none in Alkurah had ever seen. Dwarves taught the Koros to write, to take cold charcoal from doused fires and drag it along thin-shaven wood. Koro was the one who the men called chief, and whose name they took as their own, for he was strong in body and spirit, and fierce in battle with the shadowlings men had escaped by crossing the White Mountains to the east. So tall and broad is that range that there has been no crossing attempted by anyone on either side since. But the Koros traversed the great peaks even in their youth, and though this feat has never been replicated, no recording of the events has been made, as the Koros were loath to speak of the endeavor. They suffered greatly, and many were missing fingers or entire limbs, long lost in tribute to the never-ending snow. They arrived in Alkurah nonetheless.

The Koros became strong under tutelage by the dwarves, and their descendants bore the brunt of the evils of Kharat, Eskeria, and Hudun on many occasions, steadfast in their defense of their homes. Koro himself was a good friend to Karak, the legendary dwarf king, and they were seldom seen without one another whilst wandering the quarries around what would become Karakor.

To the south came a separate tribe of men that came to be known as the Haderon, or horsemen. Many thousands migrated out of Eskeria, where it was thought only centaurs and other beasts lived, and they found a friend in the Braeco, long hidden in the forest. Orum, king of all Praestan elves, welcomed the fledgling race as if they were his own children, and he sheltered them in the vast expanse of his kingdom. Eventually, he bequeathed unto them the entirety of Hadera, which men pronounce 'Hâedra' in their tongue, and they took to the great river Nazene and the plains. The Praestans taught the Haderon to ride horses and build great ships to navigate the river, and they spread across Alkurah like wildfire. And so, in only a few centuries, men spread from Korz to Vahir, Hâedra to Cirun, and they nestled into homes of stone and wood, ugly and sharp on the eyes, and through famine and cold, disease, and war they became strong.

Bol was pleased with his creation, and his children grew and prospered and erected prodigious monuments to him, which pleased him. He watched from his throne in the sun as the Eova built cities in his honor, for they have long memories and never forgot the kindnesses done them by their father. Ever they worshipped him, and would not be torn from his teachings by even the most wicked of tongues.

But the Sundering brought a waning of power for the Eova, and in their absence, men strove to hold sway across Alkurah, and they seized their moment with mailed fists. The Koros warred with the dwarves for supremacy among the foothills of the Huduns, but they were cast out and their armies destroyed. The bloodline of Koro was ended within three generations of the crossing. Koron, the last chief of the Koros, was slain in battle by Karak himself, now many decades older than any dwarf king to ever sit upon the throne of gold since.

The survivors settled across the northern plains. They would eventually come into contact with their brothers from the south, but they would do so in ragged bands of a few families or scattered individuals, so they were assimilated with no real excitement. Years later men turned to the west, across the Nazene, and had their first clashes with the Rofu, an alliance of orcs and goblins (which are essentially the same, save that goblins are simply a smaller statured race of orc) who had settled within Kharat. Kharat was a wasteland of scorching sun and burning sands, but the Rofu were accomplished diggers, and they excavated a keep below the shifting dunes called the Kharatule. The Rofu would become a bitter enemy of men and the foremost fuel of orcen hatred toward them.

The Haderon continued to live at bountiful peace with Braeco, however, and both races flourished among the towering trunks of Eskeria and the crystal Nazene. Their lifespans increased, partially due to many elven men falling in love with mortal women, for the brevity of their beauty was desirable to the Eova, as they saw splendor in the aging of mortals that they could not find among themselves. Their children were called Eovaron, or elf-men, and they lived longer lives than their human ancestors. These bloodlines would become powerful along the southern coast, away from Alkurah itself, and they were great explorers whose maps and charts are indespensible to anyone wishing to venture south of Eskeria.

Men are beloved of Bol, and he put great faith in their sense of right and wrong and, though he taught them precious little of their world on his own, they soaked up his knowledge through the Eova. They grew powerful in magic, though they soon found it came with the cost owed by their mortality, for magic is said to draw upon life as any exercise might, and they pushed their magic to its limits until they attempted what the Vulkha had failed. Bol, who had not warned them against this blasphemy, was irate. But he was forgiving, and the Lord of the Light knew that his second sons were imperfect, and he forgave them. He left their creation as it was, however, for he would not destroy any life, and he felt great sorrow for the fate he'd wrought upon the Vulkha. Men gave birth to the race of giants, and what they lacked in intelligence they made up for in extraordinary strength and resilience.

In the past, when the Vulkha were dispersed, Bol thought their attempt had failed, and he paid no attention to the *meredun*. From the residual magic was born a race of immortal beings that would call themselves Heldan. In time they would believe themselves prophets of Bol himself, and all they did was seemingly to bring about the glory of his Light. But Sypchallu lurked in the dark places, and in the *meredun* he was given physical form once more. His rebirth sent forth a ripple of destruction and fear across Alkurah, and savage wars raged across the world. Sypchallu traveled the land, touching everything he could with his many hands to corrupt and destroy. He built caverns and tunnels beneath the world, and his strength grew in the dark places. In these shadows he wrote runes of power that could not be comprehended by the minds of mortals. And though they could not understand the words, they grasped for this power now whispering in the dark, and wars were fought for the magic Sypchallu willed upon those stones, for these totems were greater even than those made by the Eova in their youth.

It was the Braeco who first translated the words upon the stones, and this furthered the Sundering. They began calling themselves Mon Eova, High Elves, as though the totems they gathered were an indication of their natural born regality. They fled their homes and built whole islands in the sea. When they finally erupted from their bastion within the sea, the War of the Sundering was undertaken in earnest once more, culminating in the Warre Eova. Many thousand elves fell over the coming decades, and Bol was saddened to watch his firstborn slip into darkness.

Men continued to build, and soon the tunnels and caves of Sypchallu were discovered and used for storage and the incarceration of prisoners of war. Many who were kept for longer stays went mad, and carved upon the walls with their blood until they could write no more. No heed was paid them, and the walls were washed clean before the next prisoner arrived. Sypchallu was patient, and he had lived since before the first dawn, so he was content to bide his time until he saw a moment to truly usurp Bol and cast the light out forever. His darkness grew in those days, when the races of Alkurah fought countless wars and the graves and pyres of the slain outnumbered those still fighting.

Eventually, Bol grew weary of the Godhall and the fellowship of his kin, and seeing the shadow spread across his creation, he took upon himself the form of a mortal and walked Alkurah as the Alkui, his kin, were wont to do from time to time. Until now he had simply observed and gently guided, unseen, from his throne. But when his feet first touched the cool grass and he smelled the salted air of the seas he had fashioned, and he passed through Eskeria and Hudun and Kharat, he knew he could not leave for some time.

For years, Bol took interest in every thing he had made, and even those made without his will. He stooped to spend hours watching the struggle of ants, spiders, or caterpillars. Days would pass him by without notice as he surveyed the flight paths of birds. Statues of mortal men he found especially interesting, and he could see his children had grown in spite of his lingering anger toward them for attempting what was long forbidden. In his time on Alkurah he witnessed the aftershock of the Sundering, and was caught in a battle between the Braecan and Praestan elves, and he saw such a number of those that he loved fall that he grew sad and there were storms, and rain, and thunder for weeks.

When his mourning was complete, Bol rose and took a new likeness, that of a common blacksmith, and he made a vow to live as a mortal. He crafted a home with his mortal hands, and hewed the wood and sanded it and made it his own. Bol married a mortal woman, whom he loved more than all his creations, but he had sworn away his power for the time he was bound to his wife, and he would not tell her who he truly was. Her name was Themyra, and she was beautiful and soft and kind in a way that Bol could not understand.

Together, they had a son. He would come to be a great warrior and the pinnacle of mortal achievement. His name was Tykus; born to push the limits of mortality, and he would do so, in time.

Bol loved his son, and was saddened by his mortality, so as he grew old and withered on Alkurah he planned a gift for his world that would be unrivaled throughout time. His final words were for his son alone, and none now know what was said, for he would not tell a soul the final statement of his father. But Tykus continued his growth as a warrior, and he forsook love and fine things for battle and strength. He was legend, in his time, but he would come to be forgotten, as all men are.

There was a rumor, however, that a precious tool had been gifted Alkurah, if only the right hand could find and wield it. It attracted men, elves, dwarves, ogres, and trolls, and all races on the face of Alkurah bloodied themselves to grasp this weapon.

Finally, Tykus arrived, and through the maelstrom he carved to the center of the violence. His sword cut swift arcs in the air, spraying blood and gore meters away. Men, elves, dwarves, and worse barred his path, each keen on claiming the power for themselves. But nothing would deflect his advance, and he battled for days to reach the epicenter of this madness.

Corpses, hacked and hewn to shreds, pulped by the iron boots of a thousand warriors, littered the plain. Whenever one would come near the armor, every soul became his enemy, and he was often simply crushed beneath the weight of their many bodies.

Finally, covered in the blood of foes uncountable, and fierce in his rage. Tykus laid claim to the armor, challenging any and all to oppose him. None came forth. All who beheld the donning of the armor of Tykus knelt and acknowledged the power the Gods had given him. No light glanced from his breast, and no shining banner or ornate carving inlaid the steel. It was forged of magic, and in Bol's hands alone the craft was undertaken, that no one might sully his gift.

But the armor was not ever in the hands of Bol, and the moment it touched Alkurah, Sypchallu felt its power and he trembled in his tunnels. The armor blazed in his mind, and even when he closed his eyes he saw its terrible might come crashing down upon him. Many of his minions coveted the armor, for they saw it as a means to overthrow him and become the new lord of darkness. It was not so, however, as the armor had been forged for the hands of Tykus alone. But the Shadow is as cunning as it is strong, and the butchering of many good men about the crater the armor laid within gave cover to Sypchallu, and he came forth in physical form for the first time in an age to grasp the armor himself. His slender fingers gripped the hilt of a sword of living magic, and he felt great fear when he learned the true power of this gift. He could not destroy it, nor wield it to its potential. But his touch was corruption, and even in the few moments he held the weapon, his mind warped its original intent.

The magic forged into the starsteel gave it properties unequaled through time, and the hands of dwarves and elves would never smith such wonders, for the armor craved battle and blood. Tykus's sword fought of its own accord and gave him strength unmatched, and when he suffered a blow the steel would plunge into the heart of the shadow and no harm was ever done him whilst he wore the armor.

What Bol could not know was that Sypchallu had wrought his own magic upon this great work, for when it landed upon the earth Sypchallu's shadows corrupted and twisted it to his own bidding. So it was that the armor offered unlimited strength, but each soul claimed gave Sypchallu another fraction of power, and the eldest God was patient, for he was darkness and had existed before time itself.

The story of Tykus is legend now, and though the armor would be worn by many through the course of time, it was always assumed a myth. The fury of Tykus was insatiable, and his sword thirsted for blood and souls, as Sypchallu had willed. He came to be known as Khagarel by the trolls and dwarves, which means Ageless King, because his body seemed to never grow old, and he lived thrice the life of a normal man, and he transcended mortality so all who mentioned him named him Khagarel, for he was truly King of all that which he sought dominion over. While he never settled to a throne, all accepted his rule by might and blood.

When Tykus grew too strong for foes on Alkurah, he ascended, with the help of his father, to the Godhall. None expected the fury with which he brought war against the Alkui. Sypchallu's curse had driven Tykus mad, and his bloodlust overthrew his reason. The Godhall shook with his fury, but the Alkui were unfazed, and they cast him from their sight.

But Khagarel's rage shattered his mortal bonds and the Alkui were propelled from their home with him. They carved a great Scar on Kharat, and they rent the world with their fall. Khagarel mounted the Kharatvil, hewn in time long passed by dwarven hands and hammers. It seemed even greater now that the land about it was sunken and crushed. Tykus' challenge was heard the world over.

The Alkui surged forth against the Kharatvil, but even the divine could not sunder the magic stones. They broke against Khagarel's wall again and again. And when the Alkui grew tired and hurled their spears in fear of the sting of his blade, Khagarel laughed and insulted them and feasted in the halls of the dwarves.

Their anger was unspent, and they frothed, still afraid to risk their eternal life at the hands of a mortal. But Khagarel's taunts wormed into their minds until finally they grew reckless once more and attacked. Sypchallu's curse upon the armor proved fruitful, and his power grew a hundred fold that day, fed by the rage and fear of the Alkui themselves. The sky raged, and war was made across Alkurah and beyond as Gods warred with their children. The battle was vicious and merciless, and though it did not last long it felt an age to those who bore witness.

None know what happened within the Kharatvil during the great battle. Khagarel opened the gate at some point, and the Alkui thought he would surrender himself to them. Instead, Khagarel burst from the Kharatvil atop a host of demons, and their fury outmatched that of the Alkui, and their rage burned hot as the sun that scorched the sands. Sypchallu had made his presence known with great vigor, and his will was done. Gods fell, and the shadow came as close as it ever has to ascension. Against Req, the god of the dead and claimer of souls, Khagarel stood in single combat. Their blows would have rent mountains, and their clash was thunder upon ears miles away. Each strike fueled Khagarel's power, and the shadow within him burst forth. Sypchallu's true form was unleashed upon Req, and he quailed beneath a truly unstoppable force.

"Is this your will, Godson?" Req asked, unyielding in the face of terror itself.

"If this was my will, it would be done." Khagarel's final blow smote Req's sword from his hand. The lord of the dead stood, unarmed, before the greatest of men, and was afraid.

"What will you do, son of Bol?" Req knelt, and his voice shook in his terror, for he had not imagined his own death. "What will you become?"

Khagarel did not hesitate, and he struck swiftly, and in that moment he became Godslayer. Req's head rolled, but his soul knelt still before his new god, the lord of the dead, Tykus. "What is your will, my lord?"

"I will rule the mortals through death, and they will worship me above all save my father."

And it was so, for he willed it, and what death wills, becomes.

Khagarel became lord of the dead, and took Req's place as the shepherd of souls. He became Alkui, the first of few to achieve such, rather than be born so.

His anger abated, in time, and he sat his throne with the honor accorded the position. He was generous and kind, but strong and would suffer no threats to mortals. Sypchallu, however, was unable to fully corrupt the new god of the dead, and try as he might his shadows never again pierced the mind of the greatest mortal. Eventually, Khagarel surrendered the armor and sword back to Alkurah. And Sypchallu's great tool fell to the earth once more, cast from a seat of power unto nothing.

The shadows grew strong in the wake of the tumult. Chaos reigned, and in the absence of progress, there was only devastation. Dragons, griffons, and fell beasts with no name retched flame and wanton death upon the face of Alkurah, and Tykus watched as his father sat idly by. But the son of Bol was not patient, and his unfathomable temper unraveled, and in anger he gave unto men the gift his father had given, and they seized it with greedy, bloodstained hands.

The armor and sword bathed in blood of all kinds, and Sypchallu continued to grow in power though his minions were destroyed. The darkness would suffer no rivals, and though Bol had given the world Light and beauty and all things good, men turned from him and worshipped war and violence, and the dusk of beauty was upon Alkurah.

So it was that the Eova secluded themselves further. They sang songs to the world, but the world no longer sang back. They felt magic leaving the land, and they grew weak. Weak enough to let the shadow in, and Sypchallu is patient and strong enough to corrupt even the most wary minds, and so began his work.

As the Eova waned, so men waxed, and they spread throughout the land, and they ruled. Under iron boots fell city after city, as wonders built by the elder race crumbled to dust. Mortal wars tore the world apart, and the earth began dying. Eskeria, which was the great wood that blanketed Alkurah of old, shrank, and the boughs of trees as old as time flowered less and less, until many became gnarled and twisted, their knotted limbs destroyed to feed the forge of war. The grasslands grew wide, and roads of stone and trampled dirt spider-webbed the world. Creatures of magic faded as their world fell from grace, for though it saddened Bol to see Alkurah die, he would not act. His children would live their lives as they would. His mind could cause great change to thoughts and deeds, but he was idle, and Alkurah suffered.

A BEGINNING

Unraveling lives and twisted lies tell tales of Alkurah's past.
A present future of ancient beginnings, over all lives is Shadow cast.
Gods, men, and those caught between, hasten to unforeseen doom.
Storms and war, thunder and gore, above all the darkness looms.
To mortals and more, the rich and the poor, is given the future of life.
Numbers deplete in vict'ry and defeat, all armies are swallowed by strife.
One may stand, may kneel, may fall, may rise, and still be made a pawn.
When will is steeped in pride and death, every choice is wrong.
Yet through ashes and fire comes life anew, and the sun e'er rises,
And even to ancients, to gods, to kings, a single moment may surprise.

"What are we doing here, sir?"

"Digging."

"Digging."

"Yes, digging."

"I see that, sir. Digging for what?"

"Treasure." Garroway's rusted shovel blade struggled to punch into the dirt. "What else would we dig for?"

Gunsel stabbed his own shovel into the ground and toyed with a splinter on the handle. "You know, sir, we may find something of value faster if we both knew what we were searching for."

Garroway stopped and drew a grimy hand across his face. Several months of living on the road had left his cheeks a shade redder than was healthy. And he never washed his hair, which was now past his shoulders and starting to get embarrassing. Still, not in bad shape for a man unused to such hard living as travelling the road for three months without a carriage between oneself and the ground. His eyebrows naturally tilted up enough to make him seem as though he never quite believed what someone was saying, and often wore a bored expression. The combination gave him a constant façade of feined surprise. "We may find something of value if you dug as much as you complained."

With a wink, Gunsel shouldered his shovel. Straightened up to the fullest of his height, he was confident that if Garroway slouched, he would be the taller. "Aye, but the gods gave me a mouth of many words, a back unfit for hard work, and a love of fine living." He patted his belly, sighing at the little work they had actually accomplished.

"So the gods made you a woman?"

Gunsel blinked a few times before returning to shoveling. "That was low, sir."

"Keep that feminine charm flowing. It's helping ease the load."

The filthy pair dug until the sun sank far below the horizon. A disgruntled moon rose into the sky in the way youth try their best not to wake up, and the stars winked with too much energy for the pair to truly appreciate. The hot winds of the plains had long since ceased, and the dampness of night settled like a cool blanket upon the grasslands of Alkurah. Tiny birds flitted between the scarce trees, and scurrying rodents curbed the edge in their bellies on tasty morsels of insect and sparse, probably inedible vegetation.

Garroway propped himself against a tree and unfoleded a scrap of parchment from his back pocket. Sweat-stained and dirty, it served only as a pathetic reminder of his inability to stick to even a single promise he made to himself. He scrabbled, 'Gunsel snores like an ox.' He stopped and scratched his temple with the quill, wiped the ink off his temple with his hand, wiped his hand off on the dirt, and ended up with dirty and inky pants. Abandoning his quest for godliness, he continued, 'Though I've never heard an ox snore. I presume it's… loud. Journals are dumb.'

He shut his journal, which contained many such brief entries from the past several years. In fact, the one sad page was the only item he had managed not to lose in recent memory. Scratching his neck and yawning, he stood and nudged the fire with his foot. It gave an indignant cough, so he tossed the journal on it. The corners of the paper folded in and the whole thing imploded before sputtering out. The grass rustled and somewhere in the distance something squealed as it fell prey to something else, bigger or more venomous. Howls drifted eerily in the nighttime breeze. Garroway shivered and took up his shovel again. Grunting and stomping it deep into the moist earth he complained to no one in particular, "Haven't slept in weeks anyway."

Chunk.

"Treasure."

Chunk.

"Treasure treasure treasure."

Chunk.

"Probably isn't even real."

Thud.

Thud was a suspicious sound for a shovel to make in dirt, so Garroway investigated. He brought the shovel down hard two more times, greeted twice more by the thud of steel on wood. "Gunsel!" he hissed. "Gunsel rouse yourself from your beauty sleep. You'll never have enough anyway."

Gunsel mumbled. Various curses on Garroway's mother were uttered. When a clod of dirt exploded on his head he rose with a furious bellow, "You're a damned savage, son of a savage, father of no savages because you're a *savage*!"

Garroway thudded the shovel twice more before Gunsel stopped cursing and thrashing. "Gunsel, if you're done with your tantrum I believe I have found my treasure."

With further cursing and muttered fuss, Gunsel dragged his shovel to the hole. He gave a weak salute before hopping into the dank earth.

Fifteen minutes of digging and scraping passed in silence. Garroway pictured his treasure and life of riches. He would never eat rodent again, he decided. There was nothing particularly revolting about the taste, but the thought seemed to object to any concept of class. Maybe he could buy a restaurant and only serve rodent but tell no one.

Gunsel thought he was too tired to think, so he didn't.

When the pair finished clearing a small area around the box, they stuck their shovels into the sides and levered it up onto the grass.

"Just feel it! It's heavy!" Garroway danced around the box tapping it with his shovel and kicking it lightly.

Gunsel pulled his leg back and smashed his toe into the box. The box didn't move as far as Gunsel's toe did. He yelped.

"Don't be such a killjoy, Gunsel. This could be our salvation!"

Gunsel flopped onto the ground and nursed his foot. "Maybe it's food."

"Tcha." With a mighty swing Garroway smashed the lock with his rusted shovel.

The shovel broke. If locks could mock, this one would have, squatting on the hinge it protected.

Gunsel's spade proved a more obstinate weapon, and yielded a satisfactory clang before the lock gave up on hiding its treasure.

Despite his moping, Gunsel sat up to watch the reveal.

Garroway paused before kneeling and reaching into the void. Metal tinkled together as he moved his hand around. He winked at his companion and pulled out the first of their treasure. The disappointment on Gunsel's face said more than his words.

"That's it?"

Garroway's smile faltered only for a moment. He quickly pulled more and more from the chest. He was finished in such a hurry that he poked around the empty chest long enough to acquire a splinter before he gave up. Head cocked to the side he squatted and picked up a gauntlet. "Armor. Huh."

"Oh, no, sir. Not just any armor. It's *treasure*."

With his lips pursed, Garroway fished around the pile of armor. He retrieved a small parchment, worn and flimsy, that read simply- *Tykus*.

The sun rose and shooed away some lingering mist as the birds began their daily clamor. Gunsel had groused and pouted before falling into a drunken slumber after quaffing a full jug of ale. Bugs tickled his ears, dew had dampened his clothes, and Garroway was flicking flower petals at him from across the remnants of the fire. A pigeon descended to sit directly on top of his head, and he sat up with a snort, slurring,

"I'm gonna hire someone to take you somewhere awful and kill you."

Garroway relinquished his handful of foliage, "Don't be silly, I pay you too much for you to want that."

"You don't pay me at all, sir."

"Quite so. Then you can't afford an assassin."

They rolled their bountiful rations of sad, empty cloths up into their packs before tying the old set of jet-black armor together. Garroway gave it a soft kick before nodding at Gunsel, "You can handle that."

"I'd love nothing more, sir."

They spent the morning trudging south. They trudged through grass that scratched everything up to their elbows. They trudged through a patch of mud that mired them in the middle of the grass, slowing their progress until they stopped for a lunch break early enough that it might have been breakfast still. Lunch consisted of forlorn looks at the vultures that circled something on the cusp of death somewhere close enough to be mistaken for the strange pair. They trudged past dilapidated homes and wild animals that gave them the kinds of glances Gunsel might give to an entire roast chicken. They saw only one other person that day, headed the opposite direction. He wore a long red robe with no pack or water skin. Garroway nodded as they passed. The stranger seemed to stare at the armor on Gunsel's back before nodding and moving quickly away. Garroway jerked his thumb over his shoulder, "What an odd man."

"I thought he looked familiar, but I suppose not."

"Relative?"

The response was a grunt that said either 'no' or something infinitely more obscene. Garroway appreciated the meaning either way.

There was no path to follow, but their destination was clearly visible. Ahead loomed the towering spires of Korz. Center of the world when even the ancients walked these very roads.

The location of the city never made sense to Garroway. It was a sprawling complex of wood and stone whose roads seemed to be actively trying to get you lost. There were no signs anywhere and he was fairly certain that there was no police force. City guardsmen lumbered around, trying to look less lost than everyone else, but never seemed to react to anything other than violent murder committed directly in their line of sight. The bars were sleazy, the businessmen were sleazier, and the women wore less clothing the closer to the center you went. Garroway had never made it to the city hall, the dead center of the expanding nightmare, but he planned to someday.

To Gunsel, the city was just another city. He knew where to go to drown in fermented grains and he was confident that he could find a woman willing to sate his appetite for other tastes. Whether or not he would be able to compensate her for her services remained to be seen. Hopefully the cheap ones still had all their limbs. Bad experiences with women of ill repute in his past left a poor taste in his mouth for more reasons than one.

Impressive spires dotted the city seemingly at random. They were slender and covered in upward-facing spikes. Some said these were to help the city fend off dragons in the old days. Garroway could think of no better use for them so he had often imagined the city at night, torches burning and the sky filled with roaring dragons bellowing spouts of flame into the darkness. Each spire was topped with a lookout and a massive torch that never stopped burning. The city was always doing business, so the lights burned night and day.

As the pair approached the shadows of the taller spires, they set up their campsite as best they could. The walls were well in sight now and they would arrive by midafternoon the next day. While Gunsel drained the last of his reserves of ale, Garroway tinkered with the armor. Nothing about it seemed special aside from the color. It absorbed the light around it. It didn't shine but wasn't dull. Turning the helmet over in his hands he pondered the name. Tykus. It sounded familiar and some forgotten meaning buzzed around the back of his head.

Gunsel interrupted his mulling. "Think it's worth anything?"

"Clearly. Someone took the time to box it up and bury it."

"What if it's cursed?"

Garroway frowned for a moment. "I don't believe in magic."

"I don't believe in servitude," Gunsel waved his arms grandly about himself. "And yet..."

"What if I wear it?"

"What if you sell it?"

Waving off his companion, Garroway unlaced the armor and started strapping the gauntlets to his hands. It fit perfectly, as if it had been made for him, and despite the growing cold around them, the steel was warm to the touch. Garroway was unable to tell if the pulsing he felt was his own heart racing or something within the armor. Even wearing only the gloves he felt powerful, as if these gauntlets gave him the strength to take on armies. Shivering, he tossed the eerie metal back to the pile.

"Sir Garroway, knight!" Gunsel chuckled.

As he doffed the armor and nestled into his blankets, Garroway grinned. Knight indeed.

Garroway dreamt that night of shadows and fire. He sweated and thrashed, unnerved by fleeting images of bloody weapons and greasy smoke, cavalry charges and magical barrages. In a night, he saw the world end and be born again in fire, so when he awoke to the gentle crackling of their tiny blaze he took no reassurance in its lingering warmth.

The pair struck out early the next morning. A vibrant sun painted the horizon and the birds let loose an incessant volley of tweets that left Gunsel stewing throughout their journey. "I love eating birds," he muttered. "They don't assault you when they're cooked."

"They might not assault you if you showered. Do they keep the bugs off you?"

"They keep something less pleasant and more odorous *on* me."

"If you didn't feed them..."

Gunsel swatted a pigeon in response.

Their casual, meandering pace caused the pair to stumble upon the road well after noon. Other travelers crashed and bludgeoned by on horseback or in carriages. Traffic flooded into the city, but hardly a trickle exited the gates. Dirty, scraggly men and malnourished children shuffled from the massive iron maw, some with hats or cups in hand hoping to scrounge from the travellers on their way into the city. A lonely guard, whose armor slouched as much as his shoulders, stopped every person as they entered. His massive halberd was propped on a crack in the stone. Bleary eyes blinked slowly, calloused hands moved even slower, and his voice gave the impression of a boulder creaking on the verge of rolling down a hillside. "Why are you coming to Korz?"

Gunsel's jaw worked on a long piece of grass as he replied, "Business."

The unhappy guard blinked again. Garroway was certain hours passed before the man waved a limp arm toward the city, "Welcome."

KORZ

Spires tall. Dark. Afraid. In times of beast and drake.
On human bone, flesh, and blood their mighty hunger slaked.
A man stood alone upon a tower, son of Thunder and War.
The city burned, her children slaughtered, drowning in blood and gore.
This man he swung his mighty axe, steel met scale and bone.
Clad in hope, cloaked in death, he conquered fear alone.
Ferocious. Vicious. Claws, teeth! They slashed, snapped, and burned.
Blood flowed forth as he fought alone, from man to god he turned.
Sun set, sky broke. The land grew dark and dead.
He stood alone, on stone, on bone, his armor stained bloodred.
Three days they raged, their scales crushed, his axe long bent and dull.
At last! A claw his armor rent. Storm descended, thunder rolled.
To a knee he fell, blood on his tongue, he roared challenge at the night.
He rose to live and they fled, escaped, the dragons all took flight!
Immortality earned, each scar a song, he strode to Godhall's doors.
His wounds were healed, his city saved. All hail the mighty Korz!

The roar of the city, previously muted by its massive walls, engulfed Gunsel and Garroway with full force once they passed the gates. Sloth-like guards bumbled among the commoners, pretending to look like they were attempting to prevent them from sabotaging or robbing the carriages of the lords and ladies that bounced across the stone streets. The filth of the city collected in reeking, knee-deep gutters beside the winding road. A young boy bumped into Gunsel but the sour man snatched his empty coin purse back before the urchin could mix with the crowd. He yelled over his shoulder, "Lovely place, sir."

"It's home," Garroway replied, torn between how much he despised the city and the waves of nostalgia, or nausea, passing over him.

Banging shoulders with all manner of scoundrels and lowlifes, Gunsel and Garroway scrapped deeper into the city. Musicians twanged on odd instruments with more strings than seemed possible to pluck. Drums bigger than a man boomed across the city from the rooftops as men with red painted faces wailed instructions to the enslaved workers through the beat.

If someone managed to get caught committing a crime in Korz, they certainly deserved any punishment dealt by the guards. Minor offenses were often sentenced to work details. Essentially slaves, they worked long hours for no pay for a number of days relatively equal to their crime. Unless the guard had some reason not to like them, or they happened to forget their sentence had been served, or really any number of reasons anyone could think of to extend their time beneath the yoke. The more prisoners were working, the less the Guardsmen had to do.

Real crimes, such as murder and other such common occurences, were met with conscription to the army. Not the glorious, cavalry-charging, heroic, statuesque army. These were known as the Dragon's Hand, heroes of old and greater than any other army ever to step foot upon Alkurah. The conscript army got to soak up arrows and the lances of opposing cavalry, ending up a puddle of bone and entrails on the field. Hopefully.

Gunsel gaped at the sights and marveled at the sounds. Lords and ladies draped in lace and fine linens smoked long pipes or cigarettes. The sickly stench of the smoke made his nose itch. Performers did their best to steal attention from their closest competitors; magicians, both legitimate and false, wowed the milling crowd.

Gunsel felt a gentle elbow in his ribs and took a deep breath to give the trespasser a wordy rebuke before he noticed it was Garroway's. He followed his master's hand to see an ogre strolling side by side with a dwarf. They were having an animated chat, and the ogre's gestures threatened to decapitate anyone standing too close. The dwarf's were less dangerous but just as wild, more likely to smash an unwary kneecap than anything. Perhaps in an attempt to make up for his stature with enthusiasm, his arms flailed in an assortment of entirely unpredictable directions. His beard was thrown over his shoulder and swept the ground behind him neatly. Gunsel was certain he saw a nest.

Half an hour of wading through assorted delinquency saw the pair in front of the door to a massive home sandwiched between a butcher shop and a tanner's rancid vats. The stench was almost unbearable. Garroway took a deep breath, gagged, and knocked on the tiny wooden side door, "I return from my travels, beloved family, and have need of lodgings."

There was a long scraping sound from within before a drawling answer, "Inn's four doors down, whelp."

Garroway's eyes narrowed. He put a hand on the latch, but before he could turn it the door flew open back into the house. A skeletal man, as thin as he was old, loomed to the side of the door. He sighed with as little welcome as he could muster into his voice, "Welcome home, young master."

Afraid to touch the frail-looking man, Garroway simply waved and grinned, "Many thanks to you, old servant!"

Gunsel nodded and grunted, shuffling his feet.

"I see you have a new," the ancient butler paused and frowned, "associate."

"Ah, yes. Gunsel, I'd like you to meet Mr. Fundwick. He's been a family servant for literally ages. You were the one who invented cleaning, correct?"

Fundwick didn't blink. "I am."

The certainty of his answer unsettled Gunsel as he sidled past into the foyer. Dull orange tiles clashed horrendously with pink walls. The vaulted ceiling was filled with decorative architecture. He counted aloud, "Buttresses that buttress the other buttresses that buttress buttresses buttressing buttresses?"

"Yes. My mother is very proud." Garroway shrugged as though it was simply a battle not worth fighting.

As if summoned, a klutzy ball of cloth and lipstick bumbled from a hidden door in the wall. Gunsel thought he saw a handkerchief waving but it may have simply been an extravagant sleeve. An aura of abundant frump exuded from the thing. Gunsel immediately felt distaste for it.

"My baby boy Rinslicanth is home!" It squealed, throwing both chubby arms into the air and latching onto Garroway for a suffocating hug.

"Close, mother, but you've missed by four."

She faltered, even unclasping her son for a moment to do the math. Gunsel thought she was counting sausages but they were just fingers. He was disappointed.

"Bornidash?" She asked.

"Other way."

She huffed and sweated, counting the other way, "Garroway?"

He threw his hands up and yelled, "Oh, you did miss me! Hello, mother dearest."

She looked mildly disappointed as she gave him a timid hug. It seemed to Gunsel that either Rinslicanth and Bornidash would have been preferred.

Gunsel started when Fundwick spoke so closely to his ear the younger man may not have had to imagine his earlobe being brushed by the servant's lips. "I introduce Master Brisborne, head of house."

As Fundwick presumably floated back to the coffin from which he had arisen, a tall, wiry, mangy man sprung into the hall. He sported an overcoat that was made for a man two hundred years older and three feet shorter than himself, a tall purple hat that tilted threateningly to the left, and a mustache that would make any dwarf proud. Bounding across the tiles, he scooped both Gunsel and Garroway into a crushing hug. Garroway winced and tried to extricate himself from the vise. Gunsel had not been hugged in quite some time. He decided hugs were just not for him anymore.

"It's nice to see you, father."

"Oh, my boy Garroway it's been just ages since you left us that silly note saying you were off to become a warrior to serve in the Dragon's Hand!"

Gunsel snickered.

"Laugh if you want, at least I didn't end up in someone else's hands as a servant." Garroway cleared his throat, raising his nose in the air to reply, "And yes, father, I did plan on joining the Hand. I was waylaid by misfortune, alcohol, and my first experience with a pair of dice."

"Aye, you're naught but skin and bones, my boy! Bumphrey, dear, go tell someone to cook something meaty and expensive!"

The bundle named Bumphrey scooted back through the wall with a quick nod. She screeched something just before the door shut, and Gunsel was actually afraid some of the glassware would shatter.

"My boy, what have you been doing these long years?"

Garroway scratched his temple and worked his mouth. "Lots of spending and not much making. Women. Drink. Drunken women. I got married. Turns out, she was with a centaur once. Couldn't please her one bit. She stole several tens of coins from me when she left with that ogre. I was saved the paperwork when she died, though. Aside from that, respectable enterprises of many sorts, as I'm sure you can imagine."

"Atta boy." Brisborne clapped him on the shoulder with a wink and led him toward a separate part of wall. It opened at his touch and showed them, with Gunsel searching, mystified, for Fundwick, into a new room.

The decrepit aforementioned bowed at the opposite end of the room with a towel over his arm. He moaned, "Dinner will be served in one quarter of an hour, Master Brisborne."

"All fabulous, well, and dandy indeed, my man!"

Fundwick nodded and disappeared once more. Gunsel marveled at the ornate picture frames and fantastic woodwork. The feet of all the chairs ended in beautiful sculpted griffons, wings flared out and beaks open wide. He poked at some of the clocks and toys that cluttered desktops. Ponderous artwork filled the walls from floor to fifteen-foot ceiling. Head cocked, he stared at a massive canvas adorned with a scantily clad dwarf doing something probably illegal and certainly uncomfortable.

He'd stopped to stare, and Garroway hissed at him, "Gunsel! Don't leave me alone here!"

Tearing his gaze from the painting, Gunsel trotted up behind Garroway and Brisborne in time for them to walk through another wall. The dining room put the entrance to shame. The ostentatiousness of the place was truly staggering.

Gunsel had never seen spires indoors, nor had he seen a porch that faced a dining hall. He later learned that was called a stage. Chandeliers dazzled and hundred of candles gave the room a pleasant fragrance as well as a stifling heat. Fundwick finishing setting the table as they walked in, looking as disapproving as ever. Gunsel caught a waft of his own stench and almost lost his appetite.

Garroway had no such reserves and began popping olives into his mouth by the handful. He whispered to Gunsel through stuffed cheeks, "They're monsters." Another handful of olives, "Mff. They live. Mff. Like they're kings. It's abhorrent"

Gunsel reached for an olive but received a smart rap on the knuckles from Fundwick. "For masters and ladies only."

Before Gunsel could react, Garroway stepped between the two, simultaneously turning Gunsel around and shooing Fundwick away. "It's quite alright, man, he's with me."

Brisborne either ignored the incident, or was too swept up in his own words to notice as he continued rambling about the lords, the court, and the market. "And then, of course she was drunk by this time, Jennet drew a rapier. A rapier! And she swung it about, decapitating a poor tapestry that had hung in the city hall for generations upon generations. By the time she passed out, I think she'd done enough damage to warrant her sentence..." His arms gestured madly and every time he knocked something off a table or desk Fundwick happened to be on hand to snatch it from the air and replace it. When he reached the end of the room he whipped around on his heel and stomped, abandoning whatever misadventure Jennet had gotten into next. With a grand smile, throwing his arms in the air he shouted, "Dinner is served!"

Nothing happened for almost a full minute, Brisborne standing like a herald of angels before a wall covered in horrendous paintings colored a ghastly shade of mucous. Fundwick materialized to his right and whispered something in his ear.

The master of the house tugged on his jacket, ripped it, tossed it in a corner (where Fundwick caught it), and strode to the head of the table. His massive chair sported griffon sculptures on both arms, the feet, and the back. Moving to flare out his coattails, he did his best to recover when he realized he was no longer wearing his coat, and sat with all the class and dignity expected of a man of means.

Gunsel rolled his eyes toward Garroway, who stared open-mouthed at his father. The energetic man fidgeted and bounced until he realized he had an audience. Clearing his throat loudly he bellowed, "Sit!"

The pair shared a glance before calmly sliding into their own chairs. Fundwick presumably pulled both of them out at the same time and it took Gunsel more than a moment to realize he was wearing a napkin as a bib. He shivered.

Just after the silence became uncomfortable, a wall creaked open and Bumphrey scooted out laden with trays. Fundwick and some other servants followed, setting their loads down neatly on the table before disappearing.

Garroway shoveled heaps of chicken, potatoes, something purple and grainy, and rolls that dripped with butter. Before either of his parents had touched their forks he had devastated an entire platter of stuffing.

Globs of fruits and vegetables with names he couldn't pronounce were washed down by the finest mead Gunsel had ever gulped. He strove to keep up with his master, consuming so many berries that his teeth would be stained for two days. Even Fundwick looked impressed for a moment before his surly mask of impassive disgust replaced itself.

Bumphrey dabbled at some of the platters but never actually seemed to eat anything. Her fork perched daintily between two meaty fingers and her knife was hardly visible beneath her fat hands. After every nibble she dabbed at the corners of her mouth with her napkin before resuming her pecking hunt. How she attained her gluttonous appearance remained a mystery to all who knew her.

The master of the house literally attacked his meal. Hopping onto his chair and wielding his knife like a sword, Brisborne jumped and parried, whirled and lunged. Piercing a chicken through the heart he roared triumphantly and devoured it straight from the blade.

No words were exchanged throughout the whole of dinner. The two travellers had not even managed to steal a hearty meal in weeks. Brisborne was busy giving well-practiced victory speeches and rousing performances of battles against assorted poultry and swine. When the dishes were vanquished and the warriors eased back on their chairs, belts tighter than before, the servants swept in to clear the table. Some of the candles were blown out to dim the room slightly and Brisborne clapped twice to summon Fundwick.

Gunsel, unaware that Fundwick had left the room at any point, started when the man asked for his napkin. He practically threw it at the sneaky servant in his fright. Gliding to the head of the table, and no longer holding the napkin, he produced a small flute from his jacket sleeve. Brisborne encouraged him and he struck up a lively dirge to kill the evening's mood. Garroway's smile faded and he began to ponder his own mortality. The soulful sadness of the music struck him deeply and he felt tears welling in his eyes. He peeked at Gunsel, who looked sad and sleepy, before wiping his eyes on a fresh napkin. When the song finished, the room was a little darker and a touch more somber than before. The flute went back into its sleeve to mourn silently and Fundwick almost seemed to smirk as he slid out of the room.

Brisborne, appearing deep in thought, snorted awake and cheered uproariously. He cleared his throat and addressed his wife, "My dear, would you mind terribly if I asked for some time alone with our son and his man. I know you've missed your son dearly and wish never to leave his sight again, but I must attend to some private matters."

She gave a fake smile, a weak curtsy, glared at Gunsel, and squeezed through a small door on the side of the room.

As soon as the door clicked shut Brisborne became serious. The hat still dangled precariously, but managed to cling to his hair seemingly through his willpower alone. He dragged Garroway to a wooden chair in the corner. Gunsel helped himself to one of the massive lounge chairs in the room. He listened to the father's urgent tone with only passing interest.

"I truly am glad you've returned, my boy. The city guard has become shorthanded and rather useless as of late. All of the strong and smart ones have joined the army to prepare for the war."

Garroway nearly choked on someone else's tea, of which he had taken a sip simply because the cup was in arm's length, "War? Excuse me, I thought you said war."

Brisborne leaned back, incredulous, "Did you not know? My boy, Korz has been gearing for war since before you left. Peace talks with the Rofu broke down and none of the ambassadors from either side, assuming the Rofu have ambassadors at all, have been able to make a difference. There's going to be a war; the only question left is where and when."

Often sell-swords, employed as assassins and thieves because of their innate appreciation of sneaking, the Rofu were less of an army and more of a nightmare made real. Few stories of battle from the Rofu were lively tales of rousing victories and powerful clashes in the open field. Often they were tales whispered in the night of entire armies poisoned, platoons of soldiers disappearing, or whole cities being destroyed under cover of darkness. The thought of Korz being destroyed didn't make Gunsel altogether unhappy.

"What do they want with us? Why does there even need to be peace? The grasslands separate Kharat from Korz, not to mention the Nazene. There's not even a border!"

Wringing his hands and glancing at the walls as if they were listening, Brisborne whispered conspiratorially, "They don't, ah, exactly want peace."

Garroway cocked his eyebrows, "Go on."

"Well, my boy, they seem to think we have, ah, some kind of protection to offer them from some apparition in the west."

"Well, have we?"

Brisborne wiped a hand down his face, suddenly looking exhausted, "I do not know. The city council won't tell me anything and the guard wouldn't know a bribe if it slapped them in the face. Trust me, I've actually hit guards with money and they didn't understand. I can't fathom something powerful enough to displace the entire Rofu, but if they're this afraid, I think it's time we be afraid as well."

Garroway whistled long and low, "Sounds like a good time for me to leave then."

Looking even more nervous, Brisborne jumped out of his chair and started to the wall they'd come in from, "Actually, ah, my boy, I've meant to tell you. There's been a military draft. You've been called. Two years ago, in fact."

Even Gunsel looked amused at the news of Garroway becoming a warrior. He grunted, "So I'm free to go, aye?"

Brisborne clapped and pointed his fingers at the servant, "Ha! Well, my boy, no. No, you'll be drafted too."

As he finished, the wall opened behind Gunsel and the ogre they had seen earlier threw the spluttering manservant onto his shoulder. His muscular gray arms flinched as much as a mountain might flinch at the stomping of a single ant while Gunsel rained punches, kicks, and insults. It mumbled, "Ah've go' a thick skin, sah. Cain't hu't me wit' words o' bloauws."

Put off by the beast's speech, Gunsel settled down, crossed his arms, and pouted. Garroway strode from his chair, indignant finger under his father's nose, "You cannot take me nor my servant for a silly war with some silly desert orcs over a silly superstition!"

"Love not to, my boy, but they've threatened much worse things than drafting my youngest son if I don't comply."

Furious, Garroway turned to address the ogre, decided he would have better luck shouting down a brick wall, and rallied against his father once more, "This is unfair! I haven't been a Korzian for years! You know people! Work out a deal! Do something!"

Another door opened. Garroway whipped around with a ferocious punch. His knuckles plowed through the air and he nearly tripped on the stern-looking dwarf that clucked at him, whiffing it high by at least a foot. "You come with me. Easy way or hard way."

With a final glare at his father and a pitiful gesture toward the dwarf, he rolled his eyes and turned to face his captor. They stared at each other for a full minute before Gunsel complained from the back of the ogre, "Can we get on with it?"

Garroway snatched the armor from his pack on the way through the front door; confident it would protect him better than the armor that had been worn by the Korzian infantry for the last five hundred years. On their way through the house Gunsel was sure he saw Fundwick grinning from a crack in the wall.

THE GUARD

The Dragon's Hand from the Guard was raised in times of open war.
The best of greats filled their ranks, an honor to serve great Korz.
Men poured forth to fight, to die, and keep their city proud.
Their armor gleamed, their minds shone bright, risen above the crowd.
Korz had long since entered Godhall, his people praised his name.
Those who fought amongst the Hand exalted his power and fame.
After years of safety, of plenty, of peace, their power waned, thinned.
The Hand faltered, it's bluff was called. Evil approached and grinned.
The Shadow never dies; it lies, and watches and waits and sees.
A crack in the armor of hope it seeks to bring good men to their knees.

Westernmost of all the many strongholds held by Korz, Brathur was a truly unoriginal design. It is the closest Korzian outpost to the Kharat Desert, a great block of stone meant to break whatever waves may be sent its way. The first line of defense. Stone barracks separated by narrow alleys lined the east side. A squat cabin housed Lord Commander Kyson, while the platoon commanders all bunked in a smaller barracks complete with their own mess hall. It had stood for centuries, built in the glory days of Korz when the Dragon's Hand roamed far and wide and won honor and gold for their homes. Its western wall was hardy and thick, and the north corner housed a massive turret that supported three ballistae. The southern wall, however, slumped slightly, and ivy crawled across the mortar. Now, it was filled to the brim with green recruits and hardened mercenaries, with little bridge between them. There had been no open war among the men of Korz in so long they had grown fat and content, unused to the trying road, hard work, and battle.

Soldiers all gathered to the Great Hall for their meals, meetings, and training that took place indoors. The massive structure dominated the simple barracks that stood behind it. Built long and stretching to the sky, it inspired pride in the soldiers just enough to offset the loathing inspired by their training. If men were capable of creating such a thing, they could certainly win any war. Gorgeous statues of fallen heroes stood as pillars, hands resting on axes, swords, hammers, and bows. Men of the east and south were depicted side by side with dwarves. Trolls of the north shown in glorious battle allied with the elves of the forests. Glorious deeds immortalized in stone to remind the men of Korz of their forebears. Modeled after the ancient interpretation of the Godhall, it was an impressive artistic work as well as a sturdy, battle-hardened keep. The ture masterpiece, however, faced Korz. On the eastern wall was a marvelous stained-glass depiction of the Legend of Tykus.

A torch flared in the damp barracks. The sudden brightness stung eyes still sticky from sleep. Mumbles and groans greeted the crusty man that stood in the doorway. Whining from the shadows at the back of the room, a voice yelled, "The hell out! Not even morning."

Stony features almost creaked as the man with the torch scowled even harder. He tossed it onto the nearest bed. The greasy sheets caught fire immediately and whoever was trying to sleep there practically exploded out of bed to stand at attention in front of his bunk. He shivered from the cold as the older man leaned close to look at him. His breath smelled like dust and his granite eyes were void of emotion. The protruding brow and strong, broad jaw made him look like he was a generation or ten removed from the smooth structure of modern human face. He cracked his neck and, through one side of his mouth, growled, "Name."

"Willoskowitz, sir!"

His scowl deepened, "Nope. You're Lo, now."

The young man was accustomed to explaining the deep cultural and familial significance of his name, so he took a deep breath, hoping to educate the military man. He had almost begun when the officer smashed his knuckles into the poor fellow's nose. Lo collapsed.

The rest of the barracks was groggily awake now and most managed to stand vaguely at attention at the feet of their beds. One man dared remain totally oblivious. At the back of the building, in the darkest corner, covered in sheets that dripped from the moisture of the room, a young man yelled again, "Not today. I'm sleepin'."

Narrowing his unfeeling eyes, the soldier stomped to the back of the room. When he reached the bed he asked for a name.

"Tykus."

The officer's reaction was instant. He snatched the wet blanket, flipped the metal frame of the bed over entirely and pulled the delinquent up by the hair. His gravelly voice seemed to chew up the words before he spat out, "I fought with Tykus." He grated his teeth and spat on the floor, "You're not him."

The confident smirk vanished from the boy's face as it was rearranged for him, free of cost, by a jarring backhand. Addressing the contingent of other guards just outside the door, the officer smiled. It was worse than his scowl. "Not even sunrise and I've performed two fist-surgeries. Hell of a start, meat."

He stomped back to the door and retrieved his torch, now sputtering in a pile of ash. As he bent down, Lo flinched, drawing a chuckle from the guards outside. Leaving his back to the bunks, the officer barked, "The courtyard. You have three minutes."

Recruits scrambled to squeeze into uniforms that had been made for men now long dead, and their crimson mail was not entirely free of rust. Garroway, who slept near the front of the room, had dozed off in his assigned tunic, giving him a headstart, so he was first out of the room. The chain mail he had been issued smelled like a dirty sponge. It wafted over him whenever he shifted. Coarse metal hung rather loosely around his shoulders, threatening to slip off at any moment. His treasure-armor lay polished in the trunk at the foot of his bed. Having witnessed the older officer's outburst at the name of Tykus being mentioned, he was nervous about showing it off to anyone, so it stayed locked in the trunk for the moment.

Already, other platoons of recruits were running, climbing, fighting, and puking on the grass. One sliver of orange was all the sunlight that had managed to crawl above the gray horizon. Gunsel and Garroway were in the same platoon, so they had been free to discuss the unfairness with which they felt they were treated. Having arrived only the day before, each recruit received their crimson uniforms and rusty, filthy, ownerless-because-their-owners-were-dead chainmail, and was sent to the barracks.

Yawning and struggling into his mail coat, Gunsel mumbled, "Morn'."

Garroway simply nodded and slapped his cheeks to wake up before the grumpy old soldier returned. He received a smack across the shoulders with the flat of the harsh captain's sword.

The man was the utter personification of a glower. Thin, gray lips, outlined by a jaw chiseled from stone. His short crop of thin hair was almost transparent in the light. The abuser bellowed to the assembled company, "Good hustle, meat. My name is Roc and I have the pleasure of breaking you," he paused and surveyed his troops, "in."

He sheathed his sword and trudged away from the front line, "Today we'll take it nice and slow. Some light sparring, basic weapons training, introductions to your comrades and officers, and so on." Kicking at a weed, he ordered, "Ten laps around the compound. Last one done gets no dinner. Or lunch. Probably not even breakfast. I hate slackers."

The assembly milled around unsure of where to start. One of the training officers lurking in their midst and gave an unsuspecting recruit a slap to the face. He barked, spittle flying, "Means go, meat!"

The herd stampeded toward the nearest gate. None of them had seen the sheer size of the encampment on their way in, and most were winded before even turning the first corner. Striking a leisurely pace, they loped straight into a group that was running the opposite direction. Garroway had the misfortune of chest bumping a troll. It didn't even react as it bowled him over and trundled off around the corner, either sneezing or howling in pain due to some injury inflicted by certainly not Garroway.

Gunsel, not a skinny man by any standard, huffed to his master's side and helped him up. "Ten laps. Ain't run ten of anything my whole life."

"Perhaps if we were eating instead of running?"

"Aye. I'd be commander of legions if that were the case."

On their ninth lap, Garroway and Gunsel had a healthy lead on the stragglers of the platoon so they eased up around the first corner. Both men dripped with sweat and were caked in mud from the knees down. A chicken was keeping pace with them, trying as hard as it might to trip Gunsel. In ragged breaths, he interrogated Garroway. "How come. Whoo. You never. Phew. Told me you. Guh. Were a noble?"

Garroway trotted easily beside his companion, "It never mattered. And they aren't nobles. My grandfather apparently worked for the city for some years and they didn't notice when he died, so they send money to the home every month. We use Fundwick as our model if anyone ever comes questioning the existence of the man, but it's been nearly thirty years now. Besides, I don't consider myself one of them anyway. I want to make my own name for myself, not be someone's son for the rest of my life, hoping no one would come to collect me for fraud and sentence me to forever in slavery to atone for my family's conduct."

"So, treasure?"

"At least I could say I earned it then. Or found it. It's different. Feels less wrong. I was hoping my father might steer me in the direction of someone to whom I might trade in my treasure for money. Alas."

Gunsel shook his head, "But the food…"

Grinning, Garroway slapped his partner on the back, "The food comes with Fundwick, and I'd like as little of him as I can get."

Gunsel almost laughed, but started wheezing instead.

Rounding the final corner, the pair was in high spirits. Confident they'd get a good meal, some time to rest and chat, and some sort of bath, they were swiftly backhanded by the cruel hand of fate. It looked suspiciously like Roc. He was lying in wait for all of the recruits just around the final corner, and he smacked both of them across the jaw as they came by. "Suck it in, weasel-dung. What's your name?"

"Garroway, sir," he rubbed his jaw and kept running.

Roc backpedaled and shook his head, clucking his tongue, "Terrible name. You're Ro." Turning to Gunsel he asked the same question.

Still in shock from the blow and exhausted from the exercise, he muttered, "Guns." The "el" didn't escape his lips audibly.

Roc swatted him in the chest and roared, "Well, damn me! A strong name for a fat man. We'll fix that in time." He chuckled, "Guns!" as he returned to his post at the corner of the wall to crack another unsuspecting recruit across the face with his mailed fist.

Garroway grinned at his companion, "I suppose we're now Guns and Ro."

They glanced at Lo getting slapped again before Gunsel answered, "Least we aren't poor Lo."

Nudging his compatriot in the ribs, Garroway eased to a stop just inside the gate, laughing. They received a cheer from their comrades upon striding into the open field.

By the time Roc jogged back into the courtyard, the group was noticeably smaller. He gave a nod across the field to a cluster of gruff-looking men that may have descended from a race of bears. The company, obviously mercenaries, swaggered toward the recruits. Massive swords rested on their shoulders, hammers tugged on their belts, axes perched across their backs, beards tangled and twisted across their chests, and the smell of liquor and death lingered about them. The leader, covered in swirling blue tattoos, chucked a handful of swords at the group. Sneering, he spit and glanced at Roc before jerking his head back at the recruits. The rest of the mercenaries tossed an assortment of dangerous metal and wood at the platoon before assuming positions behind Roc.

Raising his eyebrows, the stony commander simply said, "Well, pick one."

They gingerly approached the pile, careful lest any of the weapons begin wielding itself. The more brutish of the group grabbed massive hammers and grinned their grins that held few teeth. Those who fancied themselves classier plucked swords or spears and slicked their hair back. Gunsel hefted a pair of small axes and grunted appreciatively. Carvings of orcs and goblins decorated both, and their hafts curved slightly to a wicked sickle down and away from the blade.

Garroway saw nothing that struck his fancy until the pile shifted and a black sword slid to his feet. He knelt and stroked the plain scabbard. Just above the crossguard was a small "T" branded on either side. The sword slid easily free of its sheath and he marveled at the dark blade. It reminded him of the armor he had recently found. These suspicions were forgotten when he felt a hot breath on his neck. Roc whispered, "You choose that sword, yer destined for glory," he inched closer, "or horrors beyond imagining."

"Encouraging," Garroway answered, sounding more confident than he felt.

When the recruits figured out how to attach their various weapons to themselves through the means of an assortment of belts, scabbards, cursing, and a few incidents of self-maiming, Roc had them each pair up with one of the mercenaries. "These are your teachers. They look like animals, they act like animals," he sniffed and sidled away from the group, "and they smell like animals."

They grinned and patted each other's backs.

"They've killed more men, drank more ale, and bedded more women than the lot of you ever will. Learn from them, live like them, and fight with them."

From the back of the group a man grumbled, "Probably bedded some men too."

The lead mercenary shoved through until he found the quivering body belonging to the voice. Cocking an eyebrow he grinned around to his comrades. He nodded, "Aye, and some of those men were prettier than the women."

Various guffaws erupted from the assembly. The recruits were unsure how to react so many of them laughed uncomfortably while others simply chewed their lips fiercely hoping the conversation would end without someone dying.

It almost did. As the bearish mercenary left the group of recruits, an arrow punched deep into his chest. Without batting an eye, he pulled it out, sucked his blood off it, and handed it to Roc, "Message." He squinted at the paper, "For you, I believe." He nodded to Roc, pounded his right fist against his left arm, and collapsed. The other mercenaries made the same gesture, the looks on their faces approaching solemn.

Roc sighed and unfurled the parchment. He read aloud, "The Rofu take no prisoners. The Rofu never forgive, they never fail, they never fall." He snorted and tossed it over his shoulder. The rookies, most no longer only figuratively quaking in their boots, were too afraid to whisper. Instead, they all crouched somewhat, as if they were moving to sit on a chair, but just froze only a quarter of the way down, trying to have entire conversations by facial expression.

"Soldiers die every day. We'll find whatever scum loosed this lucky shaft, but until then, it's best to keep your own head down and your eyes open. Now it's time for your weapon's training. Pair up, meat."

Everyone eventually managed to face his own personal, hairy, muscle-bound teacher. Garroway stood face-to-beard with a man as tall as a house and wider than the street it stood on. Green eyes appeared to grow straight from his thick, brown hair. No nose could be detected, and Garroway was confident that the man simply fed his beard and had no need for a mouth. Said beard rustled, and a growl rolled out, "Got a name?"

"Ga- um- Ro. Just Ro."

"Gortrum Trollsbane."

"Trolls... Um. Is that a last name?"

"A title."

"Oh."

Gunsel was left partnerless when the mercenaries were exhausted. Shrugging, he started walking away, "Guess ya don't need me then."

Roc grabbed his hood and whipped him around into a strong backhand. "You get the pleasure o' trainin' with me."

"Pleasure is a strong word."

Roc gave one hard burst of laughter before scowling and punching Gunsel in the gut. "Strong name for a weak man."

Gunsel straightened and nodded to the corpse that lay unaddressed, "Did he have a strong name too?"

Plucking at his chin thoughtfully, Roc replied, "I can't say for sure. Never knew it."

Incredulous, Gunsel shook his head and, in the process of unsheathing his axes, hooked his belt and lost his pants.

"Not even the first date, meat."

Trying to pull his traitorous trousers over his knees without slicing a leg open, Gunsel nodded, "Well, ya know, why wait, sir?"

Roc almost smiled before drawing his sword. He bellowed to the gathered pairs, "Today we work on blocking."

Immediately the sound of multiple blows being landed was heard. A lucky few of the recruits were even holding their weapons, fewer still were able to successfully parry a blow, and only Garroway had the presence of mind to strike back. Almost of its own accord, his sword bounced from Gortrum's and arced toward his neck. It came to a quivering stop an inch from his exposed throat.

Gortrum nodded. There was a flash of toothy smile before he crushed Garroway with a mailed fist. The beard rumbled, "Block then kill, or block then block again. Never do neither."

Rubbing his jaw, Garroway straightened and gave the sword a few flips. He assumed a ready pose in time to deflect a flurry of blows from Gortrum. Steel rang on steel as the pair danced across the field. Other groups stopped to watch swordsmanship Garroway had no business being capable of displaying. He raised his sword arm high to stop a downward swing from Gortrum. The blow slid down the flat of Ro's blade, and he spun, letting the momentum dig Gortrum's sword into the ground. Following through with a full turn, he whipped the blade down into Gortrum's hair. He sliced a lock off, turned his sword and shaved a chunk from the curly beard, slapped the sword from the bigger man's hand, and drove his own almost an inch deep into the broad chest. The blade tried to sink deeper, but Ro kept a tight hold on it.

Gortrum nodded, pulled the blade from his own chest, and slammed his right fist to his left arm. He grinned and growled, "Ro indeed."

Still shocked at his swordsmanship, Garroway mimicked the movement, clutching the sword in his fist as he brought it to his side.

Roc clapped once, gave Gunsel a sidelong glance, then strode to Garroway. "Gortum, you rescue lard here. I'll take *this* one for training."

"Aye, sir." He winked at Garroway and patted him on the shoulder lightly enough to not quite knock him over.

Roc roared, "You have probably three months with the man standing in front of you. You'll hate him, he'll hate you. You'll come to love him, he'll still hate you." Sniggers rippled through the crowd, "Train hard and you might live. Weakness is rewarded only with death."

The pairs drifted off, most deep in conversation. Roc threw an arm around Garroway's shoulders. "I guess you know whose sword that was."

Garroway nodded slightly, "Aye, but I can't place how I know that name, sir."

Cocking an eyebrow, Roc led Garroway to the massive stained glass window. It dominated one side of the Great Hall. Rubies and emeralds glinted in the dawn light, diamonds cast rainbows all around, and a battle unfolded in front of the pair. A lone man clad in obsidian armor stood before a sea of foes. The figure waded among corpses, his ebony blade seemingly alive, writhing and exalting in the bloodshed. Mortal men fled his sight, unearthly beasts were hewn and broken, and only the Gods stood before him. Their magics did him no harm; their weapons were ever turned aside by his. In the final frame, the man in the black armor stood, cloaked in a thundercloud. Sword of lightning raised high in one hand, the head of a God hanging loosely in the other, he stood at the head of the army of the dead.

Roc whispered, "Tykus, Godslayer."

The next three months passed in a whirlwind of bruises, missed meals, bad meals, and curses. Every morning, Roc found a new and exciting way to provoke his platoon. A favorite, which he returned to a number of times, was to toss a handful of snakes into the room and lock the door. All of the men quickly learned to sleep lightly and with a blade nearby.

Garroway grew accustomed to his daily beating from Roc. The pair often trained with wooden swords that left welts and bruises instead of slices and dismemberments. The fat sloughed from his body and his face became hard. Mirth turned to grit. Laziness to willpower. Every day he came closer to striking Roc, but every day he was sent to the barracks with a new injury.

Each evening, after their training, Roc would help Garroway out of the dust, stand him tall in the waning light, and stare at his face. A few weeks in, Garroway asked why he made such a point of this particular ritual. Roc grabbed his shoulders and turned him about, showing the rest of the mercenaries doing the same ritual with their respective trainees. "The Korzian military teaches its soldiers to remember the face of every man and beast they defeat in battle. It is the first among our simple rules, and should never be forgotten."

"Why is it so important?"

"So no man ever comes to think of death lightly. Certainly, a warrior may boast and jest, but always remember the faces of the vanquished and you shall always be wary of the end."

"But you haven't killed me. Not yet, at least."

Roc grinned, "Aye, but I have defeated you. I would know your face, if ever I saw it in battle, as one that I've beaten."

The thought of trying to remember the faces of everyone slain in a battle seemed ridiculous to Garroway, but a faraway sadness in Roc's eyes told him that even now the old warrior was recalling painful faces from the past.

So time passed, the same with Garroway and Gunsel as with the other hundreds of other platoons stationed at the Korzian outpost of Brathur. Each went through a similar training regimen, some with mercenaries, others with veterans. But all fell under the command of Lord Kyson. Every evening, the Lord Commander would stroll the compound, pretending to look interested in the everyday duties of the soldiers. The sinew and scars he displayed showed him to be a man of war, but the easiness with which he spoke of battle made him out to be despicably prideful. A decade before, Roc had tried to teach Kyson a lesson of humility.

"Kyson!" The old man had roared over the sounds of dying men. "Kyson, get your ass back here now."
"But the war is happening up here, sir." Kyson's lilting mockery came with a background instrumental of sword slicing through flesh.

Roc stomped through the battlefield, grabbing his charge by the throat as he attempted to hew an injured troll's head from its shoulders. "How dare you ignore me, boy?"

An indignant swat at Roc's closing fist was met with steely resistance. "Let go of me, old man. My father is-"

"A terrible one." He released the young man, who gasped and clutched at his sword. "Don't even pretend, son."

"I earned this kill."

"You earned nothing here."

"None of these orcs or trolls can match my blade."

"Nor can they match your pride. And I'd have any one of them at my side over you for it."

"The skill of Kyson is worth a hundred other Korzians."

"It takes only one moment to fell one Kyson."

The young man snarled, whipping his sword back at the troll who was struggling to tear a spear from his leg. Instead of slicing through it's exposed neck, Kyson's sword clanged against the flat of Roc's blade.

"I told you to stop." Roc stomped on Kyson's sword, cracking it clean in half, before smashing an elbow into his ribs.

When the younger man stopped coughing up blood, Roc looked deep into his eyes. "I know your face, Kyson. Remember that."

Their animosity continued through Kyson's ascent through the Korzian ranks, and even to the present, Kyson was leery of the grizzled commander.

Occasionally, one of the legions visiting Brathur would offer special instruction on various weapons, poisons, fighting styles, or magics. A particular favorite were the troll regiments. They wielded clubs, abstained from petty things like clothes and bathing, and always found a way to sneak a barrel of mead into the barracks. Always. They were hard to understand until the men managed to achieve the level of drunkenness that equalizes all beings in ineptitude, but once that balance was achieved they proved to be steadfast friends.

Dwarves were a regular sight in the courtyard as well. They got along with the trolls nicely because they both had a mutual disdain of peace. The constant bickering and fighting was in good faith, and often blows or harsh words were only a prelude to stiff drinks and laughter at the expense of some poor human. Any dwarf enjoys a good argument, and the conscripted men were no strangers to hard living. However, everyone stationed in Brathur quickly developed a keen sense of debate. Dwarves are well known for picking fights over anything they possibly can. Often, these are settled with words, which they call *Werakum* (dwarvish for "word fight"). The *Werakum* is considered the paramount technique to determining truth, and if that fails, a fistfight will serve almost equally in its stead.

The particular band of dwarves stationed in Brathur, nicknamed the Iron Storm, had acquired a significant knowledge over their many combined years. They would argue over which utensil to use with what food, what color you should wear as camouflage in which country, how long it would take for an orc to bleed out if you only cut off one finger, and other such important issues. So it was that Garroway was particularly taken aback when he plopped onto a bench for

lunch and received an earful of beard at the vanguard of a
tirade against his choice of spoon, over fork.

"But it's stew." Garroway replied, after several minutes.
He sloshed it in the broth and let some of it dribble from the
wooden spoon back into the bowl. "It's actually the reason
spoons were created."

"Well," the dwarf started, yanking a new bench closer to
Garroway, "spoons help you get the broth, but it's not about
that, is it? No, see," he grabbed the bowl and sloshed it around
a bit for effect, "that's not the part you want. You want the
meat, which would be easier to get hold of with the fork. Then,
once you've satisfied yourself with the meat, you drink the
broth from the bowl. No spoon required." He leaned back,
satisfied with his opening statement.

"But it's stew," Garroway answered, certain that this
statement alone was truth enough to rock the dwarf's
argument to the core. "I like the broth *with* the meat."

"But, don't you understand?" The dwarf produced a
spoon from one of the patches of hair trespassing further away
from his face; "The broth just gets in your beard and makes
your face sticky when it dribbles off your spoon."

"I don't have a beard." Garroway stroked his bestubbled
cheeks, "And thus, nothing in which to catch broth."

The look of confusion and pain on the dwarf's face was
such that Garroway almost felt bad for him, but couldn't bring
himself to apologize, opting instead to simply continue eating
with his spoon and refuse to acknowledge the dwarf existed.

One day, a handful of orcs were brought through the
front gate. Kicking and flailing, they snarled at anything they
could, trying to intimidate everything from the hunting eagles
to trolls, stones, and grass. When Garroway asked Roc why
they were being brought in, the grizzled commander simply
shrugged, "They're orcs. The Rofu have always been orcs and
goblins. We're at war with the Rofu, so..."

Their screeches continued until they were several
stories deep in the cells below the barracks.

Gray-skinned ogres were often employed as cooks,
much to the dismay of the recruits and their trainers. Every

day the food lost flavor and color only to gain lumps and odor. They tried their hardest, however, and occasionally turned out a masterful soup or bread. They were often seen slaving over their stoves, arguing over recipes and ingredients. Sometimes they simply left the kitchen, assuming someone would take over for them. On such nights, many empty stomachs slept fitfully, unwilling to brave the incomplete dinner their ogryn chefs had not quite finished making.

Even wizards passed through occasionally. They hardly seemed to touch the ground when they walked and spent an awful lot of time muttering and shaking their heads at everyone who passed by. Most always seemed rather busy and deep in thought. All of them were too enthralled with themselves to waste time on the weaker beings scattered about them, save one. Grael Voor, an elven wizard who was old when humans were young, took great pleasure in answering the eager questions of the soldiers in training. Wisdom seemed to eminate from him, and there was a sense of calm and righteousness when he was nearby. He was neither tall, nor was he short, but his magnificent plait of white hair was instantly recognizable, anywhere.

Sometimes, he would demonstrate petty magic, show off potions and fanciful inventions, and dazzle even the most experienced of warriors with his unmatched swordplay. The swiftness, strength, and ferocity of his attacks blasted through the best defenses in seconds. His small swords flashed in the light and blurred as they cut belt loops and beards. Their beautifully decorated pommels could have been sculptures on a cathedral, and his golden armor was never even smudged by the dirt, let alone scratched by an opponent.

Grael even took the initiative in some training exercises. The old elf used his powerful magic to alter time in the center of the courtyard for almost a month, allowing the training to evolve thirty days further than it should have in only one 'real' day. It exhausted him, however, and he took a full week to rest before taking his leave of the camp.

During this time, Gunsel approached to drill him about magic, combat and otherwise. The patient elf answered all questions to the fullest extent of his considerable knowledge.

"To use magic, you needn't learn any incantations or spells or any other such nonsense. There is no required hand motion or phrase. Magic is within every being that is willing to seek it out." Grael conjured a flame in the palm of his hand, letting it crackle for a moment before closing his fist on it. He opened it once more to reveal a rose. "Magic is simply about willpower. If you believe something fiercely enough, you can make it so."

Gunsel absorbed it all. He learned rudimentary battle magic, even casting a few minor spells on his first day. By the third day he could project his force a few feet in front of himself and deflect blows of the sword with a thought. In the second week of his training, Grael took him aside. "You are strong in body. You are willing to learn. These are the traits of a warrior, and a warrior I will make you."

Filled with pride, Guns thanked his mentor and started toward the training fields. A sharp tug on his arm held him back.

"However, eagerness has many a warrior slain. Take care you do not become overzealous." The old elf frowned and turned Gunsel toward him. "The last thing I will tell you is that magic has a cost. Each spell you cast drains from your life. You'll not notice this until you advance well past projection or minor spells. Every magic has a cost, and some are quite terrible. Win battles by strength of magic only if you must. Strength of mind, and of body, is paramount."

Gunsel had not lived under one roof for three months in a row in fifteen years. Every day he felt more comfortable with his life. He kept his armor clean, his weapons cleaner, and constantly drilled his mercenary companion with questions. In a short time he transformed from porky slacker to chiseled warrior. His arms bulged, and many of his shirtsleeves had long since fallen victim to a blade, as they restricted his movement. A braided beard weaseled from his chin to his collar. He kept his head shaved bald, and even recieved a magnificent blue tattoo on his scalp. It was Garroway's family crest- the griffon.

After a morning training session, Garroway caught up with him and asked what made him choose the griffon.

"Seemed right, sir. It's a fierce animal, a noble animal," he nudged his friend, "and I suppose I have some respect for you, sir. Less so for that asshat of a father you have, him being the chief reason we're in this army."

"I'm glad of that at least. Only took three months in hell for you to realize it."

Gunsel squinted and glanced around, "It's not so bad. I can tell ya I'm not thrilled to really start fightin' though." He shrugged, "Least you have the magic trappings of the Godslayer."

Garroway chuckled, "Aye, but you've got the muscles of a troll. Look at you, ye big bull. What happened to the fat, whiny Gunsel?"

"Now he's the strong, whiny Guns, sir."

The pair was interrupted by a cacophony of bells from the outer walls. Roc rushed up the stairs of the gate three at a time before roaring to the confused men behind him, "Armor up, lads. To battle!"

TO BATTLE

Times changed, seasons passed, the Darkness waited and watched.
Orcs and goblins, ogres and trolls, beasts reeking of rot.
With the Guard asleep, the city weak, their time at last had come.
The cries of war of a vicious horde, they march to the thunder of drums.
Arrows nocked, swords unsheathed, shields and armor shone bright.
Outnumbered, outmatched, the Guard braced for attack, certain death, or
dishonor and flight.
Stone smashed stone, steel crushed bone; the screams of the vanquished rang out.
The men of the Guard, fierce, hard, brave hearts free of doubt,
Butchering, slicing, beating, breaking, the soldiers fought tooth to nail.
Their city, her halls, her sons to fall, if in this moment they failed.
The glowing moon, herald of doom, turned her eye on the fray.
Each second a year, each minute an age, the battle outlived the day.
No mercy given, no quarter gained, the blood of the dead gushed free,
The men of the Guard, fierce and hard, were broken, and began to flee.
Yet! High in the sky, a crack, a cry! Korz came forth as a man!
His blessing, attack! His armor and axe, steadied the hearts of the Hand.
With fury unmatched the Guard fought back, hope now buried their fear.
In their hour of need, he descended to lead; morning, again, drew near.

Warning bells were joined by a host of horns bellowing
into the grey sky, laden with thin clouds. A dust cloud rose in
the distance as a tremendous host materialized on the horizon.
Already drums and ritual chants rose from the camp.
Companies and legions rushed to find their commanders, trolls
knelt where they stood and began praying to their bloodthirsty
gods of war. Ogres grinned and began massing near the gates.
Dwarves strapped their plate armor over chainmail, hammers
and axes unsheathed. They trundled to their positions
alongside the engines of war brought from their homelands.
Massive catapults were loaded with chunks of stone, and
ballistae were nestled into firing nooks. Teams of men along
the walls were assigned steaming cauldrons of oils and tar to
pour on anyone daring to scale the impressive masonry.
Archers took positions behind the wall with runners prepared
to fetch more arrows from fletchers already working overtime.

Several wizards strode into the courtyard, arms waving and hair whipping about their faces as the magic they wielded manifested itself. Four groups of six wizards each began creating star patterns. After a few moments there was a snap and a sizzle through the air as if lightning had struck somewhere nearby.

A hulking monster, translucent but very real, snarled and gnashed in the center of each group. One stood almost fifteen feet tall, arms covered in bristly hair that dripped with a noxious smelling liquid. Its six eyes all jittered about randomly while a long, forked tongue tasted the air.

The next had six limbs, four on the ground, two wielding a monstrous scythe. It had no eyes and sniffed at the air, hissing.

The third stood only twelve feet tall. It was clad in a hide vest and cloth kilt, looking every bit like an over-sized human. Every inch of it rippled with muscle and the glazed eyes were white. It wielded no weapon, and began to rock its head back and forth, chanting. The longer it waited the more agitated it became.

The final monster was simply a dragon. Diamond-hard scales shimmered eerily and eyes of unimaginable depth and intelligence searched its surroundings lazily. Grael Voor stood in front of it, whispering and gesturing with his hands quickly but smoothly. The dragon snuffled and whipped its tail around before nestling below Grael's hands. He grinned and gave it a small scratch behind the jaw before resuming his chants.

Men from dozens of platoons scrambled to the armories to clad themselves in armor and mail. Grunts of greeting were exchanged. Most of the assembled men had never been in real combat. The veterans and mercenaries dispersed into the companies in order to keep the inexperienced soldiers in line.

Guns donned his massive chest plate, with assistance from some of the runners, and laced his own greaves and gauntlets. Kneeling, he shut his eyes. "I've never asked anything of any of you before, and I don't plan on doing much asking in the future, but, if there are gods of any sort listening, I'd appreciate a nudge of guidance during this. I think." He stood and rolled his neck around, swinging his chiseled arms about. His axes rested in his belt, and a dagger was tucked into its sheath on the small of his back. The braid in his beard was tight, and when he was satisfied, he nodded to one of the assistants and let his helm slide over his face. Immediately, he gasped for breath. Gortrum had told him helmets made breathing hard. He was right. Every time Gunsel slid the cool metal over his bald head, he started sweating and felt faint. Within moments Guns was on his knees, gulping air. He took a slow, deep breath in and held it. Flipping the visor up just slightly, he felt a cool rush of air tickle his chin. He smiled and knocked it shut. Taking deep breaths and staying calm, he strode to his master's bunk.

Ro stood in front of his moldy mattress appraising the armor of Tykus. It looked as if it had just been forged, cleaner even than the armor of the lords. Guns' thick hand smacked him between the shoulders, "If not now, when?"

"Aye."

The armor seemed to mold itself to Ro as he strapped it on. Guns tied the cuirass and turned his friend to face him. With an admiring punch to the chest, he grabbed Ro by his shaggy hair, "Today we find out if all this abuse has been worth anything, eh, sir?"

"Enough with the sir, Guns. I'm just another soldier, you're a comrade, and you're my friend."

With a toothy grin and a crow of laughter, Guns slid the helmet onto Ro's head. The pair strode through the open doors of the barracks and into the morning.

Commanders barked orders, their drums thudding to make hot blood run quickly. War cries went up from the trolls. They howled and grinned, head-butting each other and slamming their forearms together in gestures of respect. The ogres remained unnervingly calm as they shrugged their gargantuan weapons onto their shoulders. The air of nervousness among the recruits was palpable.

Formations shifted slightly, and coughs and sniffles rippled through the courtyard. Roc whispered something into Grael's ear. The old elf glanced over his shoulder at the green trainees, nodded, and slammed his palm into the dragon's snout. It shuddered and went rigid. Satisfied, Grael nodded to Roc once more. The grizzled warrior's whole body seemed to expand as his amplified voice roared through the soldiers. "Today, many of you see battle for the first time. Today, many of you may also see battle for the last time. Every man has his hour. Every ally, every friend, every soldier finds the blade with his name on it." He cracked a gnarled smile, "And the same goes for the damned Rofu."

The courtyard roared with approval as he shook an armored fist and pointed his sword at the horizon. "Trolls of Ictheim, Dwarves of Karakor, Ogres from… wherever ogres come from," tense nerves allowed nervous laughter to pass between the soldiers. "And you brave Sons of Korz!" The men cheered. Swords clanged on shields, mail jingled. "Allow no fear to taint your hearts this day! The men of the guard, fierce and hard, shall once more wield their iron fists with Bol's fury!"

Ro and Guns joined the bone-chilling war cry that exploded from the assembly. Drums worked at a fever pitch, drowning out the sounds of the Rofu host. Commanders found their way to the front of their platoons. Flagmen stood, unarmed, ready to die banner in hand. Guns had never seen such a striking assembly in all his life. He shuddered, thinking that he may never see the like again, but he shoved the feeling aside. For the first time in his life, Guns had a purpose. To fight and kill not only for his own survival, but for the survival of a group of men he had come to respect and care about. The thought came and went as fast as the previous one. He grinned beneath his helmet and let out a howl. His voice joined the ten thousand others sending their regards to Bol, God of fire and war.

Abruptly, the drumming stopped; the warriors became quiet, penned behind the gates. Trolls' eyes grew wide, mouths drooling. Ro swore he heard the ropes on the catapults straining.

"Fire."

Gargantuan chunks of stone hurtled over the walls, ballistae thumped and sent spears hurtling into the massed enemies, the twang of bows preceded the deadly buzzing of arrows. Fletching hissed on the wind like a swarm of barbed insects followed by a second loud *fwip!* as another volley was loosed. From beyond the wall, screams of agony and rage ascended into the dawning sun. A return volley tinkled from the massive stone walls, not close enough yet to arc into the courtyard.

Several of the dwarven machine teams were shouting in their gruff language. Ogres reloaded great stones into catapults and dwarves nestled spears into their ballistae. Two of the cauldrons of oil were dumped, followed by a torch and a rather uncalled-for curse against the collective mothers of the Rofu, to set those doused ablaze. The stench of burning hair and flesh wafted into the courtyard. Black, greasy smoke drifted from the wall. A single ladder thudded into the stones before being brutally wrenched from its resting place and tossed back onto the Rofu army. The Rofu fired a second volley of black arrows that soared over the ramparts. "Shields up!" Came the order, but too many were too slow. Barbed and poisoned arrowheads buried themselves into exposed flesh. Men screamed as their blood flowed forth. Arrows thunked into the tough hides of ogres or trolls, who ignored them or laughed, respectively. Some began foaming at the mouth and collapsed, eyes rolling back into their skulls. Others died instantly. The inexperienced soldiers, unused to the horror of war and already nervous to the point of being sick, began doubting themselves. Some turned to run while others simply knelt and began to weep. The stench of urine and voided bowels mingled with the blood and smoke.

A ram collided with the southern gate; it shuddered as the hinges strained on their morrings. Dust showered the men closest to it as the whole wall rocked with the blow. One of the wizards pacing the wall stopped directly above it. Muttering and moving his hands in wide circles he raised them both to the air before an arrow shaft stabbed deep into his throat. He gurgled, unable to finish his spell, and fell forward over the wall.

Catapults finally began to return fire. Stones crunched into the thick walls. Some slammed into the courtyard, rolling over anyone not swift enough to escape. Broken bones and gouts of blood followed in their wake. Already the healers and surgeons flooded the field, removing anyone they thought they could save. Some were beyond repair, and their suffering was ended swiftly.

Dozens of retreating men found they had nowhere to go, as the gates on the eastern wall were besieged as well. Again, Roc strode the wall, oblivious to stones, spears, and arrows hurtling about. "Would you run, now? Would you abandon all those here to a fiery doom? Cowards!" His words dripped with contempt as he hurled them at the deserters. "How dare you sully the name of Korz with your weakness. You deserve a pitiful, meaningless death. May you find it here, among the arrows and stones that presage real battle." He turned his back on the courtyard, surveying the battlefield in front of him once more.

For almost an hour the opening stages of attack went on. The ram pounded the stout timbers of the south gate tirelessly. A mountain of corpses formed a shield of meat to protect the operators from any further arrows. All the defenders could do was watch as the massive gate slowly gave way. Finally, it split down the middle. Leering faces grinned through, spittle dripping from chapped, bleeding lips. The men in front were able to watch the ram be pulled back one more time before it hurtled home, splintering the beams. The ogres blasted out before the Rofu managed to squeeze in. Terrified screams sounded beyond the gates as they bludgeoned their way through the battering ram and into the tightly packed body of orcs. Black blood arced through the air, bones crunched as limbs were smashed. Enormous swords cleaved twisted bodies in two, clubs crushed, fists tore into flesh and broke bone as easily as if it were dry grass.

The sheer numbers of the Rofu force became evident as the ogres formed a defensive circle around the outside of the gate. They fought valiantly, massive bundles of brutal death, but even an ogre cannot stop a flood. The Rofu had breached the wall.

Ro felt the armor become warm, as if it was drawing life from the bloodshed around it. He had never seen such a sight as this battle.

A blood-curdling shriek came from outside the walls before the whole north-eastern corner of the stonework was torn aside by a pair of giants flanking a dragon. It was an awesome sight. Magnificent purple scales flickered in the smoky sunlight. Its belly expanded before it belched out a jet of blue flames. The closest group of trolls was incinerated, leaving nothing but dust and fragments of red-hot metal. The dragon spread its massive wings and jumped, shaking the ground before buffeting everyone nearby with a gust from its takeoff. It roared once more and soared away from the battle. Grael whispered to his dragon, which looked as if it had been napping. Heavy eyelids snapped open and it unfurled ghostly wings. Without a sound it rose to the winds and sped after its prey.

Most of the men were too shocked to react for several seconds. Orders flew around as commanders rallied their troops toward the hole in the wall that was rapidly filling with orcs and goblins. They scrambled over stones, corpses, and felled comrades in order to fill the courtyard as fast as possible. Roc's platoon was on the opposite side of the breach, so they could only stand and watch their allies collide with the enemy. Shrieks rang out from both sides. Orcs leapt off the shoulders of their kin to dive deep into the lines of the men. Some landed well, driving rusting steel into exposed flesh. Others were impaled by swords or spears, or were caught and driven to the ground by shields or grasping hands, then crushed or hacked to pieces. The humans, bigger and better armed and armored, strong-armed the Rofu advance with powerful blows. Swords cut clean through the rotting armor of the orcs, and their weapons shattered on human steel. Troll regiments streaked across the grass to join the fray, exulting in the bloodshed and death. Ogres brutalized every foe that dared near any of the gates while dwarven machines continued to pour missiles into the advancing horde.

The sky darkened. Clouds formed out of nowhere and frail fingers of lightning began probing the ground inside the walls. Men were vaporized or set ablaze by the massive bolts. Grael yelled something and the six-limbed monster scuttled to the top of the wall. It shifted about, sniffing the air. Finally it stopped, took one deep gulp of air, and hurled its scythe. Immediately, the storm clouds receded. Ro could only guess that it had permanently silenced the one casting whatever spell had was causing the storms.

Its initial duty done, the creature crawled down the outside of the wall and joined the melee.

Across the courtyard, the Rofu giants had finally created an entrance wide enough for both of them to enter. They stood easily six meters tall, covered in tattoos, skulls of several creatures hanging from rough, leather belts. Their size belied incredible speed as they dispatched several trolls in quick succession. These were not the clumsy, lumbering boogeymen children were made to fear through bedtime stories. These were refined killing machines. They fought as a pair, rotating, and when one struck the other blocked for him; and then they switched positions, carving into the defending lines. Trolls and men fell like wheat to the harvest. The pair slowly carved a path out from the opening in the wall, gaining precious ground to let the orcs and goblins mass behind them. They ignored minor cuts and gouges on their legs as they whirled onward.

One of the wizards hissed at Roc, who shook his head threateningly. The man tilted his head, made a vague gesture toward the giants, and stabbed himself straight in the heart. His body did not fall, as Ro had expected it to. It simply hung there, blood draining down the carven handle. The translucent body in the center of the courtyard ceased its frenzied shaking. It seemed dazed, shaking its head once before glaring directly at the giants. Metal plates materialized over its forearms and shins. A horned helm obscured the burning white eyes. It attacked.

Leaping clear of almost twenty feet of allied soldiers, the apparition took one hard step and lunged at the giants. It caught one in the crook of its right arm and landed a crushing elbow to the ribs of the second. The momentum of its leap carried them to the base of the wall, where it planted sure feet on the stone and pushed once more, driving the giant's head straight into the earth. Immediately, it was in the air again, left hand grasping at the other giant's throat, right hand raining furious punches.

Ro was startled, as he had been staring at the battle within the courtyard, by an explosion of stone directly in front of him. The flaming ring blasted into the wall reeked of ozone, and Ro guessed it was the doing of some magician. Even as he thought it, he saw the six-legged monster wheel about and crash through the enemy ranks to hunt down the source. Gravelly orders shouted by Roc jarred him into action. His platoon trotted forward to plug the gap created by the explosion.

Guns reveled in the moment. Tilting his head back, he unleashed a feral howl and pounced into the orcs already flooding the gap. His axes dealt death with frightening precision. Cutting arteries in necks, slicing off limbs, crunching through rusty mail like paper. His bulging arms remained bare, and they were quickly doused in oily black blood from the hundreds of wounds he inflicted upon the Rofu force. Daggers and swords clanged from his broad chest plate, and an arrow pinged from his helm. He felt an ecstasy he could never have imagined as he tore deeper into the gap. Nearly blinded in his bloodlust, he carved an orc's ear from its head. It screeched for only a moment before the scything reverse blow severed its neck. He whipped around, forcing both axe heads deep into the chest of an unarmored goblin. It looked dumbfounded as it fell to its knees and bled out. With a renewed war cry, he leapt further into the battle.

Ro took in the scene of slaughter for only a breath. He saw his friend cleaving into the enemy. He saw Roc wielding his axe with a strength and precision he had not previously thought possible. Gortrum Trollsbane cackled madly, clearly visible over the heads of the invaders, and crunched his way through goblin and orc alike with a hammer dripping gore.

Now nearly face to face with them, Ro noticed postules covering many of the goblins and orcs. Scaly skin covered in scabs oozed black blood everywhere. Their bloodshot eyes were yellowing, teeth hanging loosely in their mouths, smelling not only of filth, but of rot and corruption as well.

Almost without thinking he whipped up his right arm, skewering an orc through the heart as it lunged toward him over the shoulder of the man in front of him. He pulled out the sword, breathing hard despite having hardly even entered combat. His mailed left fist sent blood and teeth spraying from an unfortunate goblin's mouth before joining his right on the hilt of his sword. Taking a deep breath, he stepped sharply forward with his right leg, arcing the sword down deep into a clavicle. Quickly ripping the blade free, he kicked the body out with his left leg and rotated to parry an upward swing to his left. He spun a full circle before decapitating the foe. Stopping his momentum on a planted foot, he brought the sword down onto a waiting shield. The jarring impact staggered him for a moment and the orc tackled him to the ground.

Screeching and flailing, jaundiced eyes crazed, the thing scrabbled for his neck. Drool splattered onto the dark faceplate. Unkempt, greasy hair stuck to its face. Unable to find any purchase, it sat up slightly, plunging a knife deep into the armor. Instead of being turned aside or piercing it, it was simply absorbed. Ro was almost as confused as the orc, but recovered an instant sooner. He forced both fists up into its armpits, lifting it from his waist and sending it sprawling to the ground. He rose and stabbed his blade so deep into its neck that he had to pry it from the dirt. His hands bloodied, he joined his brothers in a ululating battlecry and allowed the armor to guide his movements.

Slow attacks were turned aside, weak defenses overwhelmed. Ro felt glancing blows ping from his armor, others were simply stopped by the magical metal, but the ancient suit never suffered a scratch. The sword almost took on a life of its own, flashing in Ro's hands like ebony lightning.

The smell of blood clouded the air. Moans and screams echoed through the courtyard. Dust choked every breath. Steel rang on steel. The day was nigh over, but night had not yet taken hold. It was, as the Korzian soldiers had a fondness of saying, Battle Dusk, tinged red by the spilled blood of friend and foe.

On the opposite side of the courtyard, the summoned juggernaut continued its impressive duel with the giants. It had ridden one giant to the ground, punching the whole way, before smashing the air from its lungs with two well-placed knees upon landing. It sprang again to the opposite giant, still pulling grass and dirt from its eyes and mouth, and corkscrewed both fists into its chest. For a moment the giant didn't react, as though the blow had done nothing. Then spittle trickled from the corners of its drooping mouth before it dropped to both knees, vomiting a stream of blood. While it knelt, its counterpart recovered its feet, already lunging unsteadily at the magician's pet. The groggy attack was quickly batted aside, followed by a lightning fast strike to the giant's throat with its right forearm. It gurgled once before the metal elbow plate of the left arm drilled into its temple, crushing its brain, and the body instantly went limp on the grass. Little time was wasted on the second giant. The wraith simply walked behind it, cradled its head in translucent arms, and snapped its neck.

The Rofu flowing into the breach behind the giants had clearly expected a different outcome. As soon as the second body hit the ground they began to retreat. The trolls closest to them whooped and roared as they chased the shaken troops over the stones and into the open plains. Clubs laced with nails and shards of metal battered away shields while bare fists and sharp teeth made short work of the poorly armored Rofu.

The main gate remained unbreached throughout the day, despite three rams being sent to it, and half a dozen magical attacks. The protective ring of ogres around the south gate was slowly wearing down. Mountains of corpses littered the short distance between the shattered timbers and their hulking bodies, but their weariness showed. The orcs and goblins, rather timid following the initial battering by the ogres, had been opting to charge through the openings torn from the wall rather than confront the defenders outside the destroyed gate, began probing the bleeding beasts once more.

A final desperate charge on the ogres was rebuffed when Roc leapt from the wall to join the fray. He landed lightly, tumbling and using the momentum to slam his axe onto a surprised goblin. The blow clove the attacker in half. He took a lunging step forward and spun a quick pirouette to rip the axe from the dirt. He lopped off heads, carved bodies like meat, and crushed armor like foil. This furious assault, combined with the desperation of the few remaining ogres, roaring and mourning their slain comrades, was enough to turn the attack away.

Ro, who was able to grab a moment's respite when one of the dwarf regiments abandoned its ammunition-less ballistae and dove from the wall to attack the Rofu, turned to watch Roc fight. Through the gate he could see his teacher twirl and spin, wielding the axe as though it were one of the wooden training swords. Arrows sliced the air around him, but none ever managed to connect. Every time it looked as though he might suffer a wound, his axe was there an instant before to turn the blow aside. Even as Ro watched, he saw an arrow that could not possibly miss its target. Roc turned to the side and snatched the shaft from the air, snapping it in half with a clenched fist as he continued his almost surgical dismembering of the enemy.

Finally, a horn sounded in the distance. Its dreary tone could mean only retreat as the orcs and goblins filtered away from the walls. Those already inside tried to escape, but were mercilessly cut down. Catapults loosed their last few stones into the fleeing rear of the army. To add insult to their defeat, Kyson assumed a position on the wall, dragging a fantastically clad troll by the hair behind him. His voice amplified by magic, he roared, "Is this your army? Is this your greatest host?" He held the troll in front of the wall. It struggled weakly, but was already gravely wounded. Kyson's fist tightened on its throat before he plunged the troll's own dagger through its forehead.

"Take that back to the desert with you, scum." He nodded to Grael, who frowned and made a small succession of gestures.

The body disappeared from Kyson's hand.

All the wizards harnessing the six-limbed magic, magic hunting beast had retired a few hours into the battle, either satisfied that their weapon had hunted down all of the magical threats, or that they no longer had a being to control. The giant-slaying berserker had collapsed after carving a bloody path deep into the field before the compound. The dragon was long gone, and the other summoned creature had never been released.

Ro, dripping with sweat and greasy, unhuman blood, wondered if it cost the magicians more to unleash the beasts than to restrain them. He sat with his back on the warm stones of the Great Hall. A setting sun provided just enough light to see the carnage on display in the courtyard. Bloated corpses were already filling with maggots, and flies swarmed from wound to wound, ignoring the weak swipes of the dying. Voices of all kinds moaned for help. While the wounded defenders were taken as fast as they could be found, the Rofu were dealt with rather more harshly. Squads of restless mercenaries stalked the fields of corpses putting the more horribly injured out of their misery. Whenever they found one in decent shape, they shackled it and led it to the prison in the caves below the compound for questioning.

Strapping his helmet to his belt, Ro wiped a filthy hand across his eyes. Peering into the sunset, he saw Guns resting on a knee. He picked his way around the severed limbs and stinking corpses to grab his friend's shoulder, "That was something."

"I've never felt so," Gunsel paused to find the right word, "alive. So right, you know?" He stood, rolling his broad shoulders back and cracking his neck. "That was something."

The pair walked back to the infirmary to get checked out. Neither suffered any major wounds. In fact, Ro was untouched aside from a few bruises. Guns had suffered several deep stabs and cuts to his bare arms, but it was nothing a few stitches and a minor healing spell was incapable of dealing with. Once the healers had finished with the pair, they took a less than soothing bath in murky, suspicious-looking water. Each snatched clean trousers and a tunic from the nearby shelf. Gunsel hunted for boots while Garroway wrung his lank hair out and tied it in a ragged ponytail.

Clean, and dressed in the finest rags Korz could provide, they made their way to the Great Hall. All the soldiers had been ordered to assemble for a feast and to hear from their commanders. They gazed upon statues of fallen heroes, once so cold and distant, and they appeared almost welcoming the pair now. Warm light blazed from the windows and muffled sounds of celebration leaked through the oaken doors.

Guns stepped to the front and pulled the massive door open. "After you, sir."

"Oh, heroes first. I'd hate to overshadow your glory."

"If you insist," Guns swaggered into a wall of heat and sound.

Many long tables had been set up through the hall. Barrels of wine, mead, and ale sloshed this way and that, shoved around by dozens of cooks keeping the soldier's mugs filled. The hearty scent of cooked meat underlined the smoky aroma emanating from a dozen fireplaces. It was a welcome reprieve from the stench of battle. A massive chandelier dominated the vaulted ceiling, thousands of candles blazing to keep the room bright. As the pair entered, the assembled soldiers belted out a familiar Korzian victory tune:

> Every man's stories are bolder when the fire's brought to a smolder,
> His stories grow taller by the flagon.
> His enemies slain, his friends share his pain,
> No good story's told without braggin'.
> With mead in his belly, a pipe in his teeth,
> A child perched on each knee.
> He'll tell you of dozens he fought and he slew,
> In battle, his like you shan't meet.

Oh, the great men of Korz, the fighters, the force.
No battle that we cannot win.
So we'll eat and not think, we'll drown in our drink,
And we'll each tell our tales and sing!
Oh, for Korz, for Korz, for glory and war.
We'll all find a new day to die!

My armor be dented, my shield long gone,
Outnumbered two hundred to one.
Bloodied and battered, the enemy scattered,
The only survivors had run.
Sword torn from my hand, beset on all sides,
Giants and wizards I fought.
With only my knuckles I showed them to hell,
What horrors and havoc I wrought!
Oh, the great men of Korz, the fighters, the force.
No battle that we cannot win.
So we'll eat and not think, we'll drown in our drink,
And we'll each tell our tales and sing!
Oh, for Korz, for Korz, for glory and war.
We'll all find a new day to die!

Wounded and poisoned, bloodied and tired,
I had not slept for a week.
Still I fought on, you can't prove me wrong!
They'll tell tales of the horrors I wreak.
Alas, they all fled, the only smart ones were dead,
That I cannot revisit them soon.
I'll outdo all the lads, their brothers and dads,
My tales'll put ladies a'swoon!
Oh, the great men of Korz, the fighters, the force.
No battle that we cannot win.
So we'll eat and not think, we'll drown in our drink,
And we'll all tell our tales and sing!
Oh, for Korz, for Korz, for glory and war,
We'll all find a new day to die!

Amid the clapping and cheering, the banging of metal on wood brought the noise of the Hall to a dull roar. Lord Commander Kyson stood from his great chair. Sunken eyes glared over the gathering. His face etched in a lopsided frown, he lifted an ornate goblet shaped like a snarling bear, his house symbol. When the last dwindling shouts died down he raised his hand an inch higher, tilted his head and, with a grin, drained its contents mostly into his mouth. "To you, men of Korz! The day is won! Fret not, brothers, for the conflict has but begun. More blood will spill." He winked, "And more ale shall brew!" The hall exploded in cheers and the thunking of tankards on sturdy wooden tables. "So worry not about battles to come. This night, we are the victors, as we shall ever be! So eat your fill, drink hearty, and sleep until the crowing of the weak-livered wakes you!"

A bard twanged his foreign-looking lute once, nodded to his companions, and began crooning about the glory to come, and the honor of the dead. In moments, grease was dripping into Gunsel's beard as he devoured an assortment of meat, frequently laughing and swigging at his ale. Throughout their training food had consisted of barely edible gruel or worse, punctuated by a truly decadent bowl of stew. Having been duped into slavery twice by a buffet, he took but a moment of hesitation before gorging himself with everything he could reach. He felt truly at home here in Brathur. Here, he had friends who would never leave his side, enough food, strong drink, and battles to win. In a life of tragedy, servitude, and hunger, Gunsel had never had time to truly relax until now.

Garroway tried to keep up with his companion but was soon left buried beneath a mountain of emptied dishes and burps. Gunsel's appetite had apparently expanded with his biceps, and now bore considerable resemblance to that of a starved ogre. Even the men setting the table began to look nervous, wondering if his rampage would ever stop. Abruptly, Gunsel frowned, waved a hand over his plate, and unleashed a thunderous belch before sliding off the bench to snore loudly on the straw-covered floor. His amused comrades continued toasting his limp form as though he were still drinking and laughing with them. Upon the collapse of his friend, Garroway declared his meal finished.

He never connected as well with the other recruits as Gunsel had. There was a degree of separation that Garroway felt came from Roc being his direct training partner. Everyone had seen the platoon commander handpick him to train with, so they felt he was either being groomed for command or given special treatment. Both options created a rift between Garroway and the others. Thus, with Gunsel having been felled by a strong-brewed dose of tomorrow's headache, Ro took his leave of the Hall.

The night was cool, though not quite so as to be uncomfortable. A half moon shone wanly through meandering clouds. A few birds squawked, doing their damndest to ruin any sense of calm the evening might inspire. Looking back, in the direction of Korz, Garroway questioned if this was how he should feel. His hands were still flesh colored and calloused. His body was in one piece, his face washed, clothes clean. Should a warrior be so comfortable? With a shake, he wondered what had prompted that thought from him. Garroway was certainly not a warrior. Before a few months ago he had never wielded a sword, aside from isolated play fights as a child. This was the first time he managed to kill anything that was previously uninjured, or a fish.

No, Garroway was no warrior.

The heat-soaked stones warmed his back as he leaned against it and slid down onto the dust. Legs crossed, he closed his eyes and took a deep breath of the clear air. Grateful he was upwind of the battlefield, he imagined the smell was quite less refreshing elsewhere in the compound. The sounds from the Hall grew louder for a moment as someone else left, and light flashed onto the grass. Soon, the splattering sound of the soldier breaking the proverbial seal on the wall made Ro stand and shake the soreness from his limbs. He had never thought about the physical toll that fighting might take on him, but his whole body ached. Not a particularly strong believer, he offered a prayer of thanks to Bol for allowing himself and his friend to emerge relatively unscathed. He almost felt ashamed as he finished, embarrassed that he would thank someone he had never seen for something that would have been so insignificant to such a powerful being. Just the luck of the warrior, he supposed, leaving the thought behind.

Moans and cries still drifted from the battlefield at intervals, occasionally drowning out the raucous carrion. The healing staff was stretched trying to keep the more viciously injured soldiers as healthy as they could. Outside the walls, wizards had been at work burning corpses for hours, and Ro guessed they would be working at their grim duty for many more. Thick smoke plumed from the charred ditch and the occasional grim visage of a magician was visible on the wall, constantly chanting and waving his hands.

A clap on the shoulder startled Ro into swinging a punch. Roc batted it aside as though it were but a minor inconvenience. The grizzled commander threw a sleeved arm around the younger man's shoulders and pulled him away from the Hall, toward the battlefield. His gravelly voice seemed almost peaceful, "Quite a day, eh Garroway?"

Shocked at the use of his proper name, Garroway opened his mouth for several seconds before answering, "Aye, sir. That was something."

"So, what's bothering you?"

It took a moment for Ro to realize that there had been a thought nagging at the back of his mind. Something about the attack felt wrong. Incongruent. Why had the Rofu been so bold? And why did they look so sick? He voiced these two concerns to his commander.

"The same thought's been gnawing at my brain. You'll make a leader yet." Roc paused, "If you live that long."

The pair strode in silence for some time, heading toward the battlefield. They knelt at the corpse of an orc. Its face was twisted in pain; yellow, bloodshot eyes wide open, it already looked waxen. Roc grabbed a stick from the grass nearby and poked at the pustules on its arms. They split and dribbled sickly green pus.

"The Rofu have never been much for open conflict. The Lord Commander seems certain this was a desperation attack, but I'm not, say, of the same mind." Still prodding, he cocked an eyebrow at his companion, as if asking for the younger man's opinion.

"Honestly, sir, I thought the same thing. If they're that desperate, why attack a fortified stronghold? They had to know the garrison was filled."

"Exactly! Go on."

"And," Garroway ventured slowly, "these troops seemed almost… halfhearted. Or afraid? They didn't want to fight us. And where were the ogres, or something worse?"

Roc winked, "That's the question, eh? Why not send trolls and ogres to fight trolls and ogres? The giants were a distraction, to make us think they were giving it their all. I'm sure of it."

"Why doesn't the Lord Commander understand that? And did you see that dragon?"

Roc's face darkened. "Don't take that monster's appearance lightly. That was Ragnus Fireborn. One of few remaining dragon lines in Alkurah."

"Few? I thought the dragons had all been killed ages ago."

"It's barely been a few centuries, don't exaggerate. And there are many things you might think that can be proven wrong."

To that, Garroway could only look to the sky and pray that he might never learn any of those things. "What were those things the magicians cooked up?"

"Ah, glad you asked. The wizards call it 'yanking' because wizards are creative with all but their words. So, they take a creature from another plane of existence, or a different part of this world, and use it for a short time. The six-legged one's name was Palarius. You've surely never seen its like living in the world, but I assure you there are plenty. They pulled him from the meredun. Most of the predators there have a keen sense of magic. Palarius has long been an ally of Korz, and he's plenty capable of hunting magicians."

"So that thing was still alive?"

Roc shrugged, "Yes and no. The magic makes it rather hard to kill, but it is capable of dying. If the magicians summoning Palarius were to be killed before they could end their spell correctly, he would be slain as well. He's tied to them, and them to him. So, once he was satisfied he'd killed all of the Rofu shamans, he was free to return to the swamp."

"What about the other three?"

"I'd never seen that big spiky lad before. I'll have to ask who that was. The berserker was purely magic. I assume you saw Marvain use that infernal dagger?"

"The one who stabbed himself?"

"Aye. That is one of several of the so-called Veiled Knives. They allow the user to become one with a summoned apparition, enhancing a man's strength and speed and such for a temporary time."

"At the cost of his life?"

Roc shook his head, "Not necessarily. The dagger judges the soul of the blood it sheds. If found strong enough, one can survive the Veiling. It has been known to happen, from time to time. Usually, a man will just let a small vein of blood to control the Hunter, for that is its name, for a few moments of dire circumstance. Marvain, however, was confident enough to leverage its full extent. And it found him wanting. I've seen too many magicians die to that cursed piece of steel. Some who thought they could enhance their powers and overcome the price of the Knife, others who fell in battle, such as Marvain. All fall prey to the bloodlust."

"And the dragon?"

Roc smiled, "That was Grael just showing off. I'm sure he could have unleashed it to terrible effect, had the battle reached a dire situation, but summoning a dragon is no mean feat even for the strongest of magicians. He was content with letting it follow Ragnus for a time. I'm not certain what its name was, but I've seen it somewhere before. Oh well, an old mind often forgets names."

THE ROFU WAY

In shadows lie the creeping vines that cling to doom and dread.
Darkness hides the twisted lies and, blind, men are led.
The Rofu fight with fear, not might, and in patience win their wars.
Constant strife of Dark and Light, and so between the Rofu and Korz.
Pestilence leads to doubt and fright. Slow, the plague fights the heart.
Courage fails, honor forgot, the mind it tears apart.
A dark web of doubt, the seeds of fear, thus slow death begins.
First the eyes, the sight, the mind, the poison always wins.
Muscles weaken, bones creak, and voices drain away.
Senses dim, thoughts dull, soon comes the end of days.
At last, a gasp, the final breath, air leaves the wounded lungs.
No medicine now, no sweating brow, souls in the balance are hung.
The body revolts, turns away from life, no mortal man survives.
With the Rofu, now, to serve, to fight. With the Rofu the soul resides.
The dagger bites deep, poisons deeper, laying even the strongest low.
By tricks and slight they snuff the light. Weakness, the Rofu know.

"The risen moon would make a fool of the sun, whose Light it can only harness for a time. Yet, ever the sun seeks to catch the wily moon, and someday it shall, and the world will blaze forever in the Light." Skal the Enlightened closed his text. He shifted the red hood that nearly blindfolded him to glance at the army assembled before his pulpit. The array of soldiers on display was unrivaled in Alkurah. Elves of the sea had flocked to his teachings, and the Light had grown within them. Men from the southlands had tagged along, eager to share in the wealth and power of the elves. Beasts of unimaginable size nested, lurked, and flew overhead, tamed by the powerful teachings of the Light. This was an army not created for conquest, but for cleansing.

"My lord, the Rofu in the Kharatvil are preparing themselves for war." One of the commanders knelt, palm open on his heart, "What are our orders?"

"The Way of the Light shall not waver at the mere sight of darkness. Burn them, my children. Burn them all."

The sun was long risen before the encampment at Brathur even began to stir. Drunken men, dwarves, trolls, and ogres lay strewn about the Great Hall, barracks, and fields alike. The chill of night gave way to a thick warmth, amplified by the mist that blanketed the ground. Snores drowned out the sounds of the carrion birds ever gnawing on the fresh feast of orc and goblin corpses. The healers had yet to sleep, having worked steadily overnight to keep as many of the Korzian soldiers' lives safe as they could manage. They were not always successful. The casualties, while minor compared to the Rofu, were still enough to keep the good mood in check. The number of those dead, or too wounded to continue fighting, was of little concern to the Lord Commander as he stalked his meeting room, listening to the opinions and thoughts of his officers.

"This was a sign of desperation," offered Commander Coark. He cracked a nut in his meaty palm, picking out bits of shell. "The Rofu know they cannot hope to win a war, so they tried to strike our recruit armies here at Brathur."

Grunts of agreement filled the room.

"But what about the phantoms?" The whole room started as Commander Tristan slunk from the shadows, revealing to everyone that he had probably been there all morning.

"Another cowardly Rofu trick, nothing more." Kyson sounded almost aloof. Usually, the man waved away the concerns of his own officers as though everything they thought mattered didn't. The opinions of allies were hardly treated better. He appeared to already be forgetting the battle. "Make their army seem larger and what not, nothing new."

"Do we still believe the Rofu are after the-"

"Keep your tongue behind your teeth," hissed the dwarvish commander, Bjerk. "Who knows what ears the wind has?"

"Commander Bjerk is right, we'd best not discuss that which we do not know." Kyson scratched his head, thoughtfully, mind tuned back into the conversation at hand. "Though, we'd do ourselves a favor if we could find out.

Tristan, send to your Rangers. We need to know more about this Rofu war."

Tristan nodded, whisking through the door without even a whisper of cloth rippling on the air.

For another hour the assembled commanders discussed the battle, sipped fine liquor, and munched on warm biscuits. He stood, eventually, shaking his head, "I don't want to hear any more about the strangeness of this engagement. If the Rofu wish to fight on our terms, they will lose in spite of their schemes. Korz shall ever be victorious!"

Other statements of general agreement wafted around the room before Roc slammed a fist on the table, "Kyson, the Rofu have never been willing to engage any foe on a scale such as this. In all my considerably lengthy life, they've schemed and plotted. Blindness now would mean terrible suffering later. Something fouler than orcs is at work here, and I dread the thought of discovering treachery in the midst of a campaign. We need to be patient and consult with Hâedra. Their healers could discover something among the fallen that may be advantageous to us."

Lord Commander Kyson, though unused to being addressed simply by his name, looked unshaken at the familiarity shown by Roc. "You would have me entrust my army, Korz's army, to cowards? They are beneath forgiveness, old man."

"Did you not care to know the faces of the slain?"

This was a direct challenge to Kyson and everyone in the room knew it. One of the first things the Korzian military teaches its soldiers is to remember the face of every foe they fight that they never forget what it is to take a life, and what it is to spare one.

"I know the faces of more orcs and goblins than I care to admit, Roc. You know that," Kyson growled.

"Did you not see the condition our foes were in? Their skin was blistered, scabby. Yellowing eyes. They reeked of fear and desperation."

"Would you not also weep for your life when you came to challenge the men of Korz?"

Men around the table slugged their drinks and cheered.

"Kyson, boy, you may remember the faces of the slain, but I fear you'll soon forget who we fight." The wizened commander rose quietly and stalked from the room.

Garroway and Gunsel sat on their bunks that morning, each holding five dice. Gunsel chewed on a braid of his beard. Between them lay a fistful of sweet candies and a dagger. The wager was set, and Gunsel felt he was soon to lose his first war prize. The pair tossed their dice into mugs and slammed them on the nearest table. He peeked under his mug. "Two fours," he declared.

Ro grinned slightly, "Sixes. Four of them."

Guns shifted. He could smell the sweetness of the candies. "Five fours."

On a three-count, the pair showed their dice. Guns flopped back onto the bed, arms raised in triumph as he howled at his luck. Five fours exactly.

Garroway tossed the mug at Gunsel, allowing himself some satisfaction as it clunked off his forehead. The bald man sat up, rubbing his forehead but still grinning, "Would you like one of my delicious sweets?"

"Bol take you and your sweets. Lucky brute."

Gunsel winked, sugary saliva already sticking in his beard, taunting, "I never doubted."

"Oh, aye." Garroway stood and ruffled his lank hair. He had been to the bathhouse twice since the battle and still felt dirty. Sitting alone now, he thought back to his conversation with Roc about the Rofu, about their fondness of disease and silent warfare. Shaking off his nerves, he started to jog around the courtyard. The bodies had all been taken away, either buried or burned. Blood stained the grass, red and black, and the stench lingered. In just his trousers, the jog was a good stretch for Garroway. He had become used to making the trip in full plate and mail, which was quite a chore even on the best of days. His path took him past the infirmary, where men had been slowly trickling in and out since his arrival several months before. It seemed as if a greater number had been stricken with illness recently, but most of the healers chalked it up to poor nutrition and fatigue from the battle, as well as unaddressed wounds. Every infirmary has a stigma of misery about it, and men tend to avoid the healers at any cost, even when it means they end up losing part of a limb to infection because they waited too long to visit.

Grael Voor sat with his back resting on a barrel, one foot dangling over the stone wall, the other crossed beneath it. Sweet smelling smoke drifted from the long pipe clutched between his teeth. Occasionally, he frowned and prodded at the smoking leaves. When Garroway got close, the elf leapt fifteen feet to the ground, landing lightly and struck out at an equal pace.

His appearance quite startled Garroway, who nearly tripped over a particularly sturdy blade of grass. "Afternoon, Grael, sir."

"If you're so deep in your own thoughts that you can't see the world about you, it may be best to unburden your weary mind," waxed the old elf, philosophically.

"It's that obvious?"

Grael tucked away his pipe and grinned, winking, "It is, son. But I've had many years to learn the ways of men."

"It's just the Rofu. Everything I've ever been taught about them was violated in this battle," Garroway puzzled.

The elf's smile faltered for a moment, but he recovered without a hitch, "Aye. Open slaughter is rarely their preferred method. Methinks Lord Commander Kyson lies blinded by his own glory."

"Has Roc approached him?"

"Ask him yourself," Grael nodded to Commander Kyson's office, where Roc was exiting, fists balled. "Though, perhaps wait a tick."

The pair came to a stop by the barracks; Garroway breathing deeply and stretching out the tightness in his legs while Grael may as well just have taken a leisurely stroll. Garroway flopped onto the grass, lacing his fingers behind his head and crossing his legs. "Could you tell me about the elves?"

He asked, curious now as he realized he had learned little about the elder race.

Grael propped himself on the warm stones, lighting his pipe once more, "What would you like to know?"

"What are they like? Where do they hail from? Why are there so few in Alkurah?"

Grael's eyes closed and his brow furrowed. "Elves are vicious creatures. Vengeful, vindictive, powerful. They prey upon the weak and defenseless, though in their youth they were beautiful and kind. Many men learned in the halls of my kin, and dwarves as well. I live in a world ravaged by time and war. Alas..." he sighed. Eventually, he shrugged, "They are also heavily bound to their own sense of honor, however twisted it may be."

"You speak as though you're not one of them." Garroway probed, hoping to uncover something of the elf's past.

"If I could claim any other kinsman, I would." He chewed his pipe for a moment, blowing a cloud of smoke that turned from gray to blue, then transformed into water and splashed on Garroway's face. "As for their cities, there are two in Alkurah, now. Braeco lies to the northwest, on an island of sorts. It is quite magnificent. The very stone of the cliffs has been bent to the will of the creators there. Such wonderful sculptures you'll not see in the realm of men, I can assure you. They live largely beneath the sea, singing songs of the shimmering sands and rolling waves that lap at their doorsteps." Grael's eyes gazed into the sky at something Garroway felt he would never see. "And in the south," he added, growing dark once more, "lies Praesta. The elflords dwell there in the remains of Eskeria. That forest itself has grown to be a cruel place filled with death. Darkness seeps ever deeper into the heart of Eskeria. It is dying, and I fear soon it shall consume the elves dwelling in those ancient trees." He snorted, "Aside from those already corrupted."

"Where do you call home?" pried Garroway, wondering that he had never known these things.

Grael stood, tamping out his pipe and helping Garroway to his feet. "My home is where I choose. Ever I've dwelt amongst men, dwarves, and elves, and never have I called a place home for long."

"Well where were you born, then? And raised?"

Grael winked, "I'll save such tales for a time of feasting and drinking, as you'll need both meat and ale to truly savor my story." With a nod, the old elf strode off toward the infirmary to lend what aid he could to the hand of the healers, who were always willing to have him, leaving Garroway's patience unsated.

Gunsel kicked open the heavy wooden door to the barracks, taking a deep breath and savoring the scent of grass and dust. He almost made it into the courtyard before the first pigeon swept down to alight on his shoulder. He gave it a sidelong glare. It cocked its head and cooed. Swinging his left hand toward it, he roared, missing, and losing his balance to crash to the dirt. Several other birds harassed him as he struggled to his feet, swatting and swiping. Finally, he connected with an open hand, grabbed the poor fowl, and threw it at the barracks. If it had collided, it may have met a grisly demise. However, the door was still open, so it simply recovered and fluttered back out. Gunsel escaped with only a few scrapes and one instance of droppings. He'd had worse.

Struggling to pull a shirt over his sweaty torso, Garroway rejoined his friend. "I see you've been once more befouled by the local wildlife."

"These damn birds haven't given me a moment's rest since my last bath. I'm tempted never to clean again."

"Oh, and wouldn't that make you a fearsome sight. Guns the Grimy, they'll call you. Or Sudsless Guns. I like that one. How were your candies, oh Bathless One?"

"Ah, stow it." He gave his friend a light shove. "What were you and the old elf gabbin' about?"

"He wanted some tips on seduction."

"And you didn't send him to the greatest teacher of them all?" Gunsel feined hurt.

"No. I'm afraid your mother isn't anywhere nearby."

Gunsel growled and tackled his friend, quickly pinning his face to the dirt and pulling one arm up his back by the elbow. "Mother didn't teach you this one, eh?"

"We were a little busy to get into foreplay, sorry."

Gunsel gave a pull to cause a flare of pain.

"Alright! Okay, okay I'm sorry."

Gunsel released his hold.

Garroway stood and patted his friend on the shoulders. "I'm sorry I didn't write her after." He winked and raced to the Great Hall for lunch, Gunsel threatening worse than murder and following close behind.

Though hundreds of braziers and candles burned around the Hall, no one ever felt overwhelmed even in the middle of the afternoon. Garroway was convinced it was some kind of magic.

The pair jostled their way into the line. Gortrum sat close by, ears deep in a dish that looked like gruel and smelled like mud. He glanced up at them over the rim of his bowl, presumably for a breath, and noticed his training partner. "Oi, Guns!" He belched uproariously, "'ow come ya never eat with ol' Gortrum?" He made a heart-stabbing motion with his knife, "Breaks me ol' 'eart."

"There's no heart in ya to break, ya old sellsword!"

"You wrong me, young Guns."

"You'd eat me soon as you'd eat that paste."

Gortrum laughed, belched again, and scooped another pile of the stuff into his gaping beard. "I couldn't stomach the birds that'd chase ye down me gullet!"

"So, how fared the battle with you, old man?"

"Oh, I sent my share o' baddies to their fiery graves, lad. No need to wring yer 'ands over ol' Trollsbane." He stood, slammed his right arm into his left, as the mercenaries preferred to salute each other, and belched appreciatively. Gunsel mimicked the movement, sans belch, nodding his head slightly in respect for his teacher.

When Gunsel turned around, Garroway thought he saw something in his friend's eye. He was about to suggest he wipe it out but after a blink it had cleared itself away. While the ogres slopped muck onto their wooden plates, Garroway asked, "Did you notice the orcs and goblins?"

Through a mouthful of stale bread, Gunsel replied, "Aye. Even crossed swords with one or two."

"I mean did you see the way they looked? Frightened. Dying."

"I'd be frightened of me as well, and of a man wielding the sword of the Godslayer. And most of them were dying, though some faster than others."

"They looked diseased, Gunsel. Sickly. Like they were running from something rather than towards it."

"Would you not wish to leave the desert? Probably some plague preying upon their malnourished hides. What matter is it to you? To us? Their numberless dead laid strewn across the field come the end of the battle. We left victorious, as we shall ever be." Noticing Garroway's expression, Gunsel flicked a pinch of their lunch onto his chest. "Lighten up, friend. There's naught in Alkurah can lay low the armies of Korz."

Roc pulled the bench next to Gunsel away from the table. He looked sullenly at the slop on his plate, prodding with his spoon as if expecting it to come alive at any moment. He gave Gunsel a glance and jerked a thumb over his shoulder.

"I'll leave you two to your lunch date then." He nodded to Garroway and slid over to sit with a troll that was debating whether to eat the table or the food placed upon it.

Roc's eyes never left his food when he groaned, "Kyson will be the death of this place."

"Did you talk to him about the Rofu? About how they looked?"

"Oh, he looks, but he sees nothing. A few months' time will tell the true toll of this battle. Sickness is spreading among the men and I fear it's more than fatigue." He took a deep breath, steadying himself for his first bite, and plunged the spoon deep into the muck. Giving a slight nod of approval, he jabbed his utensil toward Garroway. "Also, when we're done here, I'd like to take you to meet some of the dwarves. They're an odd sort, prone to bickering and brawls, so choose your words carefully. If it can possibly be taken as an insult, it will be."

"Why do you want me to meet with them?"

"Because I'm sending you and your man, as well as an escort from every race represented in the Korzian military, to Hâedra. I fear the armies of Korz will be weakened before our next bout with the Rofu, and I'd like to strengthen alliances of old. The armies of men must stand together, or they'll be destroyed standing alone."

"I understand the reasoning, but why send Gunsel and myself? Aren't there others better suited to diplomacy?"

"Guns knows his way around the trolls and ogres as well as any merc. Besides, you're easy enough to get along with, and the armor of the Godslayer may do something to sway the minds of the Council of Hâedra."

"I've been meaning to ask what you know of the armor. When I wear it, it feels almost alive. I know I'm not a great warrior, though I'm confident I could hold my own, but it makes me feel unstoppable."

Roc shrugged, "Those plates were heated in the forge of Bol himself. No smith in Alkurah or elsewhere could match the magic and skill that went into that metal. And who knows, perhaps the soul of Tykus still dwells partially within, reveling in bloodshed and the thrill of the challenge. It was torn from its last wearer and scattered across Alkurah long enough ago that few now could possibly remember it."

"When the armor was sundered the first time, it was sent at random across Alkura?"

Roc raised his eyebrows and grunted affirmation.

"But I found it all in a box in a hole in the ground within sight of the road to Korz."

They talked about how that might have happened for quite some time, settling on just accepting that they may never know what really happened. Garroway admitted he had only acquired the map to find it after an encounter with an elf that had claimed to be older than the moon. He couldn't remember what the words the elf spoke when he gave him the map.

The elf had said, "Tsund magii ne tsund Tykus. Etes burii et entir." Then shoved the piece of cloth into Garroway's pocket before staring off into the distance and disappearing.

Through a mouthful of the surprisingly appetizing sludge, Garroway asked, "How long have you known Grael?"

"That old pointy-eared bastard has planted his fair share of boots in my backside. He's trained men and elves who went on to train legends, aside from both Korz and myself. In fact, he was the creator of the Dragon's Hand, centuries ago."

"Why does your name not appear in legends and songs alongside Tykus and Korz?"

Roc seemed to shrink back. "I've no need for praise and history. Victory is a reward worth fighting for. Besides, I never killed one of the Gods or any such nonsense. I'm just a man."

"How does a man who is 'just a man' have such a story?"

Roc winked again, standing and tossing his emptied plate into a nearby barrel. "Someday, lad. Someday."

Deep beneath the shifting dunes of Kharat, an orc named Grimfilth perched on a throne of bones. His head and eyes shifted every few seconds, birdlike, to glare at something or other. Grimfilth stood well over two meters tall, enormous for an orc of the sands, and rippled with taut muscle. Ritual scarring in the shapes of the faces of the orclords of old covered his olive arms. He wore no shirt. The knotted pink flesh of dozens of wounds crisscrossed his broad chest. A greasy black ponytail hung nearly to his waist, adorned with beads, teeth, and small bones.

The massive stone doors before him opened, briefly letting the chittering sounds of arguments from the mess hall into his chamber. His sharp eyes focused on the broad figure of a troll. Rigathel. He strode to the foot of the throne. He placed his right hand, palm open, to his chest, and knelt. With his left he lobbed the waxen head of a fantastically decorated troll with a simple knife jutting from its forehead. Eyes low, he laid the flat of his hand to the stone before returning it to his chest, now in a fist.

"Rise," ordered Grimfilth. "I see you've news to share."

The deep growl of Rigathel's voice echoed slightly off the stones of the chamber, "Lord, the men of Korz slaughtered the chaff as wolves among lambs."

"And?"

Letting his hand fall, Rigathel looked at Grimfilth, "This takes time. In a few months their armies will be weakened beyond repair, their bodies yours to command."

Slamming a taloned fist into the bones of his throne, Grimfilth screeched and flashed his filed teeth, "Time is *not* our ally, Rigathel. The dunes can no longer keep us safe from the terrors of the west."

"Is there bad news from the Scar?"

"There is no news from the Scar."

"Gods. You don't think-"

"We mustn't abandon hope, but soon we *will* have to leave the dunes and seek asylum in the east. The elves have time and again refuted our requests, the Ogryn Swamps would kill us before the winter passed, and the dwarves ne'er leave their mountains nor open their gates to us."

"What of Ictheim? What of the trolls? Can I not work a treaty with my queen?" Rigathel pled.

"You know orcs and goblins cannot live in the frostlands. The men of Korz dare not shelter us, and I cannot fault them for it. Our pasts are filled with battles, death, dishonor, and deception. They'll never trust us, nor we them. Thus we fight ever on. No, the men of the east will not shelter us. The great tunnels under Brathur, and the weapons that lie within, are our greatest hope."

Rigathel nodded, jaw tight. "What of Gorathel?"

Grimfilth put a hand on his commander's shoulder. "I've no news from the Scar, I told you. I'm sorry."

Shaken at the turn of events, and the lack of news of his brother, Rigathel nodded his head. "All will that be?"

"That will be all. Go get some food in your belly and some rest for your heart and mind. Months may be too long, but one way or another we will have Brathur. We will take it as our own, as is the Rofu way."

"The cowards where are?" Gorathel hissed through bloodstained gums. A storm of arrows rained onto the battlements. Uncountable shafts tinkled from stone, but many found their marks. The troll captain had been up and down the Kharatvil, the massive wall that was the only gateway through the Scar. On the edge of Kharat, four thousand Rofu soldiers had been garrisoned as a bulwark against the west.

"Keep down your heads, imbeciles!" Arrows had been raining for days, but still Gorathel held the Kharatvil. One of the first volleys had caught him dashing up the steps to see what was happening. Three shafts to the chest. While that may have done in a human, Gorathel's hide was tough and thick, and they were mere trifles to the troll.

A human munched a biscuit, huddled against the parapet, "What're the odds they ever try and fight us?"

His companion gave a loud guffaw and roared into the buzzing of arrows, "Y'hear that? We want a fight!"

The only reply was more feathered shafts whizzing overhead.

Gorathel dared a glance upon the field. Nothing had changed. The first few hours, he had been certain the elves would advance, and he felt it unnecessary to begin rationing for a siege. Of course, he also assumed his army could leave to the east whenever they chose. He had not counted on a magician strong enough to destroy the Rhiam, the eastern gate of the Kharatvil. The Kharatvil itself was protected against magic. It was built in the days before men and orcs, when dwarves came down from Karakor to explore the different earths of the world.

It is said that when Bol first carved the land, he grew tired, and one night he dropped his hammer. The impact shattered the continent, creating the mountains, and frightening the elves out of their trees and the dwarves out of the ground. The Scar was carved into Alkurah during the battle between Tykus and the gods, and the residue of their great magics made the sands nigh invulnerable when sculpted properly. Thus, the Kharatvil was forged to be impermeable to almost any facet of force or guile, save being torn down stone by stone, grain by grain. However, the eastern side of the fortress, where the Rhiam stood, was vulnerable because the earth there was weaker, further from the Scar itself.

This host of elves clearly was no stranger to the myths of the land, because they had gone straight after the eastern gate even before beginning their assault, spearheaded by an innumerable lygian horde.

Lygians, one of several races of sea creatures that had climbed onto the land in the previous few centuries, bred fast and seemed to die even faster, given the occasion to do so. Their webbed hands make for horrific archers, and their frail, scaly gray exterior is little tougher than their brittle bones. Pointed teeth jut out at crazy angles seemingly at random. But where there was one Lygian, there was another fifty to take his place.

So it was that no reinforcements, no messengers, and no supplies could reach the bedraggled defenders.

"How do they plan on overcoming the Kharatvil?" asked the first human, named Sirin.

The other human, Bern, laughed again, "Elves, man."

"Right? Here we are, tag-teamed by elves, sea monsters, and some kinda freakin' giant army, but hey, we got goddamn biscuits, right?"

"Don't forget the dragon." added Sirin.

Gorathel interjected, "Dragons."

Two of the beasts had been strafing the wall at intervals, so the defenders had sought out extra stones to sit under. Of course, eventually a dragon could heat up enough to melt through it, but for a few moments it kept them safe.

After a few minutes, the trio realized the arrows had stopped. A shouted order from beyond the wall carried on a stiff wind, "*Rhiagia!*"

As one, four thousand elves and twenty-five thousand lygians drew swords and charged the Kharatvil.

THE ROAD

The dwarves, the lords of Karakor, in mountain halls reside.
Vaulted ceilings, tombs of stone, each chest swells with dwarven pride.
Smiths of steel, tools honed, they carved the mountains tall.
Tempers short, beards long, respected and feared by all.
Frozen Ictheim trolls call home, halls hewn from ice.
Driven from Alkurah by elves of lore, cursed, they pay the coldest price.
Lovers of clubs, of drums and blood, at war they feel at home.
No pyres for trolls, no tombs of stone, they lie beneath the loam.
The men of the swamp live ever on, unknown to legend and tale.
Ogryn tribes, leathery hides, roam both sides of the Veil.
The Meredun, a place of dread where doubt first began.
Eternal life, unending strife, behind mortals the Veiled stand.
Through Alkurah all, men do dwell, newest and youngest of all.
Boundless vigor, strength and will, forgotten pasts enthrall.
Fighting hard, loving deep, short lives humans live.
At the end of the day, the end of the fray, their lives for gold they give.
Last but first, the elves of lore, in forest and cave reside.
They never forgive, never forget, friendships fickle when tried.
Long lives they lead, anger seethes, wronged by the acts of men.
The elder race by fledglings replaced, ever they've vowed revenge.

Within the week, Garroway and Gunsel had each been given a horse packed to the breaking point with various clothing and food, and other supplies. Two dwarves would be accompanying them, as well as a solitary troll, and an ogre that was supposed to be meeting them at the gates of Brathur when they left. When Garroway had first met the dwarves, he nearly lost his head to a rogue mug toss. He and Roc had apparently interrupted a rather spectacular verbal debate between the two, and their carelessness was to be punished.

The first dwarf was named Throm of the Anvilfists. His long silvering beard was tucked over his burgeoning belly and into his belt, along with an axe made of a metal like none Ro had ever seen. It glittered in the sun, but was nearly as black as the armor of Tykus. He hoped the dwarves might be friendly enough to share some of their knowledge of weapons and smithing. Throm's helmet reached Ro's elbows, and his squat frame was nearly as broad as it was tall. His bare arms were covered with tattoos of dragons, weapons, and an anvil clutched in a fist.

His arguing partner was Rorrik of the Thundercrowns. Should the dwarf King Krumrakai be killed, Rorrik would be recalled as one of the potential successors to the throne. His bearing attested to his status. His shoulders were swept back and his jet-black hair looked finely combed and washed, tucked back away from his face. His beard contained much less silver than his counterpart, and was only long enough to cover his chest. It was braided in a manner that spoke of class and means. Brilliantly colored beads and clasps tinkled together gently whenever he shook his head.

Both dwarves wore light leather armor and heavy iron-soled boots. They spoke gruffly with voices like crashing stones. Garroway thought they were both going to break his wrist when they first clasped forearms in greeting, after they calmed down about being interrupted. The pair already knew they would be going to Hâedra, and were waiting only on Garroway and Gunsel. All that was left were the ogre and the troll.

Generally, the trolls slept under the stars in the courtyard. Some tied hammocks to posts, others laid on bedrolls, and still more just flopped to the ground wherever they happened to be when they felt weary. Bendragel opted to snooze on the grass. His muscled form lay sprawled in the shade offered by the walls. A red mohawk dangled in braids down to his waist, decorated with small bones and ornate carvings. His massive underbite showcased a jaw thick as stone and twice as hard. Small fangs jutted up over his lips, and he wore a simple woven vest and trousers. No shoes. To his left was a piece of bloodstained stone tied to a long wooden pole. Garroway assumed this was his club.

Roc stopped and gave a look to Garroway, "You want to wake him?"

Commander Tristan, Hâedran by birth, though having fought with Korz from only just out of his infancy, crouched in the searing sand. Around him a full dozen of his rangers crept forward, inch by inch. They need not speak to communicate, nor signal each other. The intense training they received at the hands of the centaurs gave them a connection akin to telepathy, and the subtlest of gestures or sounds could be precise orders. The sand in front of them shifted. Thirteen rangers froze instantly, disappearing into the grainy dust without a sound.

An orc face poked out into the blinding sun. It hissed, blinking rapidly and shielding its eyes as it climbed the few remaining stairs. "Toobright the sun. Crukky doesn'likeit. Notathin everhere aways." With an unhappy grunt, it disappeared once more, not having noticed the small magic rune glowing on top of the doorway.

The rangers backed away, taking care to cover any changes they made in the sand.

Clouds drifted lazily by Brathur, obscuring the sunlight in patches that shifted across the courtyard. Dried blood caked most of the grass, but here and there patches of new, green life poked through the remnants of the dead and dying. Gunsel shut his eyes against the sunlight. Before the battle, he had experienced more than his fill of violence and chaos. On numerous occasions, he stumbled into bar fights, gangland brawls, or had simply been mugged. Nothing could possibly have prepared him for what happened at Brathur. The stench of death mingled with smoke and rot. Flashes of faces of slain orcs and goblins laid low before his axes assaulted Gunsel's waking hours. His dreams lay in dark places. Shadows flitted at the edge of his vision, whispering and taunting him as he sweated and thrashed until he awoke, gasping and terrified. Night after night the nightmares replayed in his mind, robbing him of any refreshing sleep.

"You'll slumber the day away, brother," came the familiar rumbling of the Trollsbane himself.

One eye peeked open to see the smiling beard of Gortrum. The mercenary shooed away a flock of pigeons honing in on their favorite roost before crashing to the dirt beside his friend. "How do your dreams treat you?"

"Poorly," Gunsel grunted.

"Nightmares and demons come with the trade, I'm afraid. The faces linger long after they ought be forgotten."

"Roc tells us to remember the faces of the slain."

"Aye," Gortrum nodded. "Remember forever the faces of the fallen, but don't let them haunt you."

"How can I simply ignore the leers of the damned? They taunt me, laugh at me in my dreams, and hide behind my eyes during my waking hours."

"It passes, brother. Talk to Grael. Perhaps a wise wizard such as that elf may know something I don't." He winked and patted Guns' shoulder before standing and thudding into the Great Hall.

"And what sadness dwells in your mind, Gunsel, my friend?" The quiet power of Grael's voice startled Guns.

"Where did you come from?" He gasped.

"Please." He gave Gunsel a flat look, "I have my ways of being here and there."

"Grael, it's just," the man paused, looking for the right words, "I've never felt so afraid."

"Battle has a way of reminding us of the world's woes. My first battle was hundreds of years ago, yet I remember every detail of that day. The scents, the sights, the sounds. Those things will never leave me as long as I live which, trust me, will be quite some time."

"How do you deal with that?"

"Every day I remember the one thing that holds true for every battle I've been a part of. I remember that I survived, and I will continue to do so until I don't."

Gunsel grunted, smiling. "Thank you, Grael. It seems age may indeed lead to wisdom."

"Speaking of wisdom, did you end up using any magic during your struggle?"

Ashamed, Gunsel mumbled, "I quite forgot I was even capable of it, sir."

The elf's laugh was companionable and welcome where Gunsel had expected a rebuking or a lecture. "That's not a bad thing, *fiernda*. Friend. I have one last thing to tell you before you leave, however. I've warned you that magic's cost is life, however you never questioned me on that."

"I assumed you'd let me know, in time."

"Indeed, indeed. Well, the reason elves make such grand wizards is that magic literally steals moments from your life. Since an elf is never destined to simply fade into age as humans do, their cost is simply the same as hard work. It makes us tired, but won't shorten our lives unless we try to cast a spell too advanced or powerful."

"So how many years have I lost?" Gunsel cried, legitimately shaken, as he had practiced magic quite often over his few months at Brathur.

"What you've done has been seconds, not years. Simple magics have little to no cost at all, I just wanted to warn you once more against magic unless all other avenues have been exhausted."

"Thank you again, Grael."

The elf took a slight bow and leapt nimbly to the ramparts to continue his walk.

"One more question," Gunsel called after him. "You said magic doesn't require silly hand motions or other nonsense, so why did you and the others do them when you summoned those beasts?"

"Silly hand motions have a way of calming the mind and making everything seem a bit more real."

As Grael vanished, Garroway strode to replace him. "Guns the Sudsless, where lies your flock?"

"Gods take you, Garroway."

"Someday, maybe, if they'll have me. Let us away! The dwarves, ogre, and troll await our company."

"Damn the trolls, dwarves, and ogres. Damn you, too."

"While we're damning, let's damn Roc as well. And my father, for selling us to the army, eh?" Garroway pulled his friend to his feet, brushing dust and droppings off his shoulders.

"I'd like that, too." Gunsel stretched, yawning away some of the lingering shadows that crept in his eyes.

Just outside the gate, Bendragel was losing a ferocious battle with the local allergens. The thunderous sneezes broken up by intermittent sniffles and curses seemed to greatly amuse Rorrik, who chuckled away atop his miniature horse. Throm clucked his tongue in disapproval, as if Bendragel should be tough enough to suppress his sneezes.

Garroway and Gunsel walked their horses out into the plains to greet the rest of their company. Rorrik's pony was laden with trinkets and weapons, as well as clothes and supplies. Throm traveled much lighter, and the bearing of his pony showed its gratitude. Bendragel was horseless. When Garroway asked how he would keep up, the troll managed to avoid sneezing long enough to croak, "I'll no trouble have with that. Your own business, mind, human."

Garroway glanced at Rorrik and the dwarf shrugged. "Trolls an' horses share no love, it seems."

In response, his pony snorted and swatted a fly with its tail.

Gunsel mounted his horse, giving it some pats and scratches as they milled about. "Where is our ogre friend?"

"Yew mus' be talkin' 'bout me, though friend's a word I save fer friends." Rumbled the object that everyone had previously mistaken for a rogue boulder. It turned to face them, grinning so stupidly that it would have been ironic, had it not been sincere. "Moy name is Grumbubum Lumblegurb. Yew may call me Grum."

"A pleasure, Grum. I'm-"

"Oi know yew, Raow. An' Guns, Rork, Thurm, and Bendergal."

Garroway started to correct the ogre, but Throm shot him a look that spoke with more grammatical precision than Grumbubum ever would. The dwarf whispered, "It's not worth it, son."

The other dwarf nodded congenially at the ogre, then kicked his heels into his pony's flanks. "With our company assembled, I can think of nothing better to do than leave this place."

With grumbles of agreement, the unlikely fellowship set out on their path to Hâedra.

A waning half-moon hung low in the sky, lighting the plains well enough for all of the travelers to see for miles around, though there was little in the way of landscape, and Brathur had long since fallen below the horizon. They set a smart pace, hoping to make good time to Hâedra in order to speed up negotiations. Garroway was impressed with Bendragel and Grumbubum's endurance. Both maintained a healthy jog through the afternoon, and the party had stopped only once in order to let Bendragel pass through a sneezing fit.

"These flowers damned be!" He'd said between eruptions, kicking and prodding at patches of small blue blossoms with his club. When they resumed their journey, Bendragel went out of his way to smash every patch of flowers he saw, whether they were the same blue ones or not.

After several hours of silence, Rorrik suggested, "Perhaps some knowledge about us each may ease our bonding, lads," he yawned. "And kill some time as well."

"From Ictheim come I. Tundra frozen and hostile my home is. No flowers." He spit at a distant batch of flora. "Little, the trolls speak. Battle is our home. Words bandied at the expense of lives in battle oft come."

"Oi 'gree wit' the troll. Ogres ain't much o' the talkin' sort."

Garroway cleared his throat and raised his voice, "Then perhaps I should start. I was born in Korz-" Rorrik snorted in disgust, "which I happily left when I was old and strong enough."

"Quiet!" Throm's voice cracked into Garroway's like a rockslide. "Human lives are fleeting and dull. Bendragel and Grum would rather hear tales of the immense tunnels of Karakor!"

"You see one hole, you've seen 'em all." Gunsel interjected. The implication cut the dwarf off, as he was about to launch into a tale so full of glory and debauchery that even Bendragel would have struggled not to blush. Instead, the aged and experienced arguer whirled upon Guns.

"It's been quite some time since a man dared interrupt me, boy."

"Apparently it's been quite some time since you stopped talking, then."

Now so furious that his crimson face vibrated and both sweat and spittle sprinkled into the cool night air, Throm whipped his pony around and drew an axe. Pointing it at Gunsel he roared, "I'll not have some bald child try to have words with me. Throm takes no insults!"

"Throm may want to quiet down," Rorrik whispered, grabbing Throm's axe and silencing the old dwarf's unintelligible rage. "We're not a day from the stronghold and already we're followed."

Everyone directed their attention to Rorrik's extended finger. Silhouettes of a dozen figures on horseback stood out clearly against the bright night sky. An eerie horn wailed in the distance, carried by the light breeze over the plains.

"Well, we're doomed," Gunsel groaned.

Garroway chuckled despite his apprehension. "Come now, Guns. There're only the twelve of them!"

An answering horn sounded, and the silhouette exploded into hundreds of horsemen, no longer hiding and walking. The cloud their galloping mounts made obscured the stars.

Gunsel patted Garroway on the back. "Aye. Only the twelve."

Rorrik kicked his horse into motion, yelling over his shoulder, "The first of the Heldan Hills lay not far from here. If we hurry, we may lose them amongst the dangers there."

Garroway had enough time to simply respond, "Dangers?" before his horse shot forward.

Grimfilth stared at the roof of his chamber. The dreary stones were moist and moldy. The food was moldy. The armor and weapons were moldy. Everything molded. Though the desert was hot and dry, so far below it they may as well live beneath a lake. He sighed, rolling off his deceptively comfortable bed of leather and cloth. The chittering voices of the orcs in his army had pounded his aching head ceaselessly for months now. They were all afraid to leave the caverns. Terrors of the west, the 'Blight of Light' as they had taken to calling it, were being enhanced to mythical proportions.

"Mornin' Grimfiltsir."

Every voice he heard sickened him. All orcs were so simple, so easily molded. Not Grimfilth. The name he had chosen was to remind him of the race he was trying to lead. Grim and filthy. He was ambitious, though, and had taken to learning how to lead with a will. Knowledge, to Grimfilth, was as strong a weapon as a sword, though his skills with weapons were never shabby. Trying his hardest to look proud of his army, he stalked their midst, giving encouraging pats on their shoulders and trying to simply be among his peers. He was glad to reach the steps to his throne room. The ostentatious doors banged shut behind him.

Rigathel was already going about his morning tasks of scrubbing the mold and rust from every corner of the room. It never seemed to help. No troll had ever seen this kind of tenacity from any sort of organism in Ictheim. Sometimes, he missed the frozen tundra of his home. The massive peaks of the Hudun Mountains looming in the distance, every breath was crisp and clean, every meal hard-won against the local wildlife.

"How goes your fight?" Grimfilth asked, admiring the spirit with which his captain struggled against the blight.

"With the filth here, sir? Or with the filth out there?" He waved his hand in the general direction of outside.

"Hmph." Grimfilth was in an exceptionally bad mood. Not only had he slept poorly, he was beginning to think his troops were tiring of his leadership.

Rigathel's deep voice shook him from his moping. "Restless, sir, the soldiers are."

"Remember your speech, Rigathel." He reminded his second in command of the lessons the pair had worked so hard on together. "And I know. I sense it every time I walk in their midst. They wish to fight, to feast on the warm flesh of the slain." He stroked a clawed hand down a particularly ugly example of orcish tapestry. "Send a raiding party to the plains. See if we can catch some sort of convoy on the way out of Brathur."

"There are still a number of prisoners unaccounted for on the plains, sir."

"Yes, and they'll do a job of harassing the humans as well. Even in their cowardice they shall be useful." He wondered what the battle at Brathur had been like. To see a full-scale war was something of a goal for the orclord, one he wasn't sure he would enjoy realizing. "And send a shaman clan to Eskeria. Tell them they're to disguise themselves as men of Korz." Surely the elves and centaurs would know better, but it never hurt to keep your enemies wary of one another.

"Yes, sir."

"And tell your commanders to begin troop formations. Each battalion is to head to the surface once a day to practice."

"So soon, sir?"

"Time is not on our side, Rigathel. Best to strike while we have the arms to do so."

"Do we so abandon to their deaths the soldiers, who, at The Scar, are?" Rigathel asked about his brother as discreetly as he could.

"I'm sorry. There is only silence and rumor of death."

The troll lumbered out of his chambers, leaving Grimfilth with his thoughts. He often sat alone, remembering his long life. So much of Alkurah he'd seen, yet so little of the world. Rather than hope for kingdoms in Alkurah, he dreamed of conquering far off lands, undiscovered and wild. Orcs could only lead orcs, however, and his army had never been quite strong enough. The numberless defeats he had suffered at the hands of elves, dwarves, and men, sickened him. In disgust, he cursed the only elf he ever managed to meet. "Grael, you old, scheming bastard. I long for the day centuries past when you come to meet the cold steel waiting for your throat."

The Kharatvil stood, whole and unshaken.

"These goddamn elves, man." Sirin sighed, munching another biscuit. This one was decidedly staler yet more delicious than the last.

Bern had been shot days ago. His body lingered on the wall next to his friend. Three arrows still stuck to his chest, covered in dried blood mixed with sand. The aridness of the desert kept his body in relatively good shape; his skin had stretched, his eyes closed, and he looked distinctly corpsey, but from a distance he could be mistaken as just someone ugly and asleep. Sirin chatted to his friend, "How's hell, man? Gods, it can't be worse than here." He sniffed, smiling away a tear, "Remember Vahir? I can't imagine we've earned the Godhall after that. Bol's teeth, that was a real nightmare. Shit."

The elves and lygians had charged the Kharatvil two weeks ago. Giants had been pummeling the gate nonstop with hammers as big as a man. The sound was as maddening as the threat of what would become of the defenders if the giants ever managed to break through. There were no arrows left in the Keep. They gathered and fired back the elven arrows for several days, but for every enemy felled, another dozen stepped forward to hack at the enchanted stones. Their only action had been shoving ladders away as they clanged onto the parapets. The incessant thunder of metal on stone had been grating on them for so long that dozens of the Rofu had gone insane. Sleep was impossible, so they took turns sitting on top of the wall on the off chance something happened.

Sirin looked at Bern, "Rhiagia, right? Freakin' rhiagia." He chewed thoughtfully for almost an hour, crunching through his biscuit with care and dedication. He rubbed at a sore on his arm. "I know I shouldn't, but it just itches." He whipped around to look at the gate, "I bet it means charge, right? Rhiagia, you dainty little piss drinking squids!" With his back firmly planted against the wall again, he looked at his friend, "I know they're not squids. It just felt right, y'know?"

Gorathel's mood had become increasingly foul as the siege ran on. His command was down to only two and a half thousand men, orcs, goblins, and trolls. "We must to Grimfilth word get."

Scrolls littered the diminutive command room he found himself brooding in. A chair, now in a heap of splinters from his most recent fit of rage, was the only furniture aside from a simple table. He glanced at the scrolls occasionally, never seeming to find anything useful on them. "Flee this place our only option is to." He stalked from the room, taking care to slam the door as hard as he could. "Dyrrktha, here come."

Dyrrktha, a goblin with an unusual thickness of the skull, shambled down the hallway. His knuckles dragged and he had an underbite of such ridiculous proportions that he looked like someone had made a caricature of a caricature. He was, however, roughly invincible. Whether by training or horrid birth conditions, his skin was scabrous and cracked, but tough as stone. "I to go to Grimfilth need you."

"How?"

His short, single syllabled answer was reassuring to Gorathel. The troll hated orc-speech as much as anyone else, and he could always appreciate brevity from one of them. "I'll with you send a company small to through the Rhiam break."

Only two of the scouts that Gorathel had sent to the eastern gate had returned. What he gathered from their scattered reports made him only slightly less than completely certain his plan was a bad one. There is no easy path around the Scar, so he was counting on the elves' inability to sneak a large force around or over the Kharatvil. At best, he numbered them at a hundred or less of the stealthiest, most nimble elves. Unfortunately, in comparison to orcs, a hundred elves may as well be an army.

"Go. Each of you horses with take. When the gate in sight of you is, mount and with all speed ride to Kharatule. One across the line must make for to survive us this."

Five orcs set out with Dyrrktha, and five horses they took with them. They packed only three days provisions between them. If they were to reach the Kharatule, there would be suffering in the attempt.

The horn sounded every few seconds now as the horde quickly closed the gap to their quarry. Bendragel was itching to stand and fight, knowing that if his pack-brothers ever learned of his retreat he would never regain his glory. "Quickly they catch us, and flight I admire not do."

"Oi 'gree wit' the troll."

Rorrik risked a glance over his shoulder, regretted it as he saw how near their pursuers had drawn, and turned to nudge Throm. The old dwarf had calmed enough to be reasonable, and they held a whispered conversation in dwarvish that led to the pair reining their ponies in and dismounting. Throm drew a two-handed axe from his pack while Rorrik slid his hands into a pair of massive gauntlets that glowed pale blue in the darkness. They hummed gently as he waved his arms about, stretching. Sparks jumped from the knuckles when he crunched them together.

Gunsel and Garroway spared one another a glance before following suit. The latter felt naked with his armor tied up on his horse's flank. But the sword of Tykus was warm in his hands, as ever, and helped calm him.

A feral scream ripped from Bendragel's throat as he halted and brandished his club. "No more we run."

From somewhere, Grum had materialized a hammer the size of a small mammoth. It was made entirely of wood and had runes carved into the handle that began glowing red as he growled and squeezed it tightly.

Gunsel glanced around, ashamed at the fear he felt. Every time he turned his head to look at the shadows dancing around him, he was a moment too slow. Grael's words had helped, somewhat, but here in the night he felt exposed. Weak. He flexed his bulging arms, squeezing the wonderfully carved handles of his axes. Eyes closed, he drew a deep breath. The horn sounded again, just a few feet away. For one terrifying moment, Gunsel thought he was going to turn and flee. He opened his eyes and exhaled, "Until I don't."

The horsemen dismounted a few dozen feet from the motley diplomats. Numbering easily in the hundreds, the orcs and goblins squawked and chirped at one another, slobbering at the thought of fresh meat. They circled their prey for a few moments, reveling in the scent of fear that gushed from one of their number. He would die last, and slowest. They all knew the scent of the disease that had stolen away their clans and families. Teeth gnashing, they cried out and sprang as one.

Bendragel struck the first blow, obliterating three orcs with a downward swing of his club. He followed through by snatching one around the throat and tossing him into his comrades. The club swept around, shattering legs and crushing pelvises as it came full circle to rest in a puddle of greasy black blood. Taking it in two hands, the troll brought to bear his full height. Batting orcs and goblins aside, he pulverized bones and pulped flesh with every swing. "Pay the blood price!" He roared his pack's battle cry and leapt headlong into the trembling foe.

Throm wielded his axe with an efficiency and beauty that came only with age and experience. Every slight movement led to the razor-sharp edge severing a limb, cleaving a body, or dislodging a head. The axe seemed to bend as he twirled it, turning aside blades from numerous attackers at once, and lashing out to retaliate.

Gunsel could see nothing in his frenzy. The shadows tore at his mind, screeching and pounding his skull. Or maybe that was the orcs? He didn't know anymore whether his eyes were closed or had been torn out. Had he even slain one? Were they real? The nightmares in his mind returned, unbidden, to the forefront. He lashed out, as if in a dream, stumbling and weak. Now and then he felt blades tear a piece of flesh from his body. The pain didn't matter. His blood flowed freely in the night, but he could not see it. Not for the first time, Gunsel had a sudden clarity that he would die here, alone and forgotten. Until he felt a pat on his back, "Not here, not now."

His eyes opened as if a newborn. Everything seemed too bright and vivid, like he'd stared into darkness for so long he'd forgotten the light. He looked around to thank whoever had shielded him from his weakness, but there was no one to thank save the enemy. With his rage refueled, he carved a path into the advancing soldiers as a river carves the sand.

With skill he struggled to believe he possessed, Garroway handled the sword of Tykus as though he were the Godslayer himself. No enemy came within arm's reach of him without being butchered. The sword clove wood, steel, and bone alike. It longed for war and death, lapping up the blood of the slain like a man dying of thirst. Every time it plunged into an enemy Ro felt his power grow. He realized now that he did not wield the sword- it wielded him. He was its tool, to grow stronger once again. To claim so many lives that there was only one option left. It had tasted the blood of the gods, and it longed for a second helping.

The screams of the vanquished ringing in his ears, Garroway felt strangely calm as he wondered why Tykus had cast out his armor and sword. Bol was the god of war. Perhaps, with all of the magics he had used to craft this sword, his essence had seeped into it. The sword was War. It strove to submerge itself in glory and honor. Had Tykus rid himself of it because he knew it would consume him? Because he had ascended to the throne of the dead, did he simply wish for the sword to send him more souls to rule over? A lightning bolt brought Garroway back to the battlefield, away from his thoughts.

Rorrik's gauntlets unleashed a hellish storm of electricity with every strike. He crouched low, hands close together to keep the current strong. Each hit was calculated. Perfect. A palm strike to the chest, lightning stopped a heart. A chop to the ribs; broken, punctured lungs, the orc wouldn't last the night. An elbow to the skull; bone cracked, hemorrhaging blood leaked from the goblin's nose and mouth. With a shout, the sturdy dwarf raised both palms to the sky, summoning the bolt that drew Garroway from his reverie. Containing it between the gloves, he unleashed the devastating power into the heart of the enemy charge. Those not lucky enough to be disintegrated recieved horrific burns. Skin melted, bones fused together, and the dry grass took light and soon the night grew hot as the fire surrounded the battle, licking at the backs of advancing orcs and goblins.

A hearty chuckle rumbled within Grum as he swatted his tiny foes aside like gnats. Orcs and goblins were insignificant in such disorganized rabbles. His hammer was now glowing red-hot. Knives and arrows protruded from his leathery skin, but he hardly felt them. Not one of these fools held enough strength in them to truly injure an ogre. He relished the fight, glad to be done running at least for a time, but he took no glory from this. A massacre, not a battle. Numbers alone did not account for victory. He made sure Magnicaerna sated its thirst, and allowed himself to remember when Grael Voor had gifted the weapon to him.

Pale and sweating, Grael had looked tired. "You hold in your hands a piece of my soul, Grum, my friend. Take care of Magnicaerna, and it will take care of you."

For several hours the pair had sat, talking of magic and the wonders of the world. Grum spoke of the Veil as he never had with another being. Crossing over the Veil was an experience unlike any other, and was not without peril. What he said, however, stayed only with the ancient elf. When Grael stood to take his leave, he gave the hammer a gentle pat as one might pat a dog on the head. "Be good to one another," he asked of Grum and his weapon, then departed.

The blood dripping from the glowing head of the hammer dulled its brilliance. Grum stopped for a moment to clean it, and sheath it on his back once more. He disgraced the weapon upon such weakness. Now, his bare hands tore bodies in two, catching swords mid-swing and smashing skulls and ribs like paper. An arrow grazed his cheek, drawing blood from him in a way that could mean only one thing. "Magic," He spat.

Since the ogre stood nearly a meter taller than anyone else in the battle, he had no trouble seeing the troll that stood at the rear of the army. A large staff decorated with human skulls and grotesque writing shook and twirled as he fired another magical arrow. This one impaled Bendragel through the shoulder. Willed on by his companion's howls, Grum roared and charged. Like a juggernaut, he slammed through anything in his path, wading through dozens of orcs before arriving face-to-face with the shaman. It continued dancing and spinning its staff, though in a significantly more frenzied manner than before. Grum gave the troll credit; it stood its ground against a charging ogre. That took something beyond stupidity.

Unfortunately, staring down an angry ogre is never the best option. Grum snapped the staff in his clenched fist. The magical explosion scorched his palm, but vaporized the shaman troll, leaving only a shadow of ash imprinted on the ground.

The orcs and goblins immediately began to disperse. Some ran away, others simply dissolved, screaming, into piles of dust and greasy bone.

There was a moment of calm air and heavy breathing, then a crazed laughing flooded the ears of the fellowship.

With a faint *pop,* a man appeared in their midst. Rorrik whirled to strike, and his fist crushed the wisp of smoke left by the man vanishing. Lightning crackled in his palms as he panted and whipped around, searching for his foe.

Another pop yielded more cackling, "That was a close one!"

Rorrik growled and lashed out, again hitting nothing but air. "Fight like a man, coward!"

"What if I'm not a man?"

The red-cowled figured appeared directly behind Rorrik this time, lightly touching the base of his neck. He whispered something, and Rorrik's body went rigid. "What did you do to me, wizard?"

"Oh hush now. Dwarves and their tempers," he clucked his tongue. "Now, the rest of you seem a smidge more likely to listen first and smash later."

He teleported again, to the head of the group, and appeared in a deep bow. His long red robe brushed the ground, dirtying at the hems. As he straightened up, Garroway and Gunsel both gasped in recognition. "I've seen you before!"

"Oh good! And here I thought you might be an average pair of dullard humans." He teleported in front of Gunsel, right hand outstretched. "My name is Sekl."

Gunsel shook his hand timidly, "I wish you'd just walk places."

"Walking is boring and slow," a dozen pops sounded in the night air before Sekl appeared in front of Ro. "And magic is a gift not all possess."

"Who are you? Where did you come from?"

"I am Sekl of the Heldanhood. Several dozens of years I've waited to greet a group such as yours. Travellers from Korz sent on an errand to Hâedra? But to what point and purpose?" He started pacing, occasionally vanishing and reappearing a few feet away, biting his thumb while he thought. "Do the Korzians suspect something? No, no, they're fools. Morons. Idiots. They wouldn't know a dragon if it dropped in for a spot of ale! Are they... afraid?" He stopped and stared into the distance as if he was looking at Korz, so many miles away, in order to glean some information. "The wise one knows. He sees and feels the threat, plucking threads as he is ever wont. Alas, the past holds no sway over the present."

Rorrik was sweating with exertion, trying to make his body move against the magic Sekl had used on him. The strange little man noticed it and waved an arm. At once, Rorrik lunged again. This time it was Grum who held him back. "Oi think we ought ta keep 'im 'live."

"As if you could kill *me*," Sekl snorted and glanced at Garroway. "Come now! Follow me into the Hills and you shan't lose your way."

THE HILLS

Ever fluid, change protects, the Hills never stay.
To keep their secrets, guard their charge, and turn all eyes away.
The Heldanhood in the hills reside, to turn their mysterious wheels.
Decisions made, lives paid, nations made to kneel.
How often wars were won within the Heldanhood's halls,
Before armies have a chance to fight, they are sacrificed one and all.
Magic seeped to the nearby land, warping time and life.
Creatures dragged from other planes live in endless strife.
Monks in red, warriors white, the Heldanhood study the land.
They seal its fate, lives decide, the world in their hands.
How often has Alkurah's history lay on the whim of the Heldanhood?
At the fore of crises those of the Heldanhood have ever stood.
Dwarves, orcs, goblins, trolls, elves, ogres, men.
The future and past in memories last, and break, and twist, and bend.

For another four hours they followed Sekl, wary that he may be leading them into an ambush. Every rustle of the wind on the grass sent hands to weapons. Every squawk of a bird dive-bombing Gunsel had heads turning and nerves strained. Sekl seemed entirely carefree, skipping and teleporting here and there, sometimes reappearing to chat with one member or another, sometimes simply floating over their heads.

Finally, Rorrik stopped and held up his right hand. "Enough, stranger."

"It's 'Sekl.'"

"I know your name, wizard. What I don't know is your intent. Why are you leading us through the Hills? And how can we trust you?"

"Trust is something I leave to fools and old men. I've told you I am of the Heldanhood. As a dwarf, I expected that to mean something to you."

Rorrik frowned, chewing his tongue as he thought carefully on what to say. "It can mean many things, wizard. The Heldanhood was thought to have died out an age ago."

Sekl got suddenly darker, his voice dropped. "Died out is a kind way to say it."

"Aye. Wiped out would be closer to the truth. My ancestors grew tired of the mischief of the Heldanhood, always tripping up their marvelous works just days before completion, informing enemies of troop whereabouts and formations, or just being bothersome."

"The Heldanhood has reasons far beyond the comprehension of any dwarf, Rorrik. You would be wiser than your ancestors if you were to take my advice."

The silence was loud enough to deafen any man. Clearly, Sekl was insulting this potential future king of dwarves, however Rorrik simply nodded. Throm looked as if he might actually explode at any moment, trying to quell his rage at the insults lobbed toward his race.

"And what advice might that be, Sekl of the Heldanhood?" Rorrik asked through gritted teeth.

He disappeared, popping up inches in front of Rorrik's face. "To trust me." Once again, cackling shattered the night calmness as he reappeared to lead the group.

Garroway and Gunsel, who had never heard of the Heldanhood at all, had been exchanging blank stares for most of the journey. Finally, Gunsel asked, "Who are the Heldanhood?"

Sekl slumped his shoulders, looking at the sky questioningly, as if it might have some answers for him. He turned and stomped back to the pair, forgoing his usual teleportation to display just how disgruntled he was. "Have humans so readily forgotten their past?"

Gunsel slowly turned to look at Garroway, before shrugging and scratching his head.

Sekl sighed, throwing a companionable arm around his shoulders. "Well, I can give you a history lesson as we proceed!"

Throm muttered, "Lovely."

"When the elves were the only race that dwelt in Alkurah, they built three cities. Past the Nazene and Kharat, off the coast lies the city Braeco. It was the first. When the elves left *meredun* in the south, they wandered for many years. Elves are not suited well to deserts and swamps, so they pushed through to the seas of the northwest. Here they sang to the cliffs and waters and wove their immense magical prowess into the very air. The water now lives to guard the elven city, and the sea teems with traps and tricks to confuse or kill potential enemies."

"Grael told me about some of the elves' ways. He said they were a haughty bunch. Prone to vengeance and anger." Garroway hoped he was adding to the conversation.

"Indeed! Yes, indeed, quite, yes. The Braeco became rather full of their success, and turned on the other elf tribes. The fairer Braeco began to purge their ranks of the grittier elves, trying to assume a place at the head of the elven race. 'Lords of kings,' they'd say, whiling away the hours pondering newer, viler means to supplant the other elves. Eventually, as I'm sure you can imagine, the 'lesser' elves grew tired of this genocide. They left. It only took a dozen years or so." He poofed into Gunsel's face, "Elves are slow." He poofed back to the head of the company. "And so the Braeco were left in the north. The sand and stone holds their secrets close to heart."

"And the other elves?" Gunsel asked, genuinely curious.

"Well, you know, yes, they're still around. The city Praesta stands somewhere deep within Eskeria. Come to think of it, elves are rather fond of their 'a' 'e' sounds. Lots of names like Gael, Vaer, Caed. Strange, really."

"The elves," Throm growled.

"Ah, right, yes. The elves in Praesta are slow to anger, and slower to forget. Once they'd had enough of Braeco, they left. Of course, forgiveness isn't their strong suit. The Praestan king does a lot of plotting against his eternal foe. Not a terrible amount of real war goes on, just passive-aggressive ass-holery, you know the drill."

"If the Braecan elves know it's the Praestans, why don't they just attack them?" Rorrik asked.

"How *dwarvish*. 'It's bad? Kill it!' Come now, Rorrik. If a human convoy happened across your gates, would you simply let it pass? No, of course not, no, you'd *tax* it. One way or another you'd get something from them. Much like the Praesta did with the Braeco convoys. They wouldn't kill, usually. And besides, elven cities are not like those of men and dwarves. There are no walls to breach, no castles to destroy. They live in utter safety, guarded by their magics and mysteries." He waved his hands in the air, grinning as though he knew something more than he shared.

Bendragel smashed a fist into his club. "Trolls like stones their wars fight. Strength we with win, not tricks and lies."

Sekl teleported so he was sitting cross-legged on Bendragel's broad shoulders. "And you, dear troll, are a stunning relic of barbarism. Have you heard much from Ictheim, as of late?"

As Bendragel moved to tear Sekl from his perch, the nimble wizard appeared just out of arms length in front of him. "Of Ictheim what you know do?" The troll growled

"Dark tidings come from the frozen wastes of your kingdom."

"Of the queen do you speak?"

Sekl dropped his voice, "I speak of your kin, Bendragel."

"Rigathel?"

"And Gorathel."

"Not in Ictheim either are." The troll's club shook the ground as it thudded down. "What become of my brothers has, wizard?"

"Oh, my dear troll, they both live, if that's what you're worried about. Though, life and death lie so near a thin line."

Bendragel growled, tightening his grip on the club. "Plainly speak, wizard, or your head lose."

"A troll telling me to speak plainly. I may cross that one off my list of things I never thought to hear. Worry less of your kin, they're stronger than you know."

Garroway cleared his throat loudly and raised his hand. Feeling stupid to have done so, he slowly reached to scratch his head, as if that was his plan all along. "If I may... am I the only one who doesn't know why this place is dangerous?"

Sekl chortled again, turning mid step to face Garroway, but continuing to float backwards. "Right! Mortals. The Hills here are quite literally alive, my dear human. Some of those to first leave the Ogryn Swamps came here, to the Hills. They tried hard to replicate the wondrous works of nature that had occurred in their homeland, but they failed. They brought the land here to sentience, and it hungers, dear boy. You'll have noticed no birds have attacked your friend here for quite some time. Nor have you heard even the buzzing of flies in your ear. The hills move quite often, if you took the time to watch them, and many a traveler has lost their life to the grassy knolls."

"Was it the Heldanhood that created this trap as well?"

"Oh, how quickly the man catches on. Yes, we left the Swamps to be closer to the heart of this world. We made a mistake here, and now we dwell amongst our failure to remind ourselves that not even we are perfect."

"Why did you shy so quickly away from Gunsel and me when we saw you on the plains?"

"Shy? By the gods, mortal, I did not shy. I fled! I fled your presence as the shadow flees the flame, though in this case the opposite is quite the same! Do you know what sorcery you carry with you?"

Wary that he may not have seen the armor yet, Garroway managed a convincing, "No?"

"Gods." Sekl replied. He made a vague gesture at Gunsel and everyone's assumptions about the poison inflicted upon him at Brathur were confirmed.

This all made sense to Garroway, but he asked when the thought occurred to him, "If you mean the poison, he couldn't have been afflicted before we reached Korz."

"Ah," Sekl tapped his nose, "then you'll have to forgive me for keeping secrets."

He appeared just off Garroway's shoulder, leaning in close enough that only he could hear. "Between us, I think you're too late." He winked again and appeared at the company's fore. Facing them, he held out both hands, "Alas, my history lesson must end here."

Throm rolled his eyes, "My heart aches at our loss."

"We have arrived at my humble home."

The grass and stones on the hill in front of them peeled away, laying bare a massive hall filled with crimson-clad monks and acolytes scurrying to and fro with scrolls, platters, and books. An oaken table dominated the room, littered with ink and parchment, food and drink. The monks scribbled or dictated to their assistants as they rewrote works from time immemorial for the use of future generations. Steaming piles of potatoes kept ever warm by magically heated bowls were spooned onto wooden plates. Flavorful smells wafted through the warm air. Smoke billowed from a dozen hearths, emptying through holes cut in the hill. At the head of the table stood a massive throne. Its red cushion was embroidered with a golden glove. Each finger was carved into the face of one of the major races of Alkurah- Men on the pinky, then trolls, ogres, elves, and dwarves on the thumb. On its palm was the face of an orc.

Sekl appeared on the throne, resting his chin on his right fist. "Rest, my newfound friends. Eat, drink, read if you can and the fancy strikes you. You may spend a few days and nights here before I send you on your way to Hâedra. Who knows? Maybe my brothers of the Light here can offer some insight and guidance into the world around you."

Throm and Rorrik dropped their packs. Both grumbling about the supplies they'd lost when their mounts had bolted during the clash with the rogue tribe of orcs.

Sekl waved an arm and their horses all came trotting into the shade of the hill. "My brothers found them wandering. Glad we got to them before other, hungrier things."

Gunsel was already doing his best to drown himself in potatoes and ale. With each scoop he took the bowl filled itself up just enough so that he never made any real progress. This deeply unsettled the bearded warrior, and he took it to be a personal challenge that he could not out-eat the magic potatoes.

Garroway flopped onto the bench next to him, skimming a tome titled *Men*. "You know, Gunsel, if you read as much and as fast as you ate, I can't help but shudder at the things you'd accomplish."

"Books don't taste as good."

"While I don't disagree, I'm not sure they exist for the same purpose."

"Men often talk of sating their thirst for knowledge. I don't find parchment particularly quenching."

Garroway started to rebut, but decided his friend had a fair point and instead quaffed a mug of curiously blue liquid.

"What's that?" Guns asked through a mounded bite of potatoes and beans.

"Can't say I know. It tastes... blue."

"Oh?"

"Yes. Blue is the right word."

Gunsel shook his head and continued his relentless assault on the magical bowl. Its resilience remained staunch and infuriating.

Across the table, Bendragel was struggling to understand the concept of vegetables. One of the monks was trembling, explaining how there was no meat in the hills because all of the animals were killed by the magics in the ground or the Shadow beasts that lurked in the dark places.

"If no meat there in this place is, how do all of you here live?"

"Well, uh, there are plants that we can grow and cook to eat."

"Eat meat, trolls. Animals plants eat."

"Um, technically we're all animals."

Bendragel grabbed his club and stood, flipping the bench over and staring down the monk. "Insult Bendragel?"

"I meant no offense!" The monk raised his hands and scurried away, almost crying in his fear of the troll.

Snarling, Bendragel squatted on his haunches, forgoing the overturned bench. He plucked a green bean from a bowl. After twisting it around in his hands a few times, he sniffed it. He shook his head and simply dropped it, propped his club on the table, and stretched out on the cool stone floor to doze off. Morning had come, and he had travelled quite a distance on no sleep.

Hunched in a corner, Grumbubum appeared to be reading a massive leather-bound book written in a barbaric-looking language. Thick lines and hooked letters were scribbled violently across its pages with no apparent regard for lines, spacing, or indentation. His frown deepened with every shuffling of pages. Occasionally, he glanced at Garroway and Gunsel before sighing deeply and returning to his study.

Throm and Rorrik were arguing as they removed pieces of leather armor from themselves. The dwarven tongue clashed like steel on stone in the relative quiet of the bustling hill. Clearly they were disagreeing over whether or not to stay in this place. Dwarves use their hands as much as their mouths for talking, and they alternated between Throm pointing in the general direction of Hâedra and Rorrik pointing straight down, or toward Sekl. After a heated several minutes, Rorrik grabbed Throm by the shoulders. Garroway thought he was going to punch him. He was mistaken. The younger dwarf pulled Throm in hard for a solid head-butt, forehead to forehead. They grinned, winked at one another, and swaggered to the throne to talk to Sekl.

"So, wizard, why have you helped us?" Rorrik led.

"Please, dwarf, not this again. I've told you you're going to have to trust me."

"More than once a race has rested its fate in the hands of the Heldanhood." Throm followed.

"More than once a race has tried to defy the Light!" Sekl's tone deepened as he leaned forward. "Tried."

"And the massacre of your kind?" Rorrik smirked.

"Dare I say we saw it coming? Some of us did anyway. Most of the Heldanhood had become so full of thier own power that they refused to believe any danger may befall them. Why do you think your armies were unable to cleanse Alkurah of our existence? Some of us were wise enough to simply get out of the way."

Throm growled, fingers closing around the haft of his axe. "And what's to stop us from finishing the job?"

"By all means, you're welcome to try. Though dying isn't something that comes easily to us. Your grandfathers knew more of smithing metal and magic than they were willing to teach."

A growl formed in Rorrik's throat, "What knowledge have you of our forebears, imp? Their greatness cannot be fathomed by any but dwarves, lovers of stone and earth."

"And what of those greater than mortal?" Sekl ground his teeth, clearly disturbed about the lack of respect being paid him.

Gunsel, clearly struggling to stifle a rising need to vomit, stood and asked, "And what are you? What us is there?"

Sekl was speechless for only a moment. He teleported to Gunsel's side, "The human's questions are far more intriguing than yours, dwarf." Rorrik had to forcibly restrain Throm from diving at Sekl and Gunsel. The wizard cackled and answered, "There are seven of the Chosen of the Light left. Hundreds were slaughtered by the dwarves in their," he paused, searching for the right word, "zeal, and we few remain now."

He took a deep breath and actually paced to the other side of the table instead of teleporting. "As to *what* we are, well, that's quite another answer." He took a deep breath, preparing to launch into his explanation. "We're not actually alive, in the sense that living and breathing means life. I have no heartbeat, no need to fill my lungs. No need to consume or drink anything. I exist. I have a mastery of magic that came to me from birth." He stopped, scratching his head, "Birth is the wrong word. Creation? All of us seem to have simply sprung into existence around the same time. We know not when or why. The Swamps simply spat us out, it seems. The elves were already here, and dwarves were beginning to pop up from the soil. Everything was so fresh and new! The sun, Bol's guiding light, felt warmer, grass smelled crisper. The very air was thick with the scent of knowledge and power. Magic was everywhere in this land! When the Vulkha, the banished, fell in the meredun, they used their immense magical prowess to tap into the life force of this world. It's been slowly dying since. Terrible, really, if you're keen enough to taste it on the air."

"Seems to me Alkurah would be quite better off without the pointy-eared, leaf-eating archers." Throm made sure to spit a little as he put emphasis on his final word. Dwarves have a peculiar stigma against projectiles that aren't bigger than they are.

"Maybe. Though, if the elves had not been given this place, I cannot say for sure whether any race would live here. Anyhow, that's quite more history than anyone's been told for an age. As our kind began to come together, Bol descended from the sun to teach us. He gave us a way to peer into the past, and to glimpse into the future. We have ever since been the guiding light of Alkurah, though often behind the curtains. The monks you see here are a collection of the brightest minds from all corners of this world. We hope to reestablish the Heldanhood to once more bring Light, and order, to the world."

Still on the previous train of though, Gunsel asked,"If you're not alive, how can you be killed?" The question again took the sharp-tongued sorcerer aback.

"I'd rather not delve into that particularly gruesome set of memories, if you don't mind." With that he nodded and disappeared, leaving the companions to their own devices for a time.

The morning and afternoon passed lazily. Bendragel napped on the cool stones, content enough to rest his tired legs. Grum hunkered down in his corner with a loaf of black bread to finish reading. Garroway and Gunsel prodded the monks for knowledge for a while, but both quickly tired of the puzzling answers they constantly received, and the vicious insults against mankind they were forced to suffer. So they napped through lunch.

Lying down on the bench, Gunsel laced his hands behind his head. "Seems little love is lost between every other race and ours."

"Aye. It must be our short lifespan they find threatening. Or our general lack of magical prowess. Maybe it's the profound averageness in height and weight."

Gunsel snorted, "Probably jealous that we have the pretty females."

"And here I took you for more of a dwarven connoisseur. What turned you off them? Was it the beards?" He mimed stroking broom-bristled facial hair.

A wooden spoon plunked off Garroway's head as Gunsel leaned back again, satisfied. "Course not. Dwarf ladies are a little too feminine for me." He closed his eyes, "And our women cost less at the brothels."

The pair roared with laughter, showered with disdainful glances from the monks around the table.

"So, Gunsel, tell me about your life as a lad." Garroway asked, both men now lying opposite each other on their benches.

The bald man's strong brow furrowed for only a moment before he grinned and waved his friend's question away. "I've not a tall tale to tell. Nor a short one, for that matter."

"Come now, something must have happened to force you into servitude."

"That's an easy one. I lost a bet. I lost several bets. I didn't have money, so they took myself as payment. I'd jumped from master to master for a while. Everyone got sick of putting up with my feathered followers."

"Why does that even happen, anyway? Why are they so attached to you?"

Gunsel reminisced.

Sleeping in the gutter had always been a cultural experience to him. A sort of vacation from sanity he stumbled through every now and then. It never lasted long, and everything had a way of working itself out with him getting the 'better' end of death versus endenturement. Still, he found himself in the gutter sometimes, and had learned that wading through shit does not always lead you up the ladder: sometimes it leads you to a deeper pool of shit.

Gunsel had never drowned in that deeper pool, but he had certainly gulped its waters, so to speak. The lowest of his personal, and very low, lows, was his very first, after escaping Vahir and his childhood.

His master, Mat Nicholas Bere, who insisted upon being heralded 'Lord Prince Mattenbere the Great', was given to fits of grandeur, and often his name required spicing up to keep pace with the man's own brilliance. Gunsel, who had been beneath Bere for only a few months, had yet to experience one of these such moods, in which there could be no satiating Bere's appetite for praise and adulation.

The cook warned Gunsel about the hurricane that was their master over breakfast, and Gunsel did well enough through lunch. However, it was when he made the utmost blunder of serving the cheese in his right hand that the proverbial shit deepened.

"I thought you said only last week that I had to serve cheese in the right, bread in the left," Gunsel didn't quite shout. "I remember because you specifically said you wanted the 'Right Cheese'."

"That was before my recent promotion from 'Prince' to 'Lord Prince.' Now it is only fitting of my station to be served bread from the right hand, for bread should be strong like a sword arm on the outside, and tender as a lover within!" Bere pouted, batting his powdered lashes and tutting profusely.

Gunsel bit his cheek to keep from screaming at his master, as that had only ever netted him a flogging or worse. Instead, he gave a grotesque smile, and switched the bread and cheese, then served it.

"Much better!" Bere approved between mouthfuls of food.

To his credit, what Gunsel muttered was not the worst or most vile insult the man had ever conceived, but the actual wording mattered precious little to the Lord Prince.

"You don't approve?" Bere's voice was now thin, absurdly high-pitched, and filled with implied threat. "What, slave, would you know of how the world works? You are the mud beneath the wheels of progress. Necessary, but dirty."

Gunsel took that as an invitation to cave the man's teeth in with a brisk headbutt. Bere stumbled back, bleeding everywhere and struggling to collect his front several masticators. He cried out. It was a word, maybe. Something in some foreign language Gunsel had never heard. Whatever it was, it sounded wrong. Poisonous. And then, there was only pain. It wasn't real. His flesh boiled, his bones burned, and his insides cooked, but Gunsel could only feel it in his mind.

Then Bere spoke: "Cast upon this slave a curse most foul, and let him forever be stalked by it, even in the most barren and complete suffering!"

Now, when he thinks back on it, Gunsel can almost see a rotting mouth spit the words with a wry grin. Whether or not the gods intentionally interpreted Bere's command the way they did, or if it was an innocent coincidence, Gunsel never bothered to ponder.

Then the world distorted around Gunsel. It disappeared, he disappeared, and suddenly he was alone, face down in the gutter, doing his best not to inhale the shit.

"Son, you look awful. Would you like a job?" A thin voice grated through the muck seeping into his ears, and he pushed himself up to reply.

Instead, a rogue chicken smashed into his face, beak first, and carved the first of many fowl scars from his flesh. The curse proved itself a peculiar burden, and sometimes an irreplaceable boon.

He finished his tale, admiring the incredulous expression on his friend's face.

Garroway took a moment, then replied, "And here I though they were just hoping you'd die off so they could eat your bloated corpse."

A darkness passed over Gunsel. He waved his hand in front of his face like he was wiping a cobweb out of the way before standing and storming out of the hall into a side room.

Garroway stared, dumbfounded, for a few seconds before shaking his head and muttering, "Strange."

Gunsel found himself in a sparsely decorated room partially lit by a fluttering candle stashed on a simple table in the corner. Nothing decorated the walls, no windows offered sight to the outside world. He leaned his head against the cool stones, smashing a fist once into the smooth rocks. The candle's light grew dim, as if the shadows fought to expand their borders. "Damn it, Gunsel. Damn you, coward." Memories of a time he'd hoped to forget leapt to his mind. He sank to the floor, clutching his head tightly. "Get-out-of-my-head." He slammed his head into the unforgiving walls with each word, hoping to beat the painful memories from himself. "Damn this place and its shadows." He snatched the candle from its stand, holding it close to feel its feeble warmth. Afraid to look away from the light, he clutched it near his chest.

Shadows on the wall began to encroach on the candlelight once more. They became figures of misery, gruesome depictions of horrors long past. Gunsel shut his eyes against the onslaught, but his eyelids betrayed only more horrors. "Vahir. Saree, your sister. Meren, your mother. Remember them." A ghastly voice echoed in his head.

"*NO!*"

"Remember, Gunsel." The flame from the candle vanished into a sliver of smoke.

Gunsel's eyes snapped open, wide and terrified. He shivered on the floor, incapable of fighting this foe he could not hit. He longed for the touch of another being to shake him from this nightmare. Surely, it was but a terrible dream from which he need only awake. Black tears leaked from his bloodshot eyes. He retched, body wracking as he heaved. The candle clattered to the ground as he threw his hands down to catch himself. His bile was oily black, splattering over the stones.

Nightmares erupted from the shadow, or were they memories? Grotesque visions of mutilated corpses. The scent of cooked meat. Strangers? No, he saw his hand moving through no effort of his own, to push a lock of hair away from a partially skinned face. He retched again, seeing half-burnt features of the woman he had loved so much.

The door banged open and Garroway slid to his side, patting his back. "Come now, Guns, what's this? Defeated by mere potatoes?" He helped his friend off the floor, walking him back to the table where he sat heavily on the wooden bench. "You look terrible, friend. Did you get it all out?"

The shadows receded slowly from Gunsel's mind. He nodded and opened glassy eyes. "Aye. Must've been a bad batch."

Garroway laughed and gave his friend another pat on the back. "Indeed. Or perhaps magic tubers don't go down quite as smooth, eh?"

Grumbubum kept his head down, but shot a mindful glance at the pair. He shut the massive tome with a thud and shuffled it back into its place on the shelf.

Lord Commander Kyson stalked the courtyard of Brathur. Every day, fewer men were capable of completing their daily exercises. Entire regiments were ill, feverish, and hallucinating. Dozens had already taken their own lives. The bodies were burned on Grael's orders.

"I'd rather we remember them in cinders than meet them once more in armor," he'd said.

Roc had tried to convince Kyson to send envoys to the elves, but he was denied. He didn't even bother to ask about Hâedra more than twice, having already defied orders to send the small party now holed up in the Heldan Hills. When he breached the subject again, Kyson snapped back at him: "What good would cowards do for us now, Roc? They let our armies die once, abandoned and betrayed."

"If you don't act, you've done the same to *this* army."

"I'll not seek the aid of backstabbers and pirates. Let them rot in their river."

"And us rot in our castles."

Kyson was trying to cheer up the remaining healthy men, but he knew they felt the gaping holes in their formations. When he went to Roc again, a few days later, the chiseled old soldier had simply shaken his head. "You know my advice, Kyson. I'll not sit here and listen to your own pride kill this army. Send for help, or don't come for mine."

Now the Lord Commander of an army of infirm had no one to turn to. Hâedra was home to the most skilled healers in Alkurah, but he would never go groveling to them. His ancestors had been among the army that rode to Hâedra's aid during the great wars with the Rofu. They were led to a trap and butchered while Hâedran armies hid in their barracks, paralyzed by fear. No, Korz would not ask anything of Hâedra, nor of any other nation. This was their war, and theirs alone ever since Hâedra had turned her back.

An eruption of coughing drew Kyson's attention away from his own morbid thoughts. A soldier just exiting the infirmary knelt and retched oily black fluid on the grass. His crazed eyes darted around, never focusing on anything. He flailed his arms about himself, batting at unseen and unknowable enemies. He closed his eyes for a moment, and when they opened they were black throughout. He stared into the distance, shaking in terror. "Not again. Please, no! No, no, no, *NO!* You said I would go free! You said you wouldn't hurt any- *FATHER!*" Black tears rolled down stubbled cheeks. His jaw slackened, bile dribbling between cracked lips. Face first, he collapsed in the grass.

DIPLOMACY

No strangers to war the Hâedran lords, masters of ship and horse.
Of times long past, only memories last, allies with once-great Korz.
Together they fought, and slew, and died, brothers in arms for years.
Time proved them weak, one victory seeks, the other crippled by fear.
When the Rofu struck Hâedras walls, the Korzians rushed to their side.
The men of the Guard, swift, hard, rode to turn the tide.
For Korzian men, the bravest then, the Rofu lied in wait.
The men of the Guard, swift, hard, stumbled upon their fate.
Arrows and steel made them kneel, powerless against the night.
Hâedran scouts using secret routes fled the battle in fright.
The men of the Guard, swift, hard, fought deep into the day.
Hungry and tired, in mud mired, unyielding, none turned away.
Two times the sun circled the world and still they held their ground.
Hoping for help, for Hâedra's hand, so low their numbers now.
The Council sent none, their treaty undone at the cost of Korzian lives.
The men of the Guard, swift, and hard, paid glory's price.

Time seemed to pass strangely under the Heldanhood hill. With no sun to guide them and no other way to judge time, they slept when they were tired, ate when hungry, and passed the rest of their hours however they chose. Bendragel came to terms with vegetables, eventually, and everyone else got their fill of bread and cheese.

Garroway realized he could probably learn things here, so he sat by Grumbubum one morning, clutching a warm cup of brown liquid that seemed to do nothing but move his bowels. "How old are you? And ogres, in general?"

A single eyebrow raised just enough to be perceptible as Grum shifted to look at his companion, "Ogres've been 'ere s'long as any but elves. Moiself, less than that, but more'n most, Oi'd guess."

"So were ogres the second race?"

Visibly ready to argue with the ogre, Throm posited himself next to Garroway to give him his own account on history, "The dwarves first put ink to page, laddie, and it's their histories as are considered the truest in any form!" he cried. "The elves lie too much, and there's more politics and family history than you could possibly digest. Men are simply too young, orcs have no love for writing itself, and ogres have no language of their own!"

Grum shrugged, "'E's no' ter'bly wrong."

"Dwarves came down from the mountains once they'd finished their early masterpieces in the distant past when Alkurah was young and fresh, when magic was on the air and all you need do was breathe deeply to feel the energy in the world. They sang to the stone as they carved, and such marvels have ne'er been matched, nor even approached, by the works of men or elves. The fair folk do not attach themselves to the world as do those who are doomed to die." Throm said, almost poetically, as if he had come to terms with his own mortality and relished his love for the world. His voice softened, "Dwarves wrote lore of the mountains and their stones that makes me ashamed to try. They spoke such flowery of the land as to make dust seem roses. Truly, my ancestors grew their world to suit them." His eyes grew dreamy and he halted, deep in thought.

Then, after a stretch of explosive wind-breaking on Bendragel's part during which no one slept at all, the company reassembled their gear and packed it upon their returned horses. Sekl offered as little help as could be considered polite, and seemed aloof most of the morning, as though something took precedent over the envoys from Korz. With little fanfare, the small group trotted out behind the monk who had been assigned to lead them through the treacherous hills.

A silent morning passed, and finally the monk stopped and simply waved his hand in the direction of away from himself. The procession passed him by, and he turned to shuffle his way back to the tiny hall hidden in the hills.

"Watcha want?" The Hâedran guardsman asked from the parapet.

"We're envoys from Korz sent to speak with the Hâedran Council," Garroway replied, more confidently than he felt.

"Korz? Whazzat? The city o' goddamned barbarians, yeah? We've not got time to waste witcher lot. G'home."

The bristling, ancient guardsman shook his head, muttering as he tottered away from the stout wooden gate. Hâedra was built on the River Nazene- half on one bank, half on the other. The western side was a beautiful, vast forest of towers and massive domed buildings. The east was made up of condemned homes and forsaken ruins. Moldy, decrepit, soggy wood warped beyond use made up the pitiful roofs of miniscule, sad homes.

Throm clucked his tongue. "Men's greed makes dwarves appear as saints."

"And dwarven manners make us seem kings." A low voice seeped through the misty morning. "If it's a way in yer lookin' fer, I believe ye've happened upon the right wall." As he finished, a slab of wood thick as a troll simply lifted away to the inside. "I'd be quick about it, though. Ol' rotbrains'll be back in a jiffy, having thought of a quick insult to bandy with ye."

The confused company wasted no time squatting through the hole, save Grum, whose immensity could not squeeze through the gap cut in the wall without widening the breach. After a few minutes of curses and sweat, Rorrik produced a pair of shovels, which he and Throm used to dig deep enough to allow the ogre passage. They filled in their hole just as the old sentry came shuffling back to his stand. He frowned, seeing his prey had vanished into the morning dew.

When Grum was wiped clean of dirt, the shovels rightly polished and stowed, and the horses tied up with some straw to keep them happy, the voice spoke again, this time with a face attached to it. "Welcome ta Hâedra." A dozen spear tips clanged together as they were shoved to the throats of the newcomers. "Where what's ours is ours, and what's yers is also ours." The man, a roguish grin lingering on a mustachioed lip, gave an elegant bow and flourish before turning on his heel and stalking into the fog.

Throm and Bendragel began to draw their weapons, but a stern glance from Rorrik said enough to get them to stop. Their captors, afraid to approach the warriors, kept them at spear tip on their march through the city. Moss had claimed many homes, and the damp had consumed dozens more. Here and there a filthy face would peer from the cracks in the wood. Cruel grins missing more teeth than they contained leered from all sides.

Soon the crackling of a massive fire could be heard over the crowd. It's eerie orange glow sent harsh shadows upon decaying homes. Their captor appeared once more, at the head of a platform overlooking the open square. "You see, friends. Hâedra is not so much a glorious home of the horselords anymore. Scallywags have made this their home for quite a time. Wayward seafarers with nary a coin between them, here. My name be Captain Breegan. This here's me crew." He spun a circle, arms lifted as if showcasing a work of art, if art included mangy beards, wild hair, and scurvy. "I'm not large on the term 'pirate' meself, but if that be the one ta jump ta yer lips," he shrugged, "well, it's not wrong."

The fire now roared only feet from their faces. Its warmth stung bare cheeks and roasted covered limbs.

"This here bonfire's what we call the Flame o' Truth." He winked, "Honestly." He hopped up and swung his legs over the bannister to sit and rock with his feet dangling freely. "You see, when the Hâedran army collapsed, after hearing about the death of the Korzian Guard, a magician put a stop to it. He made some cockswill tale up about curses and doom, aye? Some o' the men there didn't take kindly to 'im, and they ran 'im through with a couple o' cutlasses. Well, 'parently the ol' wizard weren't ready ta die. The body lit up all ablaze, musta been quite the show, an' cursed every soul what dared dwell here."

The crowd was creeping out of their hiding spots, stepping over collapsed fences and climbing along moldy rooftops.

"Far as I can tell, we're cursed only to a life of pillaging and freedom."

Whoops and hollers echoed back and forth across the clearing. Bendragel's restlessness was evident as his head shifted around sighting targets and judging his enemy. He sneezed once. The noise and sudden movement elicited a panicked gasp from the assembled host.

Garroway was quite taken aback by the hostility shown to their company. Surely the men didn't expect two dwarves, a troll, an ogre, and a pair of men to be carrying anything terribly precious. Their horses were a small step up from nags and their clothes a jump down from rags. The party clearly wasn't in town as merchants and they were all only lightly armed.

Gunsel chewed his bottom lip, a growl forming deep in his belly. Broad hands flexed and clenched, ready for action at the slightest confrontation.

As the cluster of onlookers tightened, Breegan raised a hand. "The old spellweaver's enchantment ne'er left this place. Any here in its presence aren't allowed to lie, lest the flames get a taste o' their flesh, savvy? So now I asked ye, in truth, what's yer business here?"

Rorrik opened his mouth to reply, but it was Grum that stepped forward. "Roc sent us to seek aid. If we are to reforge the alliances of old, than we must first *light* the forges of fellowship."

Garroway and Gunsel both started at the familiar voice that didn't belong to the hulking ogre. Grael Voor stood in front of Grum, bowing deep enough for his wide sleeves to brush the dirt.

The man's grin faltered and he leapt down from his perch. "Grael?"

"Breegan," the old elf nodded, "I see you've not changed a whisper."

"I dare say I've grown handsome in your absence, friend." The two clasped arms and let their foreheads touch softly. "And you've shrunk in your old age, Magnicaerna."

"Let us save titles for great halls, Captain. I'd like you to meet my entourage." He gestured to the gaping mouths of Garroway and Gunsel. "This is Ro, whom I believe you know of. And his companion, Guns. Throm of the Anvilfists, Rorrik of the Thundercrowns, Bendragel, and you've met Grumbubum Lumblegurb."

Breegan released Grael's hand to clasp the ogre's. "I hardly recognize you, ya leathery boulder. Gods, it's been an age and more!"

Garroway raised his hand again, remembering how stupid he felt doing it the first time, and simply let it fall. "Am I the only one present who is quite dumbfounded?"

Breegan gave a hearty laugh as he let Grum's hand fall. "Ro, you've happened into a tale so muddied and mired you can't help but drown in it."

"That's not particularly reassuring."

Grael stepped to Breegan's side, "Captain Breegan is one of six members of the Hâedran Council. What he said about the flame of truth is the truth. This is their way of weeding out brigands and thieves. All of Hâedra," he paused, "well the East bank anyway, lies under a spell of concealment to keep stray armies away." With a wave of his hand, the fog lifted. Scorched ruins became gilded halls; forlorn docks became splendid and bustling. The homes around them seemed to build themselves out of thin air, sloughing the appearance of mold and wet to stand sturdy and tall in the clear morning sun. Stained windows sent glittering reflections onto nearby buildings. Even the criminal-looking host that was descending upon them was cleaned up and outfitted in fine, tinkling mail. Billhooks and harpoons became war-hammers and spears. Cutlasses turned to sabers and broadswords.

Bendragel had been admiring the view until he saw a garden at the opposite end of the bonfire. There, it seemed, the strange blue flowers were being cultivated. "Here I knew those damned flowers were!" He resigned to his sneezes, hoping that staying near the fire would kill whatever allergens assailed him.

As if on cue, as soon as the spell was lifted a herd of chickens rounded the corner behind them and began milling around Gunsel's feet. He kicked them away, but they fluttered harmlessly to the ground, returning to their posts just in front of his next planned step.

Breegan's appearance remained unchanged. His ankle-length coat only had one of the toggles secured and its tails rippled in the wind. Noticing the disapproving glare from Throm, he flourished his arms and spun, "I told you that 'pirate' was a fair brand for me and my ilk."

Grael shepherded the travellers toward a great domed building. At its peak stood a massive golden statue of some long-dead king. Each window showed a different picture, telling the tale of the great Rofu wars, when the Korzian Guard were defeated as the Hâedran lords did nothing.

"Why make a sculpture to celebrate your own ancestor's cowardice?" Throm growled.

"You'd be wise, master dwarf, to keep your tongue behind your teeth concerning such matters." Breegan's cold tone said as much as his words, "You know little of what you speak."

Throm gave a half-hearted, "Hmph," seeming to have grown tired of arguing with everyone.

"Then tell us, shipmaster." Rorrik's eyes bored into Breegan's back. "Tell us what we do not know."

"When the Rofu attacked Hâedra, riders sped ta Korz with all haste. They also rode ta Praesta and Vahir. A siege gainst a city with wooden walls is bound ta be a short one, savvy? Our archers ne'er missed a mark nor wasted a shaft, but the infinite tide of bodies that lay strewn before our gates was ever replenished."

"The Rofu magicians specialize in spells of manipulation and duplicity. Clones of clones formed the front ranks," Grael added over his shoulder.

"Their engines of war, their horsemen, *everything* was a spell. The damage appeared real and devastating, however we suffered no casualties for a week. Finally, one man jumped the wall and strode among the swarm. With each step closer to its heart, a rank of orcs and goblins vanished. The trap was set and sprung."

"Magic," Grum spat.

"A few hours later, with the host of phantoms vanquished, our captains sought to ride out to discover the truth behind this army of ghosts. Their pleas ta the Councilmen fell upon deaf ears. So afraid of death were those six yellow bastards that they locked the armies inside the walls on penalty o' death. When riders returned with news o' the ambush, our soldiers begged ta help. A few days passed an' more riders returned, cries of sadness could not sway minds maddened by fear. The fury our scouts felt was palpable. Not even a week passed before the Council was hanged by the common folk. By the time our armies reached the ambush..." He stopped, head bowed in shame, fists balled and shaking. "Not a soul still stood. The Rofu dead outnumbered the Korzians three ta one at least. A battle that should've been recorded as a glorious victory became a shaming defeat. Our envoys ta Korz have been shunned ever since, and I can't blame 'em. We've longed fer a day where Hâedran horses and Korzian spears marched side by side again."

"And you'll soon have it, friend." Grael put a firm hand on Breegan's shoulder.

The dome loomed in front of them, imposing, but warm, like a father whose will was to be obeyed. Raucous singing sounded from inside the gilded double doors before the old elf threw them wide.

> Ye can drink yer wines with a fancy glass,
> But to me that stuff just tastes like ass!
> Ye can quaff yer mead by the pint if ye wish,
> But that stuff's so weak it may's well be piss!
> Empty barrels of ale that ye swear's strong stuff!
> Have a swig o' some o' this and we'll call your bluff!
> Rum's the best meal I've had all day!
> Rum's the only drink for the end o' the fray!
> Rum'll warm you up on any frozen cold day!
> A mug o' rum to bless me tum an' drink the nights away!

A strange silence befell the feasting host, after finishing their song, as every mug at the table was raised and the rum within downed in a single action. Pewter, wood, and clay tankards all slammed to the oaken tabletop. Belches of varying volume and pitch sounded like horns. Guffaws of laughter followed each guttural outburst. Eventually, everyone settled down. One woman had been standing on the table dancing along to the tune. The rum, it seemed, had warmed her up rather more than her companions. She slid down from the table to accost Gunsel on his way by. Her breath reeked of ferment. Auburn hair hung loosely in a ponytail. Leather armor was tied carelessly about her shoulders. "Bit young to be goin' bald, ain'tcha?"

"Isn't this a lovely day for a lady like yerself to be with your husband?" He snapped back, more wittily than he had snapped anything in quite some time. Sniggers from the nearby onlookers told him this was an accurately judged poke at her pride.

"Ain't found a man worth keepin', mate." She stood close to Gunsel, staring up over his beard.

"Any lass ever set those rosy cheeks aflame?"

She blushed, stomping a boot down on Gunsel's toe. As he howled and limped in a circle, grabbing for his axes, she kicked a bench into his knee, sending him crashing to the stones. Flat on his back, she leaned over his upturned head briefly and winked, "Ever had a lass put ye on yer ass?"

"Gunsel, you sad, bearded ox, are you going to befoul yourself by losing a bandying of words with a damsel as inebriated as she?" Garroway had deposited himself on a bench and was immensely enjoying the spectacle, as was the rest of the party.

The red-haired pirate woman was sauntering back to her own seat amid cheers and laughter.

Gunsel stood, face so flushed with anger he was sweating, "Hey, woman!"

She turned and batted her eyelashes a few times, pointing to herself.

"Aye. What's your name?"

"Lillian. Lillian Redmane. And yours, brute?"

"Gunsel."

She winked and blew him a kiss, which must have gotten soaked up by Gunsel's impressive facial hair. "I'm sure it's been a pleasure for you." She taunted, and, as if to finalize her statement, plopped onto her chair as her comrades enveloped her back into the fold.

Garroway threw a companionable arm around Gunsel's shoulders, leading him through a small side door that Grael and Breegan had passed through a moment before. "What a woman, eh, Gunsel? However, I think a battle of strength may suit you better than one of words."

Gunsel whacked Garroway on the ear but grinned sheepishly, "May be you're right. Not sure bandying is my strong suit."

"I'm not sure women are your strong suit."

"Bah," Gunsel waved a hand as they came into a carpeted chapel.

A lovely stained-glass depiction of the river wards played joyful reflections on the walls and pews. A golden statue of Ong, god of the rivers and horses Hâedrans were so fond of, dominated a decorative archway. His mane of blonde hair flowed seamlessly into a likeness of the Nazene. A crown of prancing ponies encircled his brow. Calmness projected from his stern face, while his fiercely armored body gave the viewer a sense of the ferocity of the waters that lapped the banks of the great Nazene. His right hand rested on the pommel of a sword of carven jewels, his left lay palm up, cradling a beautiful vessel of gems and precious metals. The emerald sails were tied by gold filament rigging to masts of silver. A ruby helm, as intricately chiseled as any would be on a real ship, was affixed to planks of diamond.

Rorrik and Throm both knelt before the craftsmanship of the statue. "This ship is of dwarven make."

Breegan squatted down, marveling at an object he'd seen a hundred hundred of times, yet still the majesty of it never lessened. "Aye. It was a gift from Thorriman of the Ironscales. Shit. His line held a love for horses and water that I dare say is uncommon among dwarfkind."

"You'd be right about that, master pirate. Thorriman was my great-uncle." Rorrik's awed voice was quieter than Garroway and Gunsel had ever heard.

"I'm sorry to hear of his passing. If you'd like, sometime during your stay, I would learn of his end."

Rorrik simply nodded.

Grael cleared his throat, reluctant to hurry the dwarves from their study. "I expect you'll be here for a time, and there are no shortage of dwarven masterpieces in this place. Now, however, we must explain to the Council the direness of the situation Korz has found herself in."

Garroway was able to stay his hand from rising this time and simply asked, "How are you here?"

Grael smiled, "Grumbubum, if you would."

The ogre stomped forward, kneeling slightly and giving Grael his hammer in a show of respect and properness not usually associated with ogres.

Grael lifted the massive wooden weapon as if it weighed nothing. He caressed it as one might hug an old friend. "This is Magnicaerna. The hammer itself is ordinary enough, but within it lies a fragment of my soul. I'll not speak more on this save to say it is a dangerous process that time has rightly forgotten. I can travel any place this hammer happens to be whenever I so wish."

A stern glance silenced the questions Gunsel was about to rattle off.

"Anyway, Breegan has assembled the other five council members to hear what we have to say. I trust in their judgment," he paused and gave a sidelong glance to the frowning pirate, "but there are backup plans in place."

"Backup plans for what? I'm sorry if I dozed off at some point, but I have just no idea what we're even doing here. What danger is Korz in?" Garroway's helpless glance fell on one after another of his companions, but they were either as confused as he or unwilling to share.

"Korz needs help, laddie." Breegan leaned with an arm on a set of double doors. "And I plan to give it to 'em."

"We fended off the first Rofu assault without much of a fuss," Gunsel sneered.

"How've you been feeling lately, Guns?" Breegan asked.

"Enough," Grael interjected. "That wasn't an army, it was a sacrifice. The Rofu use a poison that kills slowly, from the mind outwards. The empty shells left over become nothing but husks of meat for any Rofu shaman to control. It's a fate I'd not wish on the worst of men."

"Well, can't you stop it?" Garroway asked.

Grael simply shook his head. "Don't be daft, lad. We've tried. There's no way to fight it. In the end, the poison always wins."

Breegan kicked the double doors open. A simple hall furnished with only an ovular table set with six chairs faced the waiting group. The far wall was dominated by a tapestry of Ong, still crowned with horses and holding the same majestic jeweled ship. Breegan took his place at the seat to the right of center. None of the other seats were filled.

Garroway asked, "Are we early?"

A disembodied voice rang out. "What brings you here, elf-lord Grael?"

"I believe you know why I'm here." He accused of the empty room.

"Don't insult us with mockery." This second voice was that of a woman. "You would do well to remember you came to us."

"And you should never forget when you didn't come to us," Roc's gravelly voice answered.

Garroway, still looking for the source of the first voice, gave up when he heard his captain. Certain that he'd managed to fall asleep at some point; he just assumed it was all a dream and that he'd wake up in jail somewhere.

"Roc. A pleasure." One of the voices said, clearly implying the opposite.

"Lord Commander Kyson is weak. He'll not ask for help because his pride has swelled to a point that only death may deflate it. I'm here asking for Hâedra to fulfill oaths long forgotten. I'll not beg, nor barter. I will only say this- your decision will decide the fate of the human race. For better," he glanced at Garroway and Gunsel, "or for worse."

The shimmering apparition of Roc disappeared, leaving Garroway still unsettled by how calmly everyone else was taking this whole ordeal.

Breegan clapped his hands together, standing and flaring his coattails out. "I, fer one, think we should assist Korz in 'er plight. We owe 'em at least that."

The female voice answered, "While I don't disagree on the shame of our forefathers, we mustn't hasten into a rash war with an enemy we don't understand."

His patience obviously long worn by the long-winded talk of the council, Breegan slammed a fist on the table. "The only enemy none of ye seem to understand is cowardice. Ye milk-drinking, flower-pickin', slack-jawed, cur-brained, yella bastards 'ave let too many men die on my watch. If ye wait longer'n a week to come to a decision- the *right* decision- ye'll have more'n the Rofu to deal with."

In a manner of swagger that only pirates can achieve, Breegan exited the room, fists balled and chin in the air.

A MEAL

Hâedran lords on Hâedran thrones,
To the Rofu fed the Korzian bones.
Alliance broken at the will of the weak,
Armies sacrificed by the cowering meek.
No penance paid, nor forgiveness sought,
Behind your own walls losing battles are fought.
The poison ever-onward flies,
Deaf to the diseased and suffering's cries.
The dark in the mind it brings out to show,
Nightmares become real, fear only grows.
While blessed armor and sword wield a man,
The curse it bears in his flesh sears its brand.
His friend tries to fight the fear,
Before the darkness' head can rear.
Pride blinds and honor binds,
Invisible enemies weaken minds.
The Alakhan and the Veiled gather to fight,
They decide what is wrong and what's right.
Immortality granted but earned in full.
Races of Alkurah in blood pay the toll.
The Rofu, Korz, Hâedra, War.
The heart of Alkurah rattles and roars.

Garroway swished his hand in the crystal Nazene. Tadpoles swirled in miniature whirlpools, camouflaged by the disturbed silt. The rising sun reached crimson fingers across the gently flowing river. A gentle breeze tickled his hair and made his loose tunic flap quietly. It was the first time in months that Garroway had been able to genuinely enjoy a moment of solace. The storm clouds of war had a way of making everything seem so bleak. A thin smile split Garroway's lips. Without the armor and sword shackling his mind to thoughts of spilling blood he could take in the beautiful morning splayed before him in all its glory.

Elu and Ula, the lover-gods of art, music, and beauty, were said to paint each sunrise and sunset. Dreary mornings were a bad omen, said to be caused by a quarrel between the pair that would extend to every lover in Alkurah. A morning such as this, however, must have meant Elu and Ula had a rollicking night in each other's arms.

"A fine sunrise," Breegan's gruff voice melded surprisingly well with the quiet atmosphere.

"I've not enjoyed its like in quite some time."

"Battle has a way of dampening one's spirits. Yet even through the darkness," He sat down heavily and waved a hand through the cool waters, "such beauty shines."

"How is the Council?"

Breegan grinned and shrugged, "They bitch and moan. Their fear cripples any thoughts of victory or assistance. Bah." He slapped the water and stood, stretching his legs and rolling his shoulders around. "Those politic-minded, fatherless sons of disease-ridden whores have imprisoned our armies for long enough."

"Were you there?"

"Hmm? Was I where?"

"The massacre."

Breegan laced his hands behind his head, closed his eyes, and sucked a deep breath. "I was. I was one of the scouts that got there in time ta witness the onset of the attack."

"How many immortals are there in Alkurah?"

Breegan cocked an eyebrow at Garroway, "Walk with me and I'll give you a lesson you'd best keep in mind."

They took off at an easy stride along the riverbank. The sun was rising quickly, bathing the world in its golden glow.

"Immortality is something not bestowed on many, and never lightly. Aside from the elves of course." He gave Garroway a look that said all he needed to know about Breegan's opinion of elves. "There are methods to acquire it, barbaric an' arcane, and rightly hidden from all but the most inquisitive. Some are born ta walk the world from the dawn o' time ta the end o' days. At the risk of revealing a dangerous secret, I'll tell ya that's me. I won't delve further fer now, an' I'd encourage ye not ta dwell on that one."

"How many of you are there?"

"Oh, I believe there were six of us."

"Were?"

"Immortality is only so effective, savvy?"

Birds chittered at each other, fighting over slimy morsels wriggling from the dirt. A barge slid down the gurgling river, men lazing on the deck. Some fished, others dozed with wide-brimmed hats pulled low over their eyes.

"What do you know of the Heldanhood?" Garroway asked.

"Speaking of barbaric and arcane." He grabbed a tree branch to use as a walking stick for a moment before heaving it into the Nazene. "The Hood was a group of immortals that simply popped into existence. Personally, I think it was an experiment by the elves. They were trying to raise the dead or attempting some other folly. Stupidity sums up an impressive amount of the problems in this land."

"And they deemed themselves the guardians of Alkurah?"

"I can't say they do a terrible job, but aye, they're the self-appointed guards of the world."

The pair stopped and admired a stray gull cracking a shell on a rock. After several attempts, it popped open and the gull was rewarded with a gooey treat.

Breegan pulled Garroway close, making sure to keep his voice nigh inaudible. "And I'll tell you this. I believe we can trust you, all of us. The Alakhan, Hâedra, Korz. But not everyone feels the same. That armor you wear can lead to terrible things, and it has before. Don't lose yerself." He straightened up suddenly, ears cocked and eyes flicking back and forth. "Didja hear that?" Suddenly, he grinned, elbowing Garroway in the ribs. "Vittles." He took off to the same domed hall they had been led to the day before.

If there was anything soldiers learned it was to enjoy every meal you could get.

Rigathel spat a piece of bone onto the dirt floor of the mess hall. He eyed a loaf of bread that was a few weeks too stale for real digestion. He sided with his growling innards and did his best to bite through the stony chunk of grains. All around him the squabbles of similarly starving soldiers ground on his ears.

"Howsit that the Grimmyfilt gits 'imself tha real foods, eh?"

"De big boss eats what 'e wanna eats. Betchee's gottim summada bes'."

Rigathel could barely understand the slurred, chirpy orcish language. The other trolls, infinitely less patient than he, were already starting to finger their clubs and stretch out their shoulders, ready to put the orcs back in their rightful, lowly, place. He stood, glaring at the orcs and goblins that argued and shouted. When none of them paid him any attention, he simply cleared his throat. Of course, the sound of a troll clearing its throat sounds suspiciously like a growling predator. Those tables nearest him shut up immediately, others slowly simmered to quiet, following suit. No conversation was worth dying for.

"Do any of you care to take up your quarrels with Grimfilth?" He strode among them, relishing the quivering fear present on greasy lips. "Because an argument with our lord is an argument with me."

"We juswannagit some goodfood anahardfight wit' the cowardmen."

Grimfilth's voice rang through the chamber like a crashing symbol. "If it's a fight you want, you won't wait long. Soldiers of the Scar, brothers of Kharat, Rofu one and all, I wish you to understand that this war is not one in which we seek victory."

Avian movements of nervousness rippled through the host, orcs and goblins searching the faces of their comrades for reassurance.

"This is a war of annihilation!"

Pretending they understood, the army reacted simply to the increase of volume in their leader's voice. They cheered, swords rattling on shields, fists thumping tables, and they howled like wild creatures in the night.

"The terrors of the West have overtaken the Scar. Our advance foray into Brathur was quite a success, and I'm told their numbers have been halved or more. Within a month, we will march upon that ancient stronghold. We will pry the cold, dead fingers of a human race unwilling to fight for its own existence from the shattered gates of their garrison. And we will *survive*, as is the Rofu way."

Amid cheers and screeches praising their leader and the glorious survival yet to come, Grimfilth whispered to Rigathel, "Take your trolls to Hâedra."

"Aye, sir."

"If you see your brother, send him my regards."

Watching the tattooed back of his second-in-command retreat to the barracks, Grimfilth muttered, "Fear is the greatest enemy, and thus our strongest ally."

Gunsel's bulging stomach threatened to break his belt. The bench strained and the men around him kept moving further away, afraid he might eat them, too. Lillian Redmane sat opposite him, coolly sliding another forkful of chicken into her mouth. "What's the matter, darling? Have I bested your heroic belly?"

He grunted, not trusting his mouth, lest he open it and his enormous meal come rocketing back out. His bald head shook in concentration and pain as he put another bite down.

Lillian daintily wiped her mouth before taking another nibble. The piled plates around the pair were beginning to obstruct the view of the contest. All of the Hâedran soldiers sniggered and cheered Lillian on.

Gunsel heaved once. Everyone within a few feet jumped back, hoping to avoid any splashes of vomit. He shook his head, gritting his teeth, and popped another mouthful in. "Can't. Beat. Me."

His fiery opponent simply took another bite, and then another, and two more. She was now in a commanding lead and Gunsel looked sickened at the thought of eating anything else.

"Oh, Gunsel, it's okay to lose! Don't hurt yourself over a silly contest." She winked and smiled coyly at him.

"Nope." Chomp. "Not." Gulp. "Gonna." Chomp. "Lose-to-a-woman." Gulp.

Breegan hopped onto the bench beside Lillian, seeing her poor opponent. He clucked his tongue, "My lovely Lillian, lady of the river, you see before you a man clearly vying fer yer heart. He could not win it with his tongue, and seeks now ta do so with his belly. What's next?" The surrounding soldiers laughed and applauded.

Lillian replied, "If it's my heart he's after, he needn't rip it from my chest. He need simply ask."

At this, Gunsel stopped swallowing mid-bite, coughed once, and lost the epic battle with his dry heaves. All manner of chicken, potatoes, lettuce, and bread came up in a river of puke unchallenged through all time. He wiped his face off, looked at Lillian, and gasped, "Honestly?"

"Of course not, man. Look at yourself!" She gave him a peck on the cheek across the table, and stood up, revealing a mountain of food behind her that she'd been able to stow away with a little sleight of hand and a touch of magic from her allies.

Gunsel's seething gave way to another onslaught of regurgitation. He tried to stand but ended up on his knees, heaving out his truly inhuman meal. "That red-headed, deceiving, honorless witch." Every time he tried to stand, he was forced to his knees by another attack. "I'll kill her. I'll kill her, and I'll not attend her funeral. I'll kill her." He passed out on his back in the cool afternoon shade provided by the hall.

Roc sat at an empty table glutting himself on food enough for three men. With the poison ravaging Brathur so fiercely, the cooks always had too much food for the healthy men to eat, so they were on double rations to try and keep them as healthy as possible. It finally seemed as if the sickness had stopped spreading, but the grisly work had been doen well. A full third of the army who survived the battle were now incapacitated or dead. The remaining soldiers weren't allowed anywhere near the healers that had been working with the sick. The everlasting pyre continued to blaze outside the wall, greasy black smoke billowed into the searing afternoon sun.

"Ye mind?" Gortrum's girth plopped onto the bench next to Roc. "How's the slop today, boss?"

"The same as always. Just more of it."

"I'm not a smart guy, sir, I'm not a thinker. Yer clearly a man who knows something, though. Please tell me something, anything, about what's happenin' here."

"Gortrum, you're a good man and a great soldier. There's nothing I can tell you that will make you feel any better, so I'd rather not tell you anything."

"I s'pose that's fair. I just wish there was something to fight. It's the not doing anything, not being able to do anything."

"If we could, we would."

"Aye, we would."

The doors banged open to Kyson's barging shoulder. "Commander Roc, I'd have a word with you."

"Only one?"

"You know what's happening here. You know why our soldiers are dropping from this invisible enemy, and you won't tell me how to stop or prevent it. Commander Roc, you are a traitor to your own armies, your own country, and your own race! Give me a reason not to strip your titles from you and have you imprisoned."

"You can do what you see fit, Kyson, it's *your* army. However, remember it was you who failed to go to the Hâedrans for help. It was you who damned our army to this hell. You who ignored the wisdom of Grael and my own advice. Don't dare impugn me while you stand with so many of your own men's blood on your hands. Of all the insolence I've suffered in my long, *long* life, that which you put on display daily is borderline comical. The gods will show no mercy on the soul of a coward, Kyson."

The commander spluttered, unable to find the words venomous enough to convey his anger.

"And I warned you about this poison. I told you what it would do, and Grael did us a service by helping burn the corpses."

"Roc, I have no further need of you. Consider yourself stripped of your duty and your rank. If you are to remain here, you will do so as a foot soldier. May you find death so long cheated at the front line of a reckless assault."

Shaking his head in sadness, Roc finished his meal as Kyson stomped through the doors to the great hall.

Unfettered rage is the best way to describe Skal the Enlightened's mood after returning to his hall in the Heldan Hills. News was not something he had expected to receive, as nothing exciting had happened beneath the Hills in some time. Upon being told, mid-lunch that a strange company from Korz had passed through, he was intrigued but not surprised. When Sekl told him who was among the travellers, he struggled to prevent an aneurism. Garroway was a name he had learned through discussion with the Council of Hâedra and his intermittent spying on Korz. Mentions of the armor of the Godslayer had been rather few in recent decades, so it certainly caught his attention when it happened. By the time he arrived at Brathur, Garroway was gone on his quest to Hâedra, and the little man had hoped to catch up to the company on the road. Instead, Sekl had taken them to the only place Skal would not bother looking. For a moment, Skal forgot his restrictions and tried to strangle Sekl. His fingers were unable to close upon flesh, and he ordered a nearby monk to put a spear through his counterpart's neck.

Sekl, who was as immortal as Skal, was surprised to find himself in pain and bleeding. A spear blessed and consecrated in water from the Helseia itself tore through his throat and pinned him to the wall. Power drained from him as fast as his blood, and soon Skal was bending over his compatriot, whispering, "Who is the greatest, but the last."

Skal had the body removed and burned. The bloodstain took a voracious scrubbing from one of the unluckier monks before finally succumbing to his sponge, but the little man stood and watched the whole time. When the monk left, and several hours passed, Skal knelt and placed a hand where the stain had been darkest. "I feel it, sometimes, brother. At night, during my darkest thoughts, the voice whispers as though far away. Who I am is no longer who I was. You fed him. All of you, with your fear and your doubts. I'm not to blame here. I have been strong for so long."

He stood up, twisted violently to crack his back, and stalked away. That night he flew high in the cool air above the Hills and did not care for war or death. He allowed his mind to be distracted by the things he once found lovely, and felt bliss. All too soon, the sun rose, and the heat warmed his cheeks as a reminder of his duty.

A crimson sunrise made the Nazene glow as if ablaze. The banks of the river were strewn with assorted clothing and armor, as the soldiers and pirates spending their time in Hâedra felt little shame in stripping for a swim in the crystal waters. Some wives and children were fetching water, standing upstream of the filthy bodies of the guardsmen. Roosters crowed to the morning sun and groans of sleep spilled from open windows. The Hâedran climate was mild and warm, and there was little need for walls save privacy or defense, and many of the barracks were simply gazebos called by a different name. They were tiered, and ladders ran up their full height at each corner.

Garroway and Gunsel had managed to climb to the uppermost floor, and spent the night on mats made from rush and the broad palm leaves that fell in scores each day. The leaves were durable and plentiful, and the people of Hâedra used them for basically everything. The night before, the snoring pair was taught how to make armor from the leaves, like men did in the days before steel and leather. They still wore their creations, and in a drunken stupor, Gunsel had stabbed his friend in the shoulder to prove the leaves couldn't stop a blade. He was right, and Garroway had received half a dozen stitches as a consolation prize. Neither of them remembered this happening, because they'd had so much to drink that they had been the talk of the bars, and the Hâedran drinkers did their best to encourage the pair to further mischief. It was all in good fun until Garroway got stabbed, at which point Breegan had to restrain Gunsel from killing everyone in the bar to avenge his friend. And though they would sleep for another few hours, the Council had been up and arguing with the rising of the sun.

Breegan's frustration was almost a physical trait. He scratched at his arms, furrowed his brow, and wiped his hand down his face so often it appeared he might soon just rip it off. "For God's sake, you can't honestly believe that."

"The Council has informants throughout Alkurah. The Rofu army numbers nearly fifty thousand strong, many of them trolls, ogres, and giants. We are not willing to risk an open conflict with them."

"And after Korz?" He waved an accusing finger at the empty chair, "what then? Where do ya think the monsters turn after they slaughter our brothers, *my* brothers, *again*?"

"They are not advancing for conquest, they are retreating from something attacking them to the west." A voice touched by insanity twittered out of the shadow. "Their fear may even be stronger than yours!" It cackled madly.

Breegan slumped into a chair, covering his face with his impressive hat. "Not the Hood."

Skal teleported to him and flipped his hat to the ground, "Oh, come now Magniseia, we're not so bad!"

Growling at the use of a more proper name, Breegan simply bristled on his chair.

The woman's voice cut through the gloom, "What menace approaches, Skal? Is it an ally to men?" Her tone implied that she had spoken with the strange creature before.

"An ally? An enemy? Some are both and none are neither. This terror strips flesh from bone and leaves no survivors. The Kharatvil is simply," he made a popping motion with his hands, "poof. Gone. No Rofu made it out. Simple as that. The question is, lovely voice, what do you plan to do about it?"

One of the men spoke, "The Korzians are assembling their full strength at Brathur. They plan to meet the Rofu in open battle at a stronghold already weakened. The walls will not last a day to the assault, and I shudder to think what becomes of an army ten thousand strong trapped within a crumbling fortress."

"Hâedra's army would nigh double that number. An' with the aid of our horsemen and ships, we could make a hell out o' the Rofu march."

"Or," Skal's sing-song voice interjected, "Hâedra could do nothing! Think what you could do with a great city like Korz under your rule. With the greatest land-based trading city in Alkurah, and complete control of the Nazene there would be none to challenge your rightful rule over the dominion of men!"

A clenched fist passed through air as Breegan hit the space previously occupied by Skal's face. "How dare you, you goddamn abomination. You shouldn't even exist on this world. You're a parasitic, god-envying, swill-chugging, dusty, shit ever present on the history of this land."

"Oh, *ouch*. Though, remember, you've been here longer than I in your own eyes."

The woman spoke again, "Why are the Rofu so keen on Brathur?"

An uncomfortable pause went on entirely too long before Skal giggled once. "The tunnels."

"What will they do there?" Squeaked a new voice, effeminate, but definitely male.

"Hide. *Survive*. And maybe they'll find something they don't realize they've lost. Something men stole from the Rofu eons past. There is more to the tunnels than damp stones."

"Is it somethin' as can be used against 'em?" Breegan asked.

"Not everything worth having is some cudgel for you to beat your enemies with, Magniseia."

"Enough." The deeper male voice echoed for a moment on the cool rocks of the chamber. "Skal, tell us plainly what you mean about the tunnels."

He sighed, teleporting to sit cross-legged on the table. "Before humans came to this land, there were dwarves. Before them, orcs and goblins. Before them? Trolls and ogres. And the first of them all were elves. The tunnels of Brathur were built by the first elves, when they were timid and afraid of the world." The mockery in his voice was replaced by something close to respect as he continued his tale. "They wove such secrets into those tunnels, but hid them well. If elves are anything, it's jealous. They didn't want anyone to know their secrets. However, there were already the original immortals gallivanting about Alkurah." He nodded at Breegan. "And each sought to better the standings of his own race."

"Some sought more nicely than others," Breegan spat.

"When the elves left the tunnels, the first to enter them seeking power was an orc named Griflidunmagnifeia."

"A Rofu?" a new voice asked.

"He leads them."

"Why is this orc returning? Did he not find what he was looking for the first time?" A new voice queried in a rumbling baritone.

"He wasn't looking for it the first time. If he found it, he may not have even known." Skal snapped.

"And would he now?" asked the baritone.

Skal shrugged, "I can't say, really. Perhaps the orc is smarter than he lets on, but perhaps he's simply hoping the truth will find him."

"What is the terror of the west, Skal?" The first male voice interjected.

"Oh, that's just the best-kept secret."

Breegan pleaded to the Council, "This thing wants you to betray the only ally you have left in Alkurah. Turn your back on the Korzians and you've doomed your own race," he paused, "*my* race." He stepped from the chamber. As soon as the doors shut softly together, he let his back fall to the cool stones, sliding down to weep, listening to the soft voices from within. "I'm so sorry, my children. My brothers."

A soothing hand patted his shoulder. He didn't need to look up to know Grael. The wise elf's words rested on Breegan's soul like a balm. "Not all is lost, my friend. We have friends outside this place. Let us seek our kin."

The swashbuckler wiped his nose on his frazzled coat sleeve, "Aye. And what kinda pirate am I ta let saltwater go ta waste on me face."

ALLIANCE

A cruel world, full of death, dampening hope and light.
When thoughts arise of victory sure, the enemy shows his might.
Shadows are clever, their whispers sly, and time has proven them strong.
After so many years, so many tears, one race will right its wrongs.
Alakhan gather, to both sides they flock, following the guiding Light.
Some will live, some will die. The future is never bright.
But from the chaos, the fear, the hate, a stronger few still stand.
They see the path, kindle their wrath, but find themselves outmanned.
No more glory, no honor, no right, this war is fought for blood.
Extinction, life, an equal price, forever flows the flood.
The Light and Dark, equal opposites, marked, both begin at the end.
At the hand of the other each one suffers. Neither breaks, nor bends.
Light can grow, only Darkness knows, each moment courts with dread
In the end there can be only two, so few, that stand among the dead.
A time ever sought nears Alkurah, when all races stand abreast.
But the twisted lies of evil's cry put alliances to the test.
To fight one other, brothers, forever, and in blood find their quietus.
To trust in allies, fight side by side, and avoid the grip of Tykus.

Rigathel's trolls crept through the forests outside Hâedra. They had come so far so quickly, and without being detected, that breaking stealth now would seem almost wasteful. Trolls generally lack appreciation for quiet, but he knew his pack would do as he ordered without faltering. And they had. Every sentry, every scout, every animal that may speak to an elf or man was killed before it had a chance to pick up their scent. And they had moved onward. They made a small camp just outside the walls, deep enough in the trees that no wayward eyes would pick them out by accident. Grimfilth had told Rigathel to strike hard and fast, but also to trust his own judgment. The west bank of the city was so beautiful, so strong, even his trolls had stopped to admire it. The east bank looked dark and abandoned, however, save a great fire near the river.

"At dawn we attack shall." Rigathel comfortably slid back into the unique trolls-speak, glad he didn't have to focus on his words for a few days.

"Unprepared. Weak, men are." His second in command, Shilleril, grunted. "And bony." He stalked back to the pack to grunt out the attack order. One of the three shamans was sent to swim across the river. One of the crows he'd sent ahead as a scout had seen evidence of the armor of Tykus, and Grimfilth wished it to be investigated. It belonged to a mortal man with a strange name. Garroway. Shilleril trusted his shaman to acquire it. What greater spoils of war could there be than the armor of the Godslayer?

Rigathel knew there would be magic at work in the days to come, but he was not afraid. As the sun set, he closed his eyes and prayed to Bol. He did not pray for victory, and he never had; instead he prayed simply for glory. "If I find my equal tomorrow, let me find him at full strength. If I am slain by my lesser, take me not unto your halls. If I find one greater than me, let our duel never be forgotten."

"Bol damn it." Gunsel stared himself in the mirror, eyes narrowed. He craned his head forward, nose almost touching the rapidly fogging glass right hand sifting through his beard while his left held a menacing dagger close to a bleeding cheek. "I don't remember shaving being so hard."

Garroway chuckled, rubbing a hand over his own rough stubble. "And why the sudden interest in grooming, birdlord?"

The knife clattered away as he tossed it toward the corner. "That woman-"

"Her name is Lillian. If you used it more than you used 'that woman,' she might entertain you. As it is, she entertains me just fine," Garroway winked to his comrade.

"I've been with women before."

"Mmhm."

"But they've never been so stubborn!"

"Whores are so easy, right?"

Gunsel didn't look as amused as Garroway thought he should. "I've never been so embarrassed to have a feeling."

"Dear Guns, you've never *had* feelings." He slapped his friend on the bulging bicep. "Look, maybe she's not into the bearded manly type."

A soft voice cooed from the open door, "Who isn't?"

Gunsel's face turned so red the blood still dripping from his cheek was thoroughly camouflaged.

"I'll be going." Garroway slid off into the evening to traipse through the eastern city.

Once he was well gone, she spoke again, and Lillian Redmane glided into the room, "I heard you."

Gunsel was too ashamed to speak. He croaked once, and flopped onto the recently vacated chair. "Kill me now. Don't let me suffer." A soft hand touched his own. It took all the willpower he could muster not to flinch.

"Oh, but the suffering is half the fun!"

"And the other half?"

"Well, I'm not sure you'd want to leave the door open for that."

"What do you want from me? Tell me how to win your heart!"

"You've tried your wit. And you've tried your belly." She playfully patted his gut. "Try something else." She reached across his chest to snuff out the candle.

Gunsel snatched her hand before she could reach it. "Please, don't let the darkness in."

Lillian looked quizzical, but stayed her hand. "Afraid of the dark, oh mighty Gunsel?"

"No. Just afraid of losing this light." He grabbed her behind the neck and pulled her close, shutting the door from across the room with a flick of his hand. It was the first time he used magic since his training.

Garroway heard the door slam and grinned. "The mighty Gunsel, tamed by a lady more wild than he."

"And what about you, lord Garroway?"

Garroway suspiciously eyed a stack of hay nearby; confident it was what had spoken. "What about me?"

"Is there any lady in Hâedra that may warm herself in your arms?" A soft voice lilted at him.

"Why are you asking me this?" He wondered aloud to the haystack.

"Oh, turn around you louse."

He turned slowly, keeping the haystack in view as long as possible, lest it talk again, and nearly headbutted a small elven woman standing just behind him. "Oh, gods, I'm so sorry." He jumped backwards, unsure whether he was more surprised that she was an elf, or that she wasn't the haystack, and landed in it.

Laughter as bubbly and beautiful as the Nazene itself tickled Garroway's ears. "Who are you?" He whispered, smitten.

"I am lady... Raela." She answered, fetchingly.

"Are you sure?"

She cocked her head to the side, smiling, "Quite. Would you accompany me on a walk through the lovely city?"

"I may have to rush through, quite a busy schedule and all that, but I do believe I can spare some time for an elven maid in need of an arm to hold." He proffered a bent elbow. She took it and they headed out at a leisurely pace.

"Do you like Hâedra?"

"It's different." He spun, lifting his free arm to encompass the whole of their vision. "I've never seen a city look both busy and clean. Royal and sturdy. Usually they're either or the other, not often both."

Her eyes darted about, as though she was looking for something, but any time Garroway happened to look into her face, her eyes found his. They were unlike Grael's eyes. Not so old, or clear, there was somewhat of a fog to them that made it hard to look away.

Roars of laughter erupted from an inn nearby. The Hâedran soldiers were still unsure of their command, and drink made the queasiness bearable. The pair stopped to listen to a gentle story-song. They were playing a game the soldiers had called 'tall-tales.' One person drew a set number of ideas written on scraps of paper, from those ideas they had to create a song. If it was good, they earned free drinks. If bad, they had to buy for their opponent.

A travelling dwarf, small, wide came to my door one night,
He told me of treasure, travel, gold. Of fortune, loss, plight.
A dream he had, of many truths, that led him here to there,
Encountering beasts of the wood, the owl, rabbit, and bear.
Something taken ages ago, something thought far away,
Stolen, lost, gone from the world, it begets strife and pain.

Judging by the raucous guffaws and hearty applause, Garroway assumed the other guests approved of the tale.

Raela shivered, "I'm unaccustomed to the rudeness of men. And to the cold of the river winds."

"Well, rudeness of men is probably an accurate way to state it," he wrapped his tattered jacket about her narrow shoulders, "but I can help with the cold."

He began shivering almost immediately, and they walked in silence for a few minutes while Garroway clenched his teeth against their chattering. "Are you an envoy or a warrior, lady? I find it strange that an elf maiden happens to be in this place alone. What is your errand?"

She took a moment to steer him away from a patrol of pigeons stalking the road. "Human, there is something I must know." She stopped and looked into his eyes for the first time. Hers, like emeralds, shone as the risen moon. Her mouth opened, and a sneeze detonated from her face, shattering the calm.

Suddenly, her appeal seemed to lessen, as did her elven charm. She seemed to grow in stature as she got more agitated, snorting and spluttering, her frame deforming slightly in the bright moon. "Only once more I'll ask, human. Where the armor is?" Her voice was warped now, guttural and violent.

"I do think, madam, that it is time we bade one another good night." He tore away from her and burst into the nearby inn. The sight of a Korzian man, flustered, sweaty, and alone, must have appealed to the Hâedrans. They brought him in with haste and slapped a tankard of rum in one hand, a loaf of bread in the other, and a few pats on the shoulders for good measure.

He almost had time to enjoy it before a troll clad in an elf-maid's dress kicked the door to splinters. It pointed a gnarled finger in the general direction of everyone and growled, "You tonight die!"

Hâedrans are not often described as violent or ill tempered. They're a congenial group, but are fiercely protective of their own. The poor troll didn't even have time to swing a fist before it was bludgeoned to a twitching mass of confused clothing and splinters by an impressive assortment of stools, bare hands, and mugs.

"Th'goddamn shit-hell wazzat?" Breegan's confused voice drunkenly stammered its way across the room.

"Breegan, I do believe a troll just tried to seduce me."

"You what?"

"Well, I thought she was a haystack at first, but turns out she was an elf that's actually a troll. It's dead now." He gave a celebratory lift of his mug and drained it. He relished the cheers from the crowd.

"You what?"

A warning horn sounded from the west bank.

Rigathel had decided to move the attack up into the pre-dawn hours. He was monitoring the progress of his shaman, but placed little faith in magic. Shilleril was confident, but could not help but agree to follow the orders of his pack leader. "With the Godslayer's armor, unstoppable we'll be," the latter said, already imagining a world in which the Rofu reigned supreme.

"Aye, but for magic little love I have. Better to our chances double than lose, in one battle, two."

Shilleril grunted in acknowledgement.

The pack was agitated. Something about the river didn't sit right with them. It felt too clean, too pure. Everything should be murkier and bloodier. Steel grated on stones and leather shuffled against thick hides. Everything was about to be murkier and bloodier.

Rigathel leaned against a tree, savoring the sticky feel of the sap on his shoulder. It was warm and thick. "Brothers, it is time. Let them pay the blood price."

On the east bank, the men and women of the Hâedran guard sped to the river. Already, flames loomed across the wide Nazene, and howls of pain echoed eerily across the gurgling water. The only way across was a ferry system. It was slow and ancient, but it did the job. Only a dozen could fit on the rickety platform at a time, so most had to simply watch from the sand as their friends and family fought some unknown enemy in the small hours of the morning.

"Onward, trolls! Scale walls and burn the halls, tonight we on flesh dine!" Howls of bloodlust followed Rigathel's cry.

Shilleril grinned, sweat glistening in the rising sun. "Brother, you done well have. Unprepared the humans are, and weak."

Rigathel hefted a mallet in both hands, "Aye. But come for men we haven't. The armor find and to me it bring."

Shilleril pounded his chest with a closed fist in acknowledgement and snuck away into the shadows.

Bendragel stood on the eastern bank of the Nazene hoping to catch a glimpse of the attackers. He had heard noises only trolls could make, but was wary of which pack it was. So long he had been estranged from his own that he had no recent news of which side of the war they found themselves on. Both of his brothers were Rofu, of that he was certain, and he knew there was no hope of changing the mind of a troll who was set in his ways. Over the screams he heard a cry, "Pay the blood price!"

His lips curled into a snarl. So this was the Rofu again. "No, brothers. It is I who shall your blood claim!" His roar rent the misty morning.

Crukky, the orc assigned watch duty at the trapdoor that led to the Kharatule, spotted something. The sun was always too bright, and the heat more intense than he preferred, so he never peered into the distance for any real length of time. By now, he had learned. It was still early enough in the morning that the sun had not yet risen fully, but late enough that he could qualify this as his 'daytime' check. The instant the hatch opened, a camoflauged elf fired a single arrow. Of course Crukky didn't see this, but the dozen Rangers still lurking around the doorway did. In an instant they were on their feet, dashing toward the solitary elf. It almost managed to draw another arrow before three swords sliced off his quiver, shattered his bow, and severed the tendons in his firing arm. He tried to cry out, but found a rag already shoved inside his mouth. He tried to struggle, but his wrists were already tied.

Still straining to see exactly what was happening, Crukky poked his head over the sand. He saw men punching an elf. As soon as this registered in his mind, he was yanked violently from his post and slammed onto his back. Commander Tristan, face void of emotion, ripped Crukky's voicebox from his throat. The arrowed clattered off the stone steps where Crukky had been standing moments before. Tristan gave a disapproving glance at a fist clenched a moment slower than the arrow flew, and whistled so quietly that only his rangers could possibly have heard. They materialized in a semi-circle around him.

"A scout. There's an army coming from the west." The ranger paused, his fear almost palpable. "Sir, he said they're led by 'The Enlightened One'."

Tristan ruffled his nose. "Learn more."

The rangers disappeared, away from the rising sun, branching out to see what they could discover before the day was done.

A full-fledged battle raged around the wooden walls of Hâedra. Archers fired arrows that thudded into the loam, passing through phantom foes. The trolls had bashed a side gate to splinters, but had been relatively contained. Not much for hiding, or guerilla warfare, they were simply sprinting from street to street looking for things to kill. The Hâedran military was hardened, and tested, and kept their lines in the face of the onslaught, no mean feat against an army of trolls.

Rorrik and Throm had been arguing over the merits of hammers versus chisels for fine-tuning sculpture. Now they argued over how many real trolls were assaulting Hâedra.

"It's at least six-hundred." Throm waylaid a barrel of water as he swung his axe at a troll that wasn't. "At least."

The thunder gauntlets Rorrik wielded crackled and sizzled in the damp air. He landed a punch square on the jawline of a troll, knocking it unconscious, and backhanded the shapeless air through another decoy. "Nay, only half that. There are phantoms here three-to-one what there are real trolls." He headbutted a building, cursing the deception magics that the Rofu were so fond of. "Kror ra korrum!" He swore, fists again missing their mark against nothing.

Grael had departed after a few days in Hâedra, citing his need to be elsewhere, so Grumbubum had been given his charge of taking care of Magnicaerna once more. The hammer seemed happy to be fighting against worthy foes once more, and Grum found himself wounded more than once. His massive body clogged almost an entire boulevard, and the trolls had learned to find a new way around rather than chance their luck against the ogre and his hammer.

"Where is Crukky?"

"Crukkylate allthatimsir. Doesnlikit when the suncomes. Looks too longan moveslow."

Grimfilth was one sentence away from brutally murdering the goblin that stood in front of him. It was a simple question, and he grew irritable with the way common goblins and orcs spoke. It hurt him somewhere deep within his being whenever their grating voices raked across his ears. "Well, find him."

The goblin hobbled away, up the winding stairs that led to the trapdoor. Almost immediately, Grimfilth heard his pattering steps returning. Readying an insult of soul-shattering quality, Grimfilth was surprised to see an arrow clutched in the goblin's talons. "Foundis."

He snatched it away. It took only a moment for him to order, "We're leaving. Tell the commanders to muster their troops. We head for Brathur at noon. In three days."

An elven arrow? Certainly the elves held no love for the Rofu, but they'd never ventured into the desert to seek them out. Had the Praestan elves taken the diversionary shaman clan he'd sent to harass them personally? He sniffed the arrow. It smelled of the sea. Salt and open air. This was a Braecan arrow. No one in Alkurah had seen a Braecan elf in decades. He growled. And they picked the perfect time to come out of their shells. Was this the terror of the west that his commanders had spoken of? Surely they knew what elves looked like.

With his head bowed and brow furrowed, he didn't even notice the ranger that dropped down from the ceiling to stand in front of him. Not that he would've had time to notice anyway, had this ranger been seeking stealth

Commander Tristan placed a strong hand over Grimfilth's mouth, motioning for silence with his other hand. "Don't speak, don't struggle. There is more and worse than elves approaching this place. Take this," he handed the orclord a piece of cloth with an embroidered 'K' marked into it, "and go to Korz. Send riders ahead with flags of truce. It will take more than orcs and men standing apart to staunch the tide we will come to face."

By the time Grimfilth realized the hot leather glove had been removed, Tristan was on the move and halfway out into the blinding sun. One of his rangers rode for Hâedra, one for Korz. Two more sped to Ictheim and Karakor. He and the remaining eight would stay behind to harry the advance of this unknowable enemy.

Grimfilth wondered whether or not to heed the words of the human who'd snuck into, and out of, his lair. Surely, if this man had been seeking to cause harm to the Rofu, he'd have simply slain Grimfilth. *There are more, and worse, than elves coming.* What could be worse than an army of Braecan elves? A sudden epiphany shook the strong orc to the core. He shivered, hoping anyone who noticed would blame the chill of the caves. Could the dragons have returned? Ragnus was the only dragon he knew of, and it's favor was repaid. More giants? How many races could ally themselves with the Braecans if conquest was their aim? If Grimfilth had learned anything in his considerably long life, it was that elves were not to be trifled with, ignored, or toyed with. They should be kept at bay further than the range their bows could draw.

Not five minutes after Tristan imparted his gift to Grimfilth, a single orc capable of hastening Grimfilth's decision collapsed half a mile from the Kharatule. Dyrrktha crashed to the sand, exhausted to the point of fainting. He spit grit as he gained his feet, stumbling unsteadily against the tremendous desert gusts. His hand kept his eyes clear as effectively as a sieve carries water, and the dust soon blinded him. His heavy boots connected with the trapdoor, and he might have wept but for the cloying sands.

With a strain, he slid down the ladder, collapsing in a heap at Grimfilth's feet. Faint breath wheezed from clouded lungs, and Dyrrktha managed to explain, in enough detail, the plight facing his brothers at the Scar.

He told Grimfilth of the five orcs that fled the Kharatvil within moments of Gorathel's order. Their bags were light, their armor doubly so, and in them lay the hopes of five thousand Rofu. They rode through burning sun and blasting sands until they reached the eastern border of the Scar. There lay fifty Braecan elves in wait, bows unstrung, and minds unwary. By the time they realized what was happening, only thirty-five arrows sliced the air.

A single rider was struck, an orc from far north of the desert come to serve Grimfilth. The shaft rent his spine, and though he could still draw breath, he succumbed within hours. That night, his corpse, and that of his horse, were consumed.

Terea Vo, one of the twenty elves attempting to chase down the party, mentally kicked himself throughout the day. He would certainly be executed. The Braecan High Command wouldn't take this lapse lightly, and Skal would react much more violently than harsh words and a demotion.

His horse leapt a soft patch of sand that would have snared beasts of lesser stock than his own. He landed without a sound, as did the other nineteen sets of hooves.

They had overtaken the bones of one rider. He was buried, but the shifting sands told tales long past, and the revealing wind could not be silenced. Only four now remained, and they were not riding elven steeds.

And Dyrrktha continued: Through the maddening sun they rode again and again, urging the fullest of effort from their mounts. With nothing to spare for the horses, they did not last a third night. They, too, were butchered and gave life to the small company. The elves caught up by midmorning on the fourth day, and there was battle in the stinging storms.

Two arrows glanced from Dyrrktha's hide, and he gulped filthy air as he tried to outpace the elves on foot. Trusting his companions to do the same, he was not surprised to hear the soft thud of steel on flesh followed by a screech some distance to the left. It took only moments for three elves to descend upon the noise and hack Grinshk to pieces.

The company was now three, and though they lost their pursuers in a fierce storm that night, their respite did not last.

"We're close, Terea." An elf swept in near to his left ear, "They're on foot now, and we will ride them down. No word of this will reach Skal."

"For some reason, I fear that he will come to know one way or the other."

The elves made sure they tended their horses as often as possible, but the lives of such beasts were harder to snuff than the nags that rode from the Kharatvil. They quickly regained their prey, and the two orcs they managed to unearth were dealt with slowly, and noisily.

But the fallen orcs were strong in their deaths, and did not speak of the fifth rider. Dyrrktha alone had broken the elven line, and though his hope was thin, he was no longer pursued, and so his chances grew from none to slim. His dinner that night was a brave lizard that had assumed him dead, either by scent or by sight, and wandered too close.

It tasted terrible.

Dyrrktha had not slept, remaining alert for several hours while he gathered his strength. Daybreak saw him only ten miles from the Kharatule. He would arrive before the sun sank. And with his tale told, the hearty orc sank into oblivion for a time, before the healers finally managed to convince him he was not, in fact, dead.

The news Dyrrktha brought rattled Grimfilth even as Tristan's had. Should he move to the Scar to reinforce his army? Perhaps behind the Kharatvil was where the Rofu would break this new army. Surely they stood more of a chance there than on the open plains with an army of sick men.

He wondered if the Ranger had known what was happening in the west, if he could have managed to scout that far ahead. It was a marvel that Dyrrktha had even managed to survive the trip. Grimfilth thought of the Rofu in the Kharatvil, but swiftly came to the decision that would either haunt him for all time, or save the world as it was.

"To Korz, to men, we will ally ourselves, or we will meet the end of all things beneath their swords."

LESSONS LEARNED

The future's past is an unfinished task to those who live for war.
Every battle could be the last, or could lead to hundreds more.
By arrow, sword, or innumerable hordes a soldier's life cut short.
A lesson, promise, to every life, that death is the only thing sure.
Knowledge strengthens minds, not steel; books don't fight wars.
Only in blood can a field be won, life is the greatest force.
Men live, fight, bleed, and die. Pawns of the great Alakhan.
History of prejudice, a past of lies, can any right such wrongs?
The future's past ends too fast, and war brings nothing to close.
Violence and war breed only more, and soldiers crave their dose.

Bendragel wiped a swathe of blood from his forehead with a hairy arm. "You for the wrong side fight, brothers." He growled as he squinted through the illusory trolls surrounding him. Though they often have an innate distaste of magic, every troll is capable of sensing it. To his eyes, the phantom soldiers were as obvious as straw men. A distraction, surely, but he would not waste time attacking them. A real troll barreled around the corner in front of him. His hair was on fire, and the stench that followed in his wake was almost unbearable. A group of Hâedran guards trailed behind, herding it away from the areas of the city civilians had been evacuated to.

It only took a few minutes for Garroway to find his armor, strap it on, and become thoroughly lost in the streets of Hâedra. After crossing the river, he could hear battle everywhere. Every corner he turned, certain there would be enemies waiting, he saw nothing. An occasional corpse reminded him that every second he spent not fighting was another second they ran a man short.

Gunsel was among the first defenders to counterattack the trolls. He extricated himself from a candlelit conversation about feelings with Lillian, armored himself so fast she barely beat him out the door, and rushed into the street with no pants on. He found himself at the head of a squad of twenty or so Hâedran soldiers, all gilded and geared so obviously like pirates that he had to suppress a snigger when he first saw them. Eye patches and peg-legs were as common as beards and missing teeth.

His ragtag squadron lurked in the alleys and abandoned homes down one of the side streets that the trolls had come through. They made as much noise as possible as they burst from their hiding spots, ambushing a dozen trolls and slaughtering them so swiftly that only one had time to strike at all. His club bounced from one of Gunsel's axes. An expert parry sliced three fingers from its wielding hand. He whipped around, fear forgotten, and buried an axe deep into the troll's muscled neck. It snarled until his other axe crunched through its forehead and found something vital.

"Where're yer trousers, mate?" Breegan poked his head through a window.

"I like to be free."

The pirate saluted with a mug of rum, cut down a troll attempting to sneak up on him, and sallied into the night.

The fires were being doused. Rigathel frowned. He had wagered the cost of this attack would likely be the lives of most of his pack. Until the last moment, though, he hoped Shilleril would return swiftly enough to keep those lives lost to a minimum. He trusted his second-in-command, but trolls were trolls. He snorted as he recalled the phrase Grimfilth used so often. "Trolls are trolls. It doesn't always mean something good or bad, but it always means something."

The shamans were still doing their silly dance, so at least that meant there were still illusions in the streets. There were always a curious few among troll-kind who take to the lessons of the shaman-priests. They learn with all the zeal they can muster, and Rigathel had never seen a shaman do a poor job.

One of them pitched face-first into a tree. Rigathel grunted at the distressed look on the faces of the remaining few. Troll magic was a dirtier sort than human magic. While the latter of the two cost time from your life eventually, the former was more of a physical effort. If they magicked too hard or too long, they suffered the consequences.

Shilleril hated sneaking. It felt cowardly. Weak. Still, the armor of the Godslayer was a tool worth sneaking for. So he snuck. The troll crept past squads of men, a red-haired woman screaming obscenities while brutalizing his pack mates, a man wearing no pants, even Bendragel. It took some restraint not to lash out at his traitorous pack mate. Finally, alone, he found a man lost, bewildered, and reeking of magic.

Having backed into the same dead end for the third time, Garroway was trying to climb onto the shortest nearby rooftop to gain a vantage point in an attempt to help. He slipped on a dewy windowsill and crashed to his back just in time to dodge a wild swing from a raging troll.

How, known, could he have that I, here, was? Shilleril extricated his axe from the wall he had buried it in. *His senses by the armor amplified must be.* The troll lashed out in a brutal display of combat efficiency.

But dodging wild axe blades was simply another training session with Roc, and Garroway was excellent at dodging. He ducked, slid, and hopped nimbly around the frustrated troll. His mediocre swordsmanship was probably only going to allow him one chance to strike back, so he waited. The sword could handle itself when the time came; he was just there to point it in the right direction.

A human toying me, with, is. Shilleril was furious beyond reason. Certain that Garroway was doing his best to embarrass the troll, his rage fed increasingly wild swings. The man lashed out.

Garroway struck.

"How?" Shilleril croaked, blood gushing from a ragged tear in his broad chest.

"You're no Roc, troll." Garroway felt brazen having said it, and wondered if this was what Breegan felt like constantly.

Shilleril didn't have time to wonder what that meant before he sank to the street in a pool of his own blood.

Growling, Rigathel finally ordered his shamans to signal the retreat. Within half an hour, every troll was out of the city save Bendragel. "The Kharatule we head to. We failed have."

The contingent of trolls was somber and much smaller on the shameful trudge back to the Kharatvil. They had failed, and failure was simply unacceptable for a troll. In the old days, before Grimfilth had put a stop to the ritual, there existed a rite called *Metitunkhel*. Metitunkhel was undertaken when a troll failed his orders in war, and means literally, "Me troll kill." They would cut themselves from wrist to elbow, in no particular line or vein, and if they did not bleed out before slaying a *hrgeet* (a massive, ram-like creature that inhabits the mountains of Alkurah) in single combat, the shaman would heal them. Trolls began to dwindle simply due to the amount of ritual suicide, and Grimfilth had banished the practice among the Rofu as impractical, if interesting to watch. This only happened, however, because the trolls taught the orcs and Grimfilth's army was decimated within the month.

Instead, when they arrived back at the Kharatule, they would have to simply be branded for their failure. To live with the shame, without the chance to slay a *hrgeet* and regain their honor, was certainly the worse of two.

The next day found the Council of Hâedra doing what it did best: not satisfying Breegan in the slightest.

"More of the same is what we'll get if we don't act." Breegan failed to contain the acid in his voice. "The Rofu are coming. Whether they're retreating or attacking, it doesn't matter, they'll be here soon. And in force. We must do something."

"Skal made an interesting point," the deep male voice boomed, "about what we stand to gain if we do not aid Korz. I'm not saying we let the Korzian army get obliterated. If we were to consider a timely attack, coming to their aid as all hope seems lost..."

"We could erase our past debts while laying claim to Brathur," the female voice offered.

"You know what this sounds like?" Breegan asked, daring someone to answer him.

Immediately, a softer male voice answered, "Sounds awfully human."

"It sure does." Breegan spat, "Damn you. Damn you all to whichever hell is out there that's vile enough to stomach the likes of you scum." He gave a hasty leg and departed, slamming the doors open so hard it dented one of the sculptures.

Gunsel met up with Garroway at a tavern that hadn't quite been destroyed. One wall was rubble, and the door was in splinters, but the rest of it was relatively intact. He sat down, acting casually to cue the bartender for a round of drinks. There was no bartender, as he had gone out to fight the trolls and been knocked unconscious, so Gunsel had to sidle past a troll corpse that was a few limbs short of whole to grab a mug and a bottle that looked tolerable. " So, trolls, eh?"

"Trolls." Garroway sipped at a mug of rum mixed with some kind of fruit juice. It was too sweet for his palate, but he rarely complained about free drinks.

Breegan snatched a stool near the pair, nodding and quaffing a flask of something less fruity than Garroway's drink. "There is an end in sight."

"And what's that?"

"We will fight with Korz. To the bitter end, if need be."

Garroway hopped from his chair, was drunker than he imagined himself to be, stumbled on the rather inconsiderately discarded troll corpse, and asked, "Has the Council decided, then?"

"Screw the council." Breegan raised his mug.

"I can drink to tha'" A new man pushed himself up from behind the bar and swigged from a cracked bottle.

"So, my two strange friends, will you come with us? We will march to Brathur to meet up with the Korzian companies with as many volunteers as we can muster. Will you be among them?"

"Aye." Garroway answered.

After a few seconds, and a few drinks, Gunsel slammed his tankard on the scorched wood of the bar. "Aye. I'll fight to see an end to the fighting."

Seeing a fully mobilized army is a sight to behold. Grimfilth gazed on the endless stream of jangling steel and murky hides that snaked across the horizon. His army was stronger than any Rofu had been before. The weak had been culled ruthlessly. The cowardly had been weeded from them as runts from the litter. None but the strongest could call themselves Rofu now. The orc wished he could say the same for their intellect as he could for their physical prowess. Alas, brains were only needed in a certain measure to lead the arms of his force.

"Grimfiltsir, wemarchin quickin th'night."

"Indeed, we are." He fingered the embroidered square Commander Tristan had given him. "But we must march faster still. We have all day to rest, so use the darkness while it aids us."

"Yessir Grimfiltsir."

A horn tooted in the distance and the pace quickened, a cloud of sand and grit obscuring the stars from the horde. Orcs don't quicken pace with much finesse, and there were several minutes of swearing and tripping before they showed any semblance of training again.

"Rigathel, come here." Grimfilth chewed a piece of roasted lizard mindlessly as he contemplated what he was about to do.

"Sir?" Rigathel looked weary. After the attack on Hâedra, he had ridden straight back to the Kharatule. Immediately, the order was given to leave, and Rigathel had not been on the receiving end of a good night's sleep in far too long.

"I truly can't believe I'm about to say this," Grimfilth sighed and swallowed his leathery snack, "but I need something from you. While you were away, I received a visitor. Two, actually."

"And that, who, sir, was?"

Grimfilth started to correct his words, decided not to, and sighed again, "A Ranger snuck into the Kharatule. The Braecan elves have allied themselves with someone or something and are moving eastward. I believe this force is the scourge we've heard about. He suggested I send a rider to Korz and ally our force with theirs."

He pulled the embroidered cloth from his cloak. With his head down, he handed it to Rigathel. "He instructed I send them with this. A token, I presume, of goodwill."

The look on Rigathel's face slid from exhaustion, to sleepiness, to shock, to hunger, to a burp, to disbelief. "You want me to, this, to Korz, take?"

"Want is probably the wrong word." Grimfilth still could not believe that fear had stricken him to insanity, but he had never killed a Ranger who told a joke. "I think we need to do this. I can't find a reason for a Ranger to lie, or to sneak into my lair and not kill me."

"Can you even die?" Rigathel asked, almost seriously.

In a way, Grimfilth knew he was capable of dying. He didn't know how he knew, because he'd never been mortally wounded, and he never had died, but he was pretty confident. "Yes."

"And who the second visitor, sir, was?"

A few moments passed before Grimfilth made up his mind to tell the truth. "Dyrrktha, sent as an envoy from the Scar." He didn't give Rigathel the chance to ask, "The Kharatvil is under siege. As of five days ago, your brother still held it, but the Rhiam is taken. They will be overrun, probably within the month. Sooner, even."

Rigathel was still as death, and only the sweat glistening in the starlight distinguished him from a statue. "We are, the wrong way, marching." He said, slowly.

"This isn't easy for me," Grimfilth snapped. "There are still five thousand bodies in the Kharatvil, and I don't abandon them lightly."

"Abandon? You the blow may as well have struck."

"I know." The orclord calmed his tone, "I'm sorry."

It took some time before Rigathel unclenched his fists and looked in Grimfilth's eyes. "What do you want from me, sir?"

"To ride to Korz with this token. Answer their questions with all the truth you can, and don't spare for secrecy. I fear our feud could be the wedge on which Alkurah breaks."

"So, to Korz?"

"Yes. And if I'm wrong, I'm truly sorry."

"If you're wrong, I'm truly dead."

"Yes. Yes, you are." Grimfilth patted his lieutenant on the shoulder, gently.

Brathur was unnaturally quiet. No groans wafted through the cool darkness. No cries of pain or fear shattered the stillness. Kyson was afraid of what would become of his army. Seven thousand he took command of. What magic could cause such destruction, and who would use such a curse?

The Rofu.

Of all the campaigns Kyson had fought against the many armies of Alkurah, he relished those against the Rofu most. Each face of orc or goblin that he recalled was drenched in fury enough to distort any thoughts of reason, surrender, or peace. He buried blades, arrows, knives, and spears in all manner of hides in his time. There is only justice in the slaying of murderers.

Kyson had been privvy to stories of their barbarism all his life, and he never found a reason not to believe them. He saw good men slaughtered like cattle, women and children consumed, and corpses that deserved a hero's burial butchered for amusement. Kyson was strong, his scars attested to that. The Lord Commander of the Korzian force was great, as his many victories against impossible odds could prove. There would be no mercy given to the Rofu, nor any retreat sounded. If seven thousand Korzian men were to stand against fifty thousand Rofu, they would stand to the last man. They would stand, bleeding and broken, as only Korzian men could.

If Kyson had learned anything in his career as a soldier, it was that it is better to face the odds than surrender to them.

PRIDE

The Dragon War bred hate and spite, relentless blood and gore.
Furious dragons waged violence and fire, to cure the world of dwarves.
The only race who dared offend, dwarves, tough and stout.
Such bloodshed was seen in a dozen years, great legends are sung about
In their magical forges the dwarven lords smote their irons hot.
In mountain nests, eyries tall, the dragons' wrath was bought.
King Makkor, lord of dwarves, in insult gave a gift,
Of exiles and criminals, outcasts all, to whom prison was a poor fit.
"What's this, Makkor, that you bring here, to this, the Dragon Keep?"
"Slaves, fools, disposable beasts, to fill your appetites deep."
The dragon lords in anger roared, "You dare insult us here?"
Their fire lit the Keep that night and Alkurah cowered in fear.
"Right this wrong, Makkor, or you will feel our indignant might!"
"You spurn my gift? You insult me? No, if you will, take flight.
We don't fear you, dragons, beasts, witless, prideful worms.
I'll show you war," the king replied, and on his heel turned.
Dragon honor is too strong to murder a king and past-honored friend.
They let him leave, and a warning gave, to prepare his kind for the end.

High Elflord, Regent of the Skies, Commander Terea Vo could not manage to lift his chin any higher in the air in affront to the creature that spoke at him. Scum. Weeded from the most ravished lands, they were prisoners from endless campaigns across the seas. Filth. The host he was assigned lordship over could scarcely be called an army. His title demanded respect, but respect was not given through numbers. He held lordship over twenty-five thousand bodies, but they were neither soldiers nor hardly alive for their want of supplies.

He sighed, willing the creature kneeling before him to shut up and walk away. He thought he could smell foul breath clinging to the air in defiance of his impeccable cleanliness and hygiene. "I understand. The commanders you all appointed are terrible. I'll fix it. I'll fix everything," he preened.

The flowing brook of the Braecan tongue rippled over the gruff, chafing language of the islands.

The creature nodded, clearly pretending to feel the same disgust as Terea. As it scampered down the marble stairs a film of dirt remained to remind the Elflord of his presence.

Terea shuddered, waving a hand at one of the waiting servants. The filth was magicked away with less effort than Terea had taken to motion to the servant. Still, it was the principle of not getting one's proverbial hands dirty that counted. "Skal, enlightened of the Sun, please tell me you've something better to assign to me than the curse of being the only scrap of intellect among an army of fodder."

With a light puff, Skal was there. "And what is it you'd like? Perhaps to sit idly on a patch of stone?"

The elf bristled at the stab. He had failed at the Rhiam, and this was his punishment. Skal was aware of the totality of Terea's failure, and he would never let the elf live through the war. However, it would be a shame to miss an opportunity for so much dishonor, and also to bury such a great strategic mind. He was content to let Terea flounder among the wretches. "I'd like respect. Honor. This host will lead my house to fall out of favor with the queen! I cannot pretend I'm pleased with your assignment."

"Does your queen reign over all the lands in all the worlds in all the skies?" Skal asked, almost threateningly. "Septis, God of Gods, the Light, does. Whom would you rather please?"

The mysterious little man vanished as suddenly as he appeared.

With a sigh, Terea summoned his second in command.

Nulau Ra stepped forward without a sound. Her legend had been forged centuries past as the finest scout the elves had to offer. When Terea promoted her, several decades hence during a skirmish with the islanders, he had noticed the sadness accompanying her glowing pride.

Scouting was her life. Silence, speed, and resilience had made her story one of cold perfection, and she was worthy of every bit of praise. As a commander, however, she rarely had the opportunity to showcase her skill, and that rankled with her more often than Terea would've liked. Still, she had a mind for tactics that most only dreamed of, and her guidance had been invaluable for dozens of years.

Neither of the pair was entirely certain why Skal did not simply execute Terea after he was summoned back from the Rhiam. Instead, the elf was given charge of this massive force of fodder, and the dishonor would never be washed from his family. The queen would condemn his name, and there would be no more elves to bear the name of Terea or Vo. He would be the last, and there would be nothing sung of him in the deathsongs of the Braeco. It was the greatest punishment allowed by elven law, and Skal could act at will to smite someone who stirred his wrath.

Still, alive was better than the alternative, and Terea hoped maybe everyone would just forget about him and he could disappear. In the meantime, he had a force of fish to turn into soldiers as they killed themselves on a magical wall. "What, Nulau, am I to do with this rabble?" He asked, hoping she would have more ideas than none.

"Burn them," she offered.

He glanced at her without turning his head.

"And hope the stench kills those who turn from the Light?" Her mouth twitched almost imperceptibly.

"We have no cavalry. We have no siege engines. We have too few spears to stop a charge of rogue ants, and less discipline than the sea itself."

"At least casualties will be meaningless here," she suggested. "As disdainful as I find charging en masse, it could be our only option."

"With training on the march, perhaps..." Terea started, hoping she would suggest something.

"Perhaps they'd charge the right direction."

He sighed. She was right, of course. He never knew her not to be, and it irritated him that not even the legendary Nulau Ra could find a trifle of use amongst the assembled host.

She added, "There's not much we can do until the giants break open that door. Get the Lygian commanders replaced with High Elves as soon as possible. We'll be useless without guidance. Training will be rigid, but try not to mete out severe punishment. The islanders take offense to brutality among their army, and I think we'd best try and abide by their customs as much as possible."

The suggestion startled Terea, as he was still contemplating burning them and trying to smoke the defenders out. He gave her a knowing grin. She was always a step ahead.

"And make them bathe once a day." She finished, moping off toward her officers to give orders.

Sometimes, she was two steps ahead.

Rorrik and Throm were practiced debaters. Not only did they both take pleasure in disagreeing with everything, they spent most of their free time formulating arguments to combat facts. It was a vicious cycle of lying and swearing that few walked away from without a black eye, bruised ego, or worse.

In the face of losing an argument, most dwarves would rather devolve into violence. Should that occur with Rorrik, he could simply use his title as prince of the Thundercrowns to keep retaliation at bay. He did not like doing it, but often it was a choice between that and a vicious beating from a dozen less masterful debaters.

Without a title to fall back on, Throm had become adept at not losing fistfights that he was unable to win. This skill, combined with his impressively stubborn forehead, meant many simply gave up trying to pummel him, nursing broken hands as they were chased away by curses and victory chants.

The piratical men of Hâedra were different. Sea and salt had tempered their flesh into a cushion of callouses that meant even Throm could not outlast their abuse. After rolling onto his back and admitting he was wrong, they yanked him to his feet and thrust a mug of ale into his frowning face. Every argument had a winner, and Throm was unused to it being someone other than him.

Still, it was hard to resist the toothless grins of the scallywags, and he was soon swaying with drunkenness as he sang along to songs he had never heard, soaking up the raucous cheers of those closest to him and filling his belly with poorly salted meat.

Nearly the entire force had abandoned Hâedra, leaving behind a skeleton crew to man the parapets and keep the city safe from itself. The navy had taken some persuading, less willing to leave behind the notion of stable pay. Breegan was indeed persuasive, however, and it is not entirely without noting that he had amassed a considerable fortune. This was not a secret, and the sailors had agreed to fill the Nazene with wood and canvas.

On the riverbanks marched the ragtag army, caring little for stealth in the shadow of a fleet. It was almost certain that the Rofu knew they were on the move anyway, and though they fretted for the safety of their home, the soldiers weren't stupid. It was with heavy hearts that boots stomped the road smooth, and nine thousand men marched towards almost certain death.

"How is it," Gunsel asked one evening, when the column had stopped and fires were lit to warm cheeks ruddy from a hard day's march, "that the dwarves managed to lose a war against the trolls?"

Rorrik bristled, "We didn't lose. We negotiated."

"That sounds awfully civil for a dwarf," Garroway noted.

"What do you give a troll?" Gunsel questioned.

This time, it was Bendragel who answered, "To us, the Dragon's Keep was, in secession, given!" He roared as if he won the great prize single-handedly.

"We offered the Keep to them as a token of our good will. They keep the pass guarded so we don't have to, we supply them with iron for their rudimentary weapons."

"D'you forge it for them?" Gunsel asked, aware of the violence in Rorrik's eyes.

He spluttered, struggling to dig up words worthy of his rage. "Forge it? *Forge it?* I could forge finer steel than that with my own hot breath and a pair of spoons for hammers!"

"So, ye admit yer simply full o' hot air?" Breegan joined in, nestling beside the fire that struggled to warm everyone present. Before Rorrik could explode, figuratively and maybe literally, he added, "Ah, I'm just playin', calm yer beard."

A cool evening descended on the army. The sails of the ships had been folded away hours before, simply coasting on the lazy Nazene to keep their pace relatively even with those on the ground. They would advance soon, however, to harass the Rofu on their way across the mighty river.

With a struggle, the flame consumed a robust log and sent flares to the sky, like red fairies recently given their wings, flitting to and fro for only a moment. Everyone stared; captured by the short-lived grace and innocence they hadd not found time to appreciate for so long before now. In times of war, the simplest things often become sweetest.

"So, what actually happened in the Titûn War?" Gunsel, who never received any sort of education outside occasional whacks on the wrist for stealing, had become genuinely curious about many things since becoming a soldier. His thirst for war stories was rarely stated, and he loved learning as much of valor and brave men as he did strategy and deceit. "I've learned lies from dwarves, and nothing from trolls, and I want to know what happened. The truth."

Breegan produced a flask of liquor big enough to keep the small party buzzing and chipper for some time, taking the first swig and making a show of wiping his lips, he said, "I may be able to produce some partial truths upon that particular story." So Breegan, shipmaster of Hâedra, began his account of the Titûn War, occasionally denying assistance from Throm.

"Dwarves are lords of stone and earth, of that there is no doubt. The marvels they've wrought of simply clay and dirt are unrivaled even in the highest of elven courts. Dwarves, though, are haughty and proud, and it would simply not do to let an insult go unavenged.

When Thurg, a prince of the Stonehands, was waylaid traveling from Ictheim to Karakor, he and his twenty men fought off a force of thrice their number long enough to make the shadow of the Huduns. Thurg's cousin, Maggor, burst forth from hidden places, holes, and caves, to destroy the ambushers and welcome the dwarven convoy home.

'Thurg,' he said, clapping his kin on the shoulder and giving him a fierce headbutt, 'welcome to my home! You bring strange visitors, however, from the frozen wastes.'

'Trolls, Maggor. It seems they felt threatened by our peaceful entourage.'

'They attacked without reason, then?' Maggor gave Thurg a distrustful glance. His cousin had always been fond of war, and there had not been a great battle in nearly a century. Even dwarves grow old, and Thurg was starting to feel the tug of the years on his axe. If there was anyone more likely to start a war, Maggor couldn't name him.

'Indeed. Brigands. Filth. The king will not take this offense lightly.' Thurg started to walk away, content to bring his escort back to Karakor and drive dwarves to war.

'Whose king should be offended?' Maggor asked quietly, his voice lost to all but one in the din of greetings.

'I would be careful, cousin, of what you say next.' The fire in Thurg's tongue was his confession.

Maggor said nothing, only shaking his head and pitying all those who would die before their time. Being something of an exception among dwarves, the black-bearded chieftain had grown accustomed to peace and the idea of living his many years in such a state was appealing. War is an art form, one that Maggor certainly appreciated, but not one he wished to participate in any longer.

And so, two weeks later, when Thurg made his report to King Kurau, there was a council held in Karakor. The king met with advisors, soothsayers, wizards, and warriors in the coming weeks. His days were filled with maps, plans, and pleas. After nearly a month, Maggor made his statement before a hall filled with his peers.

'I believe,' he said, palms sweating even in the cool stone hall, 'that Thurg is the one who invented this misfortune and brings war willfully to our homes.'

It was no secret that Thurg was quick to strike first, even for a dwarf, but to accuse another of warmongering was a serious attack on their character. Thurg was present that day, and though he shook with rage, he said nothing, and was acquitted of charges, eventually. He had, of course, killed a troll family on his route back to Karakor. He made sure it was violent, so much so as to be noticed, and now he would have his war.

Dwarves crossed Alkurah to support their king. Some came from the Kharatvil, traveling through desert heat to offer immense magical weapons said to be capable of breaching even the Godhall's doors. Others came from Soriath, Vahir, and Litha. Before long, an army of tremendous might assembled in the vast reaches of Karakor, and they were armored in steel forged by their grandfathers, and sung songs of the deeds of old for many nights. It is said that they drank so much ale as to leave the city in a drought for nearly a decade, and ate so much food that the inns and taverns had to close down for a month afterward.

Three months had passed since Thurg had returned before a single trollish emissary reached the walls of Karakor. He was sent away without even being granted audience with the king. The time for negotiation was past when Kurau's court took Thurg's word as truth, and there could only be one outcome."

Breegan paused, letting his audience relieve themselves away from the fire, get some dinner from the cook tents, and nestle back into their quiet corner of the camp. Their numbers had grown quite large, he noticed, even as he gave up trying to count their heads. Whenever Breegan told a story, he attracted quite a crowd.

He continued, careful not to go too close to Throm, who was redder than the fire, breathing in such insulted puffs he resembled a bellows.

"Battle was made before the Hudun Mountains themselves. Ictheim would have been a worthy city to sack, but in a land blanketed in ice, even dwarves daren't begin a siege. So they challenged the trolls openly, and even had the decency to allow them to muster their armies. It didn't take long.

The dwarven phalanx moved ever forward, slipping on blood from hewn trollish limbs, and they could not be stopped by shaman or siege engine. Huge numbers of their ranks were crushed beneath boulders flung from trollish engines, but they continued their march, blind to their losses.
Each step took them further from the shelter of the Huduns, and trolls can be patient, if only in war.

Finally, when the first army of the dwarves overreached and separated from the rest, a battalion of ogres blasted from the nearby hills.

It so happened that Thurg was in command of the front lines, and it was he who was pinched between ogren hammers and trollish clubs. It was a slaughter, and soon only a dozen dwarves stood standing in a circle about their prince. He wielded his axe with speed and power that belied his age, and even as he realized he was growing tired and sluggish, an arrow punched through his armor and buried itself deep in his chest.

Still he fought, embarrassed that the armor of his grandfather had folded beneath such a cowardly blow, and took the heads of three more trolls before being smote by a mighty swing. On one knee, he tore the arrow from his chest. It is said by some that he killed over a hundred ogres alone, but it mattered little. He fell, and a full half of the army fell with him.

Kurau was bested, and for the first time in many centuries, the dwarves conceded defeat. He met with the troll king, Icthil, in a guarded hall in Ictheim.

'This was a war that needn't have happened,' the troll started, 'had you a tight enough hold over your subjects as to prevent them from murdering families, Kurau.'

The dwarven king was embarrassed, and could not refuse any of the orders given him by Icthil. The Dragon's Keep, the prized possession of his people, was to be surrendered. 'And in good faith, if you supply the iron for my people, we will bleed for yours upon the Keep, and no army shall ever break upon the walls of Karakor, lest it be over troll bones.'

Icthil sent Kurau away, making sure his escort led him by the graves of the butchered troll family. And when Kurau crossed the border of his land, they bade him farewell and wished him good health and long life, if only that he may dwell on the slaughter of his own people for many years to come."

Having finished his story, Breegan bade his listeners a good night and good dreams. He then coopted a tent that did not belong to him and promptly fell asleep.

The rest of the camp was subdued. It was the third night away from Hâedra, and the men were still wrestling with the fact that their home was all but abandoned. If any number of the attacking force broke off to harry the city, it would fall in a matter of hours. Occasionally a song would sail off into the night, but neither cheerful nor uproarious tunes lifted their hearts. One voice rang out, as the fires dwindled to smolders in their pits and snores had only barely started drifting out of the darkness:

> At the end of our world, what's left for mortals, when the elves have sailed away?
> Their knowledge then lost, long hidden in frost, to whom will mortal men pray?
> When Eskeria wilts and magic ne'er lilts upon the beautiful breeze,
> Will men or the rest, the worst or the best, live in pain or die with ease?
> When the flags of our world are burned and curled, when blood no longer flows,
> The dusk of an age, a turn of the page, what will you bring, tomorrow?

> When the dwarves have all gone, beneath stone and beyond, great forges no longer hot.
> When mountains grow cold, and the unborn grow old, what, then, is humanities lot?
> Lose track of the years? Be consumed by our fears? What chance does the bravest race have?

The blade of a sword can kill peasants and lords, any hand, the hilt, may grasp.
When the flags of our world are burned and curled, when blood no longer flows,
At the dusk of an age, a turn of the page, what will you bring, tomorrow?

Where do orcs go when their time here is spent? Where do trolls go to finally rest?
What memories hold the sands and the cold? What will be left of their best?
Their violence scorned, terror unborn, will it suffer them loss in the end?
When the halls of the dead ring their bells of dread, when every soul is spent?
When the flags of our world are burned and curled, when blood no longer flows,
At the dusk of an age, a turn of the page, what will you bring, tomorrow?

When memories pass, long lives outlast, what will the new dawn bring?
Will there ever be voices to carry our story, will there ever be voices to sing?
When the books and the songs are hidden and gone, what's left for men to find?
To power and change, corruption, or fame, will greed or honor bind?
When the flags of our world are burned and curled, when blood no longer flows,
The dusk of an age, a turn of the page, what will you bring, tomorrow?

Which war will be last, to destroy all the past, which battle will cover Alkurah in ash?
Will one army stand? Will we all be damned, when the battle is everyone's last?

When our fathers and daughters, mothers, and sons, all fade
away into dirt,
Does it matter which battle was lost, which was won, what
was all of it worth?
When the flags of our world are burned and curled, when
blood no longer flows,
At the dusk of an age, the turn of our page, what have you
brought, tomorrow?

The last notes of Lillian's lament for her people, and all
people, hovered in the air, hanging on the gentle breeze. Men
shed quiet tears into the night as they, too, wondered to what
end they marched.

The mental count Skal kept of his army was impressive.
Though few in numbers themselves, the Braecan elves had
managed a robust force of those captured in raids away from
Alkurah. With four-thousand elves, Skal could threaten any
army on the mainland. With a combined force of over sixty-five
thousand warriors, comprised of elves, giants, lygians, and
ogres, as well as men, trolls, and orcs: there was nothing to
stop him.

He fondly remembered the look on Terea's face when he
handed command of the twenty-five thousand reserve
members of the army, the lygians, over. Skal made sure to let
slip the number of his command first, then crush him with the
position's devastating lack of honor. Beyond Braeco, nestled
into the western shores of Alkurah, is a smattering of island
nations known collectively as 'Lygia.' Used more often than not
to denote a specific race that lived in the island chain, 'lygian,'
in this case, meant the strange reptilian race with which the
Braecan elves had warred for decades before overcoming their
almost unfathomable ability to reproduce. The scales on their
backs were the color of algae, a healthy green that shimmered
whenever they were clean enough to not resembled rocks. Pale
underbellies, webbed hands and the occasional sail-like dorsal
fin were all that identified the things. Few had names, and
fewer still even cared to use them.

Ninety-thousand total bodies had rallied to the call of the Light. A host unrivaled in all the history of the land assembled on the eastern shore of the Seia Wesrin. The only lament the strange little man had was that only three dragons had come. There were so few, and the ones who remained were so infinitely strong and wise that he hoped to crush his enemies simply through fear.

A quiet voice, unsought for, wiggled a memory of the armor of Tykus into the forefront of his brain. Skal had a habit he was never quite able to purge of talking to himself aloud. Instead of thinking things, he simply said them.

"Armor. A sword. Such barbaric tools smithed by a barbaric god, and bequeathed unto the barbaric world for all time."

Skal cared nothing for the gods, least of all Bol. The sun god was a tool that had long outlived its usefulness. If he could bring all the races in Alkurah to their utmost pinnacle of strength, the resultant clash would be devastating. What better way to weed a garden of warriors than pitched battle?

He thought once more about the dragons. "If I had dragons, there would be no need. Ten of them. Eight, maybe. That would be enough to kill everything on Alkurah. Everything but *me*."

Since his creation, Skal had dreamt of nothing but extinction, of the dusk of this and all worlds. He was created to become death. Infinitely gifted with magic and nigh unkillable. When the races of this land all took their place in the halls of Tykus, he would move on to the next.

"That spoiled little twit. The usurper. The only one who defied my power? Me! And he gets to be a god. Of course he does. His father cheated for him." He raised his eyes to the sky, "Why the Alakhan? Why give each race one? If those pests hadn't been around all this time, I'd have taken my rage across this world and the next!"

He sighed, knowing his rage was useless. "I'll figure it out. I always have."

The sullen face grew dark for a moment as he remembered the doom that befell his kindred. Atrocities committed in the name of Skal the Enlightened would never be written down, nor recalled by any but he. They were worth every moment of pain.

"Well, it'd been worth it until I realized that goddamn armor had been found. There's one unique, specific item that's been buried for centuries can keep my power at bay. Poof. Perfect. Timing."

On so many occasions, Skal had been close to his goal, only to be thwarted by some wielder of an item destined to make his life unfair. Most spectacularly, of course, by a young man claiming to be a demigod. Each time, his armies had been torn asunder by a force spearheaded by that nightmare armor.

"Korz. Tykus. Even Therian. Everyone wants to save the world from being saved. So now I've created my tool. The first of several, I'm sure, to cleanse this world of its shameful life. I will pick that armor from the bones of its newest victim as flesh from a roast. At my lowest valley, I achieve my highest peak." He looked up, as if to talk face to face with the Sun, "Bol, I'm certain you think to thwart me, but never again will I cower beneath your will, lord of lies and fools. I'm ready to bring your creations to your son, held highest of them all. I hope you deem this gift worthy of my curse, oh God of Gods."

He wanted this destruction. He needed it. For every race to be baptized in the coals of the Light, they must first burn.

The halls of Karakor defy description. Their vastness is impossible to behold in one lifetime of men, and their glory can only be encompassed in dwarvish, whose language contains many hundreds of words for beauty and grandeur. To quote Breegan, Karakor is, "Like watching the sunset over an eruptin' volcano from far enough away that yer pretty certain yer safe, but not entirely. Only louder, and underground." Golden peaks capped each building, and towering above them all, was Mount Karakor. Sunlight filtered through tiny holes drilled through the mountain and through rooms of mirrors that blazed with the sun during the day, and brilliant candles at night. There is no sunset in Karakor.

King Krumrakai's smile was lost in his beard, glad he was no race but his own. Having lived five times the life of a man, he was not young, even by dwarvish standards. Still, he was strong and vital, his hair scarcely graying around the temples. Nothing was honored more than a dwarf's beard save his ability to argue, and Krumrakai's braided mountain commanded nearly as much respect as his thorough study in filibustery.

The king muttered to himself as he soaked up the glory of halls he'd seen hundreds of times. His grandfather's grandfathers had taken up hammer and pick to rip beauty from the dull stone. And what beauty they found here! Veins of silver, thick as a man's arm twinkled in the half-light from the orange lanterns that dotted the corridor. The ceiling rose three times the size of any ogre, and carts could pass five abreast on the smooth-worn road through Karakor. Stone eyes gazed upon any who would travel there from statues carved with such skill and magic they seemed to move in any glimmer of the light.

On this day, their eyes saw only royalty.

Krumrakai was alone, his robe lightly dusting the polished floor as it swayed with his short steps. He was in no hurry. There was a man awaiting his counsel across the city, but his halls were vast, and a dwarf's legs are short and not meant for hurrying. Unless they be hurrying to a meal or a battle, so the saying goes. He grinned again. Making men wait always pleased the dwarven king. Their lives were short, and he wondered if they could feel the moments slipping away forever as they stared at the glory of his kingdom through eyes that could not possibly begin to fathom what they saw.

His good mood soured slightly when he thought about what the man might have to say to him. It was truly a surprise when a human was allowed into his home, and this exception was only made because of his training by the centaurs. Rangers were welcome, or made themselves welcome, almost anywhere. If a ranger had come to Karakor, there must be quite the hubbub jostling beneath his mountain. Krumrakai shifted the heavy cape on his shoulders, starting to sweat slightly. He found it bothersome to keep track of the events going on in Alkurah outside of his halls the past few decades. Too many civil wars, angsty kings, and mercenaries keen on betraying their employers.

Growing old made him selfish. The stubborn king mentally kicked himself for letting his knowledge of the world dwindle while he huddled on his throne. The world had grown in his absence. Perhaps this ranger brought tidings worth stretching his legs. How long had it been since he wandered the grasslands, or sailed the strong Nazene? Most dwarves would be comforted to spend their whole life encased in stone. Seeing the sky was unsettling, knowing your own intense smallness in the world was uncomfortable for most. Krumrakai was something of an exception. Like his cousin Thorriman, he loved the smell of the air over the Nazene. In his youth, he even sailed the Seia Wesrin, albeit briefly. How lovely the salt had tasted on a stiff breeze, his beard crusted over by sand and brine. He fondly remembered the nightmare of cleaning his hair after that trip. The feel of new lands beneath his boots would be solace after so many years on the most solid of stones.

"The world is cruel that allows age to forget what in youth was wondrous," grumbled the king of the dwarves.

"Remember the wonder, then, Krumrakai, son of Makkor," a voice whispered to the lonely king.

Krumrakai growled. He'd probably have to discipline some poor young soldier. Rangers were impatient, especially if they had news they thought was important. Damn anyone who thought otherwise.

"I'm sure you have a reason for neglecting my hospitality, ranger."

"Patience is something I save for necessity. If I can expedite my duties, I will by any means." The ranger stepped from a shadow, playing with a corner of his jacket. His fraying green coat seemed to camouflage him in any background, making his frame look less than solid, more of a constantly shifting morass of background foliage.

"What news from Korz, ranger?"

"I ride with strange and ill tidings from the west, king. What do you know of Septis?" The ranger pulled a wad of leaves from under his jacket and crushed them into his pipe. Blue smoke hovered in the air with no breeze to disturb it as he puffed gently in the gloom.

"Septis?" the king squinted one eye, scratching his beard. "One of the new gods, yeah?"

"*The* new god," the ranger corrected.

"Hrmph. I have no need for new gods. Mine have dealt me a hand worth worshipping."

"There's an army approaching Korz and Hâedra."

Krumrakai steeled his temper. He dealt with rangers more times than he had liked in his long life, and he never met one he enjoyed conversing with. They were vague and their knowledge of the world was rarely worth putting up with for the scarce information they offered.

"There's always an army in the dunes or grasslands. Get to the point, ranger." The king was truly annoyed. What had started as a pleasant walk through his halls had become a stagnant conversation with a thickskulled man who thought he was more important than any king. "My time matters."

The ranger gave his left arm a lazy scratch, "The Rofu are fleeing from some terror to the west; Hâedra moves to aid Korz in a war against an enemy that neither of them could possibly fight alone."

"The Rofu can't have gathered such strength as to stand against the all the armies of men. You either lie to me or tell me half-truths. I cannot stand a witless scout, nor have I the patience for your impudence." Krumrakai drew an ornate hand-axe from his belt, lightly fingering the blade as he twirled it. "Your master will certainly understand if I send back only a fraction of you rather than waste more of my time."

The ranger, trying to pretend he was unfazed, cleared his throat, "There's another army west of the dunes. They follow a leader called 'The Enlightened One' who has rallied elves, men, dragons, and more to the banner of Septis, Lord of the Light."

"Dragons," the dwarf scoffed, "are no longer part of this land. My father, Makkor, fought in the last Dragon Wars, and I'll not see that victory slandered in the slightest." As he spoke, he returned his axe to his belt, genuinely disturbed that even a rumor of dragons still existed.

"One, at least, we know still fights. Ragnus of the Fireborn was at Brathur. We have others riding to the Rofu, Ictheim, Korz, and Hâedra to attempt an alliance against this force. We need help, King. The coward elves of the south simply hide, and there are no others to turn to."

"Cowards. Accurate." Dwarven lack of enthusiasm toward elves was simply a fact. Some dwarves managed to hate themselves enough to ride to Braeco. They told stories of trees, sand, and water sung with magic to create cities and wonderlands from dunes and lakes. Disgusting. If it wasn't made with stone, by hand, it was certainly not worth living in. "So there's an army in the west? This is such news?"

"Well, it's not terribly surprising, but this 'Enlightened One' seems to reach beyond magic and logic. It's... unnerving that there are races from outside Alkurah. And, you know, dragons."

"Dragons." Krumrakai grunted in that manner only dwarves are only capable of that said a full sentence, sometimes even a conversation, with just one grizzled syllable.

"Yeah. Dragons."

"Shit."

"Yeah. Shit."

MUSTER

Where Khagarel stood with spear in hand, demons he left to guard,
The ageless one brought pain to the Alkui- givers of life, the gods!
Battle they waged on the mortal plane, Alkuin blood was spilt.
Khagarel's spear tore the world from his peers, and magic began to wilt.
Battle the storms and battle the horns, and challenge the raging sea,
But never come near, and ever revere, the thunderforged Kharatvil.

The Alkui charged, praised above all, and broke on Khagarel's stone.
That moment their last, a beginning to pasts; the Alkui fell, dethroned.
The fallen now became Gods of the sky, and Khagarel ruled the world.
But power still in Alkuin hands was a snake but writhing and coiled.
Battle the storms and battle the horns, and challenge the raging sea,
But never come near, and ever revere, the thunderforged Kharatvil.

"Roc?" Kyson stalked the empty garrison, wondering how the old man could slip anywhere unnoticed. He had been around too many years, Kyson decided. It was time for a change in the scenery of his command. Their discussions were becoming more heated and violent as the days went on. The Lord Commander found his subordinate appraising a number of scrolls and books in his study the day before. Roc, however, spoke first.

"Have you any news from the west?" he asked, clearly implying he had.

"What do you know that you're so eager to tell me?"

Roc hacked up a wad of phlegm. "Kyson, how many years have I taken orders from you?"

"Too many, if years can even cover the span of your *service* to Korz."

"Are you implying I've lost my edge?"

Face twisting with rage, Kyson spat, "You've dulled it entirely. You let this happen to me, Roc. You knew, and don't tell me I'm wrong. You had knowledge of this poison and the goings-on in the west that you failed to share with me. Now I am the commander of half an army, shepherd of souls innumerable as they fade away and burn." His sword sang as he unsheathed it, letting the scabbard clatter to the floor. "I'll have you keep secrets no more! What do you know of the world about us that is so rashly catapulted to ruin?"

"Rash indeed, though the world is not the one falling as much as you yourself, Kyson. Put that thing away." He grabbed Kyson's sword and, ignoring the blood dripping from his bare palm, drove it into the mortar of the wall. "You could not kill me, Kyson, with a hundred such as yourself."

"I don't need a hundred." Kyson lunged with a knife, catching the grizzled warrior in the arm. Roc barely heeded the strike, and his fist lashed out with a speed uncanny. With a single blow he separated Kyson's shoulder from its joint, then gripped the area like a vice, ignoring Kyson's gasps.

"There are too many 'Kysons' in this world." Roc snarled.

"And not enough 'Rocs' I suppose?" Kyson gasped.

"Too many of those, too." The old man released his commander. "I grow old, even in the measure of this land, Kyson. My time is nigh, and I can finally lie at peace beneath a world I've helped forge. I can lie with my brothers and my sons for time unending. And finally, Kyson: finally! I will know peace." Red rimmed eyes begged without words for a chance to rest. "This is the end, Kyson. Can't you see? Even you, blinded by pride, can attest to my witness that these are the hours to decide the fate of our world. It comes down to you, Lord Commander."

"And with such responsibility, I would rise up and seize glory unmatched!"

"With help from Hâedra?" Roc asked, hoping against the answer he was sure to receive.

"With help from no man, dwarf, elf, or lesser creature. We will fight and die with songs in our hearts and blood on our swords to be welcomed by Tykus himself into Godhall!"

Several things then happened in an instant. Roc's elbow crashed into Kyson's gut with speed belied by his wizened appearance. The door opened in time for Commander Tristan to witness the blow, and to make his choice.

Training with the centaurs was as mentally rigorous as it was physically. The men selected were trained to constantly outthink and outmaneuver their opponents while simultaneously out-muscling and skillfully dueling them. Tristan had succeeded in every campaign, every mission, every conversation, and every instant of body language. He was perfect, for years upon years, in his relentless adherence to Kyson and his schemes.

In that moment, however, he made his choice. For years, he felt Kyson's mind slipping from that of a competent, if rash, Lord Commander, to that of a prideful fool, ready to fall face first into the dust having reached beyond the length of his wit. Commander Tristan stood by to watch, and even gave an ounce of his will to amplify the altercation.

Furious beyond reason, Kyson wrenched his sword from the bricks. "You assault me? Is this your play, Commander Roc?"

"I'm done playing." Roc shattered Kyson's wrist against the wall with a sharp blow. He grabbed the younger man and dragged him past a Tristan that could scarcely move for his astonishment. "I'm done playing with the lives of innocent people."

The courtyard was beginning to fill up with soldiers curious about the altercation Tristan had projected into the courtyard. Nearly half the army stood in the shivering grass to watch their Lord Commander be dragged like a ruffian caught stealing pie to the center of the compound.

Kyson sputtered, unable to break the relentless grip on his collar. "You will release me! I will take my men, even those on the edge of shadow, to meet the Rofu with arms. Release me!"

Roc flung him to the earth, tossing his sword next to him. "Arm yourself. In this moment, at least, save yourself some dignity. I formally declare my dissent from this army, and any willing to oppose me are free to do so. These actions are mine alone, and I'll not sully any other man's reputation in doing so."

A soft wind blew through Brathur. It was the end of summer now, with clouds hanging low over a sun that offered less warmth than it promised. Smoke, as ever, rose from the southeastern corner of the compound. The air was greasy and heavy.

Suddenly, a breeze swelled from the west. Stillness hung in the air for a moment, but then the clouds parted and a flare of sunlight burst from their cover, bathing the world in brilliance. Kyson took a deep, clean breath for the first time in weeks. His head cleared. The world seemed a less sinister place, and all those wrongdoings that had damned his army were laid bare before his eyes with clarity he never grasped before. "I- I didn't... Roc, what have I done?"

"Nothing you can't atone for, in this life or the next."

Fumbling, Kyson grabbed his sword in his left hand. "This won't even be a fair fight." His voice was weak as he began to truly grasp his circumstance.

"It never would be," Roc muttered.

Nearly seven thousand soldiers watched their Lord Commander strike wildly. Roc parried, almost contemptuously, and flicked his wrist so casually it looked almost as though he had rehearsed the move a thousand times.

The Lord Commander of all the Korzian armies gaped soundlessly, clasping at the hole in his throat now freely spewing blood onto the grass.

Roc knelt, pulling Kyson close, "This wasn't my intention, but I cannot stand by and watch your pride be the doom of our time."

Moments passed. Seconds stretched on, and nearly five minutes passed without even the rustle of grass. The stunning silence left in the wake of the demise of Lord Kyson was broken only by the clatter of his sword against a stone as it fell from his hand for the last time. Roc opened Kyson's jacket, lifted his shirt out of his belt and felt warm fluid on his ribs. A ragged scar, rotting and oozing yellow pus, tore across his side.

"The poison always wins. I'm sorry." Roc replaced the jacket so no one else would see the infected wound. "Bury him with all the honor accorded to his position. Bury him deep, and leave a marker that future commanders may heed."

Tristan strode across the grass, sword already in hand, ready to do what his honor demanded. "Roc, you've spilled blood worthy of a far better end."

"I have."

"And I'm glad you did, for otherwise he may have met a far worse one." Tristan knelt, offering his sword to Roc in a show of submission and fealty. "I will serve you, and Korz, until the ending of my song or the ending of all songs."

As one, seven thousand Korzian men knelt and swore loyalty, on pain of death, to Roc as Lord Commander.

"I've never wished this, my friends." Roc was humbled, and ground his teeth to keep the lump from his throat. He was one of the Veiled, and though he had stood on grounds similar to those he now tread before, never had his story been remembered by any but he. "In my life, I've fought wars uncountable. I've slain men, I've slain orcs, I've slain creatures of races that longer walk in this world. Not once did I wish command over armies, so I'll be blunt, as a soldier would be to his brother in arms."

He allowed himself a sweeping glance over the assembled host. Men on crutches with gangrenous limbs bound in dirty rags, grizzled warriors clenching their jaws and nodding in understanding, healers still struggling to keep their charges on their feet. And above all, he saw men. Men with hope in their eyes and fear in their hearts. Men, the shortest lived, weakest race in Alkurah. The greatest race in Alkurah. They would prove their mettle before the end, whether their end or that of all things.

"I will ask Hâedra for their help in this war. Men will fight together, to the last, against the Rofu."

An audible gasp shot through the crowd as Grael Voor appeared at Roc's side. "And perhaps, against something even worse."

Roc managed not to look the least bit surprised, and continued on as he had started, "The strength of men will be tested. Those who come will hope to see us weak and splintered; but in our hour of trial, those who would destroy us will find that together we are iron."

With a whisper, Grael told Roc what had been learned from Tristan and the other rangers. Roc waved, and the officers of his newly acquired army jogged away to assemble their soldiers. "Do you think they've been deceived?" Roc asked.

"I trust Tristan more than I can say of almost anyone, if only because of his training with the centaurs. He would not lie on purpose, and he is a hard man to lie to."

"Will the Rofu fight with us?"

Grael scoffed, "Will your men fight with the Rofu? Either side, I fear, is afraid to trust beyond the reach of his arm."

"And rightfully so!" Roc snarled. "Is Magnifeia with them?"

"It really would seem that way, would it not?" The elf answered, not willing to ask Roc how he came to know the true name of their ex-foe. He quickly lost a battle with his curiosity, "What do you know of the Alakhan, Roc?"

The pair, hunched with lingering years and secretive tongues, made their way to the northeastern corner of the wall. Stones still littered the scorched grass. The stench of a giant borders between putrid and alarming. After marinating in the sun for quite some time, and gaining the odor of death and corruption, it simply becomes unbearable. Grael knew Roc would expect him to protect them from it, and he did, if only because he had no intention of letting the smell near himself.

"I know more than I've told you, my friend. For that, I am sorry." He took a deep breath, ready to launch into his confession, "I talked to Chithralt. It's been some years now, but I had to know, Grael. I had to know."

And so the pair went out beyond the destruction of Brathur, and past the charred pits of bodies that were scattered in the Bolepha, which is the great plain west of Brathur, stretching to the rocky bank of the Nazene, and Grael learned what this mortal man knew of his kin.

Chithralt knelt, brushing dust lightly from a leaf recently trodden into the path. "This is soot, smell," he growled.

The leaf passed hands from student to student. They savored the feeling of the air in their lungs, and the scent became known to them for the duration of their lives.

"Soot from a fire not four hours doused." Chithralt continued, whipping a fly from his flanks.

"How do you know when the fire died?" A student asked, suspiciously.

"The scent of the smoke." Chithralt's eyebrows piqued, challenging his student to continue.

"Why show us soot in the dirt when there is smoke on the air?"

A hoof pawed the ground as the instructor became impatient. His temper was legendary, and few ever dared stir it. "I would feed you shit, Roc, that you learn better the predator from the prey." His powerful equine body shuddered with bestial foresight, ready to help repel any attack.

Roc flashed a knife in the glaring sunlight, using the guise of his left handed strike long enough to draw Chithralt's gaze. His right hand was a flurry of motion cloaked in shadow and wrapped in magic.

A buckler lashed out to deflect Roc's strike, as well as grabbing the four knives he had thrown from the air.

"That, boy, was a mistake." The centaur dashed three steps forward before collapsing in a tangle of howls and blood. His mangled legs ground to a slow halt, bones jutting where they had no business being.

"I am no boy, Chithralt. I trained men who became legends and greater, in my time. You'd have had more chance fighting a dragon." Roc had traipsed through the forest that very week, maybe three days before this meeting, and nestled a number of caltrops into the loam. The next two days he spent subtly guiding his instructor to the spot, careful to leave a track of something interesting, such as soot. He made sure to blow out the fire only that morning, almost four hours ago.

"How? Who are you?" The great centaur writhed in pain, unable to gain his hooves in order to fight or flee. "Students, flee this place and bring my kind to avenge me."

The thunderstruck trainees scattered, intimidated and terrified by what they saw. All things in the forest would hear their crashing, and surely someone would hurry to check.

"Will you not just kill me, coward, *tralapar*?" Chithralt sneered.

"Oh, I will. But you're not just a trainer of Rangers. You've grown soft, ancient one."

Chithralt's eyes widened as he saw through the disguise that had cloaked his eyes so long. "You're just a man..."

"One of many, but one of few." Roc hunkered down and set about tying knots along the wounded centaur's limbs every few inches. He made sure to keep them tight, and they rubbed the thick skin beneath Chithralt's fur raw in minutes.

"If you think to have me submit through pain, Roc, you will be sorely disappointed."

"If you think to resist, you will find that you are as weak as paper to flame." Roc knelt, grabbing the centaur by the chin and squeezing hard. "You will break for me, Chithralt. Your mind, your body, and your spirit will wither and melt into the wind." The knife bit deep, fileting meat from bone with practiced speed and skill. Ignoring Chithralt's cries, Roc continued, "There are creatures in this land, Chithralt, that have been here an awfully long time. I don't know how you're connected to them, but I have a hunch" He drew his knife gently across the centaur's cheek, "And I'm an old hand at persuasion."

And so Roc learned of the Alakhan. One creature of each race was destined to live for time immemorial from each of the races in Alkurah, before centaurs fell from the grace of Bol, and dwindled greatly. Now there were fewer of the Alakhan than should be, and Roc had learned their truth. Just before the end, when his body lay carven and whittled, white bones standing out against the mud, Chithralt confessed to Roc his deepest truth.

"You'll find, mortal, that we do not die so easily." He said, trying to sound more confident than he felt.

Roc's eyebrows rose, "We?"

"My true name, as given me by Bol, the Father, is Chithraltimazomagnifindua. I am the forest, and I will never die." Chithralt taunted Roc now, growing more sure of his power or delusional from the pain.

Thus, Roc learned what it meant to kill a god, and he became Godslayer, though neither knew it. As Magnifindua passed on, so too did the centaurs and the great woods of old. Meadows and plains encroached on Eskeria, and the trees grew weak and brittle. Centaurs were scattered across Alkurah, but they no longer felt passion for life. They grew to appreciate the dusk of all things, and learned more of death than anyone ever before, and their knowledge was guarded until the end of their days, which would come all the sooner now their heart had been carven from them.

It was hours before anyone came back. They found Chithralt scattered about a clearing. His death was one of weakness, and failure. With him, the forests stilled, and sang no more to the jubilant breeze, nor snoozed with flickering stars, nor adored the sun.

Stunned as he never had been in his considerable life, Grael simply stared. Roc returned his hard gaze with stone eyes, unflinching even in the face of fire. Brathur buzzed around them, but neither group heeded the other. It seemed ages before Grael finally spoke, and the words left him as the last sigh from a corpse. "He was my brother."

Roc snarled, "He was a liar, and a fool, and is now simply another face in my mind."

"Redemption, and grace, Roc, can serve as better tools than blades."

Lord Commander Roc grated his teeth in irritation, clearly not appreciating the lecture. "Grael, I am not some hatchling who wandered from your roost. I am one of the Veiled, and I have lived a life of lives uncountable. Whosoever I deem unworthy of life is such, and will suffer their end by what means I see fit! I am history, Magnicaerna, and I *will* be remembered!"

The pair stood, each daring the other to flinch. After a few moments, it was Roc who snarled, "I will meet with you, and the rest of my officers, at noon tomorrow. We will discuss our ... predicament." He waited for Grael to leave, but the elf gave the impression that he was not ready to go anywhere. "I will not apologize for doing as I have, Grael. Magnifindua earned what he was given."

"Mistakes are lessons best learned from, that we don't commit them twice. Vanity has brought greater men than you to heel." There was a puff of smoke and Grael was gone, whisked away to some errand unforeseen. His work was plentiful, and he had many faces.

The stench of the decaying giant nearly overcame Roc's iron stomach.

BETRAYAL

Trolls, they march, and speak words wrong, and battle for battle's sake.
Trolls, they bleed, and punish the weak, and die ere bloodlust is slaked.
Trolls, they punch.
Trolls, they bite.
Trolls, they scratch.
And trolls, they fight.
Trolls live and die and never cry,
But trolls will, you, make pay.

Trolls have a monarch. As equal opportunity achievers, female trolls lead just as often as male ones. The current troll monarch is a Queen. She sits on the frozen throne sometimes, but it becomes awfully cold, so most kings and queens spent a healthy majority of their time pacing the palace and training. The current Queen, Whoorlem, was young and strong. Her black hair was shaved into three thin stripes down the middle of her otherwise bald head, and her yellow eyes were sunk deep into her skull. She recently returned from a hunt, and had brought back a dozen Hrgeet to gain even more honor. She was resting, but even with tired muscles and senses dulled by strong drink, the troll still had time to throw a knife at the Ranger who dropped from the rafters of the throne room. The ranger, named Urloc, caught the knife by its hilt and pocketed it, unconsciously weighing it to assess how much he might make by selling it. His recently, and poorly, shorn hair poked out at ridiculous angles, and he had several weeks of patchy, untrimmed stubble crawling around his face.

"It's an honor, it really is, but I must be brief, Queen Whoorlem." He knelt in the troll custom, both knees to the ground at the same time while putting his arms straight out at his sides, palms facing the queen. "I was sent by Commander Tristan, which is a name I assume you recognize, to warn you. There is an army," he began, rising from the floor and producing a wrapped piece of salted meat to graze on, "that has overtaken the Scar. The Rofu had soldiers stationed within the

Kharatvil, and they've either been destroyed or something worse."

Whoorlem was still trying to understand why her knife did not kill this human, and was torn between getting up and pulling him in half with her bare hands, or listening. She settled for listening, barely, and fidgeted uncomfortably on the frozen throne, which she hadn't planned on sitting on for very long. "And what, with me, to do, this, has?"

"Tristan fears this is an army greater than any race standing apart. He hopes for your support against them, should they advance beyond Kharat. The armies of men are divided, and Korz has recently suffered great loss to their numbers. They will not be enough to staunch the storm brewing in the west." He swallowed hard, well aware of the amount of time he spent riding here. If the trolls mobilized immediately, they would be luckty to arrive wherever they might be needed late at best. "It is urgent, Queen Whoorlem, that you give me an answer. I must make for Brathur with as much haste as can be mustered."

"Go, then, to Brathur," Whoorlem responded almost immediately, "trolls will, with men, fight, if their need that is."

Urloc hadn't imagined troll diplomacy being that nonexistent, so he stuttered something about gratefulness and shuffled out the door. His stride grew longer as he raced through the palace of the troll Queen, making for his horse and hoping to find something to eat along the way.

Queen Whoorlem chuckled, a deep gurgling in the back of her throat that sounded vaguely cough-like. It grew to a full roar, and she pounded the frozen throne with her mug, appreciating her cleverness.

"Call me daft, but I'd be willing to bet you're starting to enjoy menial subterfuge." Skal cackled from a foggy corner, floating a few inches from the floor.

"Shkaylhu's will, stronger, is, than ice."

Urloc managed to take a deep breath of frigid air, two steps beyond the swinging door exiting the palace, before a spear erupted from his chest. He reached up, as if to pull it out and therefore make it better, and managed to look confused before a second spear nearly separated his head from his shoulders. Squinting, he made out two trolls. They swallowed hard, sharing a glance of mutual disdain, unused to such honorless violence. Their queen would suffer no hesitation, however. And they were uncertain what their queen's new king would suffer, and one man was hardly worth their lives.

Krumrakai stumped around his office. In his youth, it was a lounge. Then a study. He knew himself old when he first called it an office, and since that moment the place had been a prison. Scrolls rested on shelves, intricate maps of cave systems were pinned to assorted walls and boards, and various weapons of foes he personally slew littered the floors. He had given orders to his princes to march the mass of their armies to Brathur.

Through Roc, Grael, and Breegan, information was flowing quickly. There was no communication with Karakor yet, however, and though neither party had managed to discern what the other was doing, they acted as one. Riders thundered across every road that could be reached, summoning anyone who could bear a weapon or ride a horse, with little hope being allowed that they be able to do both. They world was ending for them, whether they fought it or not, so many chose to simply ignore the call.

But many hearts were stirred. The dwarven king was among them, and he finally dug the armor his ancestors had smithed in forges as old as the world itself from a heap of leather bound books. He brushed cobwebs and dust from the ancient iron with reverence, and piece-by-piece he assembled it in full splendor. Bowing, a prayer of thanks and protection to his sires left his tongue before he bade the ranger that lurked in his tent-flap to his side.

The dwarven king, it turned out, knew an awful lot about the 'new god' before Ranger Norrin had even asked. Septis was a bastardized pronunciation of an ancient god of darkness and death called Sypchallu. He was newly risen, and Krumrakai learned all about the happenings in the west under the banner of Septis. Dwarves kept better track of history than any other race in Alkurah, if only to provide themselves an avenue of information for the sake of debate.

His neglect of world events had only taken a few days of studying to erase. Already, dwarven armies were massing in Karakor and Soriath, a dwarven city further south than the Huduns, and banners stored away for centuries took to the wind. An iron fist would descend from the north, and the armies of the Darkness would despair.

Listening to informants grated on Roc. He respected their input, and truly could not do anything without the information they provided, but every single one of them acted like they learned the secret of life itself when they happened to learn anything. The decision not to cut them off until they each said what they had to say was one made rashly, but that promise to himself was already fading. "Okay, enough." Roc dismissed the man. His patience had worn thin enough, and he knew everything men in expensive clothes had to tell him. "Grael, can you see anything?"

The ancient elf rose from a haphazard pile of cushions, and cleared his throat. "I fear, my friend, that there is magic older even than mine at work here."

"What could that possibly mean?" The idea that there was a being in this world whose prowess with magic was capable of holding Grael Voor at bay was startling to Roc, but he kept his composure.

"It could mean a lot of things, unfortunately. We know it's not the Rofu, we know it is not just elves, and we know they've been stirred into some sort of religious frenzy by 'The Elightened One.'"

"My gut tells me to have a bad feeling about that, but my gut's been wrong an awful lot. I figure it's just some poor creature wandered where he shouldn't've and got a dose of magic he couldn't control, but then again it could be the righteous vengeance of Bol on Alkurah, right?"

"Your wit strays too near the truth. That is what my gut tells me, and it isn't often wrong." Grael took a bite from a sweet roll hidden in his sleeve. "We need to leave. The sooner we combine our force with Breegan's the safer we'll all be. The Praestan elves won't help, but Norrin is in with Krumrakai. There's been no news from Urloc or Ictheim, and as far as I know Magnifeia intends to fight with us."

"And will King Krumrakai aid us?"

"Norrin got a report out, and the dwarves have begun moving into Soriath and Karakor. They will march to Brathur straightaway."

"We should leave men here to send them on our trail."

"Where are we headed?" Grael asked, keen to see how Roc would react to a subtler attempt at advice.

"To Litha." He grabbed a map, brushing a sheaf of papers to the side and pinning it to the desk. A gnarled finger jabbed onto the city, "It's roughly between Soriath, Hâedra, and here, and it will get us in a position to supply ourselves well before we move out to Gundera."

"To Gundera? Seriously?" Grael did a poor job managing his surprise, and the look on his face bordered on incredulity. "What do you hope to accomplish there?"

"Gundera has remained neutral in nearly every human-orc conflict, and they've never been openly hostile to anyone but ogres. Apparently ogres spend a lot of time complaining, and they don't like the negativity? Anyway, we could use that as a final stop to resupply ourselves before the desert."

"You're going to cross Kharat?" Grael actually scoffed.

"If we must. I don't want this battle to happen east of the Nazene, if we can help it. And from what I understand, the Rofu hold the Kharatvil. We could reinforce them there and this army would never even make landfall in Alkurah proper."

"Or the Kharatvil has already been taken, and you'll be slaughtered by storms or armies hidden in storms." Grael poked himself in the temple, "It's better to do what you think than what you feel, my friend."

"All the same, we should fight west of the river. There's no saying what a wizard this powerful could do if he made it to Brathur or Korz. Awful lot of history there."

"I don't disagree." Grael almost winced as he pushed an idea on his friend, "But I think we should hold in Litha. It's easily defensible, it's already well manned, and it has larders we can stock. There are obvious reasons we shouldn't even attempt to charge through Kharat. I assume we will be in contact with the Rofu soon enough, and we will see what they think as well. Patience, I think, would serve us in the coming weeks."

"Patience and inaction got us here!" Roc roared, shaking an open hand at the pile of papers on his desk. "Patience is what gets us killed."

"Patience does not mean inaction. Learning and observing can be as effective as swords, my friend." The elf knew his friend was coming around, as his anger often led to his coming to reason.

After a tense moment, the old man nodded, "You're right, I'm sure. But we will make for Litha quickly. Send riders to Hâedra and Karakor, and if we hear anything from Ichteim or the Rofu, tell me immediately. Please. Thank you, Grael." Roc was aware of how knowledgeable his friend was, and though he often lacked the infinite patience of elves, he could appreciate it's worth.

"I will, my friend." He pulled the door open and stepped into a stifling hallway before adding, over his shoulder, "And you're welcome."

Two days later, the Korzian army was making ready to move, and already the vanguard had marched in full splendor from Brathur. The Bolepha teemed with families and veterans clinging to one another, hoping for this last moment to last forever. They knew as little about the coming war as the soldiers, so they simply prayed to Bol for their safety and hoped he was in a listening mood. The crowd parted, however, when a solitary troll astride a massive horse mounted the horizon. He was greeted nearly a mile from the camp, and four horseman flanked him through the ranks of the crowd. He kept asking for the chief and waving an embroidered piece of linen.

Rigathel was shocked not to be greeted by a hail of arrows and a disgraceful death. He wound his way through families of men he had probably slain, and took it as a compliment that they shuddered or fled at the sight of him. The crowd rippled ahead of him as information traveled on the wind, and soon he saw a small group of riders trotting to intercept his current entourage. There was an old human in the front, riding several degrees left of center, who looked strange to the troll: the way magic looks. Rigathel was curious, but he had seen enchanted armor and clothing before, so he took no heed of it. The elf behind him was undoubtedly ancient, and the pair seemed to garner respect from the crowd, rather than fear. He scoffed at the very thought. They eased their pace to approach him at a walk, so as not to appear aggressive, he assumed.

"Show me what you hold, troll." Roc's practiced sergeant eyes drilled into the formidable hide of the troll, but he could glean little from the outside. "I hope, for your sake, it's good news."

Rigathel produced the cloth, still uncertain of what it meant. It seemed to please the old man, however, and he handed it off to a cloaked man that he refused to believe had been present before for the stealth of his approach.

"Thanks," Tristan sounded almost serious, pocketing his handkerchief, "wasn't sure what I'd do if they didn't bring it back."

"So your leader will help us, then?" Roc asked.

"His name is Grimfilth. He is the greatest orc I've ever had the honor of serving, and his peril is mine. We need help, sir. We received a single rider from the Kharatvil. The Rhiam is taken, and this army assaults it even as we speak, unless they've overrun it already." Rigathel was aware of the gathering crowd, and he began to get nervous. Trolls were strong, but he could not defeat an army on his own. He trusted his lord, however, and did as he was ordered: "Grimfilth wishes to fight with you against the coming terror, and in order for that to happen, there must be communication between us."

Piping up from behind a cloud of smoke, Grael added, "Us, Hâedra, Karakor, the Rofu. This is going to be quite a crowd."

"With what to my master should I return?" Rigathel's stomach growled, and the assembly's nervous silence was broken by laughter.

"Get off that beast, get some food, and get some rest. We'll send you and some words to Grimfilth tomorrow." Grael said, tamping out his pipe and giving his back a quick pop. A satisfied grin nestled onto his face, and remained there most of the day. Never had there even been a real attempt at peace between the Rofu and men. All it took, it seemed, was existence-threatening danger.

They led Rigathel to the stable, where he parted with his horse and recieved a mug of ale. Four men led him to the Great Hall, where he was presented with a buffet like he never could have imagined. That evening, he ate until his gut bulged and his jaw ached, savoring every ounce of meat and morsel of juice. Sweet things, savory things, sticky things, and most enjoyably none of them were moldy or perished! The men surrounding him attempted to keep up, but fell miserably short of the troll. With the ogre and trollish regiments already moved out, there was no competition to Rigathel's appetite. Gortrum politely declined, though his friends swore his ability to stuff victuals was beyond that even of a giant.

In time, Rigathel was sent to a room of his own, with a real bed made of something softer than stones. He drank water untainted by mud or filth, and he slept more soundly than he ever had. Most of his wing of the barracks was kept awake by his explosive snores. When he rose, so many hours beyond sunrise he could scarcely believe it, he received the message he was to tell Grimfilth, and rode into the setting sun with a company of four men keeping pace behind him.

Krumrakai was now in full contact with Roc, and his scouts and spies reached wide for any whisper or scent out of place. Two thousand dwarves had assembled in Soriath, with another five hundred waiting in Litha for more instructions. Thirty-five hundred more now resided in Karakor, and the bellows pumped ceaselessly to keep forges fired. A song welled up in the depths of the Korrum, beneath the throne room. The greatest forge in Alkurah burned as a star, and metal was smote to the throaty growls of the smiths:

> Low roll the mountain tones, dig, crack, brr.
> Rocks and stones, and iron bones, dig, crack, hrr.
> Under mountain, under hill, in bedrock we live and die,
> Tinker, linger, ever deeper, each gem gleams with dwarven pride.
>
> Dwarven beards and dwarven bones, dig, crack, brr.
> Kings and lords and silver swords, dig, crack, hrr.
> We march to war, we heat the forge, even mountains heed our roars.
> Axes gleam, hammers sheen, to battle come the dwarves.
>
> Shout and rumble, stomachs grumble, dig, crack, brr.
> Stout and proud, strong and loud, dig, crack, hrr.
> Thunder rumbles loud beneath the Korrum of our king,
> To war we march our armor sound, unbreakable iron rings.
> Armor, axes, hammers, clubs, dig, crack, brr.
> Drawing all but dwarven bloods, dig, crack, hrr.

Music and hammer-falls upon hot iron rang through the innumerable halls of Karakor, and dwarves joined into the tune from their homes and workplaces. There was a fervor brought on by the preparation for war. Everyone moved faster, ate more, worked longer, and slept harder; the city buzzed. Armor was mended and fitted, weapons forged by the ancestors of ancients were sharpened and buckled to belts that had seen hundreds of battles. Though dwarves had not gone to war as a race for some time, few ever went more than a few years without brushing off their equipment.

Krumrakai sat in a room whose door never closed, and all manner of men and dwarves gave him every whisper of information that had passed through the lips of any being within a day's ride of Karakor. Little of it mattered, but he had a ravenous appetite for knowledge, and he soaked it up like a bearded sponge. He remained passive, most of the time, eyes closed, jammed into his palms, until he heard someone mention there had been almost no activity in Ictheim for nearly a week.

"You there!" He stood and pointed at a dwarf standing a few feet from him, "You, what did you say?"

She came forward, comfortable as always with his gruff summoning of her through this room of fools. "I said Ictheim hasn't had garrison movements or marching orders for a week. A human rode into the city, but no one has left those gates in some time."

Norrin perked up at that, "Tristan sent Urloc there."

"That sounds like probably bad news," Krumrakai admitted.

"There should be something happening there. Certainly a few riders out at least. I would be worried, were this my army." Norrin sounded genuinely surprised and distraught.

The female dwarf who initially told Krumrakai the news butted in, "The trolls have guarded Karakor for centuries, what could change their minds now?"

"Something old." The dwarf king sent everyone away, save Norrin and the dwarf scout. "Dweera, have you heard anything about the New God?"

"Small chatter, here and there, but nothing that makes much sense to me." She shrugged, less than interested in any gods, let alone a young one.

"What's the name you heard him given?" Norrin asked, even as Krumrakai thought it.

The dwarf king had half a mind to slap the ranger across his face for speaking out of turn in the presence of royalty, already building an argument of why it's important to maintain petty rules in times of crisis. He didn't, however, and let the two talk.

"Shkaylhu. Ugly name."

Krumrakai cleared his throat, giving Norrin and Dweera a moment to remember in whose presence they bickered, "Meet me for dinner in an hour or two and I'll tell the two of you a ... story." He nodded, then motioned to the door. Dweera and Norrin left the room quickly, still murmuring to themselves.

206

When they were some ways down the hall, Krumrakai grabbed a book from a nearby shelf. It was almost as tall on the desk as the king himself, and was well read. On the cover of the massive gray binding a single golden rune was embossed. It was simple, but elegant; a single curved line with two breaks in it. *Titun.* In it was written, by hand, every single event that ever happened in Alkurah. Each chapter was dictated by a direct witness, for dwarves were stubborn about their facts. This single book was the most accurate history ever written by prophets, seers, wizards, or kings.

Krumrakai knew it by heart, as did every dwarf king. They would not be challenged by lore-masters of other races, and they never argued for long. He turned to the first chapter, only a few pages in, and recited from memory more quickly than he could read: 'Sypchallu, god of darkness and fear, grew strong in exile, for though the Eova grew in splendor, their bright light casts long shadows, and deep.'

Days passed quickly now, the way they often do on the eve of something great or terrible, and time was a blur. Horses were shod anew, blades were sharpened by the thousands, and every piece of armor and mail that could be found was polished. Alkurah was into its autumn; the days now short and cool, and a healthy wind from the east cast leaves from creaking boughs. More clouds traversed the sky than should for this time of year, and long shadows roamed the earth. In the west was a thunderhead that rolled endlessly. Lightning rent the sky and smote down upon the Kharatvil, and even from Brathur and Soriath men and dwarves saw the doom of the greatest fortress ever built.

Ictheim was nearly empty. Trolls had been whisked to the Dragon's Keep over the course of months, and the evacuation was nearly complete. A handful of guards stalked echoing hallways, and only a single cook worked the massive kitchens intended to feed thousands of ravenous trolls. The armories were emptied, and Queen Whoorlem herself had taken hidden pathways through the mountains to join her soldiers in the Dragon's Keep.

Narod, the small winding river that drips from the towering peaks of the Hudun Mountains, has no bridges. Though narrow, it careens through valleys and clefts in the rock just wide enough not to risk jumping on horseback. There is a single ford, in a low, wide valley nearly untouched by boots or hooves. No trees reach for the stars, and only patches of frozen scrub cling to the dead plains. Once, a great battle had been fought there. It was called Whyrum Garrad, dwarvish for Dragon Grave, for in that lost valley fell the greatest of dragons- Boleth Terrorwyrm- at the hands of a man named Toroc. Whyrum Garrad was the single crossing of the Narod south of the Helseia. It lay in the shadow of the Dragon's Keep, and no army had ever dared attempt to cross in hostility.

Spikes had been set in the frozen earth across the Whyrum Garrad, and killing pits dotted the road at intervals. Trolls abstained from using bows, but the keep was well stocked with javelins and boulders enough to pepper any force that dared cross against the will of the Queen. A single ford lay at the opposite end of the valley that would allow only twenty bodies abreast to pass. The deep Narod had been dammed at one point, and that single narrow boulder allowed easy passage from the Huduns to the plains. An attempt to scale the mountains in order to bypass the Keep would be insanity, for soldiers would have to travel for days atop the uninhabitable peaks.

Queen Whoorlem tossed a hrgeet over her shoulder, pouncing on him before he regained his footing, and tied his legs together. It was a statuesque example of the species, thick horns curled three full times, tightly, on either side of its flat, thick skull. With the speed and strength of a horse and the toughness of a ram, it was a worthy opponent. Course blue fur, perfect camolauge in the frozen peaks, chafed her arms and stomach. The small crowd cheered, not knowing their Queen to be staggered by any beast. In an instant, a shaman transformed the hrgeet into a dwarf, bound and gagged by rough bonds. The cheer grew. Trolls knew they would go to war soon, and the dwarves would once again suffer at their hands. Dwarven blood was coveted above most trophies of war, for they are a tough and warlike species not known to give quarter.

"My Queen, they march," came the single report that stopped any thoughts of gaming immediately. The trolls in the room moved quickly to the armory, and already horns sounded formations across the valley. Over two thousand trolls occupied the Dragon's Keep, and the Whyrum Garrad below it. The sun set early here in the midst of such great mountains, and many hundreds of torches crackled to life. Though they were still a day's march away, the column of smoke was a clear warning signal to the dwarves who would dare pass the valley.

"How many trolls are there at the Keep?" Krumrakai bounced along on his pony, lightly armored in the brisk morning. "And how did you get word to Brathur through all that?"

Dweera shrugged, "I've been places, sire."

The King waved his hand and shook his head, "You're right, I don't care."

"Somewhere around two thousand, I think." The scout cracked her knuckles absentmindedly, "It won't be easy getting through there."

Norrin, still pretending to know what was going on and trying to get a rock out of his boot, asked, "Can't we just go around?"

The dwarves snorted in unison, almost acknowledged the moment, then both looked away before Krumrakai answered, "There's a river in the mountains that's as deep as it is long, so it is said. There is a single ford, in the heart of the Huduns. It's where Toroc slew the greatest dragon ever to defile Alkurah."

"And mountains are tall, right?" Norrin had a victorious bounce in his step, having ousted the offensive pebble, and he felt a touch of confidence as the setting sun glared through a gap in the mountains.

"Impossibly so." Dweera had ongoing conversations with a handful of dwarves as they shuffled to and from her, but never seemed to miss a beat in any of them.

"This is the plot to every pre-battle speech I've ever listened to," Norrin sighed. "We are all going to die here, aren't we?"

In answer, Krumrakai simply laughed, "And what better way to die?"

Norrin muttered, "I could probably think of one or two."

To which the King replied, with raised eyebrows, "Oh, could you?"

Unwilling to be taunted into a bombastic argument with violent undertones, the ranger simply shook his head and moped along beside the king.

Soon, the dwarven army gained sight of Hudu, the great peak that held aloft the Dragon's Keep, and namesake to the whole Hudun range. The march was halted. Scouts vanished into the night, taking to the frozen slopes to keep watch on the trolls and make sure the camp stayed safe. Of course, the odds of anyone leaving possibly the most secure fortress ever built in order to attack a fortified dwarven camp were low. Thousands of torches cast flickers of light upon the face of Hudu, yet they never came even close to touching the summit. Snow started to fall, lightly, and after a few hours tents were dusted, beards frozen, and the roars of the fires did their best to drown out chants and drums.

"Still nothing?" Krumrakai chewed a corner of his mustache, fretting about attacking the Dragon's Keep. "Whyrum Garrad has not seen bloodshed since the slaying of Boleth, and I would rather not fertilize this field with dwarven blood."

Dweera and Norrin, now common sights at either ear of the King, shook their heads in unison. The ranger was straining to see the top of the mountain, admiring the choice of location for its strategic importance. "We're attacking that?" He finally asked, shaking his head.

Dweera produced a noise in her throat of mingled fear and contempt for the idea of fear, "Queen Whoorlem, it would appear, isn't at home."

"Bet your bacon she's over there." Norrin waved an arm toward the river, indicating he assumed she was prepared to actively resist the dwarven advance.

"Bol damn her." Krumrakai's rage grew every moment that passed without word from the trolls, "Our engines of war will shatter foundations older than all the cities of men. Our axes will splinter wood that has stood as long as the sun has risen to bring the dawn."

"And they will return, stronger than ever." Grael said, appearing beside Krumrakai in a cloud of powdery snow, most of which was thrown up by Norrin jumping backwards in fright and tripping on a nefarious rock.

"I never manage to be surprised at the sight of your face, Grael," said the King. "You've a hand in history that is likely unrivaled."

"And you a mind for peace against the attitudes of your sires." The old elf seemed to anyone watching as though he was the one who'd been there all along, and Norrin the one who teleported there in a flash. "I'm sorry to say that Queen Whoorlem is not as reasonable as she once was."

Krumrakai growled, "Sypchallu."

"I've heard that name before," said Grael, his interest winning over his patience, "and there aren't many who would speak it aloud."

"I don't doubt it." Krumrakai motioned everyone into his hut. It was cozy, a little cramped for Norrin in the vertical department, but it was warm and smelled like fatty meat. A carpet of pillows were herded into a corner and everyone made themselves comfortable. "My line is the oldest contiguous ruling bloodline in Alkurah." Krumrakai made a prayer of forgiveness to his ancestors and drew forward the *Titun*. "I can trace it back beyond Karak himself to the darkness before the sun, and never before have my people been subdued by the master of death and darkness. Sypchallu is what was before Bol. His full power has been banished, but ever he sows his seeds and tends his ilk. The world is on an edge, I feel, between the darkness and the light."

The camp about the hut was quiet, as though they could hear Krumrakai as well as everyone in the room with him.

"The blood that stains Whyrum Garrad will not be that of dwarves." Krumrakai threatened to his foe across the valley.

MANY PATHS

Where will you be when the thunder comes, when wind and rain gust?
Where will you be when the world ends and all kneel before Tykus?
When sky falls, and earth shakes, and rivers run with blood,
Kingdoms crumble, mountains fall, and there's nowhere left to run?
Life, in its beauty, struggle, and pain, is by death made a fool.
Crashing waves and scorching flames as the threads of fate unspool.
The weak rely on strong men's arms; they too can be slain by steel.
When all things end, and new life dawns, will the elders rule, or kneel?

The march from Brathur had a soul all its own. The men of Korz were torn between hope, pride, fear, doubt, and the concern that this battle was all somehow above them, as if their presence could not possibly come to matter, in the end. Whispers of dragons and wizards made even the staunchest men flinch. Sorcery, poison, the gods themselves were said to be involved! Roc felt this as much as any ordinary foot soldier. Tristan and Grael made rounds through the camps at night, doing menial tasks and helping the average solders, to lift spirits and show the men that everyone was digging the theoretical shit pit together.

A smattering of trolls and ogres stayed mostly separate from the men. Lack of news from their homelands was disturbing, and some wondered if their blood had been, or was going to be, spilt elsewhere in Alkurah. Most of the human companies were thrilled by the knowledge that Karakor and Hâedra had both mobilized. They questioned the idea that a full alliance of dwarves and men could be defeated in arms by any foe.

Training exercises lasted well into the night now, and the chill wind sent goosebumps up every spine. The fires were never quite warm enough, the sun never quite as bright as it should be, and the food had a way of not quite sating their hunger. Still, every man knew the stakes of the battle to come. Their history had been steeped in the ongoing events for longer than any of them could know.

Far away from the events to the east, the Kharatvil stood, still defended by the Rofu. Gorathel had no way of knowing whether Dyrrktha or any of his riders had broken the defense behind them, so he did all in his power to chip away at the tide of soldiers breaking against his wall. He counted himself lucky that he was pitted against elves, and their white-feathered shafts had slain more of their own than they had his Rofu. The giants had succeeded in putting a crack in the impenetrable gate at the center of the Kharatvil, and they did an excellent job of making sleep impossible, even still. The lygians had proved themselves incredibly thick-skinned. Their tridents were made of a metal no one had ever seen, and each mighty thrust against the gate yielded another divot from the stout wooden beams.

Gorathel was in the storeroom, taking stock of their dismal reserves of moldy food and brackish water. He sighed. A posting at the Kharatvil was supposed to be one of great honor and little action, and he had lamented the idea of not fighting often. And he was never a lover of sieges. The idea of starving to death inside a perfectly good fortress was irritating in a way he could never describe. He told his commanders the hard truth a few nights before. They wouldn't last the month, even if no one managed to find a way inside the walls.

"There in sight an end is," he said, grinding his teeth and trying his hardest not to choke up out of sheer disgust, "Ours, than theirs, is sooner."

He told them about the riders he sent, and that his orders had always been that it was better to starve to death within the walls than to open them to any foe. The world, however, was at stake here more than just the Rofu. Gorathel understood better than many trolls the concept of the world as a living entity, and that trolls were only a part of a much larger mechanism. The Rofu were just another domino, but he would not have them simply fall without a sound. So the commanders had talked it over, without Gorathel present, and they had come to the same decision he had. If the Rofu were going to fall here at the Kharatvil, it would not be behind unbreakable magic walls. The Rofu would fall warriors, and the blood of their enemies would fill their cups in the afterlife.

They reconvened the night after Gorathel's depressing status check, and one orc stood before the rest to speak openly with the troll, "Wedon' likethe'dea of dying ferbunch o' *hurga.*" There was a murmur of agreement behind him. Orcs and Korzians have always disagreed on anything remotely important to agree about, and them benefitting from everything happening at the Kharatvil was a blow to the collective Rofu pride. "But wewilln't become dust hidenbehinwalls. None may know'r names, but they rembrus all t'same." He drew his sword, and just over three thousand Rofu, orcs, goblins, men, and trolls, cheered their deaths.

Gorathel was moved by the ferocity he saw, and his heart welled for what he knew must be done. "I, behind the wall, stay, will. Someone the gate must close."

Every soul present knew this was the greatest sacrifice their captain could make, and they knelt to honor him.

The rest of the army followed suit, and that day was filled with preparations to attack beyond the Kharatvil, with Gorathel tasked to find a way to create enough separation between the gate and the giants to allow his army to attack. Every horse that could be shod and fed was tied together and piled high with food, water, and equipment for Gorathel. He would stay behind the charge, secure the gate, and ride for the eastern gate as Dyrrktha's company had. Hopefully the extra horses would spook the defenders, or at least throw off their aim, and he would make it to Grimfilth to tell him of the coming attack. *At best,* Gorathel thought, *I'll, with an arrow in my back, die.*

Hâedra vanished from sight on the second day of their march, and by now, Garroway and Gunsel were in lands neither had ever set foot upon. Lillian Redmane rode beside Gunsel astride a black horse that bore a single white spot upon his shoulder. She called him Dice, and even though he'd been struck by at least twenty arrows, three javelins, a sword, and one adventurous boar, he remained as healthy as he had ever been. Lillian considered him a lucky charm, and spent most of her time grooming him, when she wasn't challenging Gunsel's sanity. An unlikely pairing, they'd become, but not without their differences.

"I've known you two weeks and I swear to all the gods I've already told you this a hundred times, it's a curse. A real magical one!" Gunsel waved his arms wildly, lost his balance, and accidentally spurred his horse forward. She took a halfhearted step, swatted at him with her tail, and continued on as if nothing had happened.

"And it's always been this way?" Lillian was skeptical of the birds that followed Gunsel. To his credit, no one seemed to understand what it was about him that they liked, and they didn't seem keen on pecking at him. They enjoyed simply irritating him, and being in the way whenever he planned on doing anything other than sit still.

"Long time. It's been a long damn time."

Garroway, who had been snickering to himself for at least an hour straight, added, "I can't tell which of the pairing is in fouler company."

Lillian and Gunsel both leaned forward in their saddles to give him a look of utter contempt. It took a moment, but once they both relaxed, Gunsel simply muttered from the side of his mouth, "I hate you."

"Bah. So," Garroway shouted over his friend, "Lillian, where are you from originally?"

"I grew up in Cirun," she answered, adjusting a strap in her stirrup, "lived off the lake for most of my life. I love the water, and I love fish, so it made sense to move here when I left."

Gunsel, who despised fish, neglected to say so.

The dwarves from Soriath and men of Korz were expected to make Litha several days hence. Hâedra's force had fallen a few days behind, though they made use of the swift Nazene to hasten their advance whenever possible. There was an energy around the column that been missing for some time. Morning cold began nipping at exposed noses and ears, and coats were brought out of packs, reluctantly. The riverfolk often dressed lightly, accustomed to the warmth of the sun on their skin while they rode. It was a long time before the last of them finally surrendered to the cooling air and begun layering their clothes.

Breegan was one of several exceptions. Never once did his attire change from the ridiculous blue sea-coat he wore, and no one ever saw even a shiver from him. He rode a painted stallion, named Meresif, or 'Riverswift,' for his unequalled surges of speed. The pair was the head of a column that stretched some distance into the south, winding along the road long trodden into the dirt beside the Nazene. Rorrik and Throm were behind him, constantly peppering him with questions and arguments and becoming more frustrated by the hour as he stayed calm and refused to argue back.

Finally, Breegan called over his shoulder, "I remember you saying something about your uncle, Thorriman. Would you tell me how he died? In his youth, he and I sailed the same ships and fought under many of the same banners. He was a friend, and I have too few of those left now to take for granted."

The pair of dwarves faltered, having thought of a wonderful attack to crush Breegan's opinion of coats over cloaks, but they would never deny themselves or anyone else the chance to hear a story of their kin. Rorrik cleared his throat, spurring his pony forward a few feet to match Breegan's pace. "It would be my honor to speak of Thorriman's passing."

A bleak sunset offered little warmth, and even Breegan bundled his coat a little tighter as the wind picked up across the river. "Was it glorious, as he always wanted?"

Rorrik paused, searching for the best way to tell his story, and began: "It was sixteen years ago. He was a lover of water as few dwarves are, and he grew to love magic because of the power he could draw from the living waters."

There are few dwarven wizards, owing to the propensity of physical power being viewed as the pinnacle of strength.

"Thorriman was at work on a bridge to cross the Helseia to the north. He thought there was something we may find across the frozen sea, and he worked such a wonder there that I may never see it's like again. Truly unbelievable. I mean-" he started, but could not find the words to finish. It was written on his face as clearly as if it were spoken aloud, what he saw then moved him to awe. "I hope only to witness it again, in my life."

Breegan and Throm waited patiently for Rorrik to overcome his emotion, and the dwarf prince continued: "He made a bridge of ice that would never melt. It was beautiful, the greatest work in this world not hewn by the Alkui themselves, and greater than most of those as well. There are checkpoints every five miles, and there were housed a small contingent to tend fires, care for beasts, and send along messages. But the Helseia is wide, and deep, and there are creatures in the frozen north that we could not have dreamed of." The prince shuddered.

"I've heard things," Breegan started, "about monsters living in the ice."

"What you've heard are fairytales beside the truth, I can promise you." Rorrik's tone made it hard for Breegan not to pity him. "The attacks came more frequently as he worked further, and the wonder of Thorriman became a pilgrimage by many families around the Hudun's. Casualties mounted, and the endeavor became riskier to all involved. The beasts began raiding cities near the water's edge, butchering any in their path. It was awful. They used no weapons, for their claws were sharp as steel. And they wore no armor, yet even the mightiest blows simply glanced aside. The stuff of nightmares, they were." He took a deep breath, shaking the memory away, "But still Thorriman worked. There are different tales about how close he got, whether it was only miles, or maybe even feet, or perhaps he had barely scratched the surface of the vast breadth of the Helseia. In any case, he was alone working his magic when one of the monsters rose up before him. It smote down with one arm, and Thorriman turned the blow aside, slicing back with a vicious strike. Its hide was thick, though, and the blade simply stuck within its flesh and he was cast down by a mighty attack."

"Who told everyone this?" Breegan asked.

"Krumrakai himself," answered Rorrik. "When Thorriman fell, the whole bridge shuddered, and many wondered if he had tethered his life to its survival. In any case, he was tossed into the water, and there he still lies."

There was silence for a time while Breegan digested what he learned. "I find sadness and pride mingled for my friend, as I'd hoped he would find a beautiful death in a great battle. It seems that he did, and what a great one it must have been to fight the Helseia itself. I imagine he is content with his doom. He did always love the water and strange beasts, after all." There was a pregnant pause, then, "What became of the bridge?" Breegan asked quietly, as if he had simply been thinking it and the words happened onto his lips by accident.

Rorrik's eyes were low when he replied, "It's still there, anchored to the shore by massive pillars and chains of ice. None know how far it stretches, and no one is willing to cross it to find out."

When light finally became poor enough that riding would be dangerous to everyone involved, the army stopped. The tallest spires of Litha were only barely visible as miniscule bumps on the horizon, and the wind grew steadily to a roar that tore at tents and threatened to uproot stakes not hammered deep into the soft soil. A brilliant moon glimmered between swollen clouds, and those standing watch were thankful for warm pockets and steaming mead. At some point, a torrent of rain pounded the entrenched soldiers, and they huddled together, hoping their tents would stay dry and rooted to the ground. The wind howled, causing fitful dreams and a restless night to pass more slowly than it ought.

Lygian commanders screeched in their alien tongue to encourage their subordinates. Tridents and cutlasses were gradually chipping away the magical stone of the Kharatvil, but Terea Vo, and Skal above him, were not patient. The elflord himself had made multiple attempts to stir the force into frenzy, but they could never quite make their way over the wall. Still, they hacked and stabbed and made their slow progress. Even Nulau Ra was unsuccessful in her attempt to scale the wall. Three times she tried, and each time she got near the top, her hook failed and she was sent crashing onto a mat of feathers she had set below, just in case.

"Eventually, I have to imagine they'll starve to death," said Nulau, eyes closed and hands laced on top of her head. She was unused to the heat of the desert, and she wasn't much looking forward to the march through Kharat. If there was something for her to do other than watch lizards stab rocks, the heat might be bearable. She was patient to such a degree that even the holiest monk might learn a few lessons, but she hated having to be patient and also not learn anything.

Terea had spent almost three full days staring straight ahead, sitting in a white chair before a table spread with all manner of drinks. He found himself daydreaming more than he probably should have, and he kept waiting for Skal to teleport behind him and set him on fire or something. "I'm seriously going to kill myself if he doesn't do it for me. This is ridiculous."

"Oh, pity for you." Nulau rolled her eyes at him, "At least have some dignity about it."

"I need to wash." Terea announced, storming from the table and grabbing a bucket of warm water. "I hate this place."

"Everyone hates this place," called Nulau, over her shoulder. She kept her eyes closed and rubbed her palms against the cool stone table. The lygian company had taken crushing casualties at the hands of the various defense mechanisms hidden in the stone of the Kharatvil. Logs dropping, flaming tubs of pitch, and scythes designed to swipe ladders from the massive walls. Still, their numbers were ever replenished by the reserves waiting for the order. She knew there was no honor in serving above glorified meat bricks, but she would still do her utmost to keep casualties at a minimum. "Commander Yrlet," she called, summoning the lygian in charge of the front line soldiers, "bring them back. Everyone could use some sleep tonight, I think."

The lygians, giants, and elvish siege machines fell silent almost instantly, and as they retreated from the wall, their true casualties became apparent. From the parapet came a ragged taunt, some of the Rofu calling out the number of enemies slain at their hands, and some simply yelling because it felt good to have this small victory. Mountains of scaly hides littered the ground in front of the gate, and they were shoved aside more than once by those attempting to be the first to breach the fortress. One of the giants roared back, and a pair of arrows bounced from his skull.

Nulau found herself daydreaming about an army of twenty-five thousand giants and the kinds of battle she could do with a force like that. They would be more than a challenge even for a contingent of Braecans. By the reckoning of dwarves, who even the high elves had to admit kept a pretty good record of events, giants are the youngest race in Alkurah, contrary to what many humans believe, and Nulau never stopped wondering if they would ever have the chance to learn to write and build. To evolve. She shrugged and admired the Kharatvil against the sunset. Crimson tendrils snaked across the sky, and dark clouds rushed along, burgeoning with rain that would never fall upon the cracked dirt of Kharat.

She started meditating, skimming her thoughts for anything that may be stressing her in excess. Elves traditionally love the rain. They are fond of water; the idea of such perfect calmness and tranquility hiding storms of such unimaginable ferocity and strength was something they could relate to. The Braecans, even more than their kin, worshipped the sea and rain above all but Bol himself. The great water held a sway over their hearts the way salty breezes entice men to the shores, and they built across it, and within it, giving glory to Ong. Nulau remembered the wars erupting between the elves and the lygians. Elven architects are in the habit of ignoring any concept of natural habitat, and they powered through so many local species they attracted a staunch opposition.

Her father had been part of the advance team, there to clear out any living things in the zone designated for the next building. An overwhelming force of lygians, a group of beings yet unknown to all but the dwarves, had ambushed them. No survivors left the scene and, when they received no report, the builders moved forward anyway. Over nearly a decade, the reptilian lygians bit and clawed the Braeco for every inch of sand, every drop of their watery home. Finally, their queen was captured in a daring raid, which Nulau not only planned but had a large role in undertaking. The queen surrendered for her people, and they were forced to breed cannon fodder for the elves ever since. Nulau had contempt for the concept of slaving, but the lygians had committed unspeakable atrocities during the war, and she could overlook her ideals to see them suffer. Still, it would do no good if they killed themselves pointlessly attacking a wall.

The Rofu huddled within the Kharatvil offered prayers to their gods and undertook a final round of ritual scarring. Each orc, man, goblin, and troll was carved across the chest, a spot reserved for their dying epithet. It said simply, "We fight."

Ritual incense burned in every room that night, and a pillar of smoke rose for miles into the sky. The host camped outside the Kharatvil wondered if some kind of disaster had befallen the defenders, but not a whisper crossed from behind the wall that night. Gorathel counted it a wondrous blessing that the attacking army had ceased their assault that evening, and the Rofu slept soundly for the first time in weeks. They did the job of creating an opening for him, and he would be a princess before he missed an opportunity such as this. The troll commander was awake before dawn, and he paced the gate impatiently as his subordinates assembled their soldiers. He peered into the gray west, seeing an unending host of tents and sentries. This was an army bred for annihilation, that was clear, and he was damned if he was going to let them pass his gate unscathed.

Finally, after hours of jostling and several brutal ear-cuffings, the Rofu force stood in its whole. Just under four thousand bodies were present, malnourished, bedraggled, and wasting. It was certainly no honor guard, nor any sort of elite force. Their ranks bent and shivered as they stood, some slouching or simply sitting in the dust, enjoying their last few moments of life. Most of the Rofu view impending battle, and probable death, with tranquility and acceptance, in the same way humans don't. Elu and Ula displayed their dawn in dazzling fashion, and the flames of morning awoke a fire within the Rofu. They began their chant, howling and screeching at the world itself, and Gorathel opened the gate.

Nulau Ra was disturbed from a round of mediation by the awful howls of the Rofu. She stretched, checked her hair in the mirror she brought from her home in Braeco, and sifted through a selection of armor before settling on the right set. The lygians began clicking and bellowing, and she hastened from her tent to see a fully assembled Rofu host. They had exited the gate only minutes before, and had rushed the lygian camp, howling all the while. Arrows criss-crossed the sky, and screams mixed with roars and challenges as the Rofu claimed their first victims.

The two lines met with a mighty clamor, a sickening cacophony of cracking bones and splintered wood. Both forces shuddered, and the Rofu charge ground to a halt. Nulau waded into the fray, struggling to identify her commanders, who were doing a terrific job of dying. None of the Rofu were even close to contesting her in arms, and she floated through the battle in a mist of blood. Each time she thought her army was about to rally, a troll would smash through a shield wall and the Rofu would swarm the breach. She could see no commander, which surprised her, as the Rofu often were nothing without a strong-willed presence to terrify them into cooperation. Instead, this seemed like a truly coordinated light infantry charge. Cannon fodder versus cannon fodder. She saw no reason why this charge should be happening, as she was certain the siege could have been outlasted for years at least. Already, she was planning to order some of her forces to make for the gate to secure the Kharatvil. She looked up in time to see the gates slam shut, and she cursed herself for ignoring the obvious.

It was hard for Gorathel to close the gates. Harder still for him to destroy the mechanisms that allowed the ancient doors to swing. He hewed springs, chains, counterweights, and timber to ensure that the gates of the Kharatvil would never open again. He stood upon the foremost parapet for hours, watching his brothers fall in heaps before the onslaught of lygian tridents. Their ranks held, and he was proud to see not a single soldier fled or surrendered. He strained against the glare of the sun, watching the distant shadows until the frantic movements of battle ceased. Almost thousand Rofu died that day, each of them with blood dripping from their blades. The battle lasted two hours, but once a handful of giants engaged from within the lygian lines, it came to a swift end. They pummeled the exhausted attackers, standing now solely by their own willpower and habit, and the Rofu charged with defending the strongest fortress in Alkurah were defeated.

Gorathel did not weep. He was familiar with death, and though he had ultimately failed in his duty, there was honor in his defense. He would be proud to join his brothers in the halls of the damned and raise a goblet of blood to honor them. A short, shambling walk led him to the stables, and he checked the packing of all the supplies on the horses, untying and retying knots as he saw the need. Finally, when he could stall no longer, he mounted his beast and shot toward the Rhiam. He understood that the odds he might make it past the occupied gate was minute, and he hoped more than anything that Dyrrktha had survived his trip across Kharat to the Kharatule.

Not even an hour had passed before Gorathel could see a handful of elves standing upon the ancient structure, bows drawn. He was certain they would pick him out, even though he set straw riders upon more than a dozen of the horses riding alongside him. He didn't bother praying, for if the gods were watching him they had long ago turned their backs. There was no point in lying lower to his horse, or keeping silent, and as he entered bow range, he roared and spurred forward. Feathered shafts sank deep into two of his straw dummies, but he did not hesitate or falter. Three arrows passed by his ear, and one buried itself into his shoulder. He held the reins with one hand, coming close enough to the gate to make out details on the elves. Their beautiful bows were inlaid with carvings of such intricate portraits they could have passed for museum pieces. Each arrow had a word scratched into the shaft, but Gorathel couldn't read it, as reading, especially elven words, was something the Rofu took very little stock in.

One fleeting instant passed that Gorathel thought he might survive the trip. He was only feet from the gate now, admiring the looks of panic on the faces of the elves as they realized how close he came to passing them by. They began cutting down his horses now, so he knew they were truly worried, as elves only harm animals in the direst of circumstances. Another arrow sank into his shoulder beside the first, and then he crossed the gate. It lifted his heart to see the sand stretching into forever before him. Then he was unhorsed by an arrow striking him in the back from directly above. The troll sighed even as he crashed to the dust, rolling through his fall to gain his feet as nimbly as a troll could manage.

His horse was only a few meters ahead of him, nervously prancing in place. Gorathel got a hand on the reins before he received another shaft in his thigh, and two more pierced his ribs. Finally, he gave up the idea of mounting and turned, sword in hand. He knew they would never dare his reach, but he was reassured by the weight of steel in his hand. It was the end of the world, after all, and no troll would suffer their final moments unarmed. Gorathel's last regret was that he would be unable to strangle any of the elves grinning at him from their wall.

"*Relia!*" came the final order, and seven arrows hit Gorathel's chest in an instant. Now on his knees, the sword slipped from his bloodied hand. He scrabbled to grasp its hilt, embarrassed that he lost control of his hand in the final volley, and pitched face-first into the dust. The troll commander fell silently, and did not cry out nor writhe in pain as the shafts jutting from his body bent and snapped when he hit the ground. For another half hour he lay there, dying in the dust even as his army had been obliterated beyond the Kharatvil, and the elves paid him no heed.

The next day, Terea Vo brought Gorathel's back to his camp. A troll choosing not to die in battle was an anomaly he simply could not abide. The Kharatvil had been breached during the night and, having cleared out the defenders, the invading army simply scaled the wall, removed the debris blocking the great gate, and fixed the mechanism that controlled its opening. At least, that was the theory. Dozens of climbers slipped, others were unable to find a foothold at all, but, eventually, someone managed to clear the great wall. Using a single rope as their ladder, nearly four hundred Braecan elves were needed to blast the gate open, and even after the force of their magic, aided even by Skal himself, the giants had to pry the wood into a manageable hole.

The elflord brought Gorathel's body to the mobile throne room that Skal inhabited whenever he was in the mood to join the march, and Terea was surprised to find the little man on his chair, stewing over whatever was upsetting him at the moment. He stirred when the flaps opened, but did not rise or speak, instead simply looking at Gorathel's limp form, hanging in the air behind Terea. Finally, he asked with a contemptuous wave of the hand, "What's this?"

"This troll rode against the Rhiam, alone, and is assumed to be the final defender of the Kharatvil to have perished, sir." Terea answered, more militarily than he meant to.

Skal wrinkled his nose, curling a finger to summon Terea to the base of the short stair before his throne, "Come, elf, and witness the Light." He took Gorathel's body in his hands, lifting him as though he weighed nothing, and inhaled deeply. "Rise, enemy, and speak."

The body stirred, and only a moment later, Gorathel's corpse rose to kneel before Skal as though he had simply walked into the tent to give a report. His eyes were jet-black, and his skin still cold, but he gave the impression of life better than any illusion a wizard might summon. He opened his fierce jaws, still painted with dried blood, crackling and flaking to the ground as he spoke. "No more, there are. The Kharatvil has fallen."

Skal nodded, as though he expected as much, and bade Terea to watch, "The Light is powerful, and unmerciful, even in death." The body dissolved then, into an oily puddle of black liquid, and Terea Vo witnessed the desecration of Gorathel as Skal whisked the fluid into a nearby chamber pot. "Such is the power of our god, elf. Take heed that you not become my next victim. I do not look upon failure lightly, and I will not overlook it again."

The elflord understood that it was time for him to leave, and he did, shaken that Skal would take such treatment of the dead so lightly. Even the Rofu respected the dead of their enemies, and they consumed their flesh in honor, not to disgrace their foes. Usually. He climbed to the very wall Gorathel had stood upon to keep up the defense of the Kharatvil, and wondered what the troll had been like in life. He nudged a rotting corpse nestled into a nook of stone. Crumbs of biscuit were still evident on the man's coat, and he sneered even through his final moments of pain, greeting his end with insult on his lips and an arrow through his heart. Terea hated everything further inland than his home. He kicked the body away. These few weeks had been the first he spent out of sight of the Seia Wesrin in an age, and the unbearable sunlight that beat ceaselessly upon their shoulders was more offensive to him than any orc or human.

Terea Vo had lived since the raising of Lau, the moon, and he could remember thousands of years' events with little strain. He'd known Skal for a fraction of a moment in his life, and the little imp's words had transformed the world in more ways than any ever had. Faster, too. But the words were empty, as far as Terea was concerned. Any wizard could perform the tricks he witnessed from Skal, and Terea viewed him just as such: a powerful wizard. He hadn't seen a single event or action that he was unable to recreate in his own chambers, though with slightly worse resolution, and any claim of a new god that was older even than Bol was blasphemy in the eyes of any elf. He continued to be surprised that so many of his people had abandoned their homes and families for Skal's words. But, as he had done the same, he never blamed them for their choice. The power Skal wielded was tremendous, and Terea had no doubt as to the devotion of his followers, but few could claim skepticism greater than that of elves. Following Skal was simply a better idea than opposing him.

Still, the idea of attacking humans gnawed on Terea's mind. He had been a friend to the Haderon, in reaches of time few still could claim memory, and he spent decades riding across the plains and into Eskeria. Across rivers and through swamps, even unto the foot of the White Mountains, and further north than he ever dared since the last Dwarf Wars. Humans were bound to destroy themselves, were they left to their own fate. But, given a common enemy, they had proven time and again their worth in defense of their lives and their homes. The elflord took a certain pride in being the first of his name to ride with dragons, though, and his lifesong was being woven in beautiful events. Under his watch the lowest rung of soldiers in the entire army had overtaken the greatest fortress ever built, impermeable even in the face of the rage of the Alkui themselves. There was pride in that worthy of a twinge of blasphemy.

The stop in Litha was brief and hectic. Soldiers and merchants jostled about, trading precious coins for soft leather, clothing, shoes, or food for the march. On their way out, they promised not to steal anything, and hustled away from the menacing glares of the distrusting Lithan population who was certain they had been swindled.

Then, the men of Korz were on the march again. Some twenty five hundred dwarves joined the march seamlessly in the span of only three days, a feat as legendary as any ever recorded, and every heart felt bolstered by the united might of men and dwarves. Their first night out from Litha there were massive bonfires that threw dancing shadows, howls of laughter poured from every tent as stories were shared between soldiers. The mood was pleasant and fresh, as though for the first time in ages there was something to hope for even in the face of death itself.

Hâedra's soldiers then arrived, resupplied, and caught up to the Korzian force swiftly. There were stiff nods of greeting, supplemented by a smattering of terse welcomes. A handful of hearty shouts and familiar handshakes broke the sullen monotony. Gortrum was glad to see a face he recognized, as mercenaries make few friends, and keep even less. His smile wiggled free of his beard and he reached down to give a bear hug to Lillian Redmane. Gunsel, who had shaken the man's hand and had a brief conversation with him before Lillian recognized him, shook his head in disbelief and did his best not to attract any birds. He failed, of course, and smacked a curious gull square on the beak for coming too close. After separating from Gortrum, Lillian and Gunsel were challenged to a drinking contest by a dwarf couple. There were several accusations of cheating, a mug that took an unfortunate bounce off Gunsel's forehead to shatter a bystander's monocle, and everyone rested where they lay, content in the drink and company alike.

Sleep was a particular treasure that Garroway was finding hard to dig up. His dreams were of fire and death, the cracking of the world itself beneath the onslaught of some invisible force. When he woke, he felt as fearful as his dreams, and thinking about the imminent possibility of death put stress on Garroway that weighted his limbs and lined his face. This particular night, he sulked on his bed counting the holes in his tent's ceiling. He gave up at thirty-four, taking no pleasure in the knowledge that if it rained he would almost certainly drown. Standing up seemed like a chore, so he simply scooted across his bed and poked his head through the flap of his tent. He squinted against the sudden glare of the blaze. To his immediate, acute regret, he made eye contact with Roc. The old man stumped around the fire, a cheer in his wake, and finally convinced everyone to leave him alone. Garroway assumed this was achieved through vague threats of violence that probably overreached realistic need.

"Have you been avoiding me?" Roc's voice ruined an otherwise only vaguely unpleasant evening for Garroway, and the younger man groaned in general disgust.

"No."

"Well, that reassures me."

"G'night then."

"Mmhm," Roc mumbled, shoving a blanket aside to sit across the tent from Garroway. "This will be the end of things, I fear, for us."

Apocalypse talks around the campsites were beginning to decline, in response to the superstition that if they mentioned it, it would probably happen. Garroway possessed the armor of the Godslayer, and as far as he had experienced, was invulnerable while he wore it. That was something he preferred not to test, but if he stood alone before a sea of flesh and steel, he would stand as long as it took. "If you know something I don't, please share it with me. If not, I'd appreciate you not cursing my doorstep with your brimming reserve of doomsday speeches."

"You want the full truth? The weight of the truth is a burden my shoulders alone were meant to bare, but I will give you a glimpse, if you think yourself worthy. You are the heir to bear it, after all, are you not?" Roc snorted in disgust to see the man wallowing in self pity even on the eve of the greatest battle of their time. "Queen Whoorlem, the troll monarch, has barred the passage of fully half the reinforcements the commanders were expecting at Soriath. And that's not including the trolls we expected to march with us. Now I'm faced with the very real possibility of a troll army rising on my flank while I wage battle against the greatest army to march under a single banner since before the Sundering."

Garroway managed to look convincingly horrified while trying to mask the suddenly powerful urge to retch in fear, "Why would you tell me that?"

"You need to understand the weapon you wield, and you need to wield it properly." Roc sealed the tent, gaining Garroway's full attention. "I am one of the Veiled, Ro. I don't expect that to mean anything to you, but to any who would consider themselves scholars, that's important. I'm immortal in a sense truer even than elves." He drew his sword, garnering an alarmed glance from Garroway, and drove it into his own throat.

A strangled gag disguised as a cough was Garroway's sole response, until Roc withdrew the sword. A gout of blood splattered to the floor, then Roc simply wiped the knife clean, and sheathed it. The skin knit itself shut, and within moments only a faint pink scar remained. One of many.

"What was that?" Garroway managed, without vomiting all over everything.

"I cannot die. I've been present since the dawn of mankind on Alkurah"

"So what's your real name? How many stories have I heard about you?"

"None, thus is my curse made real. I won't say more on that now, but trust me when I say I've seen bad shit happen to good people. That armor you have is evil, and it is cursed, wicked, and dreadful by its very nature. To truly bond with it, you must feed it."

"I'll assume you don't mean feed in an innocent manner." Garroway tried to fake a grin.

"Souls and blood. Not petty numbers, not of the sort you've slain in your recent warriordom. It craves the death of powerful wizards, of kings and gods. You've fed it scraps when it hungers for armies. And it now stands in almost sole opposition to one. Sure, I'll kill a bunch of them, but eventually they'll take me captive and figure out how to destroy me, even me, one of the Veiled. Grael and Breegan, their power nigh limitless, will slow down and be overrun, in time. Even the Alakhan can be destroyed. I know. You, and you alone, for no other could possibly resist the future that marches toward us, will find yourself without aid at the end. In those moments, you will be consumed, and the world will change."

No witty retorts leapt to Garroway's tongue of their own accord, and he certainly wasn't going to think of any, so Roc exited the tent with no further fanfare.

In the mists left behind by the Vulkha, whose actions brought the ill will of Bol, the creator, is a powerful magic of ancient potency. Sages say it is an omen of what becomes of challengers to Bol's pride. Others believe it a weapon yet unsheathed. Still more simply think it a place of evil, and avoid it entirely.

They are not all wrong, in their own way, and, save ogres, extraordinary sorcerers, and corpses, none but the Veiled may pass through the fog. Often enough, the men of the Veil remain as they were born: unknown and mysterious. Many of the few have found work for the dwarf kings. Others fight as mercenaries, nothing but a cheap bag of gold to the outside world.

Roc found himself dreaming of a different path. The path he had walked so long ago.

A unique problem the Veiled face is that they had no individual to model their behavior and speech off of. Thus, most come across as wildmen or idiots to the outside world. Some never shake off this mantle.

But Roc learned, as had many since himself. In his youth, he ran through the wild north naked and terrified. He was hunted, wounded, and scarred. Horrendous gashes knit themselves shut in minutes. Vicious monsters stalked his every move, and he learned. The steps they took, the paths they crept upon in the night, when they inhaled sharply before bearing down upon him. Each night, death embraced him, and each morning he rose once more to be smote down.

Until one night, his fourteenth year wandering Alkurah, he heard a snap in the forest. It must have been half a mile away, but it crashed upon him like thunder. In an instant, his eyes grew sharp, and his wits doubly so. The world grew clear to him, sharper, as though it had been viewed through a fogged glass all his life. Scents of loam and the forest's decay overwhelmed him. Moist, shallow fog clung to his ankles. A shadow changed, flickered a fraction of a degree further than the rest. Gone was the scent of grass and dirt. Now there was aggression. There was hunger. There was power. And Roc smelled all of it. The pressure around him changed, as though somewhere nearby, something was rushing toward him. He trusted his gut, ducking and swinging a leg out in a wide arc.

It crunched into something that yielded a howl of pain and thudded into the frozen loam behind Roc. It scrabbled against the solid dirt, but Roc had seen this innumerable times. The monster would regain its feet and overpower him. So he had cut himself a knife of wood the night before, hardening it over the fire. It darted forward, and he lashed out with the knife. It thudded into soft flesh, lodging against bone. An unearthly scream ripped through the air, then died with a gurgle.

Roc shivered, not quite facing the monster he had slain. Hot blood dripped from his arm. The sun set on him, motionless in the clearing, waiting for the beast to leap to its feet and bear him to the ground once more. But it did not. It would never rise again.

In the coming centuries, elves passed him by, camoflauged in the mud. Dwarves cracked rock inches from his face and never batted an eye. Trolls cooked feasts with timber cut an arms length away. And Roc learned from them all. Forestcraft, cooking, cleaning, bathing, and speech. Some days he was a merchant, others a sellsword. Some days he lived to see the end of, and some days he was slain in battle, only to rise, as always, once his wounds healed themselves.

When he felt ready, Roc made himself into a warrior. The swords of great men, the bows and daggers of legendary elves, and the axes and hammers of the most stoic dwarves often learned at the knee of Roc. He took many names and lived many lives before the one he now felt rushing to an end. Whyrumdur, Tralapar, Old Tor, Roc. His dreams were of many lives: his own.

Stretching his aching knees and scowling at anyone who dared meet his withering gaze, Roc rose from the fire and stalked to his tent. Soldiers all around him chewed their dried meat, guffawed at their own raunchy humor, or flatulated offensively. Just as they had for centuries, and ages hence. And, if Roc had anything to do with it, would continue to do until the end of time.

THE DRAGON'S KEEP

Give unto me your tired and weak, in my own image shall I remake.
Open your hearts and minds to me, and your great appetite I can slake.
Worship your god and feed me the blood of those unworthy deemed.
Give unto me the souls of the damned and bathe in the gory stream.
I am the giver, the taker, the maker. In my favor stand only the blessed.
My faithful will rise and stand, and rule, as gods above the rest.
All I require is a gift no higher than battle, and war, and death.
Those who fall are honored supreme; their souls again will find breath.
I've come, I'm here, to bring honor and fear. At my feet all will kneel.
My armies: the living, the dead, are bred to grease great War's wheels.

Through the night, and the unnatural mist that choked the deep valley of Whyrum Garrad, teams of dwarves had been working tirelessly to construct five siege weapons a human could scarcely comprehend. Their workings were simple in that they threw rocks in a general direction, but their accuracy and power had been perfected to the utmost. Little known to any but a handful of the king's most trusted allies knew what happened beneath the throne of the king. His forge was of magic, and the weapons and armor crafted there would never break or dull, and most were imbued with such elemental properties as fire or lightning, that nature itself seemed to lend aid to the wielder. Each individual piece of the colossal structures being assembled on the plain had been forged, smoothed, lathed, sanded, and perfected within, and their mighty power seemed to resonate from their ancient mechanisms.

For centuries, dwarves and trolls had been at peace. But dwarves are practical, and they understand the possibility of betrayal, so just as the *Titun* passed hands through generations, so did knowledge of the *Alkui Mechi,* the God Machines. These had been handcrafted by the finest smiths and architects for an age, designed to breach the otherwise unassailable Dragon's Keep. Others, there were, designed for overcoming the Kharatvil, and even for breaking through the magical defenses elves wove into their structures. But these few were the true marvels.

Krumrakai nodded, pleased at how quickly his siege commanders had raised the engines. Each was loaded with little attempt at stealth; but if any of the defenders happened to simply look out a window they would notice the engines. Still, the dwarf king was confident they would be overlooked, as their true power was unknown to all the world until Krumrakai himself gave the order to unleash it.

A watery sun struggled to pierce a fog slow to relinquish the world from its dewy grasp. Dawn broke without much fuss, and the army from Karakor made no hurry of armoring and mustering before the ford of the Narod. Dweera was among the first milling about on the parade grounds, kicking at a pile of mud for almost an hour before Norrin slogged to her side. His hair was disheveled, and he had clearly not slept well. She didn't say anything about it, but they both knew.

Krumrakai stumped to his place at the head of the formation. He mounted his hrgeet, whose midnight-blue fur was as marvelous as a jewel. He took a moment to adjust his stirrups before finally appraising his army. The Alkui Mechi were not meant to move, so they had been built a few feet in front of the camp. Each dwarf enjoyed a moment of awe in the face of such craftsmanship, and some knelt in respect to the monuments of their kings. Krumrakai's powerful baritone echoed across the narrow corridor of Whyrum Garrad, "Before you stand the Alkui Mechi, handforged and handcrafted beneath the thrones of my forebears with one purpose in mind." He raised a thick hand, motioning to the engineers. Without a sound, he dropped his closed fist and four boulders erupted from their slings, whipped forward with enough force to destroy the machines that held them entirely. Thirty-five hundred dwarves and Norrin bore witness to two boulders smashing into stones that had been sealed with mortar thousands of years before. The first exploded, casting shards that would land as much as a mile from the impact. The second breached the Keep, and the cheers of the dwarves nearly overshadowed the sorrow of the act.

Terac had been on watch through the night, sitting in his chair overlooking Whyrum Garrad. He had reported the building of the catapults when he first realized what was happening, but that had been hours ago and nothing had changed. Watch duty in the Dragon's Keep was a necessary evil, but a boring one. Each troll within the Keep knew they would never get the chance to see a real battle, and they accepted that their few months of service would pass quickly and uneventfully.

Until Queen Whoorlem visited the Keep nearly six months before, and the numbers garrisoned were been steadily increased. Not many bodies stayed in the Keep itself, but instead were camped upon Whyrum Garrad, on the Alkurah side of the Narod. If the dwarves were going to leave the Huduns, it would be through a troll army. Those within the Keep were given charge of massive bows and slings with which to hurl stones and spears upon any army assembled below. There were markings on the ground, invisible unless high enough above them to see, and the dwarves had camped just beyond their range. Their catapults were set almost upon the range marker, but Terac's commander had assured the trolls that nothing could possibly reach the Keep.

But that was a few hours ago, and Terac was starting to get nervous watching the builders. Every few minutes, one would stop to cast a spell or pray over a joint or mechanism, then hammer it in place. The size of the boulders that had been loaded within their hearts was enough to make Terac worry, but seeing the assembled might of the dwarven army behind these engines was impressive even if those within the Keep were under no threat of danger.

Far below, Terac heard someone shout something, and suddenly he was watching a boulder the size of a house turn itself to dust on the side of the Keep. He almost had time to get out of his chair before the second shot destroyed the wall, plowing through the Keep entirely, and exiting the backside covered in limbs and blood. The wails of the wounded rose into the gray morning, and Terac glanced at the window once more. A third boulder missed the Keep, but impacted the mountain it was anchored to with such force that he swore the entire castle shifted. He could hear cheering from below as the dwarves watched their machines pulverize the Dragon's Keep, and Terac heard the evacuation order ripple across what was left of the crumbling fortress. Already, trolls were scrambling to climb clear of the wreckage, and a fourth impact set the world tumbling around them as the Dragon's Keep rattled free of its foundation, dissolving as it slid down the face of the enormous Mount Hudu.

Terac scrambled against the falling stones, slipping and leaping sideways across the mountain, hoping to reach a stable platform of the building. His foot punched through a broken beam, which ripped his thigh open to the bone. He swatted at a falling piece of glassware, roaring through the pain in his leg and now the shards of glass in his fist. A handful of his brethren had escaped and were scaling down Hudu, hoping to rejoin the rest of the army in the valley below. A bench slammed into Terac's chest, pulling his fingers from their holds, and leaving him now suspended entirely by the vise holding his leg in place. A table behind the bench that was now careening to the ground ripped Terac from his leg, and he wailed in pain and rage for twenty-five seconds before hitting the ground with enough force not to damage the mud at all. He died instantly, and the Dragon's Keep buried him.

Norrin was impressed, but he failed to see what this accomplished in terms of crossing the Narod in the face of an entire troll army. His worries were partially assuaged when he realized the final machine had not yet fired, and actually required no adjustments to its aim. Instead, it was lined up across the river at the peak nearest the opposite side of the Narod, and the one closest to the trolls.

Krumrakai's face betrayed no emotion, but he counted it a grievous wound to destroy such a masterpiece. Still, in war there would be casualties, and he preferred to inflict them rather than suffer them. He spurred his hrgeet gently, and lumbered forward. The army behind him lurched, and suddenly the valley was filled with the thunder of heavy boots marching in time. He raised his hand once more, and again it fell, and the final machine hurled the fifth boulder. The Broken Peak, or *Krak Kea*, as it would be called afterwards, cracked, and from it came a terrible avalanche that smothered as many trolls in the coming days as it outright killed by force. Stones rolled across Whyrum Garrad, but boulders rained upon the enemy encampment.

The trolls cried out, saving what wounded they could among the buried. The dwarves heard their pain, and cheered, quickening their pace in excitement to finish what the avalanche had started. Passing the remains of the Dragon's Keep was a somber, if victorious moment for Krumrakai, and the cheers redoubled.

The mountain slid to the far side of the valley, turning a once beautiful landscape to ruin. Tents and bodies did not slow falling stones, and the dirt hurtled even unto the ford of the Narod, bridging it over entirely, and temporarily damming the shallow river. This would be the bridge which a dwarven army would cross in battle, and so were the plans of Krumrakai made clear, but not in their entirety. Krumrakai, though secluded within Karakor and shying from communication with the other races, had not neglected diplomacy, and he always maintained a healthy friendship with the nearby ogre tribes.

When he sent asking if a few soldiers could be spared, the entire population had taken up arms and traveled through day and night to supplement the king. He asked that they wait three days, and then advance onto Whyrum Garrad in full fervor. Through secret tunnels his messengers ran, trading off messages and enjoying neither sleep nor food. Finally, his plan had come to fruition, and two thousand ogres burst through narrow pass behind the troll camp. Krumrakai was pleased he still had some semblance of a tactical mind, and was hoping to avoid battle altogether, for now.

Queen Whoorlem's mood had been wonderful that morning. She had risen from a deep sleep, donned her armor, and eaten a hearty breakfast of meat, raw. The world was hers to rule, and with Shkaylhu himself as her reinforcement, there could be no opposition. The building of the Alkui Mechi intrigued her, but her confidence in the Dragon's Keep was absolute, and never once did she imagine any machine made by mortal hands would breach it.

Her good mood dissolved as quickly as her confidence in the Keep, and she watched her greatest treasure turn to a pile of rubble at the foot of a mountain. Her world had changed quite drastically, and suddenly there was a reason to treat Krumrakai and beg for mercy. When the fifth machine cleft the mountain beside her camp, the Queen herself ordered arms laid down and surrendered to the dwarves. Her first thoughts were of her people, and she would suffer any wrath to protect them. She thought back to when she received a report of strange tracks behind them in the snow, assuming it was a rogue herd of hrgeet or any of the other beasts that wandered the frozen passes. Almost as an afterthought she realized a scout was yet to return that morning. He must have stumbled upon something more dangerous than a herd.

The Ogres of Sor, an abbreviation of an ogrish name that takes so long to pronounce that even the dwarves didn't bother writing it all down, crashed through a snow-covered pass behind Whoorlem's camp, full of slobber and throbbing forehead veins. She sent riders as swiftly as they could ride to surrender before their hammer strike fell. Several tense minutes passed as she struggled to keep track of her riders among the chaos. Riders bearing flags of surrender hurdled fallen bodies and debris, ignoring the cries of wounded about them, and raced the ogres to their front lines. With relief, she saw a hrgeet meet the ogres before the clash of arms. They slowed, clearly regretting the idea of missing a good slaughter, and finally stuttered to a grudging halt.

A shout echoed across the valley, and Whoorlem saw Krumrakai, in full splendor, mount the bridge of rubble now settling across the Narod. Its banks overflowed, and the ground beneath her was swamping. She hurried to the front of her army, making clear to Krumrakai that she had no wish to fight, at least on these terms. He dismounted, honoring her by not treating her as a defeated foe, and asked, "How long has it been since we were friends, Whoorlem?"

"Sorry, not, am I for the choices I for my people made, but I regret that a dear friend was, to me, lost." Whoorlem was disgraced. She was defeated utterly, dominated, and was yet to shed even a drop of the enemy's blood in her failure. Her name would be scorned among her people, and they would never appreciate the gift she gave them in saving their lives that day. "What shall we, for our failures, suffer, King?" She asked, as she knelt, proffering her club.

"Everyone fails, now and then, and who am I to say I am above temptation? The world turns, still, Whoorlem, and we breathe the free air, as free people. And so do you," he lifted her up and returned her club. "Whatever loyalty you had with the enemy, it will be severed entirely, or I will order the absolute annihilation of your kind without hesitation. Treason against me, now, is treason against life itself, and I will not abide such foolishness."

"I understand. If harm any of my people seek against you or yours, I will, them, personally execute," Whoorlem grunted, hardly daring to believe what she heard.

"Lucky for you, I believe you, because I think you're smarter than Sypchallu suspects." Krumrakai clapped her on the side, climbing back into his saddle, "I like you, always have." His day had gone exactly as planned, which is something no one yet had ever said about a battle plan, and he wasn't about to jinx it by slowing down. "We're riding to Soriath, then to Litha, then Rivit. Ultimately, I believe we'll end up fighting whatever you've sworn service to. I would feel better with you at my side rather than beneath my hammers. I would learn, before I make any decision, what you know."

Thinking about the possibility of Shkaylhu finding her made the troll shiver, but her life was not worth that of all her people, so it was an easy decision for her. She nodded.

"Then come with me, and let's lunch before the first army of dwarves to do so in four hundred years descends upon Alkurah in full armor, well-fed and furious. Makes me shiver." He was truly enjoying the day, especially as he met up with the

leader of the ogres, Dooblidum Bumbilum, and decided to call
him Id. His army was breaking up the trolls into smaller units,
hoping an insurrection to be less likely, and the ogres took
their place in the van, breaking up ice and snow to make room
for the combined armies.

Krumrakai sent Norrin off with a horse to try and find
someone who knew where everyone was supposed to be, and
the Ranger rode even before the ogres to find any clues he
could about what had happened in his short separation from
the world. Dweera was doing her best to plan rations after
gaining nearly three thousand trolls. They could mostly hunt
for themselves, she assumed, and perhaps would help keep
supplies topped up as they passed out of the mountains.
Finally, when all other things he could think up had been
tended to, Krumrakai met with Id and Whoorlem in a small
clearing, their little island of calm amid the bustle of an army.

Whoorlem spoke first, out of courtesy to her better, and
said, "What is, of the world, becoming?"

"I will share with you what I've shared with any other
when I say that I do not know what drives our enemy. Some
say he is an old god, ancient as the darkness itself, and some
call him Shadow, or Death. Whatever it is, it has assembled a
mighty force of more than just elves. We march to battle for the
very soul of Alkurah, for life itself, as I said before, so I don't
take this war lightly. There isn't time to do anything stupid or,
and curse me for bringing it up, discuss anything, so I'll simply
ask that you all trust me and learn what you can on the way."
Krumrakai took a massive bite of a piece of salted beef and
chewed it a few times on his way out. Shortly after, he stomped
back in, took another huge bite, then left for good.

Krumrakai ordered the trolls to be reassigned to
Whoorlem, and she would lead them independently of
dwarven formations. She and the dwarf king would remain in
contact, however, and they set off toward the great battle
together.

WISDOM

A poet knows it and goes it alone; a poet's words are strong.
A story untold can be heard manifold, even truths can be proven wrong.
A warrior fights and dies beside his brothers and sisters in arms,
By steel and sweat each army is met and their blood kindles fires warm.
A king might rule, or be a fool, but his word is made law all the same.
A fool might jest or fight or rest, and be content with only a name.
A god needs disciples, and zealots, and words to spread worship afar.
Defeat and heresy, loss of faith, even the Alkui can be marred.

Grumbubum Lumblegurb became fast friends with Bendragel, and the two found they agreed on almost everything, which erased any tension that might have occurred between the two. Bendragel, it seemed, was allergic to more than just the flowers that grew upon the Bolepha. The further north they went, he was relieved to see fewer of the blue blossoms beside the road. His symptoms subsided for a time, but they returned with force after they left Litha. Apparently, there was a type of tree nut that the locals ate, and their empty shells littered the road. Bendragel had to be given a horse by one of the Korzians, who was finally fed up with hearing him sneeze. The horse helped, but Bendragel's eyes were red and puffy to the point that Grum took the reins to guide him, as the troll could hardly see. "Awful this place is. Flowers damned be, and nuts damned too," was his only sentence over the course of an entire two-day period, and Grum simply nodded.

The strange pair came to find that Bendragel's father and one of Grumbubum's uncles fought together far to the south, among an army raised by the previous troll king bent upon destroying a colony of wicked humans with olive skin. They called themselves *Nieth*. Choosing a name for their people was something they had never thought about, and when they first met with the elves of Braeco, it was suggested that they should choose a name for their kind. Translations were rough, at the time, and they took the advice as a suggestion to name themselves 'Nieth.'

Warriors of Nithalin are fierce, and their women grew tall and strong in the harsh southern heat. It became normal for the men to work farms and hunt while women tended to the homes, but eventually the traditional roles were reversed, as the women found themselves with more free time than work, so they took to learning the art of war with vigor. Now, male soldiers were outnumbered, as the female Nitha were bred for war and men for a softer home-life. The company of trolls and ogres that Bendragel and Grumbubum's relatives had fought with were defeated in their first engagement. Shortly after, the troll king died, and the campaign was abandoned after only a single battle.

Grum and Bendragel talked more of their homelands than anything, reminiscing to a sympathetic ear about the differences between their normal lives and living with humans. Apparently, trolls believe themselves to be excellent cooks, capable of producing masterful flavors in their splendid kitchens. They're wrong, of course, and Grumbubum had spent time among the trolls enough to know as much, but he nodded along with his friend, content to let him complain.

The ogre missed the magic in the air of the Swamps, having lived a large part of his long life in the fen of the Meredun. Ogres and trolls have a keen sense for magic, varying in their uses tremendously. Trolls use their awareness as a defensive tool, a mechanism evolved to help them survive. Ogres, on the other hand, seem to feel magic the way one might feel a breeze on their cheek; they taste it, they see it, and they hear it, and though they can't draw sustenance from the magic itself, they can draw strength from it. Grum missed sitting alone in the pools, letting magic into his mind and growing strong in body. He missed challenges such as only the magical beasts that roam the swamps could possibly bring. More than anything he missed the great calmness of his world. Humans were always doing, going, fighting, on and on until half of them died. Then doing it all over again a few years later. It would be an insult to an ogre to accuse them of falling behind in sheer numbers of wars fought in, but humans had a way of making wars last for decades that irritated Grum. He enjoyed learning strategy, as ogre wars are generally just groups of ogres pummeling one another with trees until most of one half is unconscious, and afterwards everyone gets drunk and feasts. No politics, no hurt feelings. Just good, bloody violence.

Strategy was a novel concept of maybe hiding some of your ogres, or having some with different weapons, and so on. It held no appeal to him in his youth, and it scarcely appealed to him now. He still preferred a good beat down to an ambush, given the choice.

Eventually, Bendragel's allergies subsided again and he dismounted, picking up conversation with Grum where they left off.

Garroway continued to struggle with his fears, and the armor, packed in a trunk stashed in the corner, drew his gaze often. Saving the world was certainly something he deemed a worthy cause, but dying for it still seemed a little extreme. The world hadn't ended yet, and Garroway still felt relatively safe. He may have racked up a number of unpaid debts and probably insulted a king or two, but nothing he was thus far unable to escape. It was hard to imagine something so vast and swift that he could not outrun or outwit it.

Yet another part of his mind felt the truth in what Roc told him, and his mood soured further. This battle could be the end of dwarves, men, and orcs. Or it could be the end of everything. Or it could just be a battle, and one side would win, and nothing much would come of it through the scope of time. Still, the possibility of such destruction drew forth Garroway's inner courageous hero, which was a side he was surprised to see finally be thrust into the forefront. So he would stay, but he decided not to be idle, and took up the sword to dive into a set of warm-up motions Roc had taught him what seemed an age ago in the fortress of Brathur.

Facing staunch opposition in the form of his bladder, Gunsel was four rounds into losing yet another drinking competition. The soldiers found that drinking and gambling were the only realistic pastimes outside of training, and training felt like work most of the time, so the open grounds were often only occupied by a few groups of friends at a time.

This game was one Gunself had never played. He felt that he grasped the general concept, but the finer strategies eluded him, and he took another swig of the lukewarm liquor. It had an assortment of beer, rum, wine, and a kind of drink the trolls make, called *Stom*, the word for stomach in trollish. Traditionally, if the Stom made you throw up, it was considered good luck. Gunsel didn't consider himself well versed in troll traditions, but he managed to keep his bile at bay as he slammed the mug upon the table and passed it to his left.

Having been well trained by Gortrum, and experiencing a handful of battles already, Gunsel knew he was strong in arms and was at least capable of using magic if he bothered to remember to do it. His paunch was returning, albeit slowly and not nearly to the same capacity as it had seized his body before. The twin axes rested on his belt, nudging him gently with each step he took, and reminding him that the world was not all drinking and happiness. Sometimes, at night, he would become blind, waking from his dreams to find a world gone black. Shadows lashed out at him during the march, and as the days grew shorter, the fearful night grew long. Lillian would sometimes ask him, but he couldn't tell her the truth. He knew the Rofu had poisoned him, and though they were apparently allies now, his body wouldn't be the first thrown upon the pyres as they marched. Few wounded were left now from the battle of Brathur, and Gunsel found himself fearing the darkness ever more as time went on.

In the past, Gunsel had always been certain his life would turn out perfectly. Growing up outside of Vahir, he always longed to visit the city. Seeing the brooding towers on a clear day was a thrill that never lessened, and he would daydream about living behind the safety of the walls as he rested in the arms of the lone tree near his home. Being a warrior never crossed his mind, as he had always been somewhat chubby and better at simply blending into a scene than punching his way out. So he turned to thieving, and by the gods was he good at it. The village that sprung up near his home offered few opportunities to snatch a bag of gold, but he found things to take all the same. Some things he stole for their value, others for the thrill, but always he gave anything she might find use of to his mother, Saree, who raised her four children alone in a shack outside of the city. He never knew how she managed it, and he never got the chance to ask.

The mug passed by him once more, this time on the way to a poor dwarf who clearly was not well seasoned in the various liquors of the world. The foul concoction dribbled through his beard as he attempted to drink some of it. Gunsel shook his head, wondering why he found himself reminiscing the forgotten past at a time such as this.

East of Korz, in the plains, there was constant fear of famine. Each spring the cities would brace for the possibility of blizzards coming down from the White Mountains, or the Huduns, armies of swarthy men and women raiding from the south, and drought. He was eleven when the rain stopped. Within Vahir were storage wells that could last for years, if need be, and enough food to fill the caverns dug beneath the city. Not everyone was allowed in, however, and Gunsel remembered his mother's tear-stained face as she gathered up her skirts, grabbed his little hand in hers, and whisked him back inside her home without another word to the guard who told her that she had to stay here. He never took his helmet off, and thinking back, Gunsel was certain he had been crying, knowing that by following his orders he was killing this family. But he left without an offer of salvation, and Gunsel's mother smiled to her son, pinching his pudgy cheeks and scooting him out into the grass to play. A few weeks passed by with little change, but Gunsel noticed the plates were less full each meal. Saree would often sit on their porch in an old chair whose legs had been gnawed to splinters by wild dogs, and she looked at the city on the horizon.

This time, the mug was his to add to, and he donated a generous portion of his tankard to it. A smell that truly cannot be described wafted to his nose as he passed it back to the dwarf. Finally, the poor creature vomited. He was cheered and hoisted up onto a pair of shoulders, having lost and won the game at the same time. When the ruckus subsided, Gunsel took an absent-minded sip from his cup before throwing it across the table in disgust. He kicked his legs onto the table, closing his eyes against the setting sun, and allowed himself to remember.

An announcement was posted in the village. Everything important was nailed to the door of the same building. It was not a church or meeting hall or anything, just an abandoned house where no one lived to be upset about all the banging and nails. Gunsel couldn't read, but everyone seemed to be shocked by the announcement, so he pretended to be as well. That night, most of the villagers gathered what little they could carry, loaded packs onto their bony nags if they were lucky enough to own one, and left, hoping to find sanctuary in a city that had already denied them.

He watched everyone leave, trudging in a solemn line into the horizon. His mother told them to go to bed, and he gazed from his window at the moon shining down upon barren plains only just starting to crack from the lack of water.

A few more days passed with no incident, and Gunsel wondered if his mother had made a mistake and everyone else had been allowed into the city. His questions were answered that evening as only three people returned, their clothes ragged and torn, bleeding and hungry. One man wept and howled at the villagers who had stayed behind when they approached to clean his wounds. He died that night of infection. They buried him in the early morning hours. Gunsel tried to piece together information from the returned, but they kept silent, especially about their encounter, and often glanced about them as though someone were waiting behind every shrub to attack them.

Seven days passed, and Gunsel could see his mother wasting as she took no food for herself. He tried to convince her to eat, even stealing food from the neighbors against her directions not to. "We'll have enough, and everyone deserves a chance," she said, refusing the meat he pilfered and ordering him to return it. That evening, as the sun set upon another day,

Gunsel dozed on the roof, taking in the view of the plains whenever his eyes would flutter open.

With a jolt, he stood up, realizing he was no longer watching the sun, as it had long set by now, but a group of torches carving a path toward his home. He could scarcely breathe, hurtling to the dirt and losing precious time scrabbling with the door. He nearly tore it from the hinges, shouting, "Mother, we need to leave. Now!"

He gathered his youngest sister, Soran, and kicked open the door to the other bedroom. Saree could hardly move, having not eaten more than scraps for weeks now, and though she sensed the alarm in her son's actions, she simply could not muster the energy to get up, and instead begged her son to take his sisters and run far away. He would not abandon her, so he tried to hide her beneath a loose board in the bedroom. They often used the hidden room for games, and sometimes to store food, or odds and ends gifted, forgotten, or stolen from guests. Saree refused to hide, however, and instead took hold of Soran and shoved Gunsel down with such strength that he was caught off guard. She slammed the door shut, sliding an oaken cabinet onto it so that he would neither be seen nor be found.

No sooner had she finished telling Gunsel to hush than there came a light tap on the door, followed immediately by someone bashing it to splinters with a makeshift club made from a discarded table leg. Three men argued outside the bedroom door, and the entire household dared not make a sound. Having found no food worth pillaging, the men broke down doors, kicked open cabinets, and destroyed furniture, hoping to find a stash hidden within the house. Eventually, Gunsel heard his other two sisters scream as the men entered the room. He would never forget the night he spent beneath the floor of his home. His world had already ended, and he could only listen as his sisters and mother were used and beaten for hours.

Eternity passed him by, hiding beneath the floor of his home. Paralyzed with fear, he waited hours after the horrifying sounds had stopped before lifting the heavy board above his head and stumbling into a nightmare. At some point, someone had fallen against the wardrobe and knocked it off his trapdoor. There was blood, some dry, some still dripping. Shreds of clothing were clumped in small piles at the foot of the table. His mother had been dismembered, her gaping mouth wearing lipstick of blood, eyes open wide in terror, as though even death had not relieved her. He never told anyone what happened, nor could he have, as what he saw of his family then was indescribable. Yet still he lurched from his home, carrying what he could on his back, and never returned to Vahir, or mentioned his family again.

Lillian stood nearby, smirking at the sight of Gunsel's head flopped over the back of the chair, mouth wide open and drooling a puddle into the ground. She knew there was something he kept from her. It didn't bother her, and there were parts of her life that she thought she would keep secret from him, but his reaction was always instant when his family was brought up, or something reminded him of his past. He had mentioned his wounds from Brathur, and though she had heard the tales of the Rofu poison, they had been only tales to her, and the black bile and screams of the dying were not burned into her memory, as they were the survivors of Brathur.

Shaking his shoulder, Lillian grasped his hand as it leapt to his belt. "Syp-" was all he said, eyes wide and head jerking frantically. There was a table between his hands and his axes, however, and all he managed to do was spill a nearby drink. The crowd cheered, assuming he had drunkenly misgrabbed at his cup, and Lillian steered him away from the table toward one of the roaring fires that dotted the combined camps. "What's going on with you?"

In response, Gunsel shrugged and muttered something along the lines of, "I'm fine." Then he leaned his head on her shoulder and they sat down, letting their faces roast beside the leaping flames. For a while, they were content, and they dozed together in the warmth without fear or memories. The darkness was stilled in Gunsel's mind, and he decided he loved

Lillian then, even if he would not admit it, because he realized that she was to him what the fire was, and she drove out the shadows in his eyes. He grabbed her hand, holding it between his rough palms, and they both smiled.

Hours passed them by, without dreams or fear, and they slept together before the fire, even as it died to embers. A fierce morning surged from the east, chasing away gray clouds and the threat of rain. A calm breeze drifted through the tents, and banners fluttered lazily upon their bearings. Gunsel awoke refreshed, for the first time since the battle of Brathur, and he started to see Lillian already looking at him when he opened his eyes. "Damn near gave me a heart attack," was what he was about to say, before a pigeon dive-bombed his neck. It scrabbled with his collar for a moment before retreating, incapable of breaking through the rough jerkin.

"And like that, we are awake." She said, gently squeezing his arm and sitting up. She stretched her back, reaching to the blushing sky. Her neck was stiff, and her ponytail had a kink in it that she couldn't brush out with her fingers, so she stood up, let her hair down, and shook it around in an attempt to make it fall where it should.

Gunsel admired her. Never had he been so captivated by a woman, and he was sure everyone would notice his affection, but for the first time in his life he simply had no desire to care what anyone thought about him. He only cared about what she thought, and if she smiled, he smiled. His life had changed, and the idea of being on the warpath headed toward a battle they were both unlikely to survive gave him little comfort. "Lillian, do you think we are going to make it through this?" He watched her continued stretching, tried to stand up, put his hand on a chicken, fell, and stayed on his back, "I don't mean, like, us. I mean, like, do you think we'll live?"

With a flick of her hair, Lillian plopped next to him again, struggling to form a bun from her rat's nest. "All I know is I've never met anyone I would rather die with than die for. If some arcane god is planning to kill everything, there's nowhere I'd rather be than dying with you."

"I suppose that means a lot to me." He held her close, shutting his eyes against the blooming sunlight. "I suppose you mean a lot to me."

"Well, then let's go eat lunch." She hopped to her feet, dragging Gunsel up and shoving him toward the burgeoning food line. He followed, forgetting for the morning about the nightmare he had at the drinking table. They ate what everyone else in the camps ate that day, and it was just as appetizing as the rest of the meals they were served weren't. Day broke upon the combined force of almost thirty thousand men, women, dwarves, trolls, and assorted ogres.

Crossing Kharat was miserable beyond the words of elves. As a frustratingly prim, and whiny, race, they possessed an extraordinary ability to describe it, as their dictionaries held many words for anything from niggling to utterly implosive in terms of annoyance. The sun itself was no danger to a Braecan elf, and their skill in magic could keep them supplied with water indefinitely. Food, however, was running scarce, and though an elf can subsist on extremely limited meals for quite some time, they would eventually need to eat. The lygians trudged on, and even as an amphibious race, many were able to shrug off the incredible heat. Others simply died, their bodies shoved aside so as not to trip the legions tromping behind them. Terea Vo noticed the giants were struggling. Their massive bodies required more sustenance, and the heavy furs they sported were left in a trail behind their march. No dragons were seen the entire march through Kharat, as they flew north to hunt and stay in the cool eyries they built upon snowcapped mountains many ages hence.

There was also a conspicuous absence of their leader, and many assumed Skal would rejoin them near the Nazene, citing greater needs to attend to.

In reality, Skal was brooding. He stomped around his room in the Heldan Hills, poring over numerous tomes that were either long memorized or written in his hand. He knew his power had limits, especially around items crafted with certain magic, or in certain eras due to their magical potency. The world was evolving, and his power needed to evolve with it. The trail to his prize started long ago, and it began with a human, named Therian, who rode into battle upon a tusked monster from far to the south. Therian's kind wore only straw or leather armor, and they proudly carved a path of destruction nearly to Korz itself. They were stopped within sight of the city by a combined army of elves, men, and dwarves, as this was before the Braeco shrouded themselves in magic and mystery. Upon the thick armor of the dwarves, Therian's people broke. Alone, Therian fought and brought early death to nearly a hundred foes before being cast down by magical shackles. The armor was stripped from the fallen body, and Therian was sent to the prisons below Brathur.

Of what followed, it infuriated Skal to have learned so little. This occurrence was before the rise of the Heldan Hood, so his people had not been present. He assumed the dwarves had written it down, and his attempts to pry the secrets from them were unsuccessful to the last. The elves were too busy singing about themselves to generate worthwhile history, and humans didn't bother writing anything down not involving death, food, or sex. A single page was written in a personal diary by an elf named Oori, present at the stripping of Therian, and it read:

> 'In my memory there marks no greater a date than this. To not destroy, or to guard, or to use such a tool invites the doom it seeks. All nations will come to seek its knowledge, and there will be terrible war.'

Skal could imply, reasonably, that this date was when the armor's fate was decided. From the writing, he wondered if the elves had taken the armor, but quickly dismissed that, as no elf would let such a treasure rest idle in some secret place for long. Then he thought it was returned to the Dragon's Hand, who proved themselves steadfast in the face of great horror before the beasts of Therian. If this was the case, he wondered that such an imbecile would have managed to possess the armor at present. He plundered thousands of minds in search of information about the discovery or concealing of the armor. Not a soul could personally remember anything about it, and, until very recently, Skal had assumed the armor was lost even to those who were supposed to know where to find it.

What he had managed to recreate was a scenario that involved the sundering of the armor, by magic, to random places across Alkurah. There was a single reference in an elvish song about the *Tsund Magii,* or the "Wizards of Severing," roughly, that placed them around the time of the stripping of Therian. Each individual would then know exactly where their single piece of armor was, but no being had the knowledge of the locations of every piece. Then, either the wizards who performed this feat were set free, and they died along with their knowledge of a single piece of the armor, or they were killed before they were allowed to tell anyone anything they knew about the armor. The second option seemed most reasonable, and therefore least likely, by Skal, so he assumed the location of the armor was, in part, still known through random bloodlines in Alkurah.

Through extensive research, Skal eventually learned the location of each individual piece of the armor worn by the god of the dead. For the next century, he found himself thwarted at each site, finding empty chests, opened tombs, and unsealed vaults where each piece of the armor should lay. Having turned the final stone, he realized he would simply have to abandon his quest for the armor. Clearly, his search must begin anew, as someone had accomplished this task before him. "Unless I've been misled since the beginning," he pondered for only a moment. He was sure of what he learned of the decisions of the *Tsund Magii* to scatter the armor impossibly far from Korz. This failure was what originally began Skal's quest to cleanse Alkurah, city by city, and in time birthed the massive force now crossing Kharat.

Upon learning someone such as Garroway now possessed such a powerful weapon Skal nearly lost his mind. The little man was unable to directly influence other beings, whether physically or by magic, and this weakness was what held sway over his immense power.

Now, he was searching for any way his magic might affect Garroway even if only to tear the armor from him and render it powerless. He had recruited others to help him search, over his prolonged life, and through countless experiments he learned he could not even cause hair to ruffle or clothing to sway. One scholar suggested he try casting the spell at himself, directing the person or object in question at his own sword. Unsuccessful. Hurling inanimate objects at a living creature? Unsuccessful. Affecting the weather above or the earth below, or even wildfire all proved the same, and Skal wondered now if he was to see his plans cast down around him at the height of his power.

He paused to peer into the distance, seeing beyond the sight of men, elves, eagles, or even dragons, and he watched the great suffering of his army as they neared the end of their trek through Kharat. Terea Vo was there, appearing to look even into Skal's eyes wondering where his leader stood in this moment of discomfort and pain. For an instant, Skal felt it would have been appropriate to endure the desert with his army, even if he would be under no risk as they were. It passed quickly, and he teleported to Terea Vo's side, "You made excellent time."

The elf started, still unused to the little man appearing out of nothing and jumping into conversation as if he had been sitting right next to him all along. This was part of the reason Terea was becoming increasingly more paranoid about Skal killing him, and he truly believed Skal was surveilling him constantly, judging by his tendency to act as though he had been there all along.

Or, Terea pondered, he actually had been sitting there all along and simply invisible. He decided it was pointless to fret over it now, and responded, "Yes, sir. Though, we could have used a touch of food to tide over some of the weaker ... " he trailed off, trying to find the best word to finish his thought, "... species."

"There is little I could have done, in spite of my power, to ease this passage for my army. However, I see there has been no real damage done to my honor guard," he sniggered, savoring the disgust on the elf's face, "and for that you have my thanks. This was a successful crossing of a desert never once dreamed by your kind."

"Yet here I stand," replied Terea.

"Indeed." Skal wondered if he should take another look at the council of Hâedra, but decided against it. Another handful of men would be but fewer graves to dig in the future.

Speaking highly of Krumrakai no longer seemed like an option to Norrin, whose glowing commendation to Roc of the dwarven king was given with such respect the grizzled commander expected him to start blushing. Roc had known Krumrakai for some time now. They were friendly, and though their meetings had been few and far between, there was only mutual respect between the pair. He didn't need Norrin to wax his mustache for Roc to approve of him, so the scout was sent away to eat and sleep before returning to Krumrakai's force.

Knowing what he did about strategy, Roc was given to the impression that his army would lose simply because they were outnumbered almost three-to-one. And dragons were back, apparently. Even hoping for perfect aim, maximum magical effect, and a large dose of luck, it was hopeless. He sent a handful of scouts to a number of old hideouts, lost cities, and elusive friends in the hopes of bolstering his forces even by a man or two. Thus far, all had returned empty handed.

One scout, an elf named Irye, was visibly shaken when Roc called on him to report. He had ridden to the Nazene and peered far beyond into the burning sands of Kharat. It was not long he looked ere the outline of marching columns the likes of which he had never before witnessed silhouetted upon the horizon. He returned to Roc with all the speed his horse and magic could muster, and when he relayed what he saw, the old man simply nodded, patted him on the back, and dismissed him to allow the next scout in.

More bad news flooded Roc's ears, and finally he decided anything anyone had to say to him was no longer worth hearing. Soon, Krumrakai would be here to bolster morale, and Roc hoped it would be enough to convince the soldiers that this was all going to be worth it. He swept the flap of his tent aside, shooing away the queue snaking behind him. "Go away, I'll talk to you all tomorrow, or never." They muddled around for a few minutes, stalking him around the camp assuming he was trying to weed out the least tenacious of the group until he backhanded a brave dwarf.

Throughout his unending life, Roc had experienced hopelessness, fear, and desperation several times. The stakes of those battles had been petty in the face of this one, however, and genuine terror threatened to overwhelm him. A backbone of fierce men shielded by dwarven armor, and supported by trollish strength made his army one of the more formidable to ever to march across Alkurah. He was proud that the men of the east would stand together. Once this battle concluded, he wondered how events would play out. Would the Nieth rise up and destroy Korz once more? Perhaps Hâedra too? Would the elves return? Roc was certain he wouldn't be around. Thus far he had proved immortal, but there was an impending doom upon the near future. So deep in thought was the grizzled warrior that he passed Gortrum by without even a glance.

The bearded mercenary was struggling to mount a horse that was clearly not enamored with the idea of bearing him as a burden. There was a wagering pool on how many bones would break, between Gortrum and the horse, and thus far both had proved obstinate. He would end up losing when the stirrup snapped, and he flipped to the ground with enough force to spill his mug of ale. Seeing Roc so pensive upset Gortrum almost as much as the fall from his saddle, and he scrabbled to catch up, flipping a small bag of silver over his shoulder to settle his lost bet. "'Ey, what's nippin' on yer fretter, old man?"

Roc, ready to defend himself from another report, relaxed and welcomed his friend with a pat on the shoulder, "Gortrum, have I ever been anything but honest with you?"

"Brutally so, sir, and ya know I love ye all the more for it."

"We're all going to die. Those who survive the battle, the cowards and the deserters, they'll be hunted down and eliminated in short order."

"Shit on that." The big man reciprocated the pat on the back, leaving Roc to try and regain his stride after being nearly clubbed to his knees, "This world belongs to men now, not elves. I know ye've seen times where that wasn't true, but it is now. I'll not see Alkurah fall prey to those frilly bastards."

Even Gortrum started to hear Grael's voice behind his ear, "We're not all frilly, Gortrum, but I appreciate the sentiment."

"You know what I mean, dontcha Grael?" asked the mercenary, hoping he hadn't offended his longtime friend.

"Better than most," replied the old elf, patting Gortrum on the shoulder and steering him away from Roc. "I must talk with this wrinkled pile of bones."

Gortrum nodded his head, slamming a fist to his chest in respect to his elders. Grael turned and was less than shocked to see a stern look of impatience chiseled into Roc's face. It had been a few days since the pair talked, and they parted on a less than happy note. "So, my friend, what has been on your mind recently?" Grael asked, finally breaking the uncomfortable silence.

"Been thinking an awful lot about dying, but I suppose that's appropriate given the circumstance."

The elf made a fake frown, nodding to acknowledge Roc's pessimism, "Things are looking rather bleak. Still, there's something about the future that I find quite stimulating." He sat Roc down on a nearby bench, waiting until the commander had shuffled his armor and gloves around for certainly longer than was necessary, then looked directly at Grael and motioned for him to continue. "Long ago, when men were young and, if you'll believe it, rasher than present, the Nieth from the south ruled most of Alkurah. And one, Therian, who I believe you knew, rode against Korz."

"And was nearly triumphant, if I recall." Roc said, remembering the first great battle he fought against other humans in the long centuries of his life.

"Indeed. Do you ever wonder why the throne of the Nieth fell so low when Therian was defeated?"

"I know Therian was a monster upon the field of battle." Roc's face lit up, remembering a war story from his youth, "Death's Shadow, Demon, and Doombringer. What a legacy they carved from the flesh of their foes." His tone turned bitter, never allowing himself to forget the curse of the Veiled.

"Only four living beings know what happened to the armor when it was stripped from Therian. Four sorcerers of immense power brought their will to bear, and beneath their magic the armor was rent from flesh and jettisoned across the world."

"'But' feels like it is about to be a very important word," Roc muttered, now listening intently to Grael. He knew it was folly to ignore wisdom given freely from such a source , and he was sick of nursing his bad mood.

"The 'but' is: the armor was incomplete at the time of the stripping. A gauntlet had been replaced by ordinary metal forged with magic to bond to the rest of the armor."

"Why is this important?" Roc asked, genuinely interested now.

"Most magical objects are only at their strongest when they're complete, and though it is metal beaten by Bol himself, I think it reasonable to assume the power within it is largely untapped." Grael's hands were shaking, with nerves or excitement. Probably both.

"So, you're thinking to reassemble the armor and turn Garroway loose?"

"I never said anything about Garroway." The old elf gave a conspiratorial glance around, continuing, "I like the man, you know that, but imagine such power at your own fingertips!"

"Or yours, Grael?" Roc didn't like the direction this conversation was taking, and he aimed to steer it away from danger. "I thought we agreed he'd be the one. He found it, he's accustomed to it, and honestly, Grael, there was probably a reason the Magii didn't just keep the armor."

At this point, both were startled to hear low horns baying from the horizon. With a march like an earthquake and drums like thunder, an army of dwarves, trolls, and ogres tromped toward the encampment. At their front rode Krumrakai, his braided beard coiled in his lap, Helm of Karak adorning his brow, and the thunder hammer Rakai held aloft. Queen Whoorlem opted to forgo a mount, and instead strode abreast Krumrakai's hrgeet. A circlet of iron bound her mangy hair, and no other marks of her station were there save the respect bade her by the soldiers. Norrin didn't belong in the group, and stuck out rather horrendously with his massive horse and leather scouting armor.

The cheer that rose up from the encampment grew until it threatened to break eardrums. Swords clattered against shields, lances and clubs clanged on rocks and stumps, and a veritable chorus of musical notes rang from the weapons of the uniting armies. Dweera handled the logistics perfectly, again, and only a few moments were lost in the march during their integration into fold. She was pleased.

Krumrakai met with Roc, Grael, Id, Breegan, and Tristan, with Queen Whoorlem in tow, later that night. Their tents were all sewn together, and they closed the flaps, setting guards so none might intrude on a meeting of so many powerful figures. When all were assembled and well fed, Roc stood and bade them settle down to talk about the ending of the world. "Here we stand, against the coming darkness. Try as we have, this battle will be more important than any event since the Sundering, perhaps even before. Grael thinks the armor of Tykus is the greatest strength we have, and even as your army came upon ours we were discussing something worth bringing up in present company."

Grael stood, nodding thanks to Roc, started, "The armor was stripped long ago from a warrior named Therian and, to shorten an extraordinarily long story, it was incomplete. There is a gauntlet missing from the set, and I believe if we find that gauntlet, we win this battle."

"The problem," Krumrakai interjected, "is that you don't know where it is, do you?" His eyes twinkled, and he wondered for just a moment if this was the proper time to reveal the greatest secret that dwarves ever kept. A hush fell upon the room as each member of the meeting caught the dwarf king's eyes. "Fortunately for everyone on this world, you brought this subject up to perhaps the only being alive who does know where it is." He brought forth the *Titun* again, reading from a passage written only a few chapters in:

> *"Khagarel, King of Kings among all those races who consider themselves intelligent, Master of Death and Life, the Ageless, bequeathed unto his friends, the dwarves, a piece of Heaven. His right hand, his sword hand, that which slew Req himself on the steps of the Godhall. The hand of God and Godslayer, the greatest gift ever given, was given unto the faithful. Upon the Kharatvil he had stood, hewn by dwarven hammers and picks with blood and unbending will, and their majesty bolstered his arms to feats impossible."*

Krumrakai took a seat, raised his eyebrows a bit, and spread his hands, a black gauntlet lilting from his meaty fist.

It was Breegan who spoke first, eyes agog and face full of surprise, "Well, what the hell do ye think o' tha'?"

In truth, Krumrakai simply felt that single passage sufficed for the information his companions needed, and he was loath to offer up any more words of the *Titun* than were required. He could have told them that the possession of this item was the reason for nearly every conflict the dwarves had ever been part of, for many dwarven rulers had been slain in battle, and not all their bodies recovered. "Every dwarven king or queen has carried it on their person from the day of their coronation to that of their death, and who am I to be the exception." He slammed the jet-black gauntlet onto the table for effect. "So who wants to go get this 'Garroway'?"

POWER

To war for Korz, to war for Korz, to keep her safe and lovely!
To war for Korz, to war for Korz, to protect our wives and honeys!
Send us off with flowers and drums; we'll be home by the morrow!
With mailed fists we draw our swords, and take back debts we're owed.
We'll kill and maim and all become great, and never fail our home.
Never challenge the mighty Guard lest to your castles they roam.
Though dragons, men, dwarves, elves, or orcs be named our foes,
At the tip of our swords they join the hordes that meant a threat to pose.

  A number of trials preceded the actual reattachment of the gauntlet onto the armor. Grael was worried there would be a magical backlash, Roc was worried it would kill everyone nearby, Garroway was worried it would kill only him, and Krumrakai was simply worried they were going to run out of time. Everything was happening on the march, and they were still a day out from Rivit. No scouts sent across the river had returned for a full week, and the united army was in a dark mood. Each evening there were fewer bonfires, shorter songs, and quieter laughs. Soldiers wrote letters in the hope that perhaps someone nearby would survive and check their corpse, and each scratch of the whetstone felt a death knoll.

  Eventually, Grael and a wizard named Cuhn managed to sever the fake gauntlet from its magical bond to the armor. Some eyebrows were singed, and everyone recoiled from a tremendous pillar of smoke that lasted only about three minutes, but no one died. To reattach the severed piece, Grael simply told Garroway to put it on, so he did. The armor was familiarly warm, as if it was only recently parted from flesh, and it fit as though it had been tailored precisely. But nothing was different than usual. There was no heightened, or lessened, bloodlust, no energy, and no transformation. Everyone showed their disappointment differently, and after several hours Garroway was happy to leave them to their sulking.

  Upon ditching the glares of his betters, he was shocked to see how quiet such a massive army could be. Grousing could be done in earnest at night, and Garroway found himself irritated that anyone would waste a day to complain about the probable end of the world. He understood, of course, because their world had followed a savage dose of reality with a blistering flood of bad luck, but the principle behind it ground on him. So, he joked and smiled and did his best to bring some cheer to the end of everyone's lives. The armor was a morale booster, and Garroway had no issue tromping around the marching columns, chin held high and back rigid as a board, trying not to throw everyone off their pace. He saw Gunsel getting beaten into the dust by Lillian on the edge of a ragged platoon. From the distant snatches of verbal assault he picked up, he assumed Gunsel made a comment about her hair that was taken somewhat less than well.

Watery tendrils of sunshine set between scattered clouds on the eve of their coming to Rivit, and the somber mood lightened ever so slightly. Something about resupplying and drinking water that had been somewhere other than sloshing around a filthy canteen for a week offered some degree of respite. Plus, if there was a reason to drink and laugh, any army could find it. Scouts reported to their various officers, then joined their friends beside a fire and told them everything they had seen and heard. A waning moon rippled above swollen clouds, and the cold evening brought hands closer to the radiant heat of the flames. Rivit's Sovereign, an old Hâedran fleet commander, sent emissaries, who were met and dealt with by Dweera, as she had been put in charge of the entire army's logistics. Wagons were filled with supplies and driven into the heart of the camp, to be distributed in the morning. A group of citizens from Rivit elected a captain and hitched themselves to the rear of the campsite, hoping no one would notice. Dweera did, of course, and made sure they were assimilated into a unit that could find use for them, in spite of their curses and efforts to escape her sight. When the job was done, Dweera sent her aides to bed, and nestled into a desk full of papers written and piled precariously, without regard to the possibility of future reading.

Not as far away from Rivit as anyone, including the High Elflord himself would like him to be, Terea Vo huddled further into his blanket, swiping at a nose that had leaked so much over the past two days he was surprised it was still there but for wiping it as often as he had. Skal's army was on the Nazene, gently floating across the river nearly sixty miles north of Rivit. Terea and Skal had argued for almost five minutes about whether it was worth taking the time to march so far north to avoid detection. Terea won when Nulau Ra said she agreed with the idea. Skal was not above bowing to her wisdom in strategy, because her arguments were always perfect, and she was always right.

Now, an entire army was slowing crossing the great river, without paddles, sails, or magic to aide them, simply hoping they would mostly all make it to the opposite shore before they passed the city to the south. As far as anyone was aware, they were still at least three days from the Nazene. The rafts had been of Nulau's devising, and Terea actually forgot he was on a river for the quiet and the stillness of his ride. His body noticed, however, and he ached with the cool evening. Having lived upon the coast, and beyond, most of his long life, he was unaccustomed to the bitter autumnal cold. He took his frustration out on some nearby fish, lashing at them with spears of magic. He missed, sneezed, earned a disapproving glance from Skal for breaking the quiet, and retreated back to his blanket shell. Moping was a fond pastime of his, and the moment felt ripe for it. The plan, as far as he could glean from Skal's insane babblings, was to attack outside of Rivit and pin their opponents between dragonfire, the Nazene, and a rundown shacktown of a city.

Plans, of course, never happen the way they're planned, and Terea was certain this battle would be no different. He had seen entire regiments collapse; storming victories wither into crushing defeats on a single moment, and once even saw an entire army contract dysentery within an hour. History had warned him not to gamble on a sweeping blow to the jugular. The lygians, which he still refused to call his army, would be at risk of collateral damage, as they were slated to be the first troops to follow up a barrage of dragons and arrows. Skal cared legendarily little about friendly fire, and though he had only contempt for them, Terea felt a twinge of guilt at the thought. Still, the battle was greater than their lives, and if there was anything lygians excel at, it was reproducing.

Nulau Ra listened to scout reports, nibbling a leaf of the *ene* tree. It kept her mind razor sharp, even if she overindulged in the eyes of some of her peers. The bitter taste was worth suffering, and it made her teeth green, giving the impression of natural camouflage. There was a common magical ritual among elves that had the same effect, though, so she simply imitated several other important historical religious practices to keep up appearances. Her issue wasn't so much that she cared what anyone thought of her habit, she just had little patience for anyone telling her how she should conduct herself. So she just lied to their faces, ate all the leaves she desired, and enjoyed the overarching silence that permeated most of her days. The stem spun wildly between her teeth as she doodled on a map, giving the facade of important work in order to weed out the less tenacious of her attendees. Avoiding scouts was impossible, as most of them had trained with the centaurs more recently than she had, so she had developed techniques to convince them not to report to her unless it was desperately important. The cold night passed quickly for her, and the bite of the river winds failed to sting her cheeks due to the warmth lent them by the *ene* leaves.

In the massive raft at the rear of the army, having only just shoved off, Skal grew ever more confident. He had managed to escort his army a full day ahead of schedule, and devoting more of his power to the march had shaken loose some cobwebs from his mind. Rule over an entire world lay only a sunrise away, and his skin tingled in anticipation of the wonders he was prepared to bring about. He still hated knowing he would have no personal impact on the battle, save what the sight of him would do for morale. But Nulau seemed confident, Terea was competent enough, and he was still convinced the dragons would cause a rout before steel was even brought to bear.

Ragnus Fireborn, the youngest dragon in Skal's employ, was also the most revered due to the respect owed his bloodline. He had owed Grimfilth a debt for decades, and his appearance at Brathur was payment long overdue. Since making good on his debt to the orc, he was returned to his eyrie only a day when Skal approached him, two other dragons at his side. The Fireborn had brought about revolution numerous times, and though dragons are generally reclusive, it was not unlike Ragnus to be seen hunting around his eyrie. He was proud and strong, and his brash actions were often viewed as a dare to any and all to attempt to crack his iron scales. He had flown north for the night to hunt among the frozen wastes. He would return before sunrise, on his word, to fight for Skal.

Taur Earthbreaker, the largest living dragon, was napping as he floated across the Nazene. His head rested on a raft that was struggling not to capsize, and the tip of his enormous tail was still dry by the time his snout bumped against the far shore. His pale bulk was invisible beneath the glassy river, and his spines kept setting crews into panic when they bumped the little rafts.

Finally, Oleth, son of Boleth Terrorwyrm, greatest of all dragons ever to roam Alkurah, had rallied to the Light as well. His onyx bulk cast a shadow of death upon the ground when he spread his mighty wings. The death of Boleth left a void that would come to be filled by his son. Now, Oleth, king of dragons, donned his ancient armor for the first time since Boleth's demise upon the Whyrum Garrad. Gleaming silver, the snarling helm was inlaid with stones of more individual value than Krumrakai's entire hoard of treasure. Five giants assisted him with his massive armor, and he spent day and night steel-clad. Scars across his throat and belly told the tale of his will to survive, and his missing left eye had been replaced with a ruby the size of a wagon wheel. The startling contrast between his obsidian body and the glaring ruby easily set him apart.

Disembarking was quieter than Nulau Ra had anticipated, and only one human sentry rode far enough north to notice the army. He was dealt with immediately, a pair of shafts jutting from his throat. Ragnus returned with more fanfare than was necessary, and he strutted and posed before the troops, relishing in their praise. When the elves, lygians, giants, dragons, and ragtag bands of orcs and humans had all been assembled, at last, Nulau nodded to herself in satisfaction before sending High Elflord, Regent of the Skies, Tera Vo, his summons. He arrived on horseback, silver inlays on his ornate saddle glinting, pristine, in the burning sunrise. The traditional armor of his station featured a relief of Lau, the moon, raised above a single ship at anchor in a bay. On his hip was strapped *Vorun*, the narrow scimitar he smithed in eons past, before even the Sundering, with hammers given him by dwarvish princes. For a fleeting moment, he wondered whether his decision to serve Skal would honor his ancestors, or disgrace them to the utmost. It passed, and he grinned, flicking *Vorun* from her sheath with practiced flourish. He looked every bit the king of elves, and many who had questioned their involvement with Skal were reassured by the mere majesty of his presence. They cast off their usual smug temperament to cheer for their lord, the only elf among them ever to treat directly with the Queen. His word was law, and they cheered with abandon for several minutes before quieting down almost entirely when Skal appeared at their head.

The little man wore his red robe, as they often saw him adorned over the years of his domination. He was greeted by a silence of fear and awe, rather than respect. Skal relished it. Being unable to cause physical or mental harm to anything was a handicap he had somehow managed to circumvent to perfection, and he was proud of the lingering atmosphere of utter terror that often accompanied his sudden appearances.

His voice amplified a hundredfold as he floated before his army. Banners flickered in the strong breeze, mail rings clinked as gently as spring rain, and all of Alkurah held its breath for a moment. "You are as I am, my hands, my swords, and my heart. Dawn is coming, and in the light of a newborn sun, Alkurah will burn. Forget any oaths sworn to false gods, forget the fear and guilt that riddles your souls, and when you see the ending of the darkness may you rejoice! A new world is being born, and you will nurse it to fruition."

Taur Earthbreaker, the dragon who had been with Skal as long as his ideals let loose a towering inferno and beat his gargantuan wings against the water. Two more flaps lifted his impossible girth skyward. With Ragnus flying close behind, they allowed Oleth to assume his position at their head. A cheer followed in their wake as the army marched upon Rivit, and the sleepy camp of their foes.

When Garroway heard a horn blow from the south, he was certain they had been surrounded and were all going to die in a matter of moments. After several deep, resonating blasts, he was surprised to hear an answering note from somewhere nearby. Having already assumed the worst, he was startled to realize that this meant there were already enemies inside the camp, and not only were they all going to die, but they were going to die in the morning, which felt marginally worse. Instead of dying, however, he noticed the suspicious lack of screams and clashing steel. The horn from the south blew once more, and he climbed a nearby stack of crates to see if there was anything worth looking for that way.

A cloud of dust shimmered in the morning glow, and the lapping of the Nazene on her shores nearby gave a sense of calm before the horn of Chithralt bellowed once more. This time, however, it was answered from the east, and out of the heat shimmer came two forces, unlooked for by either side of the conflict.

Three thousand centaurs, the last of their dying race, trotted at an easy pace toward the camp. Their hooves pounded the earth with enough force to rattle any unsecured items from their resting places, and the dawn gleamed from their polished armor. Each of them carried a long bow and a pair of curved swords sheathed on their backs. Wild hair was braided with beads and trinkets, powerful muscles gleamed on their flanks, and horns blew until cheeks were flushed and dripped sweat. Their banner, a green flag embroidered with a golden leaf, whipped as they hastened toward the camp. From a distance, they had looked small, perhaps the size of a man. However, as they came near, their broad shoulders and powerful muscles bulged, and the mood shifted from surprise to awe.

Behind them, moving at a slower pace but still managing to stay somewhat nearby the centaurs, marched an army that could've been men, if men were cleaner and cared more about their physical appearance. Long braids like starlight shimmered on their shoulders, and armor speckled with diamonds glittered from their breasts. At their head, astride the legendary *Suah*, the great painted horse that would suffer no bridle, rode King Orum. His raven hair was unbound, flapping in the wind as if it were his own flag, and he held in his right hand a tuft of Suah's mane. Nearly two thousand Praestan elves followed their king out of Eskeria for the first time in an age, and the men of Hâedra and Korz knew then, if they hadn't before, that this battle would truly be an affair worthy of history.

A united army of thirty thousand men, centaurs, dwarves, trolls, elves, and ogres awaited an equal-sized force from Kharat to defend the world from annihilation.

Krumrakai was camped on the eastern edge of the tents, and his keen eyes picked out King Orum before most. He grinned to himself, wondering at what his forebears would say about allying himself with an elf for any purpose. Even Thorriman, one of the more understanding dwarves Krumrakai had ever met, had specifically told him multiple times that trusting an elf was like trusting a stiff breeze in your sail. Prepare for a change and be ready to adapt. Or, better yet, "Don't." Still, he was pleased. Their singing bows would put a fair dent in any army, and at least if they turned on the rest of his allies, he would be in prime position to destroy them before he fell.

The centaurs impressed Grael and Roc far more than the Praestan elves. It had been centuries since even a single centaur rode openly to battle, and though they trained the Rangers for that amount of time and longer; they had shied from open warfare. The precision, beauty, and raw power of a centaur charge is nigh incomparable, and their mastery of timing is renowned in every history of Alkurah.

A cheer rose from the camp. Quietly, at first, for few could make much sense of what was really happening. It crescendoed to a roar as whispers traveled at a speed that might make the breeze jealous, and suddenly armor was clanging together in greeting to the centaurs and the elves. Most of those present had never even seen a centaur, simply believing them gone from the world, or tales of nonsense entirely. The Praestan elves, whose legendary secrecy led most to believe they were extinct, were something truly out of a fairy tale. Humans and dwarves alike marveled at the scene, some weeping, others cheering, and more still simply agape at what lay before them.

When the first army slid coolly into the campsite, some of the centaurs smiled at their receptions. Others were grim, either more informed on the situation or trying to act tough for the humans. And still more acted aloof, as if this kind of greeting was the norm, and they had ridden to battle in such circumstances dozens of times without a care. They eased their pace to weave among the tents and fires, not disturbing even a single flap or hanging shirt, and wound their way through to find Grael, Roc, and Krumrakai all standing together, grinning like children.

One centaur stepped forward, kneeling as much as his equine body would allow, and spoke in a soft tenor, "Lords, I am Eskeroth, lord of the trees and wood. I offer you my people, my blood, to staunch the coming darkness with flesh and steel if you would have our service."

Grael bent at the waist, prompting Roc and Krumrakai to do the same, with mixed depths. Still, Eskeroth seemed pleased at their respect, and he whistled something only the centaurs and nearby rangers could hear. They dispersed, making instant friends with the men, women, and dwarves assembled around them. The trolls and ogres seemed unimpressed, and kept mainly away from the rest of the army anyway.

Not long after the centaurs abandoned their formation, King Orum rode into the camp. Unlike the hooves that had stepped so carefully between tents and clotheslines, his contingent simply halted on the edge of the camp while he trotted straight through anything in his path to reach Grael. The fervor and excitement around him was enough to discourage any negative reaction to his obliviousness to the destruction he was causing, but there were grumbles and insults following in his wake.

He spied Eskeroth, and thus Grael, and made his way directly to the group. Without pause, he stated, "Magnicaerna, I am not here to assist you or your ilk in battle. I am here to put an end to a threat to the very existence of my world, and we happen to have similar feelings about this individual problem. I do not trust you, nor like you, nor approve of your doings in the past." He paused, debating whether to just leave or leave with flair. He chose flair, and whipped Suah around, "I hope you all die," were his final words to generally everyone, and he stormed back through his pathway of destruction. Over his shoulder he added, "And they have already crossed Nazene. Form up your rabble if you hope to have even a sliver of a chance."

His final comment elicited a startled gasp from everyone nearby, and those who heard the gasp gasped on principle. Grael never liked or trusted Orum either, but hearing that their enemy had already crossed the Nazene, combined with the utter lack of news from scouts, led him to amplify his voice immediately and order the united army to form up on the north side of Rivit.

Roc, who trusted Orum even less than Grael, was surprised that Grael even reacted. The look on his face must have communicated his surprise, and he started talking before Grael could begin defending himself, "Because that one has never lied to anyone about anything before, right?"

"It's the end of the world, Roc, and I won't risk being attacked inside my own camp."

"Grimfilth and the Rofu aren't even here yet! There's no reason to believe this mystery army has overtaken them." Roc, who was smart enough to know that it was unwise to simply ignore advice given in wartime, immediately ordered Tristan himself to ride north to spot the army. He also summoned

Norrin, who had been asleep until Orum's horse trampled his tent, to take a boat across the Nazene to look for the Rofu. He was not worried that they had been destroyed, but he wanted some reassurance that they were still on the way and were not simply lying about their allegiance.

The camp quickly devolved into a jittery mob of screaming captains and confused soldiers. Armor was assembled, swords sharpened, and saddles thrown upon horses with haste bred by fear and practice. Soon, an army rose up from the rabble. Eskeroth's centaurs trotted in the vanguard, their lances and spears glimmering silver, and the mere sight of them gave heart to the defenders. Orum kept his elves away to the eastern flank, and they marched without a sound. What remained were thirty thousand or so various bodies that were giving a fair impression of being soldiers. With a quick double note from one of the centaur horns, the entire force lurched forward, matching pace after only a moment.

Banners unfurled, drums thundered in time, and the mood lifted in spite of the coming dread. A beautiful morning dawned upon Alkurah, and the strong sun was a good omen to any who bothered to keep track of such superstitions. Bol was watching over them, and he would look kindly upon a glorious death.

Grimfilth and his army had, in fact, crossed the Nazene already. However, they had missed their mark several dozen miles to the south, and through a combination of not having maps and having not been across the river in decades, they had become thoroughly lost. His scouts had ridden out in every direction, returning with unanimously worthless reports. Grimfilth, who was short-tempered on a good day, was as near to losing his mind as he had been in his considerably long life. Learning nothing on the eve of probably the most important battle in history was as infuriating as it was confusing, and he was certain someone should have seen something nearby.

Alas, it was Norrin's passage across the Nazene, done in a dinghy liberated from a nearby Hâedran ship after the promise that it be brought back unharmed, that finally gave Grimfilth his first hint. Skal had erected a magical barrier to the north of the Rofu army, and since they could not see the city they assumed that either they had crossed the Nazene too far to the north, or Rivit was further inland than they thought. The illusion, however, was broken when Norrin began paddling across the river. It had only been constructed to block the army and city from the Rofu, and though the ships were invisible in their moorings, Norrin managed to work his way through the facade.

Uhm, the orc tasked with bringing up the rear of the army, saw Norrin and cocked his head to survey this single human rowing a single boat across the vast river. It took him five minutes to realize he should report this to someone, and he jostled his way through the army looking for a face he recognized as someone important. He jumped and screeched when Grimfilth grabbed him by the shoulder, spinning him around, and ordered him to talk.

"Humaninboat crossinriversir!" was all he managed to squeak out.

It was enough for Grimfilth, and he ordered the army to march north double time. Horns trumpeted orders, drummers set a frenzied pace, and thirty thousand orcs, trolls, and a handful of giants managed to make a full left turn without a single casualty, duel, or even minor stabbing. Once they were pointed in the right direction, they marched at a grueling pace beneath the uncharacteristically hot midmorning sun. Grimfilth had been hoping for some cloud cover, as orcs never function well in broad daylight, but he took pride in seeing them suffer as quietly as they could. They were complaining ceaselessly, of course, but were still managing to put one foot in front of the other.

The orc leader, now cooling his temper at the thought of battle approaching sooner rather than later, muttered to Rigathel, "Come what will, I'm proud of this army and what we've accomplished. Whether we march to doom or glory, I have no regrets save what must have happened at the Kharatvil."

Rigathel's jaw tightened, but his chest swelled at the gesture, "Gorathel was proud to serve. To die. As I am proud to both serve, and to die."

No other words passed between the pair, and they prayed silently to different gods about the battle to come. Grimfilth for victory, Rigathel for glory. Dyrkktha pierced the illusory veil first, and before him rose a steady cloud of dust carried to the sky by battle cries and war horns. The rest of the Rofu cheered to see the abandoned camp before the walls of the city, smelling battle on the air. In the distance, banners fluttered in the stiff breeze, horns blasted notes across the field, and the thunder of hooves and iron boots drowned out the Rofu drums.

In spite of his trepidation, Grimfilth smiled and spurred his horse forward, quickening the pace of the army to match the quickening in his heart.

Seeing an army appear out of nothing is unsettling under any circumstance. The circumstance made it even worse, and for one fleeting moment, everyone on the march held his or her fearful breath. Roc, who was too old to be surprised, bellowed before a true stampede could form, "Steady and onward, brothers, it seems our allies are trying to keep up with us!"

An hour and a half later, Tristan returned to Roc's side. His hair was windswept, clothing torn and scorched, and both he and his horse bore wounds leaking freely. His cheeks were pallid, and though his expression was as grim as always, it seemed a lifetime had gone by to the eyes of his observers.

"My lord, Orum was right. He- they- they are come."

A nearby cloud erupted as Oleth Terrorwyrm, Taur Earthbreaker, and Ragnus Fireborn descended in hellfire.

BLOOD

Shadow lies,
Shadow hides,
Shadow vies for light's demise.
Darkness is strong,
Darkness lives long,
Darkness seeks to drown Light's song.
Hate becomes,
Hate undoes,
Hate shall ever overcome.
Fear makes truth,
Fear feeds on youth,
Fear bites deep with poisoned tooth.
Death defeats.
Death ne'er retreats.
Death won't yield,
Death completes.

Reacting to a dragon often does not take long. Reacting to three dragons appearing at the same moment takes so little time even Grael was surprised at how quickly arrows tore up to meet them. No screams of panic, no fleeing cowards with urine dribbling down their legs, and not even a moment of hesitation. Roc would have glowed with pride had there been time. Instead, he simply lowered his visor, whipped his shield overhead, and prepared to defend himself from dragonfire that rained from above.

For a moment, the world was ablaze. Flesh and metal burned, shields and armor withered before the onslaught, and when the trio of dragons' wings finally beat the air to regain height, dozens already lay dead on the field. Within moments, they were wheeling around once more, and the impossible bravery that had withstood their initial attack was draining rapidly. To the surprise of every soul assembled that day before the Nazene, a fourth dragon exploded out of the river, wet scales shimmering like diamonds. His name was Caernohath, the Deathflame, and he was ancient even among ancients. With claw, tooth, and beating wing, he hurtled into the three and tore at their flesh. Every twist they made, Caernohath was there, claws ripping scales free of their moorings. When one of the younger dragons would lash out, his razor teeth shed their blood that had not spilled in ages. They roared their frustration and pain as they danced with the Deathflame, and though he suffered gaping wounds, he gave no moment of respite. Caernohath had seen more battles than these whelps had dreamed of, and they paid for it in blood.

While everyone was ogling the dragon battle taking place in the sky, a host of lygian warriors, refreshed by the mystical Nazene, stomped through another illusion Skal had erected and appeared out of thin air within bowshot of the Praestan elves. Again, there were no screams of fear or rampant desertion, as Skal hoped and Roc feared. Instead, every bow that had been strung that morning bent and loosed a perfect volley. The lygians lucky enough not to be shredded to pulp found feathered shafts poking from every exposed inch of flesh.

Krumrakai, who had offered his own plan to the assembled leaders of the defending army only the night before, simply nodded at Roc and left, saying over his shoulder, "Best dig a bit faster, eh?"

The centaurs, spearheaded by Eskeroth himself, broke into three arms. One wheeled to the right, breaking away from the main force to try and charge down the flank of the lygian army. As the illusory wall faded, however, they realized the lygians were simply a small dispatch of the main force, which was thundering toward the now exposed heart of the defenders.

History has proven men weak in the face of insurmountable odds. Tales and truths alike told of entire armies fleeing before a dedicated cavalry charge, of kings losing their crowns and kingdoms in a single battle, and of cowards sinking low enough to sabotage their own allies. Time and again, the armies of men withered, fell flat, weak, and spineless when tested.

History was proven wrong by the men of Korz, who had suffered and bled at the hands of every army ever to march across Alkurah. Over the thunder of hooves and the clatter of spears, Roc bellowed, "Men of the Guard, hold your ground!"

A storm of steel and blood exploded from the front lines as the battle was joined in earnest on both sides. On the right flank, Orum's elves held the lygian force at bow range. Eskeroth's centaurs had scattered and regrouped to pulverize the exposed flank of Skal's cavalry. Again, they were denied their full victory as the enemy charge dissolved into a full rout, and the bloodstained men of Korz rushed through their ranks, churning the mud and dead alike to a frothy swamp.

Somewhere in the heart of the army, Garroway was doing the same thing everyone else around him was- trying to understand what in the hell was happening. It was difficult not to simply watch the sky, as the battle unfolding above them made the one on the ground feel somehow insignificant. A shockwave rippled through the ranks as they braced against Skal's cavalry charge, but otherwise he could have been at any city market populated by armor toting warriors. He was frustrated, but confident that he need only wait before his turn came.

At his side, Gunsel was doing his best to contain his bloodlust. He howled as though he were at the front line, bearing down on his prey. Those around him cheered as his ferocity infected the army. When the cavalry charge stymied, he urged those before him to charge forward. They listened, and soon their boots were carrying them swiftly toward a force they could not hope to vanquish.

Beside Gunsel, the enormous Sorian ogre chieftain, Dooblidum Bumbilum, lumbered at the head of his people. Any human ferocity seems grossly outweighed by that of an ogre, and when Id snarled even gently, those about him leapt forward.

Then, from far in front of the Korzian army, now flanked by the Hâedran cavalry and Eskeroth's centaurs, came the rumbling of drums and baritones of the giants:

To fight, to die.
To fight, to die.
The giants roar their battlecry.
With clubs and drums and leathery hides,
We walk and run and ride and fly.
To fight, to die.
To fight, to die.
The giants roar their battlecry.

To break, to kill.
To break, to kill.
The giants march to eat their fill
Of blood and flesh and bone this meal.
Ne'er a giant's blood shall spill.
To break, to kill.
To break, to kill.
The giants march to eat their fill.

To battle, to war.
To battle, to war.
The giants fill the air with roars.
Our enemy's friends shall howl and mourn.
Forever may Alkurah fear the horde.
To battle, to war.
To battle, to war.
The giants fill the air with roars.

Their voices drowned out the battlecries of men, and it was only moments before the centaurs were among them. Short bows twanged as the centaurs nimbly dodged flailing limbs, clubs, and a handful of swords. Eskeroth himself wielded his short swords to devastating effect, whistling commands to his army as they entered the fray. His arm of soldiers, one of three into which his army was now split, drove straight into the center of the giants. Cousins, brothers, and friends were crushed and trampled by the giants, and though he was carving a considerable hole in their ranks, the unit of giants itself plowed inexorably toward the now stationary men.

A second arm of Eskeroth's army was dancing out of reach of the giants, firing arrows at their heads to blind, and hopefully kill, as many of them as possible. They swatted at the buzzing shafts, and some simply allowed the arrows to accumulate in the muscled flesh of their forearms as they covered their faces.

Garroway was now shoving his way to the front of the army with Gunsel in tow. At first, it had been difficult, but seeing him encased in the armor of the Godslayer was enough to create a narrow pathway through which he shouldered toward the front. Inwardly, he was terrified, and tripped at least twice, only to be rescued by Gunsel and shoved ahead once more. He drew his sword and shouted the only thing that came to his mind. A dwarven word he had heard mentioned when talking about the armor that was said with reverence and respect. Instead, he shouted it as a battlecry, "Khagarel!"

In moments, from the throats of trolls, men, dwarves, and even ogres, the shout hit the giants like a wall. They froze, clearly understanding the word and overestimating the actual effect it would have. Garroway broke through the front line, winking at Roc as he passed his captain, and pointed his sword forward. "Khagarel!" screamed the army behind him, in response, and they engaged with such ferocity as to even cause a handful of the giants to turn and flee.

Furious at missing the intial bloodspilling, Grimfilth somehow managed to contain his army as they rushed through the surprised ranks of the Praestan elves. The elves, clearly disgusted at the idea of being so near an orc, did their best to pretend the Rofu were not entirely horrendous.

But they *were* entirely horrendous, and with snarling teeth and rusted iron they clashed with the lygian column within feet of the Praestan van. Otherworldly screeches pierced the sky as tridents skewered orcs through ragged armor, serrated daggers sawed flesh from bone, and filthy hands strangled and crushed whatever they could reach.

Knee deep in giant blood and bladder-shivering fear, Garroway and Gunsel struggled to remember how to do anything other than simply cry and defecate. To their left, they were not reassured in the slightest to see Roc and Grael whirling like a tornado of immortal steel. Still, it appeared as though the ranks of their foes were thinning. That was before six thousand Braecan arrows ripped through the melee, pinning giants, men, and centaurs to the dirt with a double-volley.

To complete the one-two punch, a troll regiment blasted into the embattled right flank, overtaking the Rofu who attempted to extend their shields in front of the charge. Iron clubs and mailed fists pulverized armor and bone while the men of Korz and Hâedra hurried to brace against the onslaught. They were painfully slow, and hundreds of them fell onto their faces, trampled into paste by the ironshod trolls. Their strongarm advance ground to a halt after plowing nearly two hundred feet beyond the furthest of the lygians.

Roc, dedicated to hand-to-hand combat but in no real danger yet, was keeping a keen eye on the battle around him. He roared orders to his flag bearers, and even took one from the ground himself, shrugging off a splinter of lance that bounced from his ribs. The ominous clanking of a well-drilled march punched through the din as Orum's elves immediately faced left and drove into the trolls' right side. Elven magic was put to the test against trollish armor, and some of the less tenacious elves even found their blows turned aside.

But it was dwarven magic that proved strongest, as Krumrakai's force finished whatever it was they had been doing. The king of Karakor made a dramatic hand signal and a full third of the combined lygian and troll advance simply vanished in a puff of dirt and smoke. He laughed, content now that his sabotage had succeeded, and mounted his hrgeet. "Forward!" he bellowed, and six thousand dwarven shields locked together. Their inexorable march to the front neither faltered nor slowed when they reached their floundering opponents, and dwarven axes hewed bones like wood, carving their way forward over the corpses of friend and foe alike. When they reached the crater made by his previous efforts, the phalanx dissolved into a brutal melee. On uneven footing slicked with blood, the trolls struggled to survive. The wounded were dispatched without hesitation. No prisoners would be taken by dwarves.

With the giants now decimated, and the extended arm of the human infantry wounded by the double volley of arrows, Skal's cavalry was reassembling. Eskeroth, two arrows jutting from left arm, took command of the third arm of his force that was kept in reserve. Only twelve hundred centaurs now stood, and those who still had bows sent buzzing shafts at whatever enemy they could reach. Powerful arms grew sluggish with fatigue, and when quivers emptied they simply tossed aside their great bows of unimaginable worth. This would be the last battle of the centaurs, but they would not leave this world unbloodied.

Several arrows found their way into Gunsel's flesh, and he roared in fury and pain as he hacked at trolls and giants alike. His blood was inky and smelled foul, and every moment made his eyes dimmer, and his hands slowed such that Garroway tried to cover for him. The sword of the Godslayer whistled and sang, relishing in the bloodshed.

Grum and Bendragel, who had opted to join in with Id and Queen Whoorlem's forces, respectively, found themselves side by side again. Bendragel and Gorathel had met up briefly when the latter delivered his message of peace to Roc and Grael, but they had grown apart. So the troll and ogre now made for a gruesome obstacle, alternately storming forward and bracing for retaliation. The rest of their kind were flooding into the weakening lines of the humans, propping up sagging sections of the front until reinforcements could pick their way over the tangle of severed limbs and armor.

Terea Vo managed not to succumb to his cold while crossing the Nazene, and even made it out of bed to watch the battle unfold. He had given Nulau her orders, careful to leave wiggle room should she see something on the field that needed to be addressed. Then he ate breakfast beneath a pleasant sunrise and felt almost normal for a few hours, resting his weary legs in the magical waters of the Nazene, armor resting once more on his bed. When horns and drums declared that battle was nigh, he did not hurry to the front, instead choosing to mount his horse and observe from afar. From his vantage point, he could witness the incredible aerial combat of Taur, Ragnus, Oleth, and Caernohath. With ink and parchment he recorded their furious encounter as it unfurled. It would be one of the truest depictions of wartime ever written by an elf, for in the face of such majesty he could write only truth lest he tarnish it with fiction.

Taur Earthbreaker had grown accustomed to not fighting simply because taking one look at a mountain-sized dragon was enough to paralyze most creatures in sheer terror. Caernohath Deathflame was not most creatures, and in his unimaginable lifetime he had slain monsters of such vastness as to make Taur seem paltry in comparison. Still, fighting three dragons alone was not a simple task, and though his scales were invulnerable to their searing flames, claws and teeth still rent the soft flesh beneath them. Uncountable lifetimes of men made him careful, and he knew his limits better than any other creature on Alkurah. When he sensed himself losing ground, or being pinned down, he brought his powerful wings close to his body and dropped to the ground daring them to continue the battle closer to the surface. Praestan and Braecan arrows both ricocheted from armored scales, and though the aim of elves is impeccable, none found their mark among the hurricane of wings, claws, and powerful tails.

Caernohath's title had not been acquired through myth, and the searing bolts of his breath vaporized scales, scalded flesh, and were so bright even the other dragons blinked. He grappled with Oleth, using his tail and hind legs to keep Ragnus at bay. Fierce talons tore at Oleth's throat, and scraps of armor crafted by the greatest smiths ever to strike hammer to anvil rained down. Even the ruby in Oleth's eye was scratched, and though it remained in place, Caernohath gouged it deeply enough to dull the crimson sheen. However, they fought on. The three younger dragons continued chipping at the ancient one, but for each blow they struck, he landed three.

Below them, Nulau Ra roared orders at her elves. The lygian front was dissolving, and though they inflicted tremendous casualties on the Rofu, the Praestan elves were nigh untouched. Now she hoped to coax one of the ogre captains into swinging his force in front of her archers. Listening, especially during a battle, is something no one has ever accused an ogre of doing. She managed, as she always does, and soon two thousand ogres stumbled in front of her line. The reinforcement gave her lygians a much-needed reprieve for a few moments, and they rallied behind the leathery hides of the ogres.

Nulau was struggling to see the human wedge that had driven into the giants. Most of the giants were gone, however, so she could only assume their force had been destroyed. The cavalry was lancing down pockets of resistance that cropped up after her elves had leveled the field. Slowly, Skal's army pushed forward. She saw centaurs galloping freely through the ranks of men, and dwarven shields rebuffed the advance of the ogres in front of her. Not without recompense, however, as massive massive hammers crushed through armor like wet paper. Magic was bred into ogryn blood, old magic no longer practiced in places of light. Arrows bounced from their hides, and even Krumrakai bloodied his axe in the rotation of the shield wall.

Brooding, Skal shook with rage at his impotence. The world needed his final push, and he had brought it to the edge hoping it would jump. This battle was not about winning to him. He needed to crush this defense. Continue his battle into the south with as many soldiers as he could manage to save. His magic was at work distracting and assisting wherever he could, but not being able to kill anything made it all seem pointless. He was furious to learn of Queen Whoorlem's defection, but when he saw how Krumrakai had managed it, he had been forced to admit the strategious mind behind the beard. Still, if Whoorlem had delayed their march for even two days, this battle would already be over.

Floating high enough above the melee that neither feathered shaft nor dragon fire could reach him, he imagined a world with no life upon it. It would start with Alkurah proper, and from the heart of the land his infection would spread until only he remained. A lifeless world, a quiet world. A perfect world. All the voices of every lifetime whispered in his ears, but even as the day went on, the voices hushed as if in respect to Skal. He eyed Caernohath warily. For the second time, the ancient dragon had glanced directly at him. There was no doubt it was coincidence, but that it had occurred twice put him on edge. Magic could protect him from nearly anything, but Caernohath was legendary for his scorching gouts of magic-fire. He had visited the ancient beast once before, centuries ago, and requested his assistance when called upon. It was the first time any creature had denied Skal, and though it would not be the last, it rankled that such a powerful dragon stood against him. Taur, Ragnus, and Oleth were fearsome, but with Caernohath at their head Skal would have been unstoppable.

Grael and Roc had been quite a thorn in the side of the Heldanhood, and Skal himself, and the impish creature could not number the times he had ordered their assassinations. Failure upon failure made him simply give up on his vengeance, and had Garroway and his company not happened upon the Hills when Skal was not present to restrain them, he would have had a boon greater than the death of either. The armor of the Godslayer was his final hope, and he placed great faith in Tykus' soul granting him the ability to take life. He had never dared hope to see it fully assembled, as he would have found himself lucky even to find a single piece. Yet here it was, wielded against him.

Making the executive decision that he should probably at least pretend to fight, Terea Vo donned his favorite shirt, fitted his hair neatly into a jeweled helm, and strolled toward the battle. He nodded to soldiers as he passed, stopping to talk occasionally, hoping to waste as much time as possible. Inevitably, he reached the ranks of those actually at risk of dying. A nearby elf had been impaled by four arrows, so Terea took her bow and quiver, making sure to thank her and her ancestors for their service to the Queen, and emptied the quiver in the general direction of the men of Korz. Now arrowless, Terea shuffled toward the front. He took care to dodge any projectile he saw coming, which slowed his advance further. Nulau Ra was only a few steps in front of him, and he hoped she would give him an excuse to ignore the battle.

Instead, a glowing red arrow punched through his cuirass, embedding itself in his lung. He took a pair of ragged breaths, more confused that his magical wards had not protected him than anything else. Still on his feet, he looked in the direction the arrow had come from. To say he was surprised to see the face of Grael Voor himself would be a lie, as the old elf had promised him so many years before that Terea's death would be swift as an arrow and sudden as a spark. To his knees fell Terea Vo, Regent of the Skies, and he pitched forward so the arrow penetrated the armor on his back.

Nulau Ra glanced behind her, having heard the gasps of shock from those nearby, but did not even acknowledge Terea's corpse. She had a battle to win, and mourning before finishing it was a good way to die young, so to speak. Beneath the boots of his own soldiers, Terea Vo was trampled into the loam.

Parry, strike, block, and reverse. Garroway danced and twirled like an onyx top of spinning death, and nothing stood before him. Blood fed the sword, and in turn the sword spilt more and more. The power within the armor crept at the back of his mind, and though he focused on the battle, a part of him had to keep whispering of the power at bay. Orcs, wicked men, trolls, and even giants withered before him, and the men of Korz and Hâedra rallied behind him bellowing, "Khagarel!" all the while.

Roc's voice plowed through the battlefield like a juggernaut, and even some of Skal's soldiers hesitated to hear him roar, "Fall back and protect Orum."

Every head turned to the right to glance at the Praestan elves. They were fine, and with the dwarven shields acting like a bulwark against the enemy advice, the right wing seemed to be doing a rather better job than the center. Still, it was hard to disobey Roc knowing that if he survived the battle he would beat the insubbordination out of anyone who dared hesitate even a moment. Garroway and Gunsel slowed their advance, letting the rest of the army form up around them, and ground through trolls and lygians alike to try and combine with Orum's elves.

Eskeroth engaged the enemy cavalry before they had a chance to run down the weakened humans, buying them time to regroup and filter into the ranks of the elves. Compacting his force was the first part of Roc's plan, and now that they had cleared the field, Skal's lygians, giants, and trolls charged forward hoping to incite a rout. Instead, they were crushed as the Hâedran cavalry rode out of an ancient tunnel, hidden in the deep riverside grasses by Krumrakai's forefathers. The centaurs joined up with the Hâedran cavalry, working in tandem to scatter pockets of soldiers that resisted the advance, and again dwarven trickery proved mighty. Lances and spears drove into Skal's army, punching clean through the infantry and leaving the wounded to be dispatched by the men of Korz as they retook the ground they had given, forming up once more. At their head were Garroway and Gunsel, urging the men at their backs to fight harder through deeds rather than words.

The dragons still clashed, and though their blood and torn scales cascaded onto the men below, their ferocity was unabated. Taur, however, was slowing down, and a ragged tear in his right wing made it fold awkwardly when he tried to regain his height. He crashed into Caernohath, freeing Ragnus from the deathgrip on his throat and giving Oleth an opportunity to strike the ancient dragon's long neck. Three massive claws raked across Caernohath's exposed collar, sheering scales and unleashing a torrent of blood. Instantly, the great red dragon latched his teeth onto Ragnus' wing and tore it off. Both beasts howled in pain, and Ragnus fell into a spin, smashing into the ground amid Skal's army.

Caernohath's flame was going out, and life drained from him even as he lost altitude. Still, the crimson dragon struggled. Once more, Oleth dragged his massive claws across Caernohath's chest, tearing it to the bone and exposing ragged muscle. With his final breath, Deathflame grasped Oleth by the jaw, holding his mouth agape as he unleashed the last torrent of fire that would ever spew from within his great belly. He fell, releasing Oleth and managing to bat Taur out of the sky on the way down.

Grael saw his friend fall, and though he had stifled his anger and sorrow many times before, he simply could not restrain himself at the sight of such desecration. From his hands exploded rivers of flame, and he bathed the nearest clusters of Skal's soldiers until they were naught but reeking piles of molten flesh and bone in a moment of absolute fury.

For a single instant, Grael Voor allowed himself to be consumed by emotion, and the devastation he wrought in that short time was colossal. Still, it was a moment his enemies had awaited for eons, and he stumbled forward with a Praestan arrow sticking through his right eye. Orum fired twice more before turning his pitiless bow back upon Skal's army, and Grael Voor faded away in the churned, bloody battlefield beside the Nazene.

Roc saw the old elf fall, and though a part of him was saddened at his passing, another part simply saw the world letting go of its ancient tethers. Change was no longer on the way- it had arrived. Grael Voor was the second of the Alakhan to fall, at least that Roc knew of, and as the ancient ones met their doom, Alkurah was given an opportunity for rebirth. Roc's sword whirled and glinted in the sun. He grabbed a nearby orc by the throat, bludgeoning it with the pommel of his sword. The body joined countless others on the field, and Roc moved on to the next foe as he had all his life.

The battle could only have one conclusion as Taur Earthbreaker joined the fight on the ground. His massive claws swept away men as if they were dry leaves, his powerful tail flattened dwarven shields, and the furnace of his breath punctured even the staunchest defenses. The Braecan elves, who had worshipped dragons long ago, rallied behind his immeasurable bulk. Their arrows tore ragged holes in Eskeroth's centaurs, whose numbers dwindled until only a hundred remained.

Still they fought, and though the thunder of their hooves was lessened, they struck terror still into their foes. Masterful strokes lopped heads from shoulders, and though they had long been bereft of arrows, some scooped up javelins or quivers from their dead and dying foes to pour as much steel into their enemy as they could.

A gallant resistance, but one done in vain. *"Centauria!"* came Nulau Ra's order. As one, the remaining three thousand Braecan elves let fly their arrows. Some missed, others pierced men, orcs, and trolls, but most found their marks. Eskeroth could only watch as the last of his kind was obliterated in a single stroke. For a moment, it seemed, the whole battle froze to bear witness to the end of the centaurs. As if in slow motion, Eskeroth watched barbed arrowheads tear the flesh of his kin, knocking them off balance or outright killing them. He saw the arrows aimed for him, and though he could sense his end forthcoming he could not avoid it. Three arrows drove into his chest, another two caught him in the flank and ribs, and before he could fall, a final arrow punctured his heart. With Eskeroth perished the blood of the kings of Eskeria, and he was the last to bear the title.

As suddenly as the battle had frozen, it was rejoined. Arms were tiring as Bol's sun traversed the sky, and the strength of minds and bodies waned. Magical attacks had appeared conspicuously absent, but as the day progressed it became apparent that there was a battle happening entirely separate from the one fought with bodies and steel. Hundreds of magicians on either side of the conflict were frozen in utter concentration, willing their magics to overcome their foes.

Occasionally, one would fall, blood gushing from the eyes and mouth, as though he had been on the receiving end of a vicious blow. The men of Korz were falling back, carefully retreating while maintaining their lines. Roc was proud to see them keep their spacing in check, all the while striking back at any who ventured too close to their line.

On the right flank, both forces of elves had run out of arrows, and while some struggled against their foes with magic, most drew swords and waded into the melee. Orum himself stood on the front lines carving his way artfully through bone and steel alike. His expression was almost bored, but sweat was beginning to bead on his brow. Seeing an elf showing signs of exhaustion was a marvel in its own right, but Orum's pace did not slow.

Krumrakai had lost his left hand early in the battle. Having pushed with his shield to gain room, he swung his mighty axe at an overeager troll. It grabbed him, trying to drag the king away from his bodyguard. Instead of struggling with a troll, Krumrakai severed his own wrist and was pleased to watch the troll trip over something and impale himself on the spiked shield. Still, he had bled more than a little by the time someone brought him a healer to staunch the flow. Entrenched on the front line, Krumrakai could no longer hold his shield, so he simply whipped his axe at any limb that happened to break through the wall of dwarven metal in front of him. A poorly thrown hand-axe bonked off his helm, so he tracked it down to stash in his belt. Wielding his great axe one-handed was tiring, and he expected he would soon need a lighter one.

He was not surprised to see Orum fighting alongside his dwarves. After all, this battle was going to determine the fate of Alkurah and no elves ever let slip the chance to write something heroic about themselves. He was surprised the battle had lasted this long, in no small part due to Caernohath holding the other three dragons at bay all morning, but the dwarf king had no illusions about his imminent mortality. It rankled that he still did not know who led this army against the people of Alkurah. Knowing who he was fighting would have no outcome on the battle; he just hated the idea of fighting a faceless enemy.

Grumbubum Lumblegurb had not seen himself in battle against other ogres for nearly a decade. His massive hammer no longer glowed, but the enchanted wood and steel had no problem crushing ordinary soldiers into sludge. Parrying an ogre blow took special consideration and timing. If you turned too quickly, the ogre might step forward and bowl you over without even using a weapon. Turn too late, and there will be nothing left of your upper body to remind your legs to move. So, Grum parried and twisted in a manner most were unaccustomed to seeing. A nimble jump forward brought him within striking distance of Nulau Ra, who was fighting with her soldiers near to the dwarven shield line. She deflected it, barely, and leapt away to hack at a nearby troll.

That troll was Bendragel, who had managed to acquire two black eyes. A dagger stuck awkwardly into his shoulder, but no one bothered to let him know, and his club had acquired a rather gruesome trimming of entrails. Nulau's sword leapt for his throat, and he simply dropped his club to reach up, catch her hand midswing, and punch her square in the face. Screaming, her nose obliterated and both eyes immediately swelling shut, Nulau could only squint in horror as Bendragel laughed at her. He took hold of both her arms, seizing a lull in the fighting around him to inflict psychological pain upon his foes, as trolls are wont to do. He lifted her from the ground by her left arm, sneering into her broken face. He brought himself to his full height, dug his claws into her right collarbone, and tore Nulau Ra in half.

This created general and disgust, with Braecan and Praestan elves alike pausing to retch at the spectacle. Orum sneered, but did not refrain from taking advantage of such a show. He challenged his foes, "This is your fate, cowards. Preening and mocking my people will end in death and you shall know only fear in the end!"

It was then that Skal revealed himself at the head of his army, floating on high. His words rattled in the minds of everyone assembled, and the bloodshed ground to a halt.

"Behold, mortals! Your greatest clamor is but mewling to the ears of God! I will show you *fear!*"

Roc and Id had discussed this moment. Neither knew who the enemy commander was, but they were in agreement that he or she would eventually appear if even for a simple morale boost. Breegan, whose horse had been shot from beneath him, twice now, happened to be nearby. The river of curses and oaths that streamed from him would have made a dwarf blush, and he hurled his sword in frustration at the little man. It fell to the earth, causing no damage whatsoever to Skal and only managing to sever a single toe from one of the remaining giants. Id, however, hurled something rather more dangerous. And when Id hurled something, it hustled.

Throughout the battle, the ogre commander had kept a position only a few feet behind and to Garroway's left. The general consensus among the leaders was that Garroway would have the best chance of killing who, or what, was leading the enemy. No one told him this, of course. He had been oblivious to Id's position until only a moment before, when the ogre took hold of him by an arm and a leg, spun in a tight circle, and hurled him as a living projectile at Skal.

Certain he had died and was flying off to the afterlife, Garroway failed to recognize Skal even as they collided. Both were certain they were more surprised than the other, and the only thing that kept Garroway's look of incredulity secret was his visor. Skal's face, however, was uncovered and agape even as the pair hurtled to the ground. An armored body landing on someone from any height was generally enough to kill them. On top of that, Garroway had the sense to not only point his sword at his floating target, but managed to shove it directly through Skal's chest. They floundered in the air for only a moment, as if the strange wizard's magic had not yet run out, before dropping the last few feet to earth. The sword of Tykus Godslayer impaled Skal the Enlightened. Shivering silence rippled through the battlefield as those nearest the crater made by their falling bodies crept closer to see what had become of the two combatants.

Garroway twitched once; content to lie on his face until at least dinnertime. When no one stepped forward to praise his glorious deeds, he dragged himself to a knee. It was a movement exaggerated not only due to his fatigue, but also because he was secretly hoping a contingent of soldiers would either lift him upon their shoulders to celebrate, or bludgeon him to death. Neither happened, so he stood, dragged his sword from Skal's corpse, and waved to the bystanders, "So, how's that?" It was the first thing that came to mind, so he said it.

Instead of the ear-splitting cheer he was expecting, there came a horrible gurgle from the corpse behind him. Skal's broken body twitched, bones cracking as limbs lurched into unnatural positions. Rising from the small crater, Skal's eyes opened as though for the first time. No longer were there colored pupils with whites and reds. Jet-black orbs now glared from the reanimated corpse as a voice no longer bubbly and mocking issued forth, "I am God! I am Death and Shadow. I am the Darkness, and my life has been longer than life itself. Witness my power."

Skal lifted his right hand, palm upward, and with it rose the dead and dying on the field of battle. No breath escaped their lips, their eyes did not blink, and they needed neither food nor water. They stood still, rigid as if still caught in the throes of rigor mortis. Blood flowed from their wounds, shattered limbs rested at unnatural angles. Then his hand closed to a fist, and the dead lashed out at anyone, on either side of the battle, their blades could reach.

As the clamour of battle rose once more around him, Garroway had an intense debate with himself about whether or not to simply run away. It was the sight of Gunsel diving in front of Lillian to deflect a blow that made up his mind. Before he could run away, however, Skal looked at him, reaching out and roaring, "Khagarel!"

Fury and hatred etched on his face, Skal took a wavering step forward as though unused to his own body. He glanced about, appraising his limbs. All who could see him watched in horror as the skin melted from his bones. Soon, Skal was gone, and in his place stood a wraith of shadows and smoke, scarcely real at all. With no more flesh, the phantom spoke once more, "You call yourself King, yet you are as weak as your claim to godhood." With shocking speed, the shadow was upon Garroway, claws of darkness tearing at the black metal of the armor.

Reflex fueled by the armor itself made the man parry, and soon the two were dancing blade to claw. Around them, the world dissolved into chaos. A thunderhead roiled above them, lightning tore at the earth, and the dead rose up again and again to drag down the living. Even through the furious duel, the Shadow spoke, "Centuries have I laid dormant in this husk of flesh, and ages have I been cast out of the world."

With each passing moment, Garroway knew he was losing ground. Its claws grazed his left arm, touching it only lightly, yet he lost his grip on the sword at the pain blooming from even the merest contact. Like ice and fire at once it burned and froze, and his horror multiplied to see the armor turn frosty and crack. Hoping to stall, which was a tactic he was better acquainted with than battle, he asked, "Who are you?"

The question brought a pause to the next blow. It cocked its head, as though the idea of being anonymous had not even occurred to it. "I am what has always been. I am Sypchallu and I will always be. You- you are protected by armor crafted thousands of years hence, and hope to defend yourself with a sword forged to wound me at my weakest." It laughed, not quite Skal's maniacal cackle, but eerily similar, and added, "Imagine how much stronger I have become since."

It paused, and Ro was certain this was the moment he was expected to flee in terror. However, he had never heard the name Sypchallu, as all mentions of it were written in dwarvish and kept singularly within the *Titun*. There was one man nearby, however, who had heard the name. Indeed it was a name he had remembered his entire adult life. From childhood, Gunsel had repressed the mention of Sypchallu, yet never denied himself hatred towards it.

When the men came to his home, during the famine that ravaged Vahir and the plains around it, they did unspeakable things. What happened during that year was never sung about, nor remembered with fondness. The harshness of men was made reality, and they filled their empty bellies with meat thus far untasted. Those who partook were cast out and named *Chall* after the words they wrote upon walls with the blood of their meals. Gunsel watched his family be consumed by men. He had seen their limbs severed and cooked, smelled the meat and felt his stomach growl, and he had watched the grease of his mother and sister dribble down stubbled cheeks. On the wall of his family's bedroom was written a single word, in her own blood- *Sypchallu*.

Hearing that name brought forth such anger and fury to Gunsel's arms that his strikes blasted steel apart and crushed bone. Over all, he had heard the monster name itself, and suddenly his ending life was given purpose. With inky blood leaking from a dozen wounds and more, the tattooed warrior barreled through the living and the dead to strike at the creature now threatening his friend. He was beyond words, with blood and foam frothing on his lips. Garroway was parrying and losing ground to the creature that called itself Death, and Gunsel ignored arrows and swords raking his flesh, hoping to strike even once at the monster responsible for the tragedy of his life. A gap opened in the fighting before him as two trolls bludgeoned an already dead elf into a puddle, and Gunsel leapt forward, burying both axes into Sypchallu's back and offering every ounce of his will in magic.

An unearthly screech paralyzed the fighting as even the dead halted their assault. Sypchallu scrabbled at the axes digging into his ethereal body. No blood leaked from the wounds, and though it clearly injured the creature, it was impossible to tell how badly. Claws of shadow tore at Gunsel, rending flesh and opening new wounds as well as old. Even with his bare hands, Gunsel pummeled Sypchallu. Each blow bloodied his knuckles, turning blue from cold, but Gunsel had long since accepted his doom. Here, at the end of his life, he struggled with memories that had plagued him every moment of every day.

Only moments into the attack, all but Garroway were surprised to see Roc drive his sword into the hazy area where Sypchallu's head would be. This time, the reaction was silent as Sypchallu froze. Roc spoke, breaking the silence after a moment, "You may have heard the tale of this sword. I don't know what you are, but nothing survives the bite of a dragon."

Around him, the dead slowly sank to the ground. Gunsel, whose wounds were mortal and whom the Rofu poison had corrupted almost entirely, pitched to the ground. His face was content, as he had sorted out the horrors of his life in his final moments, something a great majority never do.

Those who had sided with Skal were unsure of what they should be doing now their majestic leader was simply a pile of liquid flesh and a wisp of smoke. Without guidance, they were hesitant to attack again in spite of their superior numbers. Roc withdrew the sword from Sypchallu, driving it into the wraith a dozen times before its form gave way and dissipated into the afternoon breeze. Sypchallu's voice spoke, not from a body this time, and all heard his words: "Where there is light, there will always be Shadow."

For several minutes, there was scarce a breath taken in fear that Sypchallu would return. Then, Breegan shouted across the battlefield, "So, who else needs a drink an' a nap?"

DAWN

Rise through storms, pain, and death, to shine against the sky.
Rise through suffering, glory, and doom and ever-onward fly.
The eternal blaze, Bol's throne in the sun forever shines with hope.
His fiery eye burns in the sky, giving warmth, against darkness, to cope.
When the sun sets, and wan is the light, men must weather storms.
Remember that ever the dawn comes again; all that is cold will be warm.

Commander Yrlet, who managed to survive both the Kharatvil and the battle on the banks of the Nazene, surrendered for his lygians, stating that he had only fought for Skal under pain of death or worse. Krumrakai and Roc believed him, and they granted the amphibious creatures safe passage to the Seia Wesrin. Without the Braecan elves whipping them forward or threats from Skal himself, they appeared to be a pleasant race that may have been a staunch ally of men given different circumstances. They bathed in the Nazene, washing away years of oppression and fear, and glutted themselves on fat fish and rich grasses before making the grueling trek across Kharat once more.

The Braecan elves, with neither leadership nor the presence of their newfound god, struggled with what had happened. Learning of Sypchallu's identity was a blow to both their pride and their religious faith, and some committed ritual suicide in order to atone for the abominable blasphemy against Bol. Others hoped to repair the damage they had caused to the world, vowing to work against evil and darkness for the rest of their innumerable days. Still others simply refused to believe what they were told, having not witnessed Sypchallu's unveiling, and they returned to Braeco in the sea, content to live their lives as they had for thousands of years.

What was left of the Praestan elves departed as suddenly as they had arrived. Orum would not atone for the slaying of Grael Voor, and he certainly would not answer for his deeds in a court of men. He considered the slaying a retribution for past wrongs.

The ancient elf's remains were discovered, and he was brought back to Korz to be given the burial he deserved.

Grimfilth was a problem in Roc's eyes, as the orc was now at the head of an army whose entire reason for being was only a couple weeks' march away. The orc had bred the Rofu for decades in order to sieze the tunnels beneath Brathur, hoping to find some answer to an unspoken question in the magic carved into the stones. Roc met with him privately. He asked, "So, Magnifeia, what do you plan to do now?"

The orc was taken aback at the use of his proper name, and though he was accustomed to being surprised by this bristling human, it was jarring to meet one who knew of the Alakhan. He answered, "I will return to my Keep in the desert, and I will think upon what happened here that I may understand it."

"You don't plan on seizing Brathur?"

"Perhaps, in time. " Grimfilth shrugged, "I have nothing but time, old man. And in the end, what I do will mean little to this world."

"That is something I can understand, and I hope to meet with you across a table rather than across a battlefield in the future." Roc answered, content that the Rofu would not be a threat to his people for some time. They grasped forearms, putting their foreheads together in the warrior's farewell. "Something in me says we will meet again."

"Perhaps," was Grimfilth's answer, "after all, we have forever to plan for it." And he winked, stalking out of the room. He gathered his army the next morning, repurposing the rafts Skal's army had used to cross the Nazene in order to return to the desert. When he reached the blazing sands, he paused for a breath. He was home now, to a place he had hoped never to return to, and though he abhorred the retched sun and heat, he was king in Kharat, and that was enough for now.

Having survived the battle, Roc was now uncertain of his role with the Korzian army. They had suffered immense casualties, and though the men of the Guard had stood strong against every race in Alkurah, he wondered if they would be able to defend their home from any planned invasion in the coming years. There was hope, however, in the form of Hâedra, who had proven themselves valiant against insurmountable odds. The two armies parted before leaving Rivit, taking the time necessary to sort out their dead from the innumerable corpses that now polluted the great riverbanks. Four thousand Hâedran soldiers limped home, and at their head rode Breegan himself, who would suffer the mewling of the Council no longer. He met with Roc and Garroway, before his departure, at a tavern within the walls of Rivit. They sat down with a tankard of ale apiece, hoping to drown their memories. Breegan spoke first, to Garroway, and said, "I'm truly sorry about Gunsel."

Unused to death and separation, especially of someone so close to him, Garroway grieved inwardly, doing his best to appear unaffected. He shrugged and took a deep pull from his mug, "If we took the time to apologize for every friend lost, we would be among them before we were done, would we not?"

The pirate nodded, raising his mug and tipping out a portion onto the floor, "That makes more damn sense than anything else I ever heard," he toasted, "may they feast forever in the Godhall."

They drank, this unlikely trio of men, in silence for nearly an hour, save the occasional pat on the back from a nearby patron who recognized one of them. Then Roc spoke, and his words rasped in his throat as though he had been crying, "We all lost today, but Alkurah lives on, and so do we." He slugged his drink, slamming the mug onto the table, "Unfortunately, we live in a dangerous world, made worse by the weakening of our armies. Already I've received word of warlords of the Nieth hoping to overcome Korz and Hâedra. We must return quickly, both to mourn, and to rebuild."

So the three parted ways. Breegan returned to Hâedra hoping to usurp the Council, Roc led the men of Korz to a glorious reunion with their families, and Garroway opted to stay in Rivit for a time, hoping to find something that might help him make sense of all he had seen.

No centaurs galloped home to Eskeria in splendor, and their race fell away to ruin and legend. No giants lumbered to the caves they had carved into the Hudun Mountains, and the few that had survived were left with the responsibility of reviving a newborn race brought unto the brink of extinction. Krumrakai headed a column of four thousand dwarves away from Rivit. They eventually dispersed, breaking away from the army as they neared their individual homes. Some went to Soriath, and others to Litha, but most made the trek to Karakor across the Whyrum Garrad. Stones were raised in effigy to the marvels that had transpired in that great plain. Some carved tombs for their fathers, others, for their sons. The descendants of those who fell before the Nazene were honored by Krumrakai himself, and he was generous with the tremendous hoard accrued by the dwarf kings over many thousands of years. Dweera was given a position at Krumrakai's side, and he even had a throne carven beside his own that she might offer him guidance at any moment. Thus was reborn a tradition he had ended so long ago when robbed of his own greatest advisor.

Id's tribe left solemnly, making the long march to the Swamps where many of their number had not returned in quite some time. Among them was Grumbubum Lumblegurb, and though he was distraught at the death of Grael, he went away with them. He did, however, leave his massive hammer with Roc to be buried with the old elf, saying, "It's as much a part of 'im as i' is a part of me. 'E was moi frien'."

Queen Whoorlem had lost her right arm in the fighting, and though she was weakened, she still held the crown of her people. After all, she was left-handed. The trolls returned to Ictheim immediately, and though many supported the decision of the queen to fight against Skal, others decried it as an act of weakness saying instead that they should have died to the last upon the Whyrum Garrad. She was killed a few months later in a coup committed by a group of trolls hoping to reclaim the Dragon's Keep and overthrow Krumrakai himself. Bendragel did not return with his people, opting instead to go with his brother to Kharat and serve Grimfilth. There was nothing for him to be allergic to in the desert, and he hoped to find guidance and structure among the dunes such as he never had in his life as a mercenary.

Soon, each of the armies was gone from Rivit, and the graves and pyres of the dead overtaken by grass. Songs of grief and glory alike were written and recited from the most glorious halls of kings to the lowliest brothels, and those who died before the Nazene in a battle with death itself were immortalized. Children bore the names of friends and family who perished that day, and men and elves alike celebrated the births of several Eovaron.

Brathur was rebuilt, and under Roc's eye the Korzian Guard was reinforced and strengthened. The Dragon's Hand was reformed, charged with safeguarding all of Alkurah rather than simply Korz itself, and Garroway was given the title of Dragon's Head. The first such in nearly fifty years. He accepted it graciously, and though he was of no exceptional martial skill, he made a special request of Roc and Krumrakai.

"It is strange to call my former commander friend. Stranger still to even be in the presence of the king of dwarves. But I've asked you both here for a favor." He kicked open a nearby chest, revealing the armor of the Godslayer, polished and pristine save the handprint of Sypchallu clawed into the left arm. "This cannot be left in the hands of one man, and as tempting as it is, I would certainly be the wrong one to give it to."

Roc answered, interrupting him, "That's why we wanted you to keep it."

Instead of continuing, Garroway stopped talking entirely, and Krumrakai picked up the thread of his previous statement, "You want to hide it again?"

"Mostly." Garroway hefted the right gauntlet, the one that had been entrusted to the dwarven monarchs since Tykus himself wore it. "I would keep this. I'm an average swordsman on the best of days, and I fancy it may come in handy."

"Aye," Roc nodded, "but what do we do with the rest of it?"

"Perhaps we do what the elves did, so long ago." Krumrakai said, fidgeting under Roc's questioning gaze. "We separate it."

After a debate that only became heated enough for Roc to break a chair, they decided on how best to divide such a weapon. First, the helm would be tossed into the Helseia. Krumrakai offered to accept an emissary from Korz to see that it was done, but Roc opted not to send one, trusting the dwarven king to keep his word. The cuirass would be held in the Korrum of Karakor itself, entrusted to the king's protection. To Hâedra went the pauldrons, and the greaves were buried at random in the shifting sands of Kharat. Finally, the left gauntlet was buried with Grael Voor, who was now part of both great strippings of the armor. When all was done, several months after their meeting, the trio assembled in Rivit.

But Garroway had asked one last favor of Krumrakai,

"You'll be pleased to know that even Dweera didn't spot our replication." He cracked open the chest. Inside was a perfect recreation of the armor of the Godslayer. Forged with starsteel and woven with potent magics, it looked every bit the part. Even as far as the scratch on the left arm. "Much as I'd like to reminisce, I've a kingdom to run and several other things I'd like to do before I die."

So the king of the dwarves departed, leaving Roc and Garroway alone at a table with nothing but their drinks, their memories, and a pile of buttered rolls. The pair sat in silence for some time, watching the local customers come and go and enjoying a relaxed peace they had not experienced for months.

When they parted, Garroway walked beyond the gates and walked a short distance on a narrow path, off the road and behind a small copse of trees. The bodies of the Korzian dead had burned for several days after the battle, to kill the corruption within their poisoned veins, and their ashes were scattered into the crystal Nazene with great ceremony.

All but Gunsel, who was buried in the local town graveyard with a small stone that read, by written request, "Don't let the birds shit here." And his name.

They did.

GLOSSARY

Alakhan- The immortals, Grimfilth, Grael, etc. They've existed since the first spawning of living creatures of the light.

Alkui- The gods. Ong, Elu, Bol, etc. Bol was actually the second, behind Skaalu, the evil one. Bol is the father of life.

Alkui Mechi- God machines, in elvish. A secret dwarven project to destroy the Dragon's Keep if the trolls ever betrayed them.

Alkurah- Refers to both the world as a whole, and the region of the continent from the White Mountains to the Seia Wesrin.

Bendragel- The youngest brother of Gorathel and Rigathel.

Bern- A human who fights with the Rofu.

Bjerk- The dwarven mercenary commander employed by Korz.

Bol- The chief god of war and creator of Alkurah and the Alkui (except Elu).

Bolepha- The massive plain between Brathur and the Nazene.

Boleth Terrorwyrm- A black dragon, and the most powerful of all. He was slain by Toroc on the Whyrum Garrad.

Braeco- High elves often with golden hair, that have recently been overtaken by the worship of Septis. Also their city in the Seia Wesrin.

Brathur- The furthest Korzian outpost to the west. The elves carved tunnels under Brathur in the past, weaving great magic into them.

Breeganazenemagniseia- Breegan, the human Alakhan.

Brisborne- Garroway's father.

Bumphrey- Garroway's mother.

Caernohath Deathflame- A red dragon, and the oldest and most powerful living dragon. His breath is said to be as hot as Bol's own forge.

Centaurs- Half horse, half man. The centaurs train the rangers in stealth and strategy. They reside in Eskeria.

Chithraltimazomagnifindua- Chithralt, the centaur Alakhan.

Cirun- A human city.

Coark- A Korzian Commander.

Dooblidum Bumbilum- The chieftain of the Ogres of Sor.

Dragon- A large, winged, reptilian creature of magic. Assumed extinct by most.

Dragon's Hand- The original elite guard of Korz. Ancient heroes, no Hand has been formed in fifty years.

Dragon's Keep- A dwarvish stronghold on Mount Hudu, overlooking Whyrum Garrad. Now held by the trolls as part of a secession by the dwarves.

Dweera- A dwarvish scout.

Dyrrktha- An orc.

Elu- The only Alkui not created by Bol. She was born from the Eova. Lover of Ula.

Ene- An elven tree whose leaves produce a mild high.

Eova- Elves. The first race born of Bol.

Eovaron- The children of elves and humans.

Eskeria- The massive forest that separates Korz and Hâedra from Nithalin.

Eskeroth- The king of the Centaurs.

Fundwick- The butler to Brisborne's home.

Garroway- A Korzian man.

Giants- The newest race to emerge on Alkurah.

Goblin- Another name for orc. A small humanoid creature with birdlike mannerisms.

Godhall- Where the Alkui sit, and where fallen warriors join the feast of heroes.

Gorathel- The oldest brother of Rigathel and Bendragel.

Gortrum Trollsbane- A human mercenary employed by Korz.

Graelvoorimagnicaerna- Grael Voor, the elven Alakhan.

Griflidunmagnifeia- Grimfilth, the orcish Alakhan.

Grumbubum Lumblegurb- An ogryn mercenary employed by Korz.

Gundera- An orc city close to the west bank of the Naznee. Often neutral in Orc-Human conflicts.

Gunsel- A servant to Garroway.

Hâedra (Hadera)- A human city that sits on both sides of the Nazene.

Heldanhood- A race born from misused magic that took upon themselves the role of peacemakers.

Heldan Hills- The hilly area, also warped by magic, through which one must pass to cross the Bolepha to Hâedra.

Helseia- The sea north of the Hudun Mountains that freezes for most of the year.

Hrgeet- A ram-like beast of burden found in northern Alkurah.

Hudu- The great mountain upon which the Dragon's Keep was built.

Hudun Mountains- The range that forms the northern border of Alkurah, against the Helseia.

Hurga- Human, in orcish.

Ictheim- The troll kingdom.

Icthil- The troll king during the Titûn War.

Karak- An ancient dwarven king.

Karakor- The seat of the dwarven throne, and the greatest dwarven city in Alkurah.

Khagarel- Ageless King, in both trollish and dwarvish.

Kharat- The desert west of the Nazene.

Kharatule- The Rofu keep hidden beneath the Kharat Desert.

Kharatvil- The immense magical wall, now held by the Rofu, that forms the western wall of the Scar.

Koro- The king of the Koros.

Koros- The first men of the north.

Korrum- The great magical forge beneath the throne room in Karakor.

Korz- One of the ancient kingdoms of men, formerly known as 'The Center.'

Korz- A legendary warrior who defended The Center from a dragon attack and rose to Godhall.

Krak Kea- Broken peak, in dwarvish.

Krumrakai- The king of the dwarves.

Kurau- The dwarven king who lost the Titûn War.

Kyson- The Lord Commander of the entire Korzian army.

Lau- Moon, in elvish.

Lillian Redmane- A Hâedran sailor/soldier, originally from Cirun.

Litha- A human and dwarven shared city.

Lygian- A reptilian creature from the Seia Wesrin enslaved by the Braeco.

Magnicaerna- A snippet of Grael Voor's full name, refers to a hammer made from a piece of his soul.

Makkor- The late dwarvish king, father of Krumrakai. Believed to have slain the last of the dragons in the Dragon War.

Meredun- Dark water, in elvish. Refers to the area of wayward magic left behind by the Vulkha, also called the Ogryn Swamp.

Meren- Gunsel's mother.

Metitunkhel- Me troll kill, in trollish. Refers to a ritual in which trolls cut themselves from wrist to elbow, then slay a hrgeet to be healed, or die in the attempt.

Narod- The small, fast, deep river in the Hudun Mountains.

Nazene- The river that bisects Alkurah and flows north, into the Helseia.

Nieth- The female warrior-tribes from south of Eskeria.

Nithalin- The Nieth kingdom.

Noc- The Alkui of magic and night. Her horse, Satara, is associated with shooting stars.

Norrin- A human ranger.

Nulau Ra- A legendary elven scout.

Ogre- A large, gray-skinned creature that is nearly immune to magic.

Ogryn Swamp- Refers to the Meredun.

Oleth- A black dragon, and son of Boleth Terrorwyrm.

Ong- The Alkui of beasts, wild and tame.

Orc- Another name for goblin. A small humanoid creature with birdlike mannerisms.

Orum- The king of the Praestan elves.

Palarius- A hunter of magic born of the Ogryn Swamp.

Praesta- The city in the Eskeria where the 'lesser' elves dwell. Often fairer skin, but darker hair.

Ragnus Fireborn- A purple dragon, born to a well-respected bloodline.

Relia- Fire, as in (to fire) a weapon, in elvish.

Req- The Alkui of death and the underworld before being destroyed by Tykus.

Rhiagia- Charge, in elvish.

Rhiam- The weak eastern gate of the Kharatvil.

Rigathel- The middle brother of Gorathel and Bendragel.

Rivit- A small human city.

Roc- One of the Veiled.

Rofu- An alliance that consists mainly of orcs and trolls, with some members of other races.

Rorrik of the Thundercrowns- A prince of dwarves.

Saree- Gunsel's sister.

Scar- The great valley carved into Kharat protected by the Kharatvil and the Rhiam.

Seia Wesrin- Western Sea, in elvish. It forms the western border of Alkurah.

Sekl- One of the last of the Heldanhood.

Shilleril- A troll commander under Grimfilth.

Shkaylhu- The trollish name for Sypchallu/Skal.

Sirin- A human who fights with the Rofu.

Skal- Known as 'The Enlightened." Chief priest of Septis, the new god. One of the last of the Heldanhood.

Sor- The area around Soriath that several tribes of ogres inhabit.

Soriath- A dwarven city.

Stom- Stomach, in trollish. Also refers to a troll drink of choice.

Suah- A legendary painted horse ridden by King Orum.

Sundering- Refers to the era when elves initially split and went to war with one another.

Sypchallu- The first of the Alkui, even before Bol. He is darkness and evil incarnate.

Taur Earthbreaker- A white dragon, and the largest dragon ever known.

Terea Vo- The elven Regent of the Skies, formerly a great commander.

Themyra- The mortal wife of Bol, and mother of Tykus.

Therian- A mortal who once possessed the armor of Tykus.

Thorriman of the Ironscales- A dwarf known for his love of the sea. Said to have died building a great bridge across the Helseia.

Throm of the Anvilfists- A dwarf bound in service to Rorrik.

Thurg of the Stonehands- The dwarven prince who incited the Titûn War.

Titun- The dwarvish history of Alkurah.

Titûn War- Truth War, in dwarvish. Refers to the great war between trolls and dwarves

Toroc- The human who slew Boleth Terrorwyrm and made a sword out of his largest tooth.

Tristan- The commander of the rangers.

Troll- A warlike creature that seems to have no natural preference of climate or company.

Tsund Magii- Wizards of Severing, in elvish. Said to have torn Tykus' armor from Therian and scattered it across Alkurah.

Tykus- The mortal son of Bol who ascended to godhood by slaying Req and taking his place.

Ula- The Alkui of beauty and music. Lover of Elu.

Vahir- A city of men close to the White Mountains.

Veil- Refers to a place of harsh magic in the meredun through which only ogres, and the men of the Veil, can pass.

Vulkha- The elves who created life in the meredun.

Werakum- Word fight, in dwarvish.

White mountains- The enourmous mountain range that forms the eastern border of Alkurah.

Whoorlem- The troll queen.

Whyrum Garrad- Dragon Grave, in dwarvish. Refers to the plain overlooked by the Dragon's Keep, and the only ford of the Narod.

Yrlet- The commander of the lygian force under Terea Vo.

www.ingramcontent.com/pod-product-compliance
Lightning Source LLC
Chambersburg PA
CBHW031248170626
46807CB00001B/47